Cover Design: Jay Aheer

Editing done by Jenny Sims Editing4Indies

Proofing Julie Deaton by Deaton Author Services

To everyone who struggles and fights for tomorrow.

Serenity Prayer
Reinhold Niebuhr
God grant me the serenity
to accept the things I cannot change;
courage to change the things I can;
and wisdom to know the difference.

THIS IS WILD

THE THIS IS SERIES

One

Viktor

"And they said you couldn't do it." I look up at the door to the voice of reason. My therapist, Alain, comes into the room where I've stayed for the past ninety days. The only thing in this room is a king-size bed, a six-drawer oak dresser, and a side table that holds a nightlight. Don't get me wrong, it's the classiest rehab facility I've seen, and one I never thought I would be in. I even have my own private bathroom. I look back down at the cream-colored marble floor. My black boots a stark comparison to the lightness. I'm sitting on my bed with so many things going through my head. "You look deep in thought. What are you thinking about?"

I shake my head and laugh. "Is this another session?" My tone is definitely sarcastic.

"Nope." He crosses his arms over his chest and stares at me exactly like he does in his office and in group therapy.

"This one is totally free."

I roll my eyes. "Nothing about this place is free."

Now he's the one laughing. "This is true, but this, right here, is all free. You did it, Viktor. That ninety-day chip you earned, is all you."

I think of the chip in my pocket that I got at the end of the group meeting. "I didn't have a choice."

"Everyone has a choice," he says, his voice calming. "You had a choice every single day. You could have walked out of here at any given time."

"Then I would have lost everything." I sigh.

"So you chose not to lose," he says, and I swear, sometimes I just want to tell him to fuck off. Actually, most times.

"You chose to get up and fight." He slides his hands in his pockets. "Don't ever forget that. You have the tools you need to be successful."

He looks at his watch. "I have to go, but I wanted to come and wish you well. And to tell you that I am here for whenever you need me." He smirks, leaning in and whispering, "For free." I laugh as he turns and walks out of the room.

I still have so much I need to get off my chest, so much I need help with, and fear is the first thing. Fear that I will fuck it all up, fear that I am not strong enough to fight the urges, fear that I will see the disappointment in my parents' eyes. My phone beeps, letting me know it's time to check out. The car will be here in ten minutes, so I make my way to the common area.

If I wasn't in therapy or doing my daily plan, I was hitting the gym. I wouldn't let anything hold me back. They already had enough on me not to believe in me, so showing up for preseason and not being able to skate would have been just another reason to toss me aside and cross me off the list. Gone was the scrawny little guy when I started; I was now thirty pounds heavier, and it was all muscle.

The room is almost empty, which is no surprise since it's almost eleven o'clock, and everyone is probably in class. Only two people are watching television, and they are both new here.

I walk over to one of the empty seats and sit down, plopping my bag beside me. I don't know what else to do. If I was still in rehab, I would head over to the treadmill and jog out the anxiety I feel creeping up. I know how to recognize it now and know what to do with it, or at least what not to do with it. I can't get on the phone and call my dealer. I can't go to my secret stash and take a hit. No, not this time. I look at the door, waiting for my car to arrive, and then I spot him. Matthew Grant.

"Well, look at this. I get the VIP treatment." I smile and get up, holding my hand out to him. The nerves appear in full force. I wait for the inner doubt to creep in also, telling me I'll never be good enough.

"Figured I'd give you a lift home," he tells me, and I just nod as I turn and pick up my bag. It holds the clothes I have here that fit me, and from the time I started, the pile got smaller and smaller. My mother did send me a couple of pairs of jeans but nothing more than that. I told her not to bother, and I would get everything once I got to New York. My new home.

"Have you been discharged?" he asks, and I nod at him again. "Then let's hit the road. The plane is waiting."

We pass the receptionist on our way out, and I give her a smile and a nod. When I see her sigh, I know I've still got it. I knew I always had it, but it's just a little confirmation that everyone looks for. I get into the black truck right next to Matthew, and we stay silent. When the truck takes off from the facility, my heart hammers in my chest. It's so loud I look over and see if Matthew can hear it. When I see him looking out of the window, I know it's just the echoing in my ears. I take a deep breath in and then exhale, counting to ten in my head, then to twenty, and then finally to a hundred. The beating slows to a normal pace, and I breathe a sigh of relief, thinking about how I just saved face from having a full-blown panic attack in the front of my new boss.

The car ride to the plane is silent, and when we get on the plane, I take the seat in front of Matthew. The attendant comes over and asks if we would like something to drink.

"Water, please," I answer. She just smiles at me and then turns her attention to Matthew, who orders the same.

I'm not expecting Matthew to say anything, or at least to wait until we are in the air, but again he throws me for a loop. "I bet you're wondering why I signed you?" he asks me, and I just stare at him.

"I know why you signed me," I tell him, trying to hide the fact that I am, in fact, wondering why in the world he actually signed me. "You'd be a fool not to sign me."

I look at him while he puts his head back and laughs out loud. "You think very highly of yourself," he says, and I just shrug. "But I can't ignore that when you're on fire, *you are* on fire."

My thumb taps the table "And that's why you signed me."

The plane finally takes off, and I look outside and then look back at him. Sitting there in his suit, the new general manager of the New York Stingers has been on the job for two years. Before retirement, he was the captain of the team. If you ask me, he still had a couple more years left in him. The attendant comes and places two glasses of water on the table. I pick up my glass and pray that my hand doesn't shake.

"You're right, but I didn't sign you for the bullshit you've been pulling for the past two years," he tells me, leaning back in his seat. "Listen, I've been down. Fuck, my career was nonexistent when I went back home with my tail between my legs, but I got a second chance." I don't say anything as he spills his story. "And now I'm giving you yours." I don't know what he expects me to say, so I just wait for him to finish. "We are piss testing you weekly until I think it's good enough. If you don't like the terms, you can leave now." I glare at him.

"I need to find a realtor," I tell him. "I have my stuff waiting to be shipped from LA."

"Already ahead of you there. My sister Zoe will meet with you tomorrow afternoon," he tells me. "She is the best there is, and if there is a house out there, she knows about it. You can stay in Max's loft for the next month until you get your stuff settled." I nod my head and then turn to the attendant as she comes over and places two plates on the table. Each of them contains a steak with potatoes and a side of lobster tail. We don't talk while we eat because, really, what more is there to say?

When the wheels finally touch down, I look at Matthew.

"Welcome home, Viktor. Welcome to New York."

What he doesn't add, but I can hear loud and clear is *don't fuck this up.*

Two

Zoe

"I HAVE THREE houses to show you tomorrow." Pressing my shoulder to the phone, I say, "All are in your budget." I make sure to mention that since it's the first question he'll ask me.

"I will tell the missus," he says gruffly. "She was talking about switching firms and maybe having better luck with someone else." I roll my lips and say a silent prayer to whoever is listening at this point. This will be the seventh time we are seeing houses, and they have said no to the previous twenty listings I've shown them.

"That would be a shame." I pinch my nose, closing my eyes. "I have one that was just emailed to me. It's not even listed yet, and it's in the exact neighborhood you wanted."

"Okay, dear, we'll give you another shot," he mumbles, and I open the listing that came to me two hours ago that I was going to turn down.

"Perfect. I will see you tomorrow." Hanging up, I toss my phone on the desk, then lean back and stretch. It's almost five o'clock. I can't believe the day is almost over.

Looking out the little window in my home office, I close my eyes for just a second, but my mind doesn't shut down. Instead, it makes mental notes on what I have to do next. My job is my number-one priority in my life, and I work my ass off. Four months ago, I closed on twenty-two houses in one month, a top record for my firm. I'm one of the top players in the real estate game in New York City. It's fucking cutthroat, harsh, and it's anyone's game. I may look nice with my long strawberry blond hair and angelic blue eyes, but you fuck with me, and I'll cut your balls off. I will also use my charm to get the deal and close it. I will flip my hair if you want and bat my eyes as long as I know you will be signing on the dotted line.

The house I live in has gone from one family member to the next, starting first with Karrie and Matthew, who fell in love at first sight. Then Allison took it over only to fall in love with Matthew's enemy, Max. Finally ending with Zara, my twin, who ended up with Evan and lives in Long Island in the mansion I found them. Now not only does she live an hour away from me, but she's also expecting her own baby. We can't explain our bond. It just is. Pushing off the desk, I grab my phone and make my way downstairs to the kitchen.

A collection of photos of all of us line the whole wall going downstairs. It started with Matthew and Karrie and slowly got filled up with everyone who's lived here.

Walking into the kitchen, I open the fridge and find it half empty. I take my phone out and order a pizza.

My phone buzzes in my hand the minute I press confirm. "I swear I didn't do anything." I smile, grabbing a bottle of water and walking to the couch.

Matthew's laughter fills my ear. "Hey, squirt."

"You know I'm almost twenty-four, right?" I make my way to the living room throwing myself on the couch, sinking in, and then reach over to grab one of the throw covers to cover my bare feet.

"Almost twenty-four is still in squirt age," he says, and I hear honking in the background. My brother is seventeen years older than us. My dad fell in love with our mom when he showed up at her arena to train. From all the stories they've told us over the years, it was one look and he was gone. Matthew was fifteen, and Allison was five. Their father is long gone, out of the picture, but no one will ever tell me or my family that my father isn't his father. Blood or not, they are the same person. "I need a favor."

"Holy shit, is hell freezing over?" I laugh, grabbing the remote. "Remember last year when you got mad at me and said you weren't ever asking me for anything again?"

"You put Karrie in a bikini and had her pose next to a pool for one of your real estate ads," he hisses. "You made it sound like she was single."

I roll my eyes; my brother is a caveman. Actually, all the men in my family are a bit to the extreme. "I'm surprised you didn't walk around town with her beating a hand to your chest saying mine."

"I thought of doing a billboard of us in Times Square," he says quietly. "But she vetoed it."

I roll over in laughter. "Why am I not surprised you would suggest that?"

"Anyway, I have a huge favor." His tone turns serious, but with him, you never know.

"What now?" I ask him.

"Can you come to the arena tomorrow at three?" he asks me, and now he's piqued my curiosity. "I'm working with our new guy tomorrow, and it's the perfect time for you to meet him." Matthew is or was the hockey "It" guy until he retired two years ago. He hung up his skates, but that didn't mean he wasn't in the game anymore. He's now the general manager for the New York Stingers. Where Matthew was the "It" guy in hockey, our father is the hockey god. He still holds some of the highest titles, and everyone wants to be him.

"Are you setting me up on a date?" I ask him, knowing that'll irritate him. He hates the fact we, his sisters, date. He hates the fact we have sex, and if it was up to him, we would live in a bubble. "I haven't been out in forever."

"Are you crazy?" he hisses. "Don't even talk like that, especially when you are here. The last thing I need are the rookies going apeshit over you."

"You are such a buzzkill, Matthew," I moan. The doorbell rings, so I get up and walk to the door. "So what do you need me for if it isn't to rock his world?"

"Jesus Christ," he groans. "You are going to give me a heart attack." I smile, knowing he is probably standing wherever he is and rubbing his chest, believing this. "The new guy needs a realtor," he says. I open the door, smiling at the guy, and grab my pizza.

"Thank you." I block the phone while greeting the six-foot-three hunk in front of me. He just nods and turns to walk down the stairs. I stand here appreciating his backside. Hey, men aren't the only ones who can look.

Matthew's voice brings me back from my daydream. "Anyway, he's living in the loft for now," he mentions. I lived in the loft my brother-in-law Max owns before I moved in here. It was amazing until the guy upstairs left his water running and ruined everything. It's now back to what it was, if not better, but I'm in the brownstone in Brooklyn now.

"What budget do you think I'm working with?" I ask him.

"I have no fucking idea," he says. "Don't ask me anything. Just can you please help me?"

"Okay," I say, putting the pizza on the table in the living room. "But it's going to cost you."

"Remember when I got the hottest guys in hockey to take you and Zara to prom?" he says, thinking he's smart.

"They wouldn't even hold our hands," I snap at him. "We had plans to lose our virginity that night."

He laughs. "You're lucky they sat next to you."

"Asshole," I say to him and then take a bite of pizza. "I'll be there tomorrow only because I love my job."

"You'll be there tomorrow because you know the commission is going to be sweet."

I shrug. "This is also true."

"And can you make sure you dress properly?" he finally says. "Nothing too revealing and shit."

"I always dress properly," I point out. "I'm going to tell Zara you said that." My sister is a personal stylist to some of the biggest stars out there. She even started her own company called Zara's Closet. Most of my clothes come from her, and most are the ones that Evan doesn't want her to wear.

"Later, squirt," he says, disconnecting, and I spend the rest of the night watching Netflix.

The next morning, I'm slipping on my lace thong when my phone rings, and I see it's Zara.

"Hey," I say, putting it on speaker while I finish dressing.

"Hey, yourself," she says, and I know she's in the car. I grab the white cotton button-down blouse that is tight on the chest and then hugs my waist. "Do you have plans for dinner?"

"Not as of right now," I tell her, slipping on my gray suede Louboutins. "Why, what's up?"

"I have to join Evan and one of his teammates, and I don't want to have to pretend I understand what they are talking about." I shake my head. We have grown up with hockey in our lives, yet we both hate it. From the time when we were little, we would cry when we were put on the ice. There are pictures of my dad trying to coax us up, and all we did was lie on the ice. When my mother had enough of the tears and tantrums, she would only allow us on the ice as punishment when we did something we shouldn't have. I can say it really didn't work because we would just kneel there on the ice, which would get my father trying to tell us how much fun hockey was. It was not. I went to every single hockey game I could, but it was always to socialize more than watch the game. I don't know icing from offside and neither did Zara before Evan.

Our younger brother Justin, now he is the opposite of us. He lives and breathes for the sport and was just drafted this summer, and Matthew is trying to move heaven and earth to get him to New York, but Edmonton is holding strong.

"I'm already spending the afternoon at the rink," I tell her, grabbing my light gray jacket.

"Good. I'll see you there," she says. "This whole captain's wife thing is getting a bit out of hand. I swear I call Karrie seven times a day."

I laugh at her. "You love it."

"No," she says. "I love him, and I'll do what I need to do for him, but—"

"But nothing," I interrupt. "Fine, I'll go to dinner, but I'm ordering the most expensive thing on the menu."

"Deal," she says. "See you soon."

I shake my head and slip on the jacket, finally looking at myself in the mirror. "Presentable," I say with just a twinkle in my eye because the minute I move, you see my full long leg. "This should be fun."

I hang up and meet the Flanerys to go over the listing that I had, and in one hour, they fell in love with the house that was emailed to me yesterday. I get back to the office and draw up a contract. When my phone beeps, telling me my driver is here to take me to the rink, I wrap up everything and grab my bag. As soon as I sit down, I shoot Matthew a text.

Me: On my way, where do I meet you?

Matthew: I'm in my office. See you soon.

I tuck the phone away and look outside at the leaves slowly changing, not knowing that the leaves aren't the only thing changing this season.

THREE

Viktor

I WATCH THE clock turn 6:00 a.m., the alarm ringing and my hand coming out to slap it off. I lie in the big king-size bed, looking out the windows all around the room. I've been up since 3:30. I tossed and turned most of the night, but I'm used to that. My longest time asleep, according to the Fitbit I wear to bed, is six hours and forty-seven minutes. Another thing recovery gave me was sleep. Instead when I was high I would just snort a couple more lines to stay awake, sleep was never a necessity.

My eyes focus outside on the rising sun as my mind wanders back to that day four months ago and how much my life has actually changed.

No one ever intends to overdose. No one ever intends to do so much cocaine that they are hanging onto the ledge by the tips of their fingers. No one ever wants to be so fucking far gone that all we can do is watch ourselves from above.

For two years, I pretended I was just having fun. Hey, I was riding the fucking wave. I had just won the Stanley Cup at nineteen as a rookie. Hockey was in my blood from the minute I was born. My father was a star in his own time. Though he was not as lucky as me to be drafted, he did play in the States. He met my mother at one of his hockey games. After he picked her out of the crowd, they dated for a whole three weeks, and then he married her. Nine months later, I came into the world at the same time my father's hockey career was taking a nosedive, at least for American standards.

He then took on teaching roles and coaching, which had us going around the globe and never staying in a city longer than a few years. Teams switching up coaching staffs often.

When I was seventeen, the KHL in Moscow drafted me twenty-fifth. My Russian father was pissed that I was drafted so late, especially after I had spent the year in Chicago and was drafted first into the Ontario Hockey League. I didn't care where I played; I just wanted to fucking play. He worked my ass to the bone. *Skate harder, push faster, move your feet, feel the puck. No one likes a quitter, Viktor.* It was every single day. Not just when we were on the ice and not just when it was the two of us. No, he would tell me in front of whoever was there. He didn't care. He thought it would make me better and make me stronger, but I just resented him.

One year later, the NHL drafted me third overall. At eighteen years old, I was living in Los Angeles with no one looking over my shoulder telling me what to do or how to do it. I knew I was going down the wrong path, but I did it anyway.

Four years later, my drug problem was out of control. If I'm honest, toward the end I didn't even try to hide it. We didn't even make it to the playoffs, and on the last game of the season I was high on the ice. I cringed when I saw the replay in my room a month into rehab. Watching myself skating around and around the fucking puck and then falling, was embarrassing to say the least.

Coach benched me for two periods, and I still didn't give a shit. That night, I pushed too far and did too much. When I finally woke up or came down from my high—whatever you want to call it—they gave me the ultimatum. It was either go to rehab or never play again. So I went to rehab, but it was for them and not for me. Then I got traded. I didn't even understand after everything that I did, why any team would want me, but apparently, Matthew Grant fought for me.

When we walked off the plane last night, I expected him to nod at me, say, "Don't fuck up," and then take off. Instead, Matthew got into the car and drove me to my new place. I didn't even look around last night before I dumped my carry-on and went to bed.

I roll out of bed now, trying to forget yesterday. *Think about today*. I remember what the therapist said. Tomorrow is not something you can change, but today, today is the day to change what you would have done differently yesterday. I used to groan inwardly when he said it and think it was a crock of shit. But each day the fog would be lifted just a touch. The days got clearer, it made more sense.

As I pull on a pair of shorts from my bag, I'm thinking with the time change, I should still be asleep, as I walk out of the bedroom and head to the kitchen.

I walk into the spacious kitchen right off the living room. The island is stark white with black countertops and stainless-steel appliances. I open the cupboards, looking for anything that will make me coffee. Another thing I do now is see things differently. Whereas before I didn't give a shit, now I have to fill my mind with other things or I'll go crazy. Filling the gap of emptiness keeps me from thinking about the drug that still lingers at the back of my mind and almost made me lose it all. I'm stronger than the pull.

I finally find the pods to go into the coffeemaker, and when I open the fridge, I see it's fully stocked. Taking out the milk, I make my coffee and go sit on one of the stools at the island. As I take a sip of the hot coffee, I feel the burn go down my throat. I look around, and my hands tap the counter. I know what this means; it means I'm bored and need to get up and move. Take my mind off the pull of scoring my next fix. I walk to the couch and turn the television on. My phone rings again, so I go back to the bedroom and turn off the second alarm.

Looking down, I see I have a couple of texts. The first one is from my mother.

Mom: Good luck tomorrow.

The next one is from my little sister, Natalia.

Natalia: God, it's good being the favorite child. Just kidding. Good luck, bro.

I smile and shake my head. The next is from the therapist I worked with in Arizona.

Alain: Here are the names and numbers of the sponsors I found in New York. Don't give up on yourself. No matter how much you think you don't deserve it, you do. We all do.

Tomorrow is gone, so make today count.

Going through the names, I send a text to all the numbers he sent me. I take a deep breath and sit down, looking out the window while the television plays in the background. I have to be at the rink at noon. I lie down, trying to shut off my mind and tune out all the noise. All the doubts, all the shit that shouldn't be in there.

I doze off, and when the third alarm sounds at eleven, I get up and get ready. The bathroom is right off the walk-in closet that is empty except for my little bag in the middle. Walking to the shower, I open the glass door and step inside. The shower walls have the same marble as the counter, and the white tiles on the floor blend perfectly. When I turn on the shower, two waterfalls start over me. Leaning my hands onto the wall, I let the water wash over my back.

After I dry off, I grab a pair of dress pants and a white button-down shirt. They are the only clothes that fit me besides the jeans I wore yesterday. I need to go shopping, and I need a house, so that should be enough to keep my mind busy.

I grab my jacket and head down to the waiting town car. The driver stands beside the car with a smile. "Good morning, Mr. Petrov."

"Morning." I nod at him as I slide into the open door. I look out the window while we make our way to the arena. He makes his way to the underground garage, and when we come to a stop, I get out and meet him at the back of the car.

"If you go through that door"—he points at the blue metal door—"you will be near the locker rooms."

"Thank you," I mumble and make my way into the new locker room. I pull open the door and walk into the back hallway. The small corridor leads to a wider hallway with blue carpet, and as I walk down, I pass huge pictures of Matthew hoisting the cup. Another of Matthew and Max celebrating said cup win, and a picture of the whole team in front of the cup. Another picture of Matthew taking his last skate around the arena and another one of Max. The team legacy hangs down the white walls of the hallway. I finally walk past an open door and peer in, seeing it's the locker room.

Looking around, I spot my name and sit down on the wooden bench. Since it's still summer break, no one is here, and I just take a deep breath. "There you are." I look at the doorway and see Matthew. "I see you found your spot," he says, coming into the room. He's dressed pretty much the same as I am, except his shirtsleeves are rolled up.

"Just getting the lay of the land." I smile at him, putting my elbows on my knees.

"I know how that feels," he tells me, and I just look at him, thinking he's talking out of his ass. "I walked in here with the biggest bubble over my head."

"I doubt it's as big as the cloud following me around," I finally say to him softly.

"The only way they would sign me was if I had a chaperone with me," he says, and I'm shocked. "Luckily for me, she was hot, and well, let's just say … four kids later, it was the best thing to ever happen to me."

"Really?" I hear another male voice, and I look over to see Max come in the room. "I thought I was the best thing to happen to you." He slaps Matthew's shoulder, then turns to me, sticking out his hand. This guy is a fucking beast even without equipment. "I'm Max. I was the one who tortured him and pushed him to be better." He laughs while Matthew just shakes his head.

"He also dated my sister under my nose," Matthew hisses.

"Guilty." Max holds up his hands. "Also eloped with her." He looks at Matthew. "Might as well get it all out there. There are no secrets in this family."

"Jesus," I say, laughing for the first time in ninety days because something was funny.

"Oh, these two are a riot." Another voice cuts in, and I swear it's a group meeting; something we only had on the other team when shit was getting bad. "Hi there, I'm Evan, team captain," he says, coming in wearing a blue suit and holding his hand out. "I see you've met M&M."

"That fucking name," Matthew says. "What are you doing here?"

"I asked him to come," Max says. "I figured it was a good time for us to get to know each other."

"Good idea," Matthew says to Max and then looks back at me "Let me show you around." I nod at him and get up.

"Jesus, you've been hitting the gym," Evan says. "Good. I need to know the guy next to me can hold his own," he jokes. "I'm going to go say goodbye to my wife while she talks to Oliver about what she wants to do with the foundation." He turns and walks away.

"Stay away from my sister!" Matthew shouts at him.

He turns back and walks backward. "Not a chance in

hell. Besides, it's a little late for that since my child is in her." I try not to laugh when he winks at Matthew, who just throws his head back and groans.

"It's a battle I lose every single time. Thank fuck, Zoe is a hard ass and too busy building her empire to care about guys." I hear him mumble under his breath, knowing I'll meet her soon.

"That's what she has you thinking," Max teases him. "She was out the other night with that reality guy." He snaps his fingers. "What's his name?" Matthew has a vein in his forehead that looks like it's going to pop when Max points at him and teases him. "Fucking with you," he says, laughing and turning around to walk away.

"Asshole," he hisses at Max's retreating back. "Be in the conference room at one."

"Is it always like this?" I ask Matthew while we walk down the hall, and he points out things like the kitchen and the gym.

"You will come to see that we're not just a hockey team," he says, beaming with pride. "We're a family." I nod. I thought the guys on my team in LA were family, but when push came to shove, they all dropped me. I mean, some still talk to me, but it's on the down low. No one wanted to be associated with the guy in rehab.

I meet all the coaching staff, and the head coach and the assistant are both happy to have me on their team, or so they say. The equipment manager and I go over all the how I like and want my equipment set up, and he already has my equipment shipped over from LA.

When we finally get into the conference room, Max and

Evan are already there sitting down. I sit down on one of the empty chairs right next to Evan, facing Max, and I notice they left the seat at the head of the table empty. Matthew sits in it and looks around the table.

"Well, let's get this started," Matthew says, and I almost hold my breath.

"I, for one, am happy you're here," Matthew says.

"I'm not going to lie and sugarcoat shit for you," Max pipes up. "I did not agree with him at the beginning."

"We know you can play hockey," Matthew interjects.

"No shit," I say.

"Now you have to earn the trust to play hockey," Evan says. "No one is going to want to have your back on the ice if they think you don't have theirs."

"I always have my team's back," I say, my throat suddenly dry.

"Really?" Max says. "Because after Matthew showed me those two games where you played your heart out, I showed him the last game of the season you played." I sit up straight now, and Max must see it, but he just leans back into his chair. "We want to make sure that guy doesn't follow you here."

"I'll fight for you," Evan says, "because I'm your captain. It's my job, and that is what we do."

"Bottom line," Matthew says, "I want to fucking win. I want my team to win. I want them to hold up the cup. I want to give that to them, and I know with you as a piece of the puzzle, it just may happen."

"I know this means nothing," I finally say, "since I have to prove it to you, but I want to be that guy who holds up the cup. I want to be the one who fights with a team and not just myself."

"Then," Max finally says, "you are at the right place. We aren't just a team as you can see. We are a family. If one of us is hurting, the rest of us help carry that burden. But what we don't do is go down with someone who isn't willing to fight."

"With your speed, your build, and your hands, I'm betting that you are going to take pretty boy's spot on the leader board this year," Matthew says, pointing at Evan, who just throws his head back and laughs.

"I'd like to see him try," Evan says. "I've held that title for three straight years."

"That's only because I hung up my skates," Max says, shaking his head.

"Delusional," Evan says.

We are almost done with the meeting when a knock sounds on the open conference room. I look up, and I stop and just stare.

"So, this is where the party is at," the woman says. Her long reddish-blond hair sways as she walks in, the slit in her skirt giving a nice view of her long, toned leg. My eyes watch her every single fucking move. She walks into the room, knowing she owns it and that all eyes are on her, including mine. "Sorry to interrupt. Did you want me to come back?" She looks at Matthew and smiles while he glares at her.

"Did I not say to dress appropriately?" he hisses. Her blue eyes just glitter as she throws her head back and laughs.

"This is conservative," she says to him and then approaches Max, who gets up and hugs her. She moves flawlessly from one to the other, never lingering more than a couple of seconds with each.

"Was that Zara's skirt?" Evan asks her when he gets up and give her a big hug.

"No." She shakes her head.

"Good. Don't ever lend it to her either." He smiles, and she walks over to Matthew.

"Hey, old man." She jokes with Matthew, who doesn't get up, and then she turns to me. Fuck if she isn't the most beautiful woman I've ever saw, and I've lived in Hollywood. "Hi there. You must be the new guy." She holds her hand out. "I'm Zoe."

I don't say anything, or better yet, I can't say anything because Matthew knocks her hand down. "He doesn't need to touch you."

"Oh, good God," she says. "He's my client." Now she turns to me, and I stop and watch her.

"Okay, I'm out," Max says. "Let me know when you want to work out." He walks out of the room.

"I have to go meet with Oliver about some charity and other shit," Evan says, pushing away from the table. "We still on for dinner, right?" He looks at me, then looks at Zoe. "Your sister is here somewhere, she said she'll come looking for you when she's done."

"Perfect," she says, and she puts her bag down on the table and then takes off her jacket. She turns to Matthew. "You can go also."

"Why can't I stay?" he asks her, leaning in his chair.

"Because one, it's confidential, and two, I don't want you

to." Zoe smiles at him. "You can even leave the door open."

"Fine." He gets up. "But there are cameras in this room."

"Oh, damn," she says, looking at me. "So no sex in the middle of the table."

I don't know what to do or say, but the laughter that escapes me fills the room. Matthew stops and turns around to glare at me and then scold Zoe. "Don't talk about sex in this building," he says through clenched teeth, then turns to me. "In case you didn't know, she's off-limits."

I just nod and hold up my hands. "Won't be an issue," I say. Fuck knows the last thing I need is to be chasing the sister of the one guy who took a chance on me. I also know that if I didn't have so much shit hanging over my head, I might ignore him.

"I don't date my clients," Zoe says. "Though once they sign a contract, they're fair game." She winks at me, and I swear she knows how to get under Matthew's skin.

"I'm calling Dad," Matthew says while Zoe laughs.

"Okay, you go do that." She shoos him away with her hand. When he's out of the room, she turns to me, and I stop breathing and even blinking. "I was just kidding about all of that." I don't bother answering her—one, because I'm not sure I could find my voice, and two, because I don't know what I would actually tell her.

"Now, are we ready to get started?" she asks. Grabbing a pen and paper, she looks me straight in my eyes.

"As ready as I'll ever be," I answer her, and for a minute, I just hold my breath and watch her.

Four

Zoe

HIS LAUGHTER FILLS the room, and I'm suddenly feeling just a touch better. Walking into the office, I did a quick sweep of the room and put on my biggest poker face to date. My eyes wanted to go back to the stranger in the room and look him up and down, and no matter how I told them not to, they did it on their own. My eyes met his, and I let my gaze linger for just a second longer than I should. His blue eyes are dark like the deep end of the ocean.

"I'm sorry." I look at him and finally have a reason to stare at him. The gruff of his beard fills his face as though he hasn't shaved in a couple of days. His shirt pulls across his chest, and I'm wondering suddenly if he is tatted under there or is he bare. "I didn't get your name."

"Viktor," he says gruffly with just a touch of an accent. He leans in, extending his hand, and my hand disappears in his. His hands aren't soft like the ones I shake every day. No these are hard, rugged, and callused.

"Let's get started," I say, putting his name at the top of the legal pad. "First, let's start with your budget."

"I have no idea," he answers honestly. "I just sold my house in LA for four point five million."

I nod my head. "LA is not the same as New York," I tell him. "I just sold a one-bedroom, one-bathroom condo for one point two million." His eyes shoot up, and I laugh. "Exactly."

"I'm almost afraid to ask how much a four-bedroom home will go for," he says.

"Prime New York location, you are looking at anywhere between eight and twenty million." I tap my pen on the pad, and his eyes go to it. "But if you move more toward the middle, you're looking at four to six million."

"Is that a house or an apartment?" he asks, and I have to laugh again.

"There are no such things as houses in New York." I see his thumb tapping the table. "Listen, why don't I ask you a couple of questions, and then we can talk budget. How many bedrooms were you thinking?"

"Two bedrooms are good," he says, and I write it down.

"Are you married, with a girlfriend, or have kids?" I ask the standard question I ask every person. But with him, this particular question bugs me, and I don't know why. Maybe, I'm just really curious.

"Is that on the questionnaire?" he asks. Looking at me, he leans back in his chair and folds his hands on his stomach, pulling his shirt tight.

"There are some apartments that won't sell to a family with a crying baby," I tell him honestly. "And if you have a girlfriend or a wife, she will have more specifics than a single man who just needs a couch and a bed." His face doesn't show anything. "Just as I don't want to waste your time, I'm sure you don't want to waste mine."

"I'm alone," he says. My heart suddenly kicks up just a touch more than normal, and I see that I'm throwing too much at him.

"Relax." I smile, but he just stares at me. "These are the easy questions."

"I bet." His tone is now dry, but his stare so intense I want to look away, yet don't.

"What type of neighborhood did you want?" I ask him the loaded question. "See, a lot harder, right?"

"I've been to New York a total of maybe ten times and each time for two days, maybe three," he says. "Each time, I stayed in a hotel." He puts up his hand to stop me from asking where. "I don't know where. I don't remember half of the shit that went on in the past couple of years."

I see the confusion on his face. I also see that he is help-less in this matter. "I don't usually do this," I tell him, putting down my pen, "but how about we spend Saturday going around New York, so you can get a feel of things?" I fold my hands together. "We can check out different neighbor-hoods, and you can see where you feel most comfortable. What feels like home to you."

"Why?" he asks, leaning back in his chair.

"Well, for one, I take my job seriously." I sit up. "I want you to find a home, not just a house where you come and go." I take a breath and continue. "If you don't want to, that's fine.

Also, I just thought I would offer a helping hand."

"Is this to piss off Matthew?" His eyes get a deeper blue, and a smirk fills his face now.

Leaning back in my own chair, I smile. "No." I shrug and kind of smirk. "I mean, it doesn't hurt to rile him up."

He's about to say something when I hear a knock on the door and look up to see Zara. "Hey, I heard you were here." She smiles and looks over at Viktor.

"Holy shit, there are two of you?" He looks at me, then at Zara, and then back at me.

"Yes, but I'm the better-looking one," we both say at the same time, making me shake my head, and Viktor bursts out laughing.

"Fine, I'll go with the smarter of the two," I finally say, and she walks in and extends her hand to him.

"I'm Zara Richards." His eyes finally light up when he puts two and two together.

"You're Evan's wife?" he asks, and she smiles so big I think her face will crack. She also puts her hands over her stomach, something she started doing the minute she discovered she was pregnant. It's a secret no one really knows, and because she isn't even showing, no one asks any questions. He leans over the conference table to shake her hand. "I'm Viktor," he tells her.

"It's nice to meet you," she says, then turns to kiss my cheek and sit in the chair next to me. She sees the pad in front of me. "Oh, was I interrupting something?" She starts to get up, but Viktor just shakes his head.

"It's fine," I tell her. "We were done anyway." I look at Viktor. "I'll get a couple of things set up for Saturday, and we will go from there."

He nods his head and gets up. "I will see you two later," he says gruffly and turns to walk out of the room. I look over at Zara, who leans back in her chair and waits a full minute before turning to me.

"Holy fucking shit," she whispers and hisses at the same time. "Did you see that ass?"

I shake my head. "The question is, what do you think your husband and father of your child is going to say if he hears you?" I don't answer the question but yes, yes, I did see that fine ass. Who could ignore it? His pants are tailored perfectly to that ass.

"It's not my fault," she says, putting up her hands. "I have so many hormones, it's insane."

"I'm not sure I want to hear this." I put my hands to my ears. "Honestly."

"Hey, you two. I'm coming in to say goodbye," Matthew says, walking into the room and then looking at me. "What's with her?" he asks Zara.

"She doesn't want to hear that I have extra hormones now that I'm with child," Zara says with just a twinkle in her eye. Looking at Matthew, I see the exact moment it clicks, so I fuck with him too.

"She was checking out Viktor's ass," I say, and he covers his face. "I, for one, didn't get that great a look at it," I say, looking down, so no one can see I'm lying, "but your sister, here …" I point at Zara. "She almost fell off her chair leaning back."

"This isn't funny, you two," he finally says, then looks straight at me. "I know I give you guys a hard time."

Zara slaps her hand on the table. "You don't say." She rolls her eyes at him.

He doesn't laugh or do anything; he just stares at me. "What are you looking at me for?" I ask.

His face never cracks. "Listen to me," he says, his tone tight, and we both look at each other and then back at him. He's always been on our cases, but his tone is different this time. "I'm dead serious about this. You don't want to go there," he says, pointing at the empty doorway that he just came through and Viktor just walked out of. "There is shit you guys might have heard or seen on the news." He holds up his hands, knowing he can't just lay that down with us and not give us something. The more you tell us no, the more we think yeah, it's a great idea. "I'm not telling you anything because it isn't my story to tell. But I will say, Zoe, that you don't need that."

"Oh, good God." I throw my head back. "I don't even want that," I say, pointing at the door. Max comes in and assesses the situation, looking at Matthew who now stands there with his hands in his pockets and then at us. Zara sits with one hand on the table and the other on her stomach.

I sit with both elbows on the arms of the chair. "What did you two do?" Max asks.

"Nothing," both Zara and I answer simultaneously.

"They were checking Viktor out," Matthew says, and now it's Max's turn to groan.

"You're married." He points at Zara. "And you"—he points at me—"no fucking way."

I shake my head, grabbing my things on the table and putting them away. "Okay, for the last time, I don't want to date him." I glare at Zara. "She was the one who was look-ing."

She looks at Max and Matthew. "There is nothing wrong with appreciating a good backside," Zara says. "It was in passing."

"I swear, you guys are going to give me a whole head of white hair," Matthew says, and now even Max laughs. His hair is so black with not one little white hair in it.

"You need to calm down and relax," I tell him. "Now, what time is this dinner?" I look over at Zara.

"Should be any minute," she says to me, then looks back at the guys. "Relax. Honestly, I was just messing with her." Zara then says quietly, "He's her client."

"Yeah, well, keep it like that," Matthew says and then looks at Max. "Ready to go?"

"Aww, did you two carpool?" I make a joke. "Isn't that cute? I swear you two have the best relationship ever."

"My car is in the shop," Matthew says, then mumbles, "Asshole."

"We will see you guys on Sunday," Max says, then puts his arm around Matthew. "Come on, love bug, let's take you home."

I roll my lips together when all I want to do is burst out laughing. "The question is, will he open the door for you like Evan does for Zara?" I yell at their backs, but they don't an-swer. I just see them shaking their heads.

"Jesus, that was fun," Zara says, and I just nod.

"How are you feeling?" I ask her, and she just smiles at me.

"Amazing." She puts her hand on her stomach. "I can't

wait to start showing. I can't wait to feel the baby kick." I watch her with the love written all over her face, and I swear I'm so happy for her.

"There she is," Evan says, and then I look behind him at Viktor. His eyes find mine and then quickly dart away. Zara looks up at her husband standing right next to her chair now. He leans down and kisses her lips softly. "Love you."

"Barf," I say, rolling my eyes and putting all my papers away. "Where are we going for supper?"

"I thought we could hit up one of your sister's favorite restaurants," Evan says, and I laugh.

"That's only because you don't want her sending you into the city tomorrow for it."

"Are we all going for supper?" Viktor asks, confused.

"Yes," Evan says. "I invited Zoe to keep Zara company."

"Aww, Evan," Zara says with a soft voice and stands.

"I swear to God, she's just so mushy about things ever since she got pregnant." I look at Viktor. "You should have met her before. She liked hockey, and she was amazing."

"Hey," Zara says, "I'm still amazing. And hockey is fun." She puts her arm around Evan's waist.

"Okay, who's driving?" I ask, not even getting into this discussion.

"I'll drive," Evan says, putting his arm around Zara. "Let's go." He turns with her and walks out of the room past Viktor, who just stands there looking at me.

"Go ahead," he says, motioning with his hand, and I just nod at him.

We follow Evan and Zara, and Viktor just watches him when he opens the door for Zara and waits for her to get in.

He moves forward not sure what to do. "If you open my door, I am going to stab your toe with my heel." I side-eye him as he stops mid-step. "It's a door. I get that Evan is the most chivalrous person, but I can get my own door," I explain.

Evan walks to Viktor and slaps his shoulder. "Her bark is worse than her bite."

"Want to bet?" I say, opening the back door of the truck and looking at Evan.

"Stop trying to scare him, Evan," Zara says. "I promise you, I won't let her hurt you."

"She got pissed off at me once and put bronzer in my body wash," Evan says to Viktor. "I was orange for two days."

"A day and a half." I laugh. "So dramatic." I close the door, and now it's just me and Zara in the truck. "You're lucky I still haven't told him that you helped me."

"Silly girl, we did a 'twins' promise. It goes to the grave," Zara says, and I grab my phone in my pocket when it buzzes. I ignore the door opening and Viktor getting in. I ignore that I feel his hand next to my side. I ignore that I want to turn and watch him. I ignore it all, and I do it perfectly.

FIVE

VIKTOR

WHILE EVAN ZIGZAGS through traffic on the way to the restaurant, I stare out the window, trying like hell to ignore the siren sitting next to me. I should be taking in the buildings and getting my bearings in a new city, but the buildings glide by in a blur of steel and brick. Instead, all I see are long legs, long hair, a great ass—

No, this won't work. The woman is my realtor. I can't ignore her, but I can talk to her like the professional she is. "What section is this?" I ask, turning to Zoe, who looks up from her phone.

"Did you see something you liked?"

You, spread out on my bed. "Not really." Buildings. Think buildings. Blocks and blocks of buildings. I clear my throat and focus outside again, really looking this time.

I should have made an excuse and bailed on dinner, but when Evan texted me the night before, I thought it would be a good idea to make an effort. But then he brings his wife and her sister, who is now my realtor. Who, if things were different, I would be the first one to make a move on. But she's off-limits. I add her to the mental list of *really bad ideas; don't go there* I have in my head and force myself to look out of the truck window and not back at her.

The block we're on is a spread of businesses on the ground floor with apartments above them. Iron staircases cling to every façade. "It looks like something out of a movie set."

"Yeah, it's a pretty nice neighborhood. You have Washington Square Park not too far." She points out the window, and I finally see that there are trees but no grass. The trees planted in the concrete sidewalks have just a small circle to grow out of the ground. "I sold a studio apartment for one point one."

"Million?" I ask. Shocked, I look around, then back at her and see her sly smile.

"His living room was his bedroom. He had a murphy bed in the wall," she tells me, doing something on her phone and then turning it to show me. "But look at his kitchen."

"He slept in his living room," I tell her, looking through her pictures. "That's a no."

"There is one." She grabs her phone from my hands. Our fingers graze, but I ignore the tingly feeling that shoots up my arm. "Just came down in price. Three bedrooms, three bathrooms, three million. There is a little bit of a catch."

I roll my eyes now. "My bed is in the kitchen?"

She laughs again. It's so carefree that she must do it often. Her eyes turn a crystal blue when she does it, and I can't help but want to make her laugh more. "No, it's not a regular size apartment," she finally says and pulls up the floor plan. "It's long. You have the length, just not the width."

"What in the world is going on back there?" Zara says, turning in her seat.

"I'm showing him houses in the neighborhood," Zoe says. "Not everything is about sex."

"I'm just making sure." She smiles and then looks at Evan. "I'm starving."

"We're almost there." He grabs her hand and brings it to his lips. I can see how much he loves Zara and worships the ground she walks on. I think about if I've ever had that, and I know I haven't. I was too busy chasing the high to care about if I had someone beside me to love.

"There is an open house tomorrow," Zoe says, and I blink my eyes and look back at her, getting out of my thoughts about Evan and his wife. "It's a penthouse, and it's nine million." I'm about to say something, but she holds up her hand. "I just want you to see what you get for that price."

"Fine," I say gruffly, turning again to look outside at the street. He turns down this street, and I see bricks again and businesses for lease. I love how it goes from a two-story building to a six-story building and then again to a three story. It looks almost like Lego blocks. The car slows down, and he slips into a parking spot and shuts off the truck. We get out of the truck, and I'm waiting for Zoe and Zara to do the same, but they just sit there. Evan walks around the car and opens Zara's door first and then Zoe's. She looks at me while I watch.

"If he doesn't open her door, she sits there and pouts

like a child," she says, smiling and then gets out. I close my own door and walk around the truck while he helps Zara out of the car. "He tried helping me out once." She shakes her head.

"She tried to knee me in the balls," Evan says while he links his fingers with Zara's and shuts her door. "She missed, thank God."

I take in the street, then the restaurant across the street with a red and white sign. "Cornelia Street Café," I say out loud and see the white tables with red chairs outside.

"They have good coffee," Zoe says from beside me. When I look down at our feet, we are walking in sync, and I see her long leg flash me each time she puts her right foot forward. "But you can get better coffee near the loft, and they also have fresh croissants."

I stop walking when I see Evan hold the door open for Zara and look up at the yellow awnings hanging over the front windows. As soon as you walk in, you are immediately salivating from the aroma of spices. I see Evan wave to the girl behind the bar as we walk past it. Bottles are all lined up against the mirrored back wall. After passing a couple of tables, we step down into a back area with wooden tables. It looks like a garden, and when you look up, you see it's all glass to stop the rain from coming in. We walk past the tables to the side and then walk up a flight of stairs. "Don't worry," Zoe says, looking over her shoulder. "We aren't bringing you somewhere and chopping your body up."

I shake my head. I've never seen a woman who can make jokes at the drop of a hat like that. When we finally make it up the stairs, I stop at the entrance. "Is this someone's house?" I lean in to ask Zoe, the smell of her perfume filling my nose. Three windows let light into the room. Four bookcases fill in the walls to the windows. But it's the huge square table with fourteen chairs around it in the middle of the room that makes me stop. On the back wall are stairs leading to another floor.

"This is the private area," Zara says. "We came once and sat downstairs. This is a big hockey town and the fans are amazing, but it was a little bit over the top when Evan had to stop every two bites to talk and take pictures."

"This way, we get to enjoy the food, and it's quiet," Evan says, walking over to the table and pulling out a chair for his wife to sit down. He looks at Zoe, who glares at him and walks to a chair and sits down, putting her purse on the empty chair on her right leaving the left chair open. "The table is huge, but we can all sit on one side."

"Aha," the woman from behind the bar says, walking into the room, her chest heaving at having climbed the steps. "The Richards and Signora Zoe," she says. "You finally got a boyfriend," she says, looking at me. I don't know what to say, and I actually don't have to say anything because all three of them shake their heads.

"No," Zoe says, shaking her head. "He's a hockey player."

"What does that mean?" I look at her, and I'm surprised that I even care she said that. I shouldn't care. She can call me whatever she wants to call me; it makes no difference.

"It's mean that you play hockey." She turns to look at me. "It also means I will never date you."

"Because I play hockey?" I ask, confused, and now all eyes are on us as we go back and forth.

"Well, that's strike one." At least she's honest about it. "Strike two, I work for you, and strike three—"

I hold up my hand. "I don't care," I say and then look back at the lady. "Can I have a water please?"

She tries to hide her wide eyes and smiles. "Sure thing. I get some water, and then I'll bring some food, yeah?"

"Perfect," Zara says, trying to cut through the tension we just created in the room.

"I didn't mean anything by it," Zoe says. "I was just trying to say"—she uses her hands to motion between Evan and me—"that you and Evan are co-workers."

"It doesn't really matter," I repeat. I don't even look at her. I can't get involved with her, and this, right here, is another reason. She doesn't want me anyway. I turn to look at Zara who sits beside Evan on the side of me. "What do you recommend?"

"Everything," Zara says, and then I feel the chair next to me scoot back from the table.

"Excuse me, I have to use the bathroom," Zoe says, and she gets up and walks back down the stairs.

"I don't think she meant anything by that," Zara says. I look at her, and then I look at Evan. I know that if I upset his wife, he's probably going to deck me. "It was just taken out of context." I just nod at her, and thankfully, the woman comes back with some water and then hands us the menu.

"I am starving," Zoe says when she returns and pulls in her chair. "Do you think they're bringing us some calamari?"

"Oh, God, I hope so," Zara says, and just like that, the big elephant in the room and the tension from the talk before goes to the corner. Though it lingers. I want to ask her what exactly she meant. They teach you to talk your feelings out in therapy and not hold it in to where it festers inside you.

"I think I'm going to go with pasta tonight," Zoe says. "What about everyone else?"

"I'm going meat," Evan says.

"I might do meat and pasta," Zara says, and I look up at her. "I'm eating for two."

I look at Evan, who sits there beaming with pride as he puts his hand on her stomach. "Congratulations."

"Thank you so much. We really aren't telling anyone yet," Zara says to me with a smile, "but it's hard to keep the secret."

"What do you do?" I ask.

"I'm a professional shopper," she says. "Zara's Closet, that's me."

"I've heard that name before," I tell her. "One of the hockey wives was raving about it because you just dressed Carter Johnson and his wife. What's her name?"

"Erin," Zara says, nodding. "That was me."

"I need clothes," I tell her, and the waiter comes up the stairs and goes to the wall. I just noticed it's a hole in the wall, and he presses the button, and then the food comes upstairs.

He puts plates of mozzarella sticks, fried zucchini, meatballs, and mussels in a tomato sauce, some fried calamari, and then some grilled calamari. The food just keeps coming. "Who ordered all this?" I look at everyone at the table, and they chuckle.

"They always do this; it's their way to woo you. They are doing this because you are new," Zoe says. "They want to impress you so you'll come back."

Everyone reaches in and grabs different things, and I cut into the round plump meatball covered in sauce and the smell of the spices and garlic hits my nose right away. But it's nothing like it is when it hits my tongue and melts in my mouth. "After a bite of those meatballs, I knew I was going to be coming back." I lean in to Zoe. "This is going in my pros list for buying a house near here."

"You can also just come when you want them." Zoe smiles, and unlike before, I feel it's forced. Ever since the dating topic came up, our conversation feels forced. That she's feeling uneasy about what she said.

We remain quiet for the rest of the meal. No one says anything to start new conversations, and when the bill comes, everyone except Zara tries to get it. In the end, Evan won. Pushing from the table, I'm the last one to walk down the stairs. I nod to the woman behind the bar and grab a business card on the way out.

"I'll catch up with you guys on Sunday." I hear Zoe saying, walking to Evan and giving him a hug.

"We can drop you off," Evan says.

"No." She shakes her head, walking to Zara and giving her a hug. Then she shocks me when she bends and kisses her stomach. "That kid is going to love me just as much as you guys," she says, then she turns to look at me. "You have my number if you still want to go to that open house tomorrow. Let me know." I nod at her. "And if you find someone who you want to go with"—she smiles—"no hard feelings."

"I'll text you guys when I get home," she says, and she walks around them.

"Where is she going?" I ask them, watching her make her way to the corner and then turning the corner and out of sight.

"She is going to catch the subway," Zara says and then walks to the truck.

"Is that safe?" I ask them, not sure if we are in a good area or not. I'm irritated with her, but I don't want anything to happen to her. I look at Evan and Zara, wondering why they even allowed her to walk away from them and at night, no less. I don't move from the spot in the middle of the side-walk as I look at them and then at the corner where she just disappeared around.

"She does kickboxing and Kung Fu," Zara says over her shoulder.

"Plus, she's crazy as fuck," Evan says. "I feel bad for the guy who tries to attack her." My eyes never leave the corner she disappeared around. I watch Evan open the door for his wife and then kiss her.

"Actually," I tell them, "I'm going to catch up with her and talk about the open house." I look at Zara. "It was nice meet-ing you," I tell her, and then nod at Evan. "Thanks for dinner. I'll see you Monday," I say. Taking off at a light jog, I turn the corner, looking around to find her.

She's already three blocks ahead, so I step up the run and then call her name. She stops walking and turns to look and is shocked when she sees me. "What are you doing?"

"It's nighttime," I tell her, looking around while I try to slow down my breathing.

"Yeah, it usually happens when the sun goes down," she says, and then we hear a honk and look to see Evan and

Zara waving as they drive away.

"I didn't want you to be alone at night, and I thought we could talk about the open house," I tell her, and she turns to continue walking, her heels clicking on the concrete side-walk.

"You could have called me." She looks over at me, ignoring the fact I didn't want her to walk alone at night.

"After all that food," I say quietly, "I need to walk." Looking down at our feet, I watch as our steps becoming leisurely. "This was a good choice."

"Do you even know how to get to the loft from here?" she asks me, and I shake my head, looking down to smile.

"Not a fucking clue," I say laughing, looking at her.

"It's about a thirty-minute walk from here," she tells me. "If you don't mind, we can walk it."

"Yeah, that's good. It will give me the lay of the land," I say, then look at her. It stays quiet for a couple of minutes. "So you don't date hockey players?"

She laughs nervously. "Are you asking me out?" She pushes my arm with her shoulder. Because she is wearing heels, she comes a little past my shoulder.

I shake my head. "No, definitely not."

"Good. That's a relief," she says. "It would have been awk-ward as hell." I laugh now at her bluntness. "But to answer your question, no, I don't."

"Too much for you?" I don't even know why I care.

"They are just not the type I usually go for," she says hon-estly. "It's just like for a guy. If he likes big boobs, he isn't going to go out with someone who has small boobs."

"I don't think that's the same thing at all," I tell her as we leisurely walk down the street at a snail's pace.

She rolls her eyes. "I was trying to think like a man. It was the only thing that came to mind."

"Guys don't just go for boobs, you know," I tell her. "I mean, I like a girl who can have a conversation with me." I shake my head now. "Wow, I didn't even know that was what I liked."

"I take it that you don't date girls often." She looks sideways at me and puts her hair behind her ear.

"I don't think I've ever really dated," I answer honestly. I don't tell her that the reason was because I was chasing the high, and the girls that went with the high were just interested in getting my dick and the high. "So you date guys in business?" I ask, and she shakes her head.

"Not necessarily but I have a strict rule about hockey players," she tells me. "As much as I love to irritate my brother by joking about it, I just stick to non-hockey players."

"Ah, this makes sense now, and I get it." I stop walking, and she stops with me, turning to look me. "You got burned by one of them?" I ask her.

"Have you met my brother?" She looks at me, raising her eyebrows, then turns to walk again, and I follow her. "He would not be okay with that."

"But your sisters are married to hockey players," I point out.

"And my father is Cooper Stone," she says. I stop walking because I can't believe I didn't put two and two together. "You knew that, right?"

"I mean …" I start saying. "I knew it, but it just didn't really connect until, well, now." She laughs, and then we start walking again but this time a bit slower. "Jesus, Cooper Stone." The greatest hockey player to ever play.

"Well, I get to call him Dad," she says. "But yeah, Cooper Stone. See why I don't date hockey players?"

"I can see it," I finally say. "Well, the good news is I'm not in the market for a girlfriend."

"What's your story, Viktor?" I'm not even sure where to begin with that question. "You don't have to answer the question."

"It's not that I don't want to answer it," I tell her.

"You just aren't ready," she says, nodding. "I get it. This is a big step, right? Getting traded and then meeting your new team."

"You really don't know any of my story?" I ask her, somewhat shocked.

"I really don't know anything except Matthew was super pumped when he signed you, and that you are looking for an apartment," she answers me, and I breathe a sigh of relief that she will learn about my past from me and not through hearsay. She could go online, and all the details are there for her to read, but I want to be the one to tell her. I mean, I don't care how she feels or if she accepts it. I'm the one who has to accept it.

"I was in rehab when I got traded. I'm a recovering cocaine addict," I say, and I know she will find that part if she looks it up, but at least I got to tell her. I inhale deeply and then tell her, "Last game of the season, I went on the ice high as a kite." I don't look at her; instead, I just walk ahead. "I mean, I've been on the ice high before, but this time, it was just so obvious." I look over at her, but she doesn't say anything. "I chased the puck in a circle four times before falling into my goalie." I laugh bitterly, rubbing my face and trying to erase that memory. "To top it all off, my parents were in the stands watching, and well, when I got pulled off the ice and benched, I couldn't care less. When I got into the car that night, I expected my parents to ream my ass, especially my dad, but he said nothing, and then the next day when I got up, the GM to the team was there, and it was basically go to rehab or lose my contract. So"—I shrug—"I went to rehab."

"That must have been a very scary time," she says softly and I don't know how to answer her. "This is you," she says, stopping, and I look up at the building that is now my temporary home. "I'll text you the address for tomorrow," she says, continuing to walk, then turning. "Thanks for making sure I was okay." I don't say anything to her as she turns around and walks, her hips swinging just a touch. She is the first one that I actually admitted all that to and she didn't say anything, didn't judge me, didn't ask me, didn't blame me. I don't know how I feel about any of this and I stand here for longer than I should and finally walk up the steps to the iron door.

Six

Zoe

I TOSS AND turn most of the night, and when I finally wake up, I feel slightly hungover even though I had nothing to drink last night. I drag my ass to get coffee and decide to hit a boxing class to get some energy in me. I'm locking my door when the phone rings, and I have to dig deep in my purse to find it. "Hello," I say finally on the sixth ring.

"Zoe." I hear my name in his light Russian accent. "It's Viktor."

"Hi," I say, walking down the steps and making my way over to the gym four blocks away.

"Sorry, I didn't know if it was a good time to call," he says, and he sounds weird like rushed and disconnected.

"I'm just walking to the gym," I tell him, "so it's a good time."

"I was wondering if we could go to that open house?" he asks me. "We got sidetracked last night when we talked."

"We really did." I laugh. "I guess other issues were more important like my dad and why I don't date hockey players."

"Don't forget to add in my rehab. That is always a great topic to derail any conversation," he says, and I hear him drink something.

"I guess we had lots of things to discuss that were more important than you finding a house," I joke with him, looking at my watch. "My boxing class ends at eleven thirty, but I can meet you at the apartment at twelve thirty."

"That sounds good." His voice is so husky. "Send me the address."

"I will, and I'll see you there," I tell him and disconnect. Opening my messages, I forward him the address.

The workout was just what I needed to rejuvenate. When I take out my phone to check my messages I see a couple of emails need my attention and also my father just called me. Without fail every single Saturday, he calls wondering if I will be coming home for Sunday family lunch.

I start walking toward the open house, and when I finally turn the corner, I spot him right away. I take the time to look at him while his eyes are on his phone. He's casual in a blue sweater, sports shorts, and black and white Nikes on his feet. His dark brown hair curls out of the back of his Stingers baseball cap, he has scruff on his face, and I can't see the blue of his eyes yet. But I can see his crooked nose, something that you can only see if you look at his face. It's something I noticed while we were walking. I also noticed his plump lips that look perfect, too perfect. He's actually very much a pretty boy except his attitude is all hockey. I don't know if I can describe it really; it's just the cockiness, the attitude.

He must sense someone is looking at him because he turns his head in my direction. I don't know what I'm expecting to see, but what I'm not expecting are the circles under his eyes or the way he just looks exhausted. The blue of his eyes is so dark they look black. I smile and raise my hand to say hi, and he just nods and then turns back to his phone. "This is going to be fun," I say to myself.

When I'm finally close enough, I speak up. "Hi, have you been here long?"

"No," he says gruffly, keeping his eyes on his phone.

"Okay, we should get started," I tell him, waiting for him to finish whatever he's doing on the phone. He finally closes it, but he doesn't put it away; he holds it in his hand, tapping his index finger on it.

"Lead the way." I just nod at him. He's still paying me to do this job.

"I was doing a little research last night," I tell him when we walk up the stairs to the front door. "It's actually three floors, and it's at the top of the building. There are ten floors, and five are used for office spaces," I say, opening the door and walking over to the elevator. "There is a night security guard, but during the day, it's an easy access in."

"Okay," he says. The elevator pings, and we get in. I press the button for the seventh floor.

"You can only access your floor with a key, but since it's an open house, it's accessible." I turn to find him nodding his head. He hasn't said more than five words to me, and all his answers have been curt. Maybe I was too nosy last night, and he didn't want to open up to me, but I just kept pushing.

I don't have much more time to think about it before the elevator doors open and we are faced with the apartment right away. He holds out his hand for me to walk ahead of him, again not saying anything.

"Hi, welcome to our open house," Nicole, a fellow real estate broker, says to me, and then she must recognize me. "Hey, Zoe, I didn't know you were in the market?"

"We aren't really," I tell her. "He is new to the city, so I'm showing him the area and saw it was an open house." I smile at her and look around. "High ceilings are really nice." I look over at Viktor who has walked to one of the three windows and is looking outside.

"A little bit to know about the penthouse," Nicole states and hands Viktor a paper with everything on it. "It's a four-bedroom, four-bath built in nineteen eighty-two. But renovated last year. It's one thousand eight hundred square feet."

"My closet in LA was that size," Viktor says and then comes back to stand next to me.

"Yes. New York is nothing like Los Angeles," Nicole says with a nervous laugh. "There is an HOA."

"Great," Viktor says sarcastically.

"It's almost nine thousand a month," Nicole says. "Please feel free to look around, and if you have any questions, I'm here. Be sure to check out the rooftop terrace," she says before she walks away.

"Why don't we start downstairs and work our way up?" I suggest to him. Again, he waits for me to lead the way, so I walk down the modern stairs that look like they're hanging from strings to another little sitting area. "There are three bedrooms on this level," I tell him and wait for him to walk around. He walks into the master bedroom and then in the other one while continuing to check his phone every second. His eyes rove around the room, but you can see he really isn't looking.

"How much is this?" he asks while he walks to the third one. His fingers either tap his phone or he's looking at it.

"Eight point seven million," I remind him.

"Insane." He shakes his head, glances at me, then looks back at his phone again. "Plus, the kitchen is upstairs."

"Yes." I nod and see his hands start to move nervously. What is going on with him? I want to ask, but I'm afraid to.

"I don't even want to see anything more," he says, then his phone pings in his hand. "I have to go. I'll text you later," he says and then jogs up the steps, leaving me alone in the middle of the house. I walk up the stairs and hear the elevator door close.

"Well, that was quick," Nicole says, and I put on my game face.

"He had a meeting he had to run to," I tell her, "but I'll let you know if he wants a second round." I walk to the elevator.

Putting my head down, I make my way out of the building, and I'm a bit pissed off and a lot irritated. I hold my hand up and flag down a cab the same time I get my phone out and send a group message to my sisters, sister-in-law, and her best friend, Vivienne.

Me: Coming home tonight and I need a drink. Who is with me?

Everyone answers yes, so I put my phone away. I get home and when I finally take it out again, I see that I have missed over a hundred notifications from the group chat that was not tabled, and I also see one from Viktor. I contemplate opening it, but I choose against it; instead I grab my laptop and my overnight bag, and when Vivienne rings the bell, I'm ready to go.

"I have a car waiting, and I already have the wine," she says, running back down to the car, and I get in with her.

"Where is the wine?" I ask her.

"In the water bottles," she says, reaching into her bag and grabbing the "water bottles."

"It's yellow," I point out.

"We can say it's Crystal Light," Vivienne says, uncapping the bottle. "Yup, tastes just like it." I open my own bottle and take a sip.

"Yup, this should be perfect." I cheer her with my bottle and take a gulp.

"Good news. I brought six just in case." She winks at me. "It's going to be a fun night."

I smile and look out the window as the driver takes us to Long Island. The whole time, my phone gets heavier and heavier in my pocket.

SEVEN

VIKTOR

I HIGHTAIL IT so fast out of that open house, I'm sure I look like the cartoon coyote. This morning was shaky after getting off the phone with Zoe. There was this sudden burden and then an even bigger urge to use, so I texted every person on the sponsor list to talk to, and when one finally answered me, I bailed on the open house. I walk down the street, looking down at my Google maps and following the blue fucking arrow. I look around, checking to see the numbers on the doors.

"You must be Viktor," someone says from the side, and I look over at a man sitting at a cast iron table right in front of the coffee shop I'm looking for.

"Jeffrey?" I ask him, and he just nods as he sits up, pushing his rounded glasses up on his nose. His salt and pepper hair is short on the sides and long on the top, his white goatee a little long. He is dressed in jeans and a white linen button-down shirt.

"That would be me." He smiles and then motions for me to sit in the empty seat in front of him. "Please sit down."

I pull out the chair, the metal scraping across the concrete walkway, and I sit down. "Sorry about the urgency," I finally tell him.

"Not a problem. It's what I signed up to do," Jeffrey says and then stops when the waitress comes over and asks for our order.

"I'll have an ice coffee please," Jeffrey says.

"I'll have an ice water." I force a smile, and she turns and walks away with our order. I look around and find the street crowded with a lot of people walking. A man with fifteen dogs walks down the other side.

"How long?" Jeffrey asks, and I look over at him. An older man, he has brown hair with white in it, his beard matching the hair on his head. His sunglasses cover his eyes, but with me looking at him, he takes them off, and I see he has brown eyes.

"Ninety-two days," I say softly. My stomach hurts, and my thumb strums on the table. Unlike Jeffrey, I'm sitting up in my chair, but my shoulders are slumped over.

"Not even at the tip of the iceberg," Jeffrey says. "You are two days out of rehab, right?"

"Yes," I say tightly. "Last night was the worst night I've ever had since I've been clean."

"How so?" he asks me, and I look up at him. "What did you feel?"

"I tossed and turned the whole night," I tell him honestly. "Every time I shut my eyes, the only thing I could hear was the voice in the back of my head telling me I just needed a hit."

"Did you do anything about it?" he asks me, and I shake my head. "Because you didn't know where to get it, or because you fought it off?"

"Both." I sigh. "At first, I fought it off. Then I got out of bed and walked around the loft," I tell him, recounting last night to him. But I can't even put into words the despair I felt, the helplessness, the heart palpitations, and the images in my head of me sitting on the couch with my head back feeling nothing because I did just one line of the drug. "I walked in circles for an hour," I spit out. "Maybe even two."

"Did you have your phone?" he asks me the odd question.

"I did," I answer him. "I mean, it was somewhere in the house." I try to remember where it was. I don't say anything because the waitress comes over and places our order on the table.

"Thank you," Jeffrey says, sitting up. "What stopped you from using your phone?"

I look at him oddly, and I swear I'm starting to sweat. I feel drips of sweat forming on my back. "You could have gotten drugs in a snap," he says, and I know this. "You could have picked up your phone and messaged just one person, and they would have had that number you needed." I never thought of that, never thought that all I had to do was text someone. "But you didn't do that."

"I didn't think of it." I shake my head. "I sat on the couch after walking around in circles." I close my eyes, and I'm right back in the middle of the loft on the couch, wearing just my boxers. The only light streaming in the pitch-black loft was from the full moon through the window. "In front of the couch was my chip," I tell him. Taking it out of my pocket and rubbing my fingers over it calms my heart just a touch. The red coin with the words "Clean and Serene for Ninety Days" in gold.

"Why didn't you call me?" he asks. "That is what a sponsor is for." Yesterday, he was the only one to respond to the texts I sent looking for a sponsor from the list I got.

"I didn't think it would be a good idea to call you at four o'clock in the morning because my head was fucking with me. Alain also gave me a list of therapists, so I'm going to reach out to a few this week."

"You know why your head was fucking with you," he finally says, and I just look at him. "It was fucking with you because for the first time in ninety days, you didn't have anyone else stopping you from scoring that drug. You were sent into the wild, and your body knew you didn't have to look anyone in the eyes today." I take in his words. "Your subconscious is the devil on your shoulder when it wants to be." He smiles and almost laughs. "You didn't think this would be easy, did you?"

I shake my head. "I didn't think it would be easy." I take a sip of the water, and the cold water feels fresh in my dry mouth. "But I didn't think it would be this hard." He reaches in his pocket and takes out a white chip and hands it to me. I look down at it seeing the words "Just for Today" in gold.

"That is for today," he says. "All you can see is today."

"I thought that if I wasn't around the people who I partied with, it would be easy." I laugh bitterly. "But I'm my worst enemy."

"That, my friend," Jeffrey says, "is almost like step one."

"I thought step one was admitting I have a problem," I counter him with the stuff I heard at rehab.

"Repeat the sentence," Jeffrey asks me.

"Step one was admitting I have a problem." I stop speaking as the words finally sink in. "I have a problem."

"If I had a sticker, I would give you one," he says. Leaning back in his chair, he smiles while he crosses his arms over his chest.

"Fuck off," I finally say, and I finally feel the pressure on my chest start to get a bit lighter. The crushing part doesn't feel so heavy. "I really should have called you. It would have saved seven hours."

"What did you do to fight it off?" he asks me. "Besides sitting in the dark."

"I went to work out," I tell him. "Left the house at six and then met my realtor."

"Have you eaten?" he asks me, and I shake my head. "I had a muffin."

He gets up now, tossing a five-dollar bill on the table and putting his cup on it so it doesn't fly away. "Let's get some food in you. I know a great burger place not too far from here." I get up with him, putting the phone in my pocket along with the two chips. "Then we can hit up a meeting."

We walk to the restaurant and take turns talking to get to know one another. You always think you have it worse than the other person, but then you hear their stories, and you realize you don't. He tells me that he's been sober for thirty years and that he just celebrated his sixty-fifth birthday. His wake-up call was when his six-month-old crawled onto his needle. "I will always remember that day. I was in that space where the high was just starting to hit me and I was feeling euphoria. That feeling of nothing can touch you, but then I heard the wailing of my daughter. I saw what was happening, yet I couldn't do anything because my hands were just too heavy to raise. She cried for twenty minutes until my wife came in and saw." My heart breaks for him. "For twenty minutes, I had no control over my body. I had no control over anything. The drug had the control. It was my rock bottom. I pleaded with her to forgive me, which she did. Eventually. I went away to rehab, and we tried to make it work, but I needed to heal myself before I could love anyone."

"Where is she now?" I ask. "If it's not too much to ask."

"She's living in Atlanta with her second husband who is the opposite of me. A soft-spoken minister," he says, almost laughing. "It was for the best," he says softly and puts his hands in his pockets as we walk up to the restaurant. "I have a brand-new life. I have a wife who loves me and who I cherish with every single fiber of my being. I am a father to four children, including the six-month-old who is now a mother of three kids herself."

"So, there's a light at the end of the tunnel?" I ask him. "After the dark, there is light."

He nods his head. "There is light, Viktor. You just have to work to get there. Then you have to work harder than everyone else to keep it. Some recover easier than others, but every day that you fight is an extra day with the light."

I don't say anything else and neither does Jeffrey while

we order our burgers. We discuss baseball as we eat, and then when we finally make it to the meeting, I know that I'm going to make it to ninety-three days. But I know that getting to ninety-four will be another hurdle.

When I finally leave him at the end of the night, I hand him back his white chip. "This is for you," I tell him. "Save it for next time."

"I will," he says and then looks at me. "Go home, Viktor, and get some sleep." I nod at him. "Use my number if and when you need it."

"I will," I say, then turn and walk away. My hand goes to my pocket, and I grab my phone. I sent Matthew a text right before I went into a meeting asking to sit down with him. I also sent one to Zoe apologizing for my mood today. I scroll and see that Matthew is the only one who answered me.

Matthew: How about you come out and spend the day tomorrow? It's Sunday; you can meet the family.

I don't know if I should go or not, but I know I have nothing else going on, so I answer him.

Me: Sounds good. What time and what can I bring?

I see the button with three dots come up.

Matthew: Anytime after ten and bring yourself.

He follows that with his address. Bring myself. I don't think they really want a recovering drug addict who just feels like he went ten rounds with Mike Tyson. The same guy who was a total dick to Zoe, and she didn't deserve it.

I open my map and put in the address to the loft. I see that it's a forty-seven minute walk. I spend the forty-seven minutes listening to the noise of New York City—the honking, the zooming of the cabs down the street, and the sirens. So many fucking sirens.

When I finally open the door to the loft, I'm exhausted. I barely make it through the shower, and by the time I collapse on the bed, my body gives in. I finally get the sleep that evaded me last night, and this time, I keep my demons at bay.

EIGHT

ZOE

"I LOVE MY girl time," Karrie says from beside me as she lies on the couch with one eye open. I look over at her and then back at the coffee table in front of us. "I need my girl time," she says, looking at all of us one at a time.

After I texted them about drinking, they were all up for the challenge. We've all spaced out on the couches in Zara's living room. She has three huge couches with deep cushions. You just sink into them and think you're in heaven. They are so big that we aren't even touching each other.

"I haven't had sex in six months," Vivienne says, and we all look at her with mostly shock on our faces. Vivienne has been Karrie's best friend since forever. She moved over from France so long ago, but her accent is still there.

"What do you mean you haven't had sex in six months?" Allison sits up on her side of the couch on the other side of Karrie and me. Vivienne lies on a couch all by herself with one leg hiked up on the back of the couch while the other leg is flat on the couch, and her arm dangling off the couch holding her wine glass.

"I mean, I haven't had sex in six months," she says, rolling to her side and taking another sip of wine. "I'm thirsty." She looks at her wine glass. "For cock."

"But why?" I ask her. "You have sex all the time."

"I don't know why, Zoe." Her voice comes out a touch higher.

"Have you tried to have sex with someone lately?" Karrie asks her. "You are always out."

"I am trying. Just none of them are"—she starts snapping her fingers, trying to come up with the right word—"eligible."

"That isn't the right word," Karrie says to her, and she glares at her.

"Who cares what the right word is," she says, flabbergasted. "My vagina is probably full of cobwebs."

"It's not that bad," Allison says.

"When is the last time you had sex?" She looks over at me.

"Three weeks ago," I tell her, and everyone looks at me. "What?" I shrug. "It was with another agent. We just pulled out the deal of the month, and well, we had pent-up tension that needed to be released."

"Only you would talk about sex like it's a merger," Zara says, and I ignore her and look back at Vivienne.

I shrug my shoulders while I get up and pour myself another glass of wine. The whole thing needs my full attention since I can see more than one bottle, and I'm trying not to spill any. I wonder when the last time Viktor had sex. My eyes open wide, and then I look around to see if anyone is looking at me. After a couple of glasses of wine, you sometimes say things instead of think them. Thankfully, I didn't verbalize that thought.

"I'm so confused," Allison says. "I need to just close my eyes."

"This is when the party is over," Zara says and gets up from the couch. "Evan, can you call the men to come and wrangle their women?"

She goes to the table and starts picking up the bottles. "Wrangle their women." I giggle to myself. "Like they are cattle."

"You need help upstairs?" she asks me, and I just shake my head. It takes about five minutes for Max and Matthew to arrive.

"Jesus, why does she smell like she bathed in wine?" Matthew asks when he picks up Karrie.

"The last three glasses of wine spilled on her before she got it to her mouth," Zara tells him, and he just shakes his head.

"Vivienne," he barks at her, and she sits up. "You need me to carry you, or are you good?"

"I'm good," she says, standing and then falling back down. "Just go ahead. I'll catch up."

"Hey there, good looking," Allison says when Max leans over her and kisses her lips. "Take me home and have your way with me."

"That is so gross," Matthew says, coming back into the room and watching Vivienne try and get up. When nothing helps, he puts her over his shoulder.

"You have a great ass, Matthew," she says when her face is up close to it. "I'm so thirsty,"

she moans, and I roll my lips so I don't laugh.

"I have some water bottles in the car," Matthew says and then shouts over his shoulder. "See all of you tomorrow."

"Are we going to get busy in the car?" Allison asks Max who just laughs. "Remember the last time?"

Zara and I both groan. "Can you stop her from talking?" Zara asks him, and Allison just smiles.

"We had sex in the back seat of the car," she says in a whisper, but since she's drunk, it comes out in a scream. "In the driveway."

"Why didn't you just go inside?" I ask her.

"Because it's taboo," Allison says, and Max just shakes his head. "Also, he's super-hot."

"Okay, Angel," Max finally says, calling her by her name that he always calls her. "Let's not scar them anymore than you already have," he says, walking out of the room.

"Seriously? In the car?" Evan says, shaking his head. "I've sat in that back seat."

"I was on top," Allison says, putting up her hand, and Evan puts his hand to his mouth. "I'm a rodeo queen."

"Jesus fuck," Zara says. "Why am I not recording this?"

"I think I'm going to be sick," Evan says. "I put my hands down on that seat."

"Which side?" Allison asks right before Max walks out of the door and the door slams.

"You two okay?" Evan asks us, and I just nod while Zara goes over to him, hugging him around the waist.

"I'm going up to my room," I say, walking out of the living

room.

The next morning, the sound of banging pots in the kitchen rustles me from sleep, and when I finally roll out of bed and make my way downstairs, Evan is making his special hangover cure. Just for me. Evan knew very early on that Zara and I had this insane bond we couldn't explain. He also knew it would never be severed, so he did the only thing he knew how. He accepted me with open arms. I mean, honestly, I'm perfect, but it helps that he tells me on occasion.

Breakfast is smooth sailing, and I eat everything on my plate, and then we lounge on the couch while Zara puts headphones on her belly and plays classical music. After putting on my light pink bikini, I slip a dress over it and slide into my flip-flops. I grab my stuff, knowing I'm going straight home from Matthew's house.

When we pull up, it's almost noon, and the driveway is full. "Who the fuck did he invite? The whole team?" I ask, getting out and placing the sunglasses on my face. "I can hear kids screaming from here," I groan, and we walk around the side and go through his cast iron gate. "Jesus, who are all these people?" I say, looking around the yard at what must be at least fifty people.

He has a huge property with a massive pool on the side of the yard. But what is the coolest is the Olympic-size rink he has set up on the other side. In the winter, it's ice, and in the summer, he has this shiny surface so the kids can use their roller blades.

"Hey there, I was wondering when you guys would get

here," Matthew says when he meets us coming out of his house. "You look like shit." He hands me a water bottle.

"Bite me," I say, grabbing the bottle. "Who are all these people?"

"Some are from Mini Cooper's hockey league. The rest are coaching staff and a couple of players are here. Some rookies," he says and then stands straight and crosses his arms over his chest. "Don't get any ideas."

"Did Max give you a ride to the rink last week?" I ask him, and he just nods his head. "He banged Allison in the same car."

"Motherfucker," he says, turning and walking away from us with Evan laughing beside me, and Zara holding up her hand.

"Oh my God, I think I'm going to die." I spot Vivienne while she comes up to us, and she is wearing a checkered bikini.

"You look like a checkered flag," Zara says.

"Gentlemen, start your engines!" she yells, turning around, and no one really notices her but Max, who laughs at the joke.

"Oh, look who's here. Viktor," Evan says. "I'm going to go say hi to him."

"Evan, can you put in a good word for me?" Vivienne asks him. "I've been trying to get his motor running, but he's too busy ignoring me." She then turns to us. "I'm so thirsty." She winks, and my stomach suddenly knots and burns. "I've been saying that all afternoon, and Matthew and your dad have been getting me drinks."

I shake my head with a laugh. "I'm going to go say hi to my parents." I turn to walk toward them, but my head is down, and I smack straight into a white shirt. I'm about to bounce off the hard chest, but his hands come out to catch me before I lose my footing.

"Sorry," I say and then finally look up into Viktor's blue eyes. Eyes that taunted me in my dream all night. "Sorry about that. I wasn't looking where I was going."

"It's okay," he says, and then the noise from all around us stops him. "Listen, about yesterday …"

I'm not sure I want to hear why he was a dick. I'm not ready for this conversation, least of all not with everyone here. "Forget it. It's fine," I say, and I don't wait for him to answer. I just walk around him and into my father's open arms.

"You look sick," he says, kissing my head. "Are you sick?"

"Yes," I tell him, "of wine." I try not to look around and see where Viktor went off to. I shouldn't care, and I don't care. Maybe if I keep repeating it, my brain will finally get the memo.

"Did you girls drink too much last night?" he asks, and he doesn't let me go. I don't tell him that I was drinking to forget about what a dick Viktor was.

"Where's Mom?' I ask, and then I feel a little finger on my thigh.

"Auntie Zoe," Alex, my niece, says softly. Her whole body drips with water because she just came out of the pool, and she still has her floaties on her arms. "Will you come in the pool with me?"

I squat down in front of her. "Why? Is this a trick?" I ask her, and she just shakes her head.

"Mommy won't let me swim without my floaties," she says, and I understand it now.

"So you want me to take you in the pool and take off your floaties?" I ask her, and her face fills with a huge smile that looks exactly like her mother's. "You're lucky I love you," I say and peel the dress off my body.

"I'll be back, Dad," I say, walking away to the pool holding Alex's hand.

"Where is the rest of that bathing suit?" I hear my father shout, and I just shake my head.

"Zara is wearing it," I say over my shoulder. Looking at Zara, I see she's talking to Viktor, but their talking stops while they watch me. "Zara, show Dad your suit." She throws her head back and laughs, slipping the dress off and showing us that she is wearing a one piece. "Traitor," I say, and then I spend the next hour in the pool, pretending to be carefree except the heaviness of Viktor is weighing in.

NINE

VIKTOR

"HEY, NICE TO see you again," Zara says as soon as Zoe walks away from me, but I can still feel her in my arms. She wasn't even looking where she was going. She just had a head-on collision and then she looked up, and even though I couldn't see her eyes, I knew she must have been shocked it was me. I tried to apologize, but she wouldn't let me and shrugged it off.

"It's great seeing you again," I answer Zara, and then I spot Evan coming over. He stopped to talk to me on his way to get his wife a drink. When I walked into the yard two hours ago, the last thing I expected was a circus. I thought it would be a low-key affair, but I should have known that Matthew didn't know what low-key meant.

"Here you go, sweetheart. I got you a water bottle," Evan says, handing her the bottle, then going to stand next to her. "How long have you been here?"

"A while," I answer honestly, and then my eyes go back to the pool. I spot Zoe with her hair tied up on the top of her head while she talks to Max's little girl. When she pulled her dress off, I thought my mouth would hit the floor. Don't get me wrong, I knew she had a smoking body, but what I didn't know is that everything is defined and toned. Her ass is hands down the best ass I've ever seen on a woman. "He told me to be here at ten. I figured getting here a bit later would be good."

"There she is," a man says and when I look up, he comes to hug Zara and kisses her head. He turns to Evan and gives him a side hug. "We haven't met yet," he says, but he doesn't need to tell anyone who he is. "I'm Cooper."

I try to stay cool and not get tongue-tied. I mean, if you play hockey, you know who Cooper Stone is. Every year, you go out on that ice and try to beat or reach one of his records. Fuck, I think I have a jersey of when I was in school with his number on it. "It's nice to meet you, sir," I say and then hear Evan laugh.

"Cooper is fine," he says, smiling and shaking my hand. "You must be Viktor."

"I am." I nod at him. "It's a pleasure to meet you."

"I've heard some good things," he says, and then he turns back and starts talking to Zara. "What's wrong with Zoe?" he asks. Looking back at the pool, I see that she's standing in the pool with the water up to her waist talking to some guy who I don't know stands there with his perfectly coiffed haircut and wearing shades. He looks like he's a model.

"She got trashed last night," Zara says, laughing. "Karrie, Allison, and Vivienne were all over the wine bottles last night."

"Allison!" Cooper yells, and she looks up from the chair where she's sitting. Max looks up from beside her. Her face looks just a touch better than Zoe, but she also has her glasses on.

"I thought you said you woke up with a migraine?" he asks her, and she smirks and looks down. "Incredible that she lied to me."

"It's okay, Pops," Zara says to him. "I can be your favorite now."

"No way in hell," a male voice responds. I look behind Cooper, and it's like I'm looking at twins. Justin is a touch bigger than his father in height, and he is also bigger in size. His eyes are a light blue exactly like his sisters.

"Well, well, well, look at what the cat dragged in," Zara says. "The prodigal son."

"Justin," Cooper says, and now I know that's Justin Stone who was drafted last year first overall for Edmonton. He gives Cooper a hug. "You know your mother stayed up all night."

"I told her not to, Dad," Justin says and then walks over to Zara. "Hey, preggo," then nodding at Evan. "Where is the yang to the yin?"

"You are so lame," Zara says loudly at her mother who is across the yard. "Mom, look who it is? The sly one!"

Justin looks at Zara. "For once, can you not bust my balls? I'm nineteen, and I don't even live at home."

"Interesting, since I saw Mom washing your laundry last night," Zara says. She doesn't say anything else because their mom comes up to him with a scowl on her face.

"I told you to text me your plans," she tells him as soon as she's close enough.

I lean over to Evan, asking him, "Is it always like this?" I'm taking it all in. This whole family dynamic.

"No," he says. "You should be here at Christmas. It's a madhouse."

"Oh my God, what is that on your neck?" Zara shrieks. Walking over to Justin, she moves his collar away to reveal a huge hickey.

He moves away from her. "Can you fuck off?" He looks at her. "You are so lucky you are with child or I would have you over my shoulder and toss you in the pool."

She crosses her arms over her chest. "Dude, you wouldn't lay a finger on her," Evan says.

"Hey, buddy," Matthew says, coming over to us and shaking Justin's hand and giving him a side hug. "Good to see you."

"You are six hours late," Allison says, joining them. Max stands behind her, holding her shoulders in his hands. "Is that a hickey?"

"No way. Where?" Matthew says and then sees it. "You dog," he says, pushing Justin away with a beaming smile.

"Let me get this straight," Zoe says, walking to us as she wraps a towel around herself. "He comes home after a night with a bunny, and it's all okay." She looks at her father and then at Matthew. "But if I do it"—she points at herself—"it's the end of the world?"

"Zoe," Cooper starts and then looks down at his wife who just crosses her arms over her chest. "I just don't want you to be put in that situation." He tries to be diplomatic about it, but there is no turning it around because it's borderline sexist.

"Yeah, and you're a girl," Matthew finally says. "Not okay. Never okay. It's bad enough that one is pregnant."

"By my husband," Zara says, and then the whole group starts talking at the same time.

I walk away from them and go to the side table, grabbing a water bottle, and then I'm cornered by the crazy French lady, Vivienne. "They are nuts, aren't they?" she says, getting close to me. "So how do you like the city?"

"It's good," I say. "I'm just getting to know it really."

"You should take my number and give me a call. I can show you around." She smiles at me and inches even closer. "I know my way around."

"I'm sure you do." I smile at her, and thankfully, I'm saved when a kid starts crying. When she turns her head, I run away to the side where I sit in a chair and just take in the backyard.

An hour later, most of the kids and parents have left, and the only ones lingering seem to be the immediate family. I look at my watch and see that it's almost dinnertime. I also realize I haven't wanted to use today. I spent the whole day socializing, and not once did I feel the need to get high. Not fucking once. Also, no one treated me differently or watched what they said or how they acted. As I look around, I realize I haven't felt comfortable in my skin in the longest time.

"There you are. I was wondering if you had left without saying goodbye," Vivienne says, finding me again, and before I can even answer, Zoe walks over.

"Vivienne, there you are," Zoe says as she walks over, wearing her dress again. "The car just got here."

"Already?" Vivienne says. "Let me go and get my things." She walks away from us.

"Are you guys going back to the city?" I ask her, and she looks up at me, and I can see that she got some sun on her nose.

"Yeah." She nods. "Would you like a ride?"

"Yeah. That would be great." I smile at her and look around to see if anyone is close by. "Listen, about yesterday …"

"It's all right. We all have crappy days," she says. "Today is mine. I swear I'm never drinking wine again."

I laugh at her now. "I bet you'll forget that by next Saturday."

"Wow, you really give me credit. I was thinking by Tuesday," she says, laughing. She stops talking beside me and looks over at Justin. He's just taken his shirt off and has fingernail marks all down his back.

"Mom, Justin got attacked!" Zara shouts, and Justin looks at her weirdly. Matthew goes up to him, turns him around, and whispers something in his ear. He puts his shirt right back on. "Cover it up." Their mom stands up and then walks to him, and all you can see is Justin shrugging his shoulders.

"I'm ready!" Vivienne yells, and then Zoe looks at me.

I say goodbye to Matthew and his wife, thanking her for having me, and make plans to be on the ice with Max and Evan the next day. "Can I sit all the way in the back?" Vivienne asks, looking at the Suburban that has come to get us. "I need to lie down." The man stands by the side with the door open and nods at Vivienne as she makes her way into the back. The driver puts the seat down, and I get in and look out the window, seeing Zoe carry her big bag with two bottles of water under her arm.

"Here," she says, tossing the water at Vivienne. "My mother didn't want you to get thirsty." She laughs and then puts her bag in next to me and then sits down. The car door closes. "We are going to drop Vivienne off first if that's okay."

"I'm the one tagging along," I tell her, and she just nods. She then takes out her phone and her fingers move a million miles a minute. "Do you work every day?"

"No," she says, not looking up. "Or maybe I do." She finally looks up. "If a deal is on the line, I work every day. If not, I take Sunday off."

"That makes sense," I tell her and then look out the window when she looks back down at her phone.

"Look at this," she says, moving the bag next to me and coming over with her phone. "It's going on the market tomorrow."

"Then how do you know?" I ask her, and she shrugs.

"Someone sent me the listing. It's in Tribeca. Two bedrooms, three bathrooms, three point two million," she tells me, all excited. "One thousand eight hundred square feet of living area." I grab her phone and swipe through the pictures. "Are you busy tomorrow?"

"I'm available in the afternoon. I have work in the morning," I tell her, and then she grabs the phone back, typing something in.

"Okay, I told him to hold off on posting it until tomorrow," she says, looking down at her phone. "I'm going to owe him one." She looks at me. "Which means you're going to owe me DF."

I look at her shocked. "I know what DP is. I definitely don't know what DF stands for."

She laughs hysterically now. "Oh my God, DF means double favors. Get your head out of the gutter." She looks at me, her eyes a crystal blue.

"Double favor," I repeat, getting it now. "But explain to me again how I owe you now," I ask her as the SUV turns a corner and she falls onto me.

"I'm going to have to go on a date with this guy for keeping the listing a secret until tomorrow," she says honestly, and I ignore the little ping in the pit of my stomach. "And I don't really like him because he's creepy and oily." I watch her face as she explains what oily means. I don't push her away from me, which I know is mistake number one. For the next forty minutes, she doesn't move from beside me, her body heat on me, and her smell all around me. I pretend to be interested in her story, but the only thing I look at is the way her lips move, or the way she always uses her hands while she talks. She tells me story after story about all the times he's tried to make her owe him. When we drop Vivienne off, I look around and then open my maps app while they hug goodbye. Knowing I need to get as far away from the two of us being alone as humanly possible.

When she gets back in the SUV, I look at her. "I'm going to get off here. It's a forty-minute walk, and it's a nice night," I say, not disclosing the real reason I want to get out of here. She tells the driver to pull over, but she doesn't get out like she did with Vivienne.

"I'll send you the address and the time," she says, and I just nod when the SUV pulls away. I make sure it's out of sight before I make my way over to the church on the corner. I walk in the side door and down the stairs with the smell of incense all around. The wooden walls lead into the light room that even smells dusty. The curtains on the window look like they were white, then yellow, and are now a tint of brown. Hand-drawn artwork sticks to the white concrete walls.

I walk in and spot the circle of chairs; the meeting has already started, so I do my best to sit quietly while the woman tells us a story about how she was one digit away from scoring her next fix. But then her son called her, and his face appeared on the phone. When she finishes talking, the man running the meeting looks at me and smiles.

I nod at him and start. "My name is Viktor, and I'm ninety-four days sober." They welcome me. "I went to a party today." I look down at my hands. "Not that kind of party, a family party. I was there for six hours and not once did I think about getting high." I smile. "Not once did I get the itch, but I know the night is coming, and with it comes the devils." I look around while everyone just nods.

"One day, you'll see the guy before the recovering addict," the man in charge says, "and it's going to be glorious."

The rest of the meeting is uneventful. When we finish, I don't stick around for the bad coffee at the back of the room nor do I talk to anyone. I walk out and make my way home, enjoying the semi quiet of the night. I walk into the loft and don't bother turning on a light while I make my way to the shower. The night is a success if you count sleeping for four hours straight a good night. I mean, I can't complain, and even if I do, no one is there to listen. I don't get out of bed; I just toss and turn, and somewhere around three a.m., I fall back asleep, jumping out of bed when my alarm goes off.

I'm so excited to be getting on the ice today that I skip breakfast and make my way to the arena. I don't know what I'm expecting when I walk in, but what I'm not expecting is for it to be so empty. I mean, no surprise here the preseason only starts next week. The tryouts are already underway, but contract players are asked to show up starting next week. I get up and make my way to the kitchen, seeing that at least the chef is there and so is Max.

"You're here bright and early," he says to me, grabbing the shake that the chef just handed to him. "Bernie," he asks the chef, "is there enough left for another shake?"

"Yes," he says, turning and getting a glass to pour me one.

"Thank you," I say to him and then take a sip. "What's in here?"

"Fruit," he says. "I tried the green celery thing." He grimaces. "Not my cup of tea."

"In LA, it's all about the juices," I tell him. "Celery, kale, beet root."

"LA is its own brand of living," Max says, and I nod. "Now let's get on the ice and see how shaky the legs are."

I laugh at him. "Are you talking about me or yourself?"

"Both," he says, laughing. We walk back into the dressing room, and I sit at my place. I undress and start getting into my gear. When I slip my feet into my skates, it's almost like a sigh of relief. Everything is like it was the first time I started skating. "I'll be on the ice," Max says to me. Getting up, he grabs his gloves and helmet and walks toward the door.

Slipping the blue jersey on, I look down and see New York in the middle of it in red letters. "Don't fuck this up," I say to myself, grabbing my helmet and gloves and making my way out. I stop where all the sticks are lined up against the wall. Each of them are separated by player, so I grab one of my custom sticks and make my way through the door to the arena. I look around for the first time; the stands are empty, but it's a huge building. It's quiet, so eerily quiet, and when I glide onto the ice, it's like that first time. The smell of the dry ice hitting you right away. I don't know why I thought I would forget how to skate. I don't know why I thought it would be like that first time when I was three, and I couldn't get my skates to skate.

I skate around the rink a couple of times, getting my skates used to the ice. Max is taking shots at the goal down on the other side. "Well, well, well …" I look up to see Matthew. "You don't look too bad," he says, pushing me, and I smile and see he's in full gear.

"Yeah, I didn't fall yet," I tell him, holding the stick in my hand and then seeing someone else get on the ice. There is no mistaking who it is; the man is a legend and his skating is just as good now as it was when he retired.

"Hey there," Cooper says, skating to us and then stopping. My heart speeds up just a touch as I stand on the ice with him; it's every little boys' dream, and now I can proudly say I did it. "Smell that," he says, lifting his head. "I used to call it freedom," he says to me and Matthew. Someone else joins us on the ice.

"You aren't allowed on the ice," Max says to the guy. "Traitor. Take that jersey off before I wipe my ass with it," he jokes with Justin who skates to the four of us, wearing his Edmonton jersey.

"What are you doing here?" Max asks Justin when he joins us.

"I had to escape my mother," Justin says, then looks at his dad. "Sorry, Dad, but she was all over me last night about the nail marks."

"If you don't want her all over you, then you don't come home with those marks," Cooper tells him. "That is step one."

"Okay, enough of this bullshit," Matthew says. "Let's see what he's got." He looks at me.

"We rustled up some of the guys," he says, and I finally see more and more people stepping on the ice. "Thought we could play some three on three."

I nod at him, looking around the ice. First time really back on it since that disastrous game, and I'm going to be playing with greatness. I'm intimidated, but I am not going to let them see it. "That sounds like fun. Think you can handle it, old man?" I wink at him and then skate away to shake off the nervousness in my stomach. Max's laughter fills the quiet arena, and then I skate to the bench where Evan's sitting. I skate side to side to get a feel of the skates and to make them not as sharp.

"You look rough," I tell him and see him yawning. He just shakes his head.

"Zara wanted fried pickles at three a.m." He looks at me. "You know where I can get fried pickles in Long Island?" he asks me, and I shake my head. "Nowhere. I had to make them myself. And she didn't even eat any." He grabs the water bottle that he brought out and sprays it in his mouth and then on his face.

Matthew comes over with some practice jerseys. "I can't wear a New York jersey," Justin says. "Someone might take a picture of me."

"I'm going to take a picture of my skate up your ass," Matthew says. "Tuck it into your pants."

I skate to the right of Evan and take my spot, waiting for everyone to get in place. I'm so nervous I might puke. I haven't been this nervous since I got drafted. I skate in circles while I move my head side to side. "Relax, it's not a real game," Evan says, and I just nod at him. One of the coaches comes out with a puck and a whistle, and he drops the puck. I try to skate around Justin, but he's on my ass the whole time. I try to deke him from left to right, but with every turn, he's on me. I try to protect the puck and pass it over, but it gets intercepted, and we hustle back to the other end of the ice. The first shift is rough; my heart speeds up, and I'm out of breath by the time I get to the bench and switch with the second line.

I watch them play and see Matthew go toe-to-toe with his father. He tries to read his father, but he doesn't, and just like that, he has a breakaway and scores with his back hand. He isn't even on my team, and we get up and tap the board with our sticks. I climb over the boards and take my place again on the right of Evan, and this time, I don't wait for him to win the face-off, I just take off to the left of Justin. Luckily for me, Evan wins the face-off, and I'm just a touch out of reach from Justin when the defense guy sends me the puck. Landing on the blade of my stick, I handle it like glass, gently skating into the zone with Justin so close I can feel him. I make it to the left and then slip the puck back to the outside of the blade, and when I'm just on the side of the goalie, I lift it just a touch and it falls behind him. I know it's just a pickup game, but that goal is everything.

TEN

ZOE

I RUN OUT of the house and down the stairs to the waiting car. I smile at the new driver and get in, putting my purse next to me. I am running late, which I never do, but I just closed one of my biggest deals, and I'm on cloud nine.

I send Viktor a text that I'm on way, and he doesn't reply.

When I finally pull up in front of the address, I spot him on his phone. He is wearing black jeans and a white T-shirt with a leather jacket and boots. I swear, if you didn't know any better, you would think he was a biker. When the car finally comes to a stop, I grab my purse and get out, smiling at him when he looks up. "Sorry I'm late. It was a last-minute deal, and I couldn't leave."

"I just got here," he tells me and puts the phone in the back pocket of his jeans. Being this close to him, I can already smell his musky cologne.

"Let's get in there." I turn and lead the way up, ignoring

that I'm even thinking about him when I pull the gray door right next to a bookstore. "This is on the fifth floor," I tell him over my shoulder, buzzing the number 5E, and the door buzzes to let us into the lobby. I look around and see a sitting area on the right, and when you walk in a bit more, you see that the mailboxes are on the left. I walk to the elevator located right in front of the door. We get off on the fifth floor and see all the doors are painted with gold numbers on them. When we get to the apartment, I knock and then turn to Viktor. "Put your poker face on," I tell him. "This guy can smell when you want things, and if he knows you want this, he won't budge on his price."

"I don't know if I have a poker face," he whispers, and I look over at him and see his face looking at me a bit scared. He closes his mouth and looks away and then back at me. No matter how he puts his face or how he looks at you, he's hot as fuck, but I cannot tell him that. "How was that?"

"Just don't make eye contact," I tell him. The door opens, and my poker face comes out along with a fake smile. "George," I say when he opens the door. I take him in from head to toe and cringe inwardly. He's wearing a custom-made suit, which isn't the problem; it's the amount of hair gel he puts in his hair. You see exactly where the comb brushed through it. His fake tan makes me almost gag in my mouth because he looks almost orange. This is why he looks so greasy.

"There she is," he says, stepping away from the door to let us into the apartment. Viktor looks around. I take in the walls right away with the exposed red bricks, the ceiling high with wooden beams sticking out and a skylight in the middle of the room. The sunroofs on the ceiling bring in the extra light. It's almost got a loft feeling. "This must be your exclusive client," he says to Viktor. "I'm George." He puts his hand out, and Viktor takes it.

"Viktor," he introduces himself and then drops George's hand.

"This is nice," I say, walking around, taking in everything. "The windows bring in a natural light," I say, walking over to the three windows at the far end of the room. "It makes the room seem bigger than it actually is." I look over at Viktor and I point at the huge mirror against the wall.. "That is why they put up mirrors against the wall." Turning to smile at George. "It's also a four-minute walk from the subway, so the traffic is lighter in this area."

"This is the living and dining room," George says, and I look at the long wooden table that is on the left-hand side of the room. "All furniture is an option," he tells us, and I look over at Viktor, who is looking at me.

"I like that the kitchen is open and leads out to the living and dining room," Viktor says when he walks to the kitchen just off the dining room. "It's a good size." I take in the kitchen that is big for New York and actually has some counter space. "It isn't stated that appliances come with the apartment?"

"It can be looked at," George says to him, and I walk into the kitchen and look around.

"The cabinets are custom made to the exact fridge and stove." I look at George. "Which means that it limits my client and his choices."

"I can talk to the owners about this," he says, knowing I

have him on that one. We walk down the narrow hallway and find one of the bathrooms. We walk into the master bedroom, and we have closets on both sides and then to the right is the bedroom and to the left is the master bathroom. The bedroom is a good size with two windows bringing in more light, the high ceiling so it doesn't feel as small. The bathroom is all marble and comes with a claw tub and double vanity sinks.

We walk into the master bedroom and I look around and see it's just the two of us. "What do you think?"

"I want it," he says to me quietly, almost in a whisper. I nod, and I knew the minute that I saw the pictures that this place was for him. It was bright, airy, and centrally located. I can picture him sitting in this room or even downstairs in the kitchen.

"Let's see the other bedroom and the loft area," I tell him, and it just seals the deal. The second bedroom is across the hallway from his, and then when we take the six steps to the loft part of the apartment, it's a huge theater room complete with the chairs. "This can be a bedroom," I mention of the little office in the back of the room. I close the door and then turn to Viktor. "It's three million."

"That's fine," he says, and I just smile at him. "I have the cash."

"That is even better," I say and then open the door. "Let's dance."

I walk out of the room and down the five stairs and see George there on his phone. "So what is the verdict?"

"It's good," I start to say. "Just a couple of things really."

His eyebrows shoot up. "Like?"

"The appliances need to stay since it's custom, and if he needs to get another one, he is going to have to redo the kitchen."

"I got the approval. They will include the appliances," he says, and I smile.

"Okay, so here is our offer. Two million eight cash offer. Escrow for fourteen days after that we leave."

"It's going on the market for three million two," he says to me, and I look over at Viktor.

"Just because it's going on the market for that doesn't mean you're going to get it. And if you do, how long will that take?" I play my cards. "The last time an apartment in this building was up for sale, it took six months. This hasn't even listed, and you already have an offer." I look at Viktor. "I guess we can continue looking and see what happens." I walk over to George with my hand outstretched. "Thanks for letting me see it." I tilt my head. "I owe you one."

"You are killing me, Zoe," he says. "Let me bring them the offer and see what they say. But I know that they weren't looking to go that low."

"I'll go as far as three million but not a penny more." Then I pull out the facts. "There are thirty-one houses in this area going from two million to three million."

"Let me go make a call," he says, going to the steps and the upstairs loft. I look at Viktor who just shakes his head.

"What?" I ask him.

"You just bamboozled him, and he had no chance in hell," he says quietly, shaking his head.

"I didn't bamboozle him. I gave him an offer," I tell him. "And in the end, I saved you two hundred and fifty thousand," I tell him, and I hear steps coming back.

"Okay. Three million final and they can be out in two weeks," George says, and I smile, looking at Viktor who just looks at me.

"Congrats, Viktor." I look over at him with a huge smile on my face. "Welcome home." I look over at George and tell him to send over the contracts, and when I walk out of the place, I am beaming with happiness for him.

"I'm starving," he says, looking at me.

"Want to grab lunch?" I say, looking at my watch. "Late lunch, early dinner."

"Sure," he says. His phone beeps, and he starts typing. I point out the restaurant at the corner, and we are seated right away when we walk in.

"Your server, Josh, will be here shortly."

"Thank you," I say to her while I grab the menu she holds out for me. "I'm starving," I say to him while I look down at the menu.

"Did you have breakfast or lunch?" he asks me while he reads his own menu.

"No," I answer. "I started putting a bagel in the toaster, but then my phone started ringing and one thing led to another." I look up. "That bagel is now cold and toasted." The waiter comes over to take our drink order and tells us the special of the day.

"I have a question to ask, and I don't want to offend you," I say, and he just looks up at me. His blue eyes not showing anything. "Would you be offended if I got a glass of wine?"

"I thought you gave up wine," he starts, and then I shrug. "But the answer is no," he says. "I am not an alcoholic. I'm a drug addict." My heart stays in my throat when he says that, but I try not to show any reaction. "It's not anything that's a secret. The joys of hitting rock bottom while in the middle of a hockey game on national television." I watch him, his eyes going back down to the menu. "Have the glass of wine if you want, Zoe."

I look down at my own menu now, his words replaying in my head over and over again. The waiter comes over and puts down our two glasses of water with two straws. "Did you guys decide what to order?" he asks us, and I look at Viktor, who just looks at me.

"I'm going to start with the mini meatballs, then I'm going to have the arugula"—I hand him the menu—"with a side of french fries." I smile at him, then look at Viktor, who orders some wings to start and then a meat lover's pie. Josh smiles and walks away.

"Why didn't you order wine?" Viktor asks, grabbing his glass of water and taking a sip.

"Because it's rude if I do, and I don't need it to eat," I tell him. I'm not sure what the right or wrong answer is.

"It's not rude—"

I hold up my hand. "I don't know what you're going through or what you went through. I mean, I know when I was younger, Matthew went through something, but I was too young to know." I look down at my hand and then up. "If at any time I offend you or even—"

He cuts me off now. "Zoe."

"Seriously." I tilt my head and push my hair behind my ears. "It's a huge deal."

"What is?" he asks. When he shrugs off his jacket, I see

that his arms are bigger than yesterday.

"Hitting rock bottom and admitting you have a problem," I tell him honestly, and before I make a fool out of myself, Josh comes back and places our plates in front of us.

"Thank you," he says while he grabs a chicken wing and takes a bite.

"For what?" I say, biting into a mini meatball. "This is so good." I put one on my fork and hold it out for him. "You have to try this. It's like you died and went to Italy." He looks at my fork and then looks at me. "I don't have cooties." He leans in and grabs the meatball in his mouth and starts chewing. "Isn't it good?"

"It is, but I don't think it tastes like they do in Italy." He laughs, grabbing a napkin to wipe the sauce from his wings on. "Have you ever been?"

"No." I shake my head. "We were supposed to go during graduation year, but Zara and I got kicked off of the trip."

"Should I ask why?" he asks me, trying not to laugh.

"You can, but it's dumb," I tell him. "I mean, how were we supposed to know that if you cut a little hole in football pants, they can split right down the middle." He throws his head back. "Zara was dating the quarterback, and she thought he was cheating, so we just cut a small hole in his pants to give him a breeze." His laughter gets even louder, and I roll my eyes. "It's not that funny. Anyway, he got sacked or tackled, whatever they call it, and when he got up, he bent down to grab the ball, and his whole pants split open." He holds his stomach now. "Again, why wasn't he wearing boxers?" I grab another meatball. "And well, apparently, the jock strap is sewn into his pants, so we got the whole ball shot." I close my eyes, trying to forget it. "Needless to say, we didn't make the trip."

"You two together is almost scary," he says, and I don't try to tell him it's all Zara.

"Technically it was all Zara's idea." Smiling at him. "Do you have any siblings?" I ask him, taking a bite of the salad.

"I have a sister, Natalia, who is two years younger than me. She's a model," he says, and I look at him with my eyes wide. He grabs his phone and finds her picture. "There she is."

"She is gorgeous," I tell him honestly. "You guys look alike."

"Are you saying I'm gorgeous?" he jokes. When I raise my eyebrows, he says, "She is way better looking than me."

"Are you as annoying as Matthew?" I ask him, leaning back in my chair. I have to stop eating or I'll be full by the time the pizza comes.

The rest of the meal goes off flawlessly without us touching on his past or his addiction. When the bill comes, we fight over it, but agree that I will get it next time. When we finally walk out of the restaurant, it's packed.

"Are you going home?" he asks me once we walk out of the restaurant, and I stand in the middle of the walkway.

"Yes. I have two contracts to look over," I tell him. "What about you?"

"I'm going to hit up a meeting," he says, his voice lower than it should be. His eyes avoid mine, and I smile, knowing it wasn't easy for him to tell me that.

I walk to the corner of the sidewalk and hold up my hand for a cab. "I'll text you when I get the final contract for you to sign." A cab stops, and I start to walk away.

"Thank you, Zoe," he says, and I look back at him. "For everything."

"No worries, Viktor," I tell him, and he smirks. I turn around before I question anything else. I get in the cab, and I don't look over at him. I know he's standing there, I can feel it, but I'm not going to go down this road. I can't, end of story, no matter how much my heart is telling me to just try it.

ELEVEN

VIKTOR

"DID YOU GET the schedule?" Evan asks me, sitting next to me three weeks after I bought my house. We just got off the ice at practice, and I'm huffing and puffing.

"I did," I tell him, thinking back to the email I got that morning. It was right after I got an email from Zoe telling me she is going to have my keys ready for me at five. I haven't seen her since the day I bought the house.

"You excited?" he asks me, unwrapping the tape from his socks.

"I am. It just sucks that I'm leaving the same day my furniture gets here." Ever since I signed the contract, it's been an endless amount of time and energy trying to get my shit out of storage and delivered to me. If I'm not on the ice, I'm organizing the moving truck or doing something else for the apartment. I should have sold it all and just bought new stuff here.

"Let us know if you need help," he says and walks away. His family and this organization have accepted me with open arms, and my life is slowly coming together. The nights are still the roughest, but now that hockey has started back, it fills my time during the day, and the nights have been slower than usual. I attend up to five meetings a week, and so far, I've only needed my sponsor that one day. I know that it isn't going to be this easy as time goes by, but I'll take it one day at a fucking time.

I get up, get changed, and walk into the weight room where I spend two hours lifting weights and switching it up with cardio. When I finally walk out of the arena, it's quarter to five, and I make my way over to my new house. My phone vibrates as soon as the cab pulls up to the apartment.

Zoe: Just buzz when you get here.

I walk to the gray door and press the number five, which is already changed to V. P. She buzzes me in right away, and I nod at the woman walking out of the elevator with her dog. I press five and make my way to my new apartment. I haven't been back here since the open house three weeks ago. I knock on the door, and then hear Zoe yell, "Coming!"

She unlocks the door and then throws back the door, and yells, "Welcome home!" as she throws her arms out to her sides. I'm in shock when I look behind her and see that the apartment is empty, but the balloons at the end of the room tied together spell out:

W-E-L-C-O-M-E H-O-M-E

"What is all this?" I say, looking around once I walk in and see baskets on the counter that separate the kitchen from the living and dining room.

"Well," she says, and I watch her as she closes the door. She's wearing tight dark blue jeans with holes in the front and a long-sleeved white sweater. It's a normal outfit, and I shouldn't even be looking at her in that way, but I can't help it. Plus, she is barefoot, her gray strappy heels tossed beside the front door. I don't let my mind linger on the bubble gum pink she has painted on her nails. "I knew this place would be empty, and I knew your stuff was coming on Monday, so I added some decorations."

"You didn't have to do this." As I look around, there must be a hundred balloons just hanging there with the ribbons.

I walk to the counter and look at the baskets. There is a fruit basket and then one with champagne in it. "And just because I'm an awesome person," she says, stopping beside me and grabbing the bottle. "The very best non-alcoholic champagne money can buy," she says, and I swear her face is like a kid on Christmas morning. She pops the bottle and then pours it into two crystal glasses that are also in the basket. She puts down the bottle and hands me one of the glasses and then she hands me the key that is on a key chain. "Congratulations," she says. I grab the key and place it in my pocket next to my chip.

I hold up my glass. "Thank you to the best real estate agent I know." I click her glass, and she takes a sip.

"Not too bad for twenty bucks," she says. "And I'm the *only* real estate agent you know. I mean, in New York."

"This is true," I tell her and then hear the buzzer and look at her surprised.

Her eyes twinkle bright. "I may have one more surprise up my sleeve," she says, and I walk to the door and press the buzzer to let the person in. I open the door and wait for the elevator door to ping, and then I spot the guy coming down with food. "Delivery from Daluggi," the man says and hands me the two pizza boxes with three bags on top.

I shut the door and look at her as she takes paper plates out of a bag along with plastic utensils. "You thought of everything," I tell her and place the pizza on the counter.

"Well, not really. I didn't go out of the box with the order," she tells me, opening the boxes. "I ordered you exactly what you had when you got the house. Almost like you've come full circle."

She smiles, and I don't know what to think or to say or to do. There are so many things I want to do like lean over and kiss her lips or touch her face. The endless possibilities run through my mind along with all the reasons not to.

She must notice the change in my demeanor, and her face falls. "I'm so sorry," she starts to say and closes the box. "I shouldn't have assumed you were free." She grabs her jacket from the counter. "I'll just leave the food here for you." She picks up her purse, and I watch her walk over to her shoes. She doesn't even put them on; she just grabs them in her hand, and she's turning the handle of the door. She is moving so fast I can barely get the words out.

"Where are you going?" I ask her when the words finally come to my throat. "I was just ..." I shake my head. I can't tell her what I was thinking or what I wanted to do. "This is just very nice and thoughtful of you." I watch her as she stands there. "Thank you for doing all this, Zoe." She smiles and then looks down. "Please stay and help me eat this food."

"Only if you're sure," she says, and when I nod my head,

she puts her shoes, jacket, and purse in a pile next to the door. "This was a stupid surprise," she says, almost sounding defeated.

"It was a perfect way to come home," I tell her and grab the boxes and open them. "You got me chicken wings. And today is my cheat meal day," I lie to her. As soon as the season starts, I go on a lean diet, and chicken wings is not on that list. I'll just do extra time on the treadmill tomorrow.

"I got you what you ordered that day," she tells me. "I feel like a dork."

"Don't." I shake my head and look around. "I don't have any chairs."

"We can have a picnic," she says, picking up the food and looking at me. "Grab the rest." She motions to the two pizza boxes and then sits on the floor under the skylight. I follow her lead and sit in the middle of the room. She grabs a slice of pizza and eats it. "What time is your stuff going to be here on Monday?"

"Probably after I leave," I tell her. "We got the travel schedule for the year today, and we leave on Monday at noon."

"Shit," she says between bites. "If you want, I can come over and open the door for them."

"Would you really?" I ask her. "I don't want to impose on you." I take a bite of pizza and look around. No frilly blankets, no table, paper plates on the floor in the middle of my condo, and I'm okay. Content. Happy even. "But if you would"—I smirk—"I would owe you one."

She groans and throws her head back. "Why does that phrase always sounds so greasy?" Her eyes roll, making me laugh. "I'm paying off my I-owe-you to George tomorrow afternoon."

"Afternoon?" I ask her. "Isn't that strange?" I look down at the chicken wings, making sure I don't look at her just in case she can see how much this news bothers me. *You can't have her*, I remind myself.

"No." She shakes her head. "I have my kickboxing class at eleven, and then we are meeting at twelve thirty." She looks down and then looks back up, and she has a twinkle in her eye.

"What am I missing?" I ask her.

"Well, I definitely won't be showering after my workout." She raises her eyebrows.

"You could just tell him you aren't interested in him," I tell her.

She shakes her head while she chews. "Been there, done that. It was more of a challenge for him."

"I can see that," I admit. "Work hard kind of thing."

She tosses her pizza crust down. "I have no idea, but I owe him one, and I pay my debts." She gets up now, and I watch her every single move. "With that said, I'm going to take off." I'm about to get up, but she shakes her head.

"Don't get up. I know the way out." She walks over to her pile of stuff and slips her feet into the strappy heels, and just like that, her outfit goes from comfy to hot. I shake my head. I can't think of her like that. I won't think of her like that. I have bigger things to tackle before I can even go there with her and admit I want her. The last thing you do while in recovery is get involved with anyone.

"Text me all the information, and don't worry about

a thing. I'll be here." She smiles, and I just nod at her. She opens the door and walks out of the apartment, leaving me by myself. I get up and clean up the mess and do a walk-through, seeing that it's much bigger without anything in here. I think back to all the furniture I put in storage and hope it matches.

I put the pizza and leftovers in the empty fridge and store the fruit. The only thing I'm not bringing from LA is a bed, but that will be delivered tomorrow morning. I turn off whatever lights are on and take the key out of my pocket to lock the door and then I finally see the key chain. It's gold and a circle; it looks like a coin. On one side is a picture of the sun and then the earth with engraving on the bottom.

One day at a time.

I smile, flipping it over, and my heart stops, or pulses, or skips—fuck if I know—but I stop for a second and read the words.

Grant me the serenity
To accept the things I cannot change;
Courage to change the things I can;
And the wisdom to know the difference.
Viktor 2019

I rub my fingers over the words and take out my chip from my pocket. It's going too good; shit is too calm. I pull out my phone and make a phone call.

"Well, well, look who finally called," Jeffrey says, his voice booming in the phone.

"Hey," I say, running my hand through my hair and then squeezing my neck. "I got a new place."

"Did you?" he asks in a lower voice than his greeting.

"I did, and then someone gave me a gift," I tell him, my hands starting to shake on the key chain. It's the most meaningful gift I've ever gotten. "Things are too calm."

"Where are you now?" he asks me, and I look around.

"In my empty apartment," I tell him. "Would you like to come visit?"

"I would love to," he says. "How about you send me the address, and I'll come right over."

"You don't have to come right over," I say, going to the window and looking down at the street.

"Beats the shit out of watching *Jeopardy* and *Wheel of Fortune*," he says, laughing. I try to laugh, but it doesn't come out. "Send me the address."

"Will do," I say, disconnecting, and then I send him the address. I sit with my back against the white wall as the apartment darkens as the sun sets. The buzz getting me up and then I hear a soft knock on the door and yell for him to come in.

The door opens, and he stands there looking around. "Is this a surprise party?" he says, looking around and then turning on the light. "Jesus, it looks like prom." He closes the door. "If you asked me here to take my virginity"—he gives me a pointed look—"you're a couple of centuries too late."

That makes me smile, and I look down at the key still in my hand. "Zoe did it," I tell him. "She had this whole thing as a surprise and welcome home."

"Zoe?" he asks, coming over and sitting next to me with his back against the wall.

"My realtor and my GM's sister," I tell him. He sits there quietly, waiting for me to play it out in my head. "She's nice, and she's gorgeous," I admit. "But she's untouchable."

"To who?" he asks, trying to get me in the right frame of mind.

"To me," I tell him. "I'm a broken man." I close my eyes and lean my head back. "I take it back; I was a broken man. Now I'm trying to piece all the pieces together, and I don't have time for this."

"Does she want to date you?" Jeffrey asks me, and I look at him.

"No." I smirk. "According to her, the fact that I play hockey is a big strike, and she doesn't date anyone who does. But I don't want to lead her on."

"Have you told her?" The question I don't know where to go with.

"I told her I'm in recovery." I take a deep breath. "And that I'm a recovering addict."

"And …?" he asks me.

"And nothing. She didn't seem fazed by it," I tell him. "It's all going too smoothly. I'm back on the ice, and even that is so much better than I remembered it was," I say, which is the main reason I called him. "It's all going too good. I'm in a good place. I'm healthy, and I'm semi happy. I'm sleeping five hours straight at night. My hands shake at most only twice a night once I wake up." I look down, my heart beating a touch faster. "The pull to get high isn't as great as it was last week. I have friends who actually care about my well-being, but that means nothing."

"Well," Jeffrey says, "I do believe you've just completed step four."

I look at him, confused. *Searching and fearless moral in-*

ventory of ourselves.

He smiles. "You just taken an inventory about yourself, and it wasn't all negative." I let his words sink in. "You've been here a month—one month—and it's been hard. But no one said it would be easy." I nod. "But you are starting to see the moments when the walls start closing in. The moment your heart speeds up just a touch. The moment your hands start to twitch right before they start shaking." Jeffrey takes a deep breath and then lets it out. "One day at a time."

I hand him the key chain. "Zoe got the keys to my place today, and she got me that key chain," I tell him, and he looks at it and flips it over.

"Looks like you made a good friend," he says, handing me back the key. "Want another piece of advice?" He doesn't wait for me to answer. "Talk to her. Make sure all the cards are on the table. Things aren't always black and white. Sometimes, a little gray slips in."

We spend the rest of the time sitting next to each other without saying much. He knows I'm letting everything we just said play over in my mind. When I feel more like myself, I get up and so does Jeffrey. He helps me lock up my place, and then we walk down the street. He gets on the subway, and I continue back to the loft. My mind is finally clearer, but I know I have to talk to Zoe. I have to nip this thing in the bud.

Twelve

Zoe

"Hello?" I ANSWER my phone while I wait for the light to change from red to green so I can walk across the street.

"Hey there." Viktor's voice fills my ear. "Am I interrupting the coffee date?"

I groan. "It wasn't a date." I take a sip of the refresher that I left with. "It was a twenty-minute sit-down of me trying to catch my breath from my workout." I leave out that the only thing I kept thinking about was him.

"Listen, I was wondering if you could come by and pick up the key for Monday?" he says. "If you have time either today or tomorrow."

"Yeah, I can head there now," I tell him. "I was just going to go home, but I can swing by your place before I head back home." My heart starts to pick up just a touch, knowing I'm about to see him.

"Perfect," he says and disconnects. I make my way over

to his house, trying to keep my mind off the nerves starting in my stomach or the fact that my heart beats faster than it should. I also make a mental note to get my head out of the clouds and stop overthinking Viktor. I use the buzzer and then walk to the elevator. Seeing my reflection in the mirror, I can't believe I left the gym like this. I should have changed from my black yoga capris and gray long-sleeved hooded sweater. It goes long in the front but is cut in the back. I threw on the sweater on top of my sports bra after the workout. My braided hair hangs over my shoulder. I get in the elevator, and I look up, seeing the numbers move from floor to floor. I try to calm down just a bit, my stomach feeling weird almost like flutters.

I don't have to knock because Viktor is at the door waiting for me. My smile appears automatically when I see him, and I want to kick myself, so I look down, then up to bring the poker face back. "You weren't kidding about being in workout clothes."

I roll my eyes. "I was not kidding." I smile at him and walk into the house. The balloons are still all over the place. "I like what you did to the place," I joke with him and put my bag on the stool.

"I just finished in my bedroom," he says. "Want to see?"

"Is this a trick?" I ask. *This is good,* I think to myself. I'm going to joke with him like I would any other guy who I wasn't interested in. "Are you going to ask me to lie on it naked to see if it's comfortable?" I fold my arms over my chest. "Because I have to say I've heard that one before."

He throws his head back, and he laughs, the sound making me smile even more. "Well, this makes the second part of why I asked you to come over a little easier." I look at him and see that his eyes are a lighter shade of blue today, and the circles under his eyes have slowly started to disappear.

"Wait, you asked me to come over to get the key and get naked?" I joke with him, not wanting that smile to disappear from his face.

"Jesus, you are a nut," he says. "I just … I didn't want …" His mouth snaps shut, and he shoves a hand through his hair.

"I think you need to relax," I tell him, reaching out and grabbing his arm. "Just relax."

"We can't date each other," he says. I don't know why it bothers me, but my hand falls from his arm. "I mean, you're hot and all that, but I can't date you."

"Um …" I start, ignoring the echoing of my heart in my ears. Ignoring that crushing feeling in my chest. I pull out the Zoe that just lets things not bother her, the fake Zoe, the Zoe everyone has met. "One, thank you, I guess, for think-ing I'm hot." He smiles, and now I put on my fake smile, but he doesn't seem to notice. "And two, when did we say we would date each other?"

"I …" he starts. "Never really but I wanted to make sure you knew it was never a possibility." I nod at him because I can't say anything. The lump in my throat just gets thicker. "You can't fall in love with me."

I laugh and look down at my feet, giving myself an inter-nal pep talk. *Put the poker face on, Zoe.* I channel it as much as I can. "I am a touch confused with this conversation, but just so we are perfectly clear"—I hold up my hands—"I don't want to date you. You are good looking, but you aren't any-thing that I …" I try to find the words.

"I play hockey," he says, and I start to make a list of why I don't like him.

"Yes," I say louder than normal because I'm nervous and that is also number one on my list. "You play hockey, and I don't really get hockey." I use my hands. "It's just something that I don't ever …" Then I stop and look at him. "Did I say anything that made you think I wanted to date you?"

"No," he says, shaking his head, and I at least breathe a sigh of relief that I wasn't that transparent. "I mean, you got me dinner, and you gave me a key chain."

"Um, yeah, because we were celebrating a big step," I tell him. "I mean, the key chain was something that I saw and figured it would be a nice thing to do." I shake my head. "You know, for a friend."

"I'm a recovering addict, and I have to focus on me. I don't have time for a relationship," he says and then looks down at his bare feet. "God, this is the most awkward conversation I think I've ever had."

"I mean, if it makes you feel better, I had an even more awkward conversation about an hour ago." I smile at him, and he smiles back.

"Okay, well, now that we got that out of the way," he says, and I put my hand up.

"Viktor, I think you are a great person." It feels like a breakup, but we weren't even together. "I don't know what happened with everything that went down in LA, and I think them tossing you aside and looking for a trade was a crappy thing to happen. I think you got dealt a shitty hand and then you decided that shitty was what you deserved. That key chain was just a little reminder to let you know I don't agree. I think you deserve more."

"You sound like my therapist," he tells me. "And my sponsor."

"Well, I don't know how to be a therapist," I answer, "but I know how to be a listener, and I know how to be a friend. A *friend.*"

"Okay, I get it," he finally says. "Now, come see my room." He turns to walk down the hallway, and I follow him. I stop at the doorway, not stepping inside. "Come in."

"And just to be clear, I will see your room with all my clothes on." I wink at him, and he groans and puts his hands over his face, and I laugh. "Okay, that was the last time. It was just too good to pass up."

Walking in the room, I see the huge king-size bed in the middle of the room with a dark brown leather headboard, cream-colored covers, and matching light brown throw pillows. The nightstands are also a dark brown almost chocolate color with side lamps. Above his bed hangs a sun with a mirror in the middle.

"I saw it in the showroom and just bought everything," he says, and I laugh. "The sun was just like tomorrow is another day kind of thing."

"That is exactly what I was thinking," I tell him, smiling at him. "It's perfect."

"I hope so because I moved out of the loft," he says, and I look over at him shocked.

"But you have no furniture," I tell him.

"I have a bed," he tells me. "A fridge, a stove, and a television in the movie room. What else do I need?"

"You have a point there," I tell him and then look at him.

"I should get going."

"Is being in this room with me too much for you?" he jokes with me, and I like it. "I know how tempting I can be."

"Yeah, that must be it," I tell him, walking to my bag. "But truth be told, I have a date tonight."

He raises his eyebrows. "Really?"

"Really," I repeat after him. He really doesn't need to know that's a lie. I am going out for dinner, but it's with Zara and Evan.

"If only you said that first, then we wouldn't have had that awkward conversation." He laughs and then walks to the counter and hands me a key to the apartment. I try to keep my poker face intact and my emotions hidden.

"But then how else would I know that you found me hot?" I joke with him to keep my disappointment buried. I just want to hurry and get the hell out of here. "I promise not to defile your home while you're gone."

"Please try to refrain from smelling my shirts," he jokes, and I walk to the door.

"I will try my hardest," I tell him, forcing a smile on my face and then walking out the door. I close it behind me so he doesn't make it even more fucking awkward by coming out and watching me. I almost run to the elevator, and when it finally closes, I let out a huge sigh as the disappointment shows on my face. I keep my head down the whole way home, not even sure why I'm so disappointed by what he said. He was being honest and I wasn't even that interested in him. *Lies*. Fine I was interested in him, and I liked him and.. And nothing, I tell myself, it was time for me to get Viktor out of my head once and for all.

I'm putting on my shoes when I hear the front door open. Standing, I look at myself in the mirror. Okay, it's a bit risqué but whatever. The one-piece black dress has a plunging neckline, spaghetti straps, and no back, and then the dress part turns to leather, stopping mid-thigh on one side and then long on the other. I paired it with a simple black shoe with a strap around my toes and another around my ankle. I ignore the fact that I chose this dress as a huge *up yours* to Viktor. Even though he won't see me in it, I'll know.

"Are you almost ready?" Zara yells.

"Yes," I say. Grabbing my shawl to cover myself, I walk out of the bedroom and then down the stairs.

"I'm ready," I say once I get to the last step and turn to look at them in the living room, except it's not just the two of them.

"Oh my God," Evan says, but my eyes are on the man I'm trying not to think about; the man I literally can't get involved with. "She needs to go change," Evan says, looking at Zara.

I change my face and then look at Evan. "It's a night out," I tell him. "Besides, this is Zara's." Looking back at Viktor, I feel my mouth go suddenly dry, my heart beating so fast I look down to make sure it isn't coming out of my chest. "What are you doing here?" I try not to stare too much at him standing in the middle of my living room a couple of hours after telling me that nothing would happen between us. A couple of hours after I told him I was going on a date. This can't be happening.

THIRTEEN

VIKTOR

STANDING IN THE middle of her living room, I have to put my hands in my pockets to keep from going over to her and covering her with my body and burying my hands in her hair because she looks hot as fuck. I look down at my feet and give myself an internal talk. *You can't date her*, I repeat three times just in case. The minute she closed the door to the apartment after our talk, I sat on the couch. Or better yet, my legs were shaking, and I slumped onto the couch. I knew I had to talk to her and put all the cards on the table. I knew this, yet it stung harder than I anticipated.

"What are you doing here?" she asks, and I wonder if this is such a great idea.

"Yeah, I called Zara about tomorrow, and Evan forced me out," I tell her, and she turns to glare at Evan.

"That isn't Zara's outfit," Evan says, giving me a chance to catch my breath. "I won't even have backup tonight," he says. "It's just me. How am I going to fight off all the men?"

"Our reservations are in twenty minutes," Zara says. "Let's go." She turns around to join Zoe, and they walk out of the living room, leaving just Evan and me.

"This should be fun," he says sarcastically and walks out of the room, and I follow him. I think about ways to bail or different excuses I could use to get out of this and go home. Especially if we are going to be meeting Zoe's date at the restaurant. I walk out of the house and see that both girls have gotten in the back seat. "Dinner and dancing on a Saturday night, who planned tonight?" Evan says, complaining when we get into the front seat.

"Your wife," Zoe says. "I would have been more than happy with pizza and beer."

"We could always go somewhere else." I look over at her.

"You know where we can go? That new Korean barbecue restaurant that I've been dying to go to," she says with a huge smile, looking at Zara.

"I think you need reservations," Zara says, then looks at Evan. "I mean, I could name drop."

"Ugh with the name drop. We should mention Matthew or Doug," Evan says, mentioning Karrie's dad and the owner of the team.

"Good call," Zara says and then calls the place. "Hi, I'm wondering if you have space for four people tonight?" she says, and then she just listens. "It would be for the captain of the Stingers and his wife." She smiles. "We will be there in twenty minutes." She smiles, looking up. "They will make a place for us. Now let me call and cancel the other reservations."

I wait for her to finish and then tell her, "You know what that means, right?" Zoe turns to Zara. "Someone just got shafted on their date night. Sorry, honey, that night out is canceled because the captain of the hockey team wants a table."

"It is not," Zara says.

"That is exactly what that means," I say, now turning to look at them in the back. The way she's sitting, her skirt is pulled up just a touch, baring even more leg. "I've seen it happen before in LA." I quickly turn back to face the front.

I feel a hand on my seat, and then I hear her whisper beside me, "I can't not drink tonight."

"Have one for me," I tell her and then turn to the side to face her. "And I'm sorry for showing up. They wouldn't take no as an answer."

"I mean, this still doesn't mean I want to date you, FYI. Even though it's like a double date." She smiles at me, but her smile doesn't reach her eyes.

"Will I ever live that down?" I ask her, and she shakes her head and sits back in her seat.

"Not anytime soon," she says and looks out the window, and I turn to look out mine as well. I wonder if she's nervous about me meeting her date. I wonder if she's thinking about what we spoke about. I wonder if she feels that little burning in her stomach that I'm feeling. I don't have time to think about it or dwell on it because ten minutes later, we are walking into the restaurant, and I let out a huge sigh of relief knowing it's just the four of us.

NATASHA MADISON

"That is a definite yes," Zara says to me as I stand in the middle of a room with mirrors all around me. "Do you like the fit?"

I look down at the blue suit I'm wearing, and it's almost like the blue suit I tried on right before this. It's also the same as the black suit she made me try on. I'm about to answer her when I hear Zoe behind us. "It's the same suit."

Zoe lays with her head on the armrest of the couch in the waiting area, and Evan is next to her on his phone. "Why am I here?" she groans and looks at Evan who just smiles. I look in the mirror right at her, so it's not obvious I'm really looking at her.

"You're here because you owe me for carrying your ass to bed last night," he says, and I shake my head. Last night, I sat next to Zoe and ignored my body's reaction to her. I ignored every single time our hands grazed. I ignored when the wine started hitting her, and she would lean in a touch too close and talk to me. Zoe drank way too much wine, so much wine that it was her idea to hit up a karaoke bar.

"I don't owe you anything," she says, raising her head. "I was perfectly okay with sleeping on the stairs." She then stands up. "I need some water," she announces, walking out of the room.

"Evan," Zara says, "go with her, or she'll go to the furniture floor and nap on one of the beds." He shakes his head, puts down his phone, and then goes in search of Zoe.

"Will she really go find a bed?" I ask, concerned she'll be kicked out of this posh store.

"No." She smiles and shakes her head. "Okay, maybe." She shrugs. "It happened one time, but in her defense, we were furniture shopping for my parents."

"I …" I start to say. "I …"

"You have no words. I know," Zara says. "Now, besides suits, do you have active wear?" she asks me. "What about casual wear? Beach wear? Nighttime wear?"

"Nighttime wear?" I ask, confused, thinking it might be something else.

"What do you wear to bed?" she asks, then holds up her hands. "If it's too personal, it's fine."

"Boxers," I answer her, and she crosses her hands over her chest.

"Interesting," she says, and I'm about to ask her what she means by that, but Zoe comes back in followed by Evan.

"If you aren't out of that suit in three minutes, I'm going to go and crawl on the bed on the sixth floor," Zoe says, sitting down on the couch

"Calm down. He's done," Zara says and looks at me. "You can undress. I'll go speak to them about everything else now that I have your sizes."

Stepping into the changing room, I'm done in under two minutes. When I walk out, the only one left in the room is Zoe who lounges on the couch. "I think I'm going to die," she moans. "I'm breaking up with wine," she mumbles. "For good this time."

"Why?" I ask, trying not to laugh.

"Evan showed me the video of me singing I am woman, hear me roar." She closes her eyes and covers her face. "But it explains why my groin hurts. I haven't done the splits since I was fifteen."

"I'm just thankful that one part of your dress was longer

than the other or else it would be a whole different show." I sit next to her. Since I've told her we couldn't date, it's been lighter and more of a joking thing. Though it did sting a bit when she told me I wasn't her type. It should have been a weight lifted off my shoulders, but it wasn't. I mean, when she walked downstairs yesterday, my jaw pretty much hit the floor. She was the most beautiful person I've ever seen, and I've lived in Hollywood. She just oozed sex, beauty, and ... *fuck*, those legs.

"You know what I need?" She's sitting next to me, but today's outfit of black leggings and a sweater is the total opposite of last night. She piled her hair on her head, and she wore her sunglasses the whole time.

"What do you need?" I ask her even though I know I shouldn't.

"A burger," she answers. "A greasy burger. A burger so greasy it's running down your arms."

"What are you two doing?" Zara says, coming back in. "I have been waiting for you two at the service desk." She looks at me. "I put in a rush for the suit so it will be done by tomorrow, and the rest will be delivered by Thursday."

"Zara," Zoe says from beside me. "I want a greasy burger."

"Oh, God," she says. "I was just telling Evan that. We should hit up that Firestones. I'm going to tell Evan," she says, leaving, and Zoe stands up and looks at me.

"Are you coming with?" she asks, looking down at me. I think about hitting up a meeting instead. "Did you have other plans?"

"I was going to hit up a meeting," I tell her. "You know, before I go away."

"Oh my God," she says softly, sitting down next to me. She rips off the glasses. "Is it because I got drunk last night?" Her eyes almost look like she is tearing up, and worry fills her face.

"No." I shake my head and put my hand around her shoulder to bring her closer to me. "It has nothing to do with you." I smell her right away, almost like a field of berries, and my mouth suddenly goes dry.

"Are you sure?" she says softly.

"I thought we went through this," I say. "I don't like you like that." She turns and pushes away from me. Her touch stays on me long after she stops touching me.

"You're a jerkface," she says, angry.

"I leave tomorrow," I tell her, "and even though temptation is everywhere, it is usually stronger on the road."

"Do you have someone you can call?" she asks me, and I nod. "Why don't you call him?"

"It's Sunday, and I don't really want to bother him, so I was just going to go to a meeting." I tell her the truth. "But I could hit up a meeting after I have one of those burgers."

"Yeah," she says. "Are you sure?"

"I think I'll be good. Worst case, I tap out early," I tell her, getting up and holding out my hand for her. This is what friends do, right? "Let's go get some grease into you, so you can get back to normal." Turning, we walk out of the room. And when her hand slides out of mine, my hand itches to take it back.

"I swear, never ever again," she says, putting her glasses back on. "Ever."

When it's finally my turn, I start. "I've been clean for one hundred and twenty-two days," I say, thinking about what a milestone it is for me. "But tomorrow, I leave town and," I say, and my hands suddenly shake just a touch, so I rub them down my thighs, "I'm worried I'm not strong enough not to go out searching for it." I look around the room and see a couple of people nod their head like they know how that feels. "I'm just scared," I tell them, and then the next person speaks. I stay until the end and walk out into the crisp air of New York; it's starting to get a bit chilly at night.

I decide to grab a cab instead of walk, and as soon as I flag one down and get in, my phone buzzes. Taking it out of my pocket, I see that it's from Zoe.

Zoe: Hey, so I found out that you were going to Philly, and I did a little research. These are some meetings next to your hotel. Just in case.

I shake my head. *This woman*. She went out of her way to get me the name of meetings near me. She didn't feel sorry for me when I told her. No, she first blames herself, and then she helped me. I smile at the phone and see the three dots pop up and then go away. She's either texting me, or she's erasing everything. I look down, and this time, something comes through.

Zoe: That was pushy, right? I didn't mean to be pushy. Just trying to help. I'll stop now.

I look out the window as I think of what to text and finally just go with my gut.

Me: Not pushy, very thoughtful. You should stop doing things like that, or I might think you have a crush on me.

I laugh at that and then laugh more when she answers

me.

Zoe: Barf.

I don't bother answering her. Instead, I get home and take a shower, then slip into bed. Lying down, I look up at the ceiling, then turn and get comfortable and wait for sleep to take me. I don't sleep as good as I have been. I go a full four hours before I wake up in a puddle of sweat. I get up and strip down the bed and look at the clock to see it's 2:00 a.m. I grab my phone and go to the movie room and play a movie. Sometime during the middle, I doze off, only waking at six a.m. right before my alarm is going to go off.

When I walk into the rink after one, I look around and see that it's very different from when I walked in here a month ago. Everyone is back to the grind. I'm also wearing my new suit that got delivered to me this morning along with two outfits that Zara rush ordered. "Hey," I say to Matthew who comes out of his office and hits me head on.

"Hey," he says, looking me up and down. "That the new suit?"

I look at him confused. "How did you know?"

"Group text," he says and then shakes his head. "The girls are in a group text chatting back and forth about suits. Zoe was planning to murder Zara, and she was going over different ways to do it. Anyway, you ready for tomorrow?"

"No," I answer him quietly and look around. "I guess it's the nerves."

"Yeah," he says and then looks down. "It's just the monkey on your back. As soon as you hit the ice and score, it'll be fine." I think about what he says, and for the first time in my life, I think about what it would be like not to score. To be sober and suck on the ice.

"Let's hope," I tell him, and he grabs my shoulder, squeezing it and walks away toward another office. I finally get in the locker room and sit down when Evan struts in.

"I hate road trips," he says, sitting next to me and putting his bag on the floor. He then looks over at me. "I just dropped Zara off at Zoe's."

"She isn't staying home?" I ask him.

"No, she has some appointments in the city, and it's easier for her. Plus, I have reassurance that someone is taking care of her." He grabs a drink off the cart in the middle of the room. "Don't tell her I said that, or I'll deny it."

"Your secret is safe with me," I say, sitting here and waiting for everyone to gather.

Oliver, our public relations man, comes in, clapping his hands "Put away all important packages." He laughs at his own joke, covering his private area with his hands over his bright blue suit with white stripes. "Listen up, gentlemen. We are leaving in twenty minutes. The bus is already here, so you can load it now if you would like. Once we get to the hotel, the manager will be there to give us the keys to your rooms. Rookies, good news. You get roommates," he says, and then I hear the rookies moan.

"Count yourself lucky," I say. "LA always has that policy," I tell them, and some of them raise their eyebrows. I was always with my partner in crime. Easier to be roommates with someone who was also an addict and easier to hide when you would get up and snort a line of coke instead of having to hide in the bathroom every ten minutes to get a hit.

"See," Oliver says, pointing at me. "It could be worse.

There is also a team dinner tonight. More on that to follow," he says, turning. "See you out there."

"Here we go, boys," Evan says, walking out of the room, and the rest of us follow his lead as we make our way out to the bus. Once there, I store my bag in the bottom hatch and climb the stairs onto the bus. Sitting in an empty seat, I grab my phone and go through my emails. I have to start answering some of these. "Holy shit. You have twenty-one thousand emails?" Evan says once he sits in the seat next to me.

"Yeah," I say, scrolling through them and not knowing where to start.

"You should hire someone to take care of that." I look over at Evan who shakes his head. "My sister Candace takes care of all mine plus my social media account. The only thing I work is my Instagram."

"Really?" I ask him.

"Yeah. At first, she only did me, but then when I left, she started her own company. She has about twenty clients now. If you want, I can ask her if she's taking on any other clients."

"I think I need it," I say truthfully. "Let me know what she says." I put my phone away because just the thought of it makes my head spin.

The bus ride goes by fast, and the flight goes by faster. The only ones really excited about this are the rookies. When we get to the hotel, I grab my key and go to my room. It's a standard room with a king-size bed and a desk. After dumping the bag on my bed, I sit down next to it. I'm out of my comfort zone and out of my safety net by not being at home. My heart starts to beat just a touch faster at first, and then it's pounding while my hands get clammy. I rub them together and ignore the burning in my stomach and the weight on my chest. I reach inside my jacket pocket and grab my chip. My fingers rubbing over the words 90 days over and over again. I start to count to ease my mind when the phone rings in my pocket. Taking it out, I see it's a FaceTime request from Zoe.

I think about pressing the red button to reject it, but my fingers have other plans.

"Hey," she says when her face finally fills the screen, and my heart rate slowly returns to normal. "Are you busy?"

"No," I tell her and look at her face, and my anxiety is kept at bay now. She has tiny, tiny freckles on her nose that you can barely see. "Just got to the hotel."

"Oh, good," she says. "The movers just left," she tells me, and I see she's in my apartment. "It looks like everything is here." She turns the screen, and boxes cover my whole apartment. "I made a couple of executive decisions with the furniture."

"What kind of executive decisions?" I ask.

"Well, I figured that since the boxes were labeled, they should go in their designated rooms," she says, and I just watch her. "I made them set up the couch and the dining room in the area," she says, showing me.

"Oh, I didn't know they did that," I say, feeling a touch relieved I don't have to move the boxes. "I thought it was just dump and go."

"They don't usually, but when you bat your eyes and act helpless, it gets people moving," she says with a smirk.

Looking into her eyes, I know I would do it for her if she asked me. "Anyway, it looks like it's all here."

"I definitely have my work cut out for me this weekend," I tell her, wondering if she has any plans this weekend. Is she coming to the game? "We have a game on Saturday, but then we are off for three days."

"Well, if you need help, let me know," she says. "I'm going to leave now."

"Where are all the balloons?" I ask, trying to keep her on the phone. I notice that they aren't there even though I left them there this morning.

"That's another executive decision I made. I cleaned up," she says.

"You didn't have to do that," I tell her. "I have someone coming in to clean the house twice a week."

"Well, it was either clean up or go and smell your clothes," she jokes, laughing. "I figured it would be safer to clean."

I shake my head, laughing. She just saved me from having a panic attack, and she didn't even know it. "So are you saying I won't find your hair in my bed?"

"I never said that," she teases. "I didn't smell your clothes. I never said anything about your pillow." She laughs. "Anyway, my car is here, so I'm out."

"Thank you," I say. She did even more than she knows. She salutes me and disconnects. It's only after she hangs up that I notice that my heartbeat is back to normal, my hands are dry, and the weight that was on my chest is lighter.

"She's just a friend," I remind myself. "Just a friend." Though my brain doesn't really agree. "Just a friend who talked you off a ledge without even knowing it," I say, getting up again. This time, it's without the weight on my chest.

FOURTEEN

ZOE

"WHY, WHY DO we have to watch the hockey game?" I groan from my side of the couch. "You've already scored him." I look over at Zara who lies on her side with a huge cover over her. We just finished eating Chinese, and she switched on the game.

"Because I always watch the game," she says. "If you watched, you'd like it, too."

I glare at her. "You hated hockey for twenty-two years, and now, all of a sudden, it's a great thing," I point out to her and get up, heading to the kitchen. I grab a water bottle and then walk back into the room. When I hear the announcer says Viktor's name, my eyes shoot up to the television screen to watch. This is not helping with me frantically trying to remind myself that he is off-limits.

"He's back in the lineup," the announcer says. "No one thought it would be possible for him to come back." I watch him skate up the ice, and I wonder if he's nervous. "Petrov takes the puck out of the zone and brings it up, passing it to Richards who sends it up over the glass."

"What does that mean?" I ask Zara who's now looking at me with her head tilted to the side.

"It means they are going to have a face-off in the neutral zone," she tells me. I roll my eyes, but my eyes go right back to the screen as I watch him skate down the ice. My finger starts to tap the water bottle nervously.

The announcer continues talking about Viktor. "I didn't think anyone would pick him up after his disastrous season with LA."

"Well," another voice says, "I'm not sure what Grant is thinking by signing him." I want to yell at the screen and tell them to shut the fuck up, but I don't. Instead, I just scoff.

"Time will tell," the other guy says, and now the referee drops the puck.

"What's going on with you two?" Zara asks, and I look at her. In my whole life, the only person I've never lied to is Zara. Not that I didn't try, but she always spotted it. She would know.

"Nothing," I tell her, looking back at the television. It's not a lie because there really isn't anything going on. "We're friends."

"Bullshit," she says, and I look at her.

"He's a recovering addict who can't get involved with anyone," I tell her. "That's what it boils down to."

"But if he wasn't recovering, would you go for him?" she asks, and my heart starts to speed up. I don't want to admit it because I don't want to put it out into the universe. I want to deny, deny, deny.

"He plays hockey," I tell her. "You know my stance on that." It's not that I don't like hockey players; it's just that I'm not interested in dating a hockey player who is going to go on and on about my family name.

"It was one guy," she says, bringing up the one who fucked me for all other hockey players. "And he wasn't even good."

"I loved him!" I shout at her.

"You were fifteen!" she shouts back.

"I practiced my name with his." I tell her about the insane amount of times I changed my last name to his.

"Oh, please," she says, rolling her eyes.

"Liam broke my heart. All because he wanted to be in Dad's stupid summer league hockey camp." He started dating me on March 17th, St. Patrick's Day. I was totally head over heels in love with him after a week. He started coming over more and more, our make-out sessions started getting shorter and shorter, and he started spending more time in the family room. Then he tried out for the team and didn't make it. Well, five minutes after he got cut from the team, I got cut from the girlfriend role. "Asshole."

She shakes her head and then a horn from the television makes us both look up, and we see that Philly just scored and are celebrating while Viktor and Evan skate off with their heads down. "Fuck," Zara says, tossing me my phone. I watch the television, mesmerized by the replay and how it went off Viktor's stick and into the net.

"Well, I guess he can score goals for the other team," the announcer says, and when it shows Viktor on the bench, his head is low as he looks out over the ice.

"How much time is left?" I ask her.

"I thought you hated hockey?" she says, and I answer by giving her the finger. I turn and watch the screen as it goes to intermission. I grab my phone and scroll through Instagram, and I'm not paying attention "It's not a good idea," Zara says, and I look at her.

"What are you talking about?" I ask her.

"You and Viktor and the whole let's be friends bullshit." She doesn't waste any time with the bullshit, and I want to kick her, but she's pregnant, so I don't. "You need step away from the whole situation. You got him his house, so it should end there."

"There is nothing more," I tell her. "Honest." She raises her eyebrows at me. "Okay, fine, he's hot, and he's sexy as fuck. But"—I tell her—"and there is a huge but, it's never going to go anywhere. I know that. The cards are on the table."

"Yeah, well, the house of cards is going to fall soon, and I don't want you to get crushed by it," she says and then laughs. "Fuck, that was a good line. I'm going to put it in my notes."

"You're an idiot. You know that?" I laugh. The game comes back on, and for the next seventeen minutes, nothing happens. They get several chances to score, but it's always stopped. When they have two minutes left, they pull the goalie. "Why, why are they leaving the net empty?" I ask her.

"So they can have the one-man advantage," she says, but I stop talking when the announcer's voice starts to go a bit louder.

"Intercepted by Petrov." The announcer's voice gets louder with anticipation, and then I sit up. "He makes his way around Gustoff who tries to check him into the board, but he's a second too late. Petrov skates to the center, and he scores." I jump up out of my chair with my hands in the air.

"He just scored," I say, grabbing my head with both of my hands. "Holy shit, that was so good," I say, but I don't take my eyes off the screen as Evan goes to Viktor and jumps on him. "I don't know about you, but if my man was looking at another man like that, I would be a little worried." I wink at her, and she now flips me the bird.

"Now what happens?" I ask, sitting back down.

"Now, they go into overtime three on three," she moans. "You are literally there at every single game. Have you not ever watched?"

"I've watched," I say, "between my sips of wine."

"Your Instagram consists of all selfies from the games," she points out.

"Yes, because obviously I'm there," I say. "You are so annoying."

The overtime comes, and they lose, but at least Viktor isn't on the ice, so he won't feel bad about it. I mean, he probably will feel bad about it.

"Oh, well, maybe next time," I say and then turn the television off. "Where are you sleeping tonight?" I ask, knowing she usually shares my bed when Evan isn't here.

"I was going to cuddle you," she jokes, and we walk up to the bedroom and then her phone rings. "It's Evan."

"Go into the spare room and come back later," I say. "The

last thing I want to do is be nauseated before I go to bed." I walk into my room as she walks up the stairs to the third floor and goes into the spare room. I get ready for bed and try not to think about him. I try to clear him from my mind, but my dreams all night are of the fucking hockey game.

———

Sunday morning, I slide my eyes open right after eight o'clock. Reaching for my phone, I see that the Stingers won their game last night. It's been almost five days since I've thought about him. I'm super proud of this. Getting up, I decide to go take the expert boxing class, and they don't call it expert for nothing. I swear, I think my arms are going to turn to jelly. I can't raise them to take off my sweaty bra. I put on my maroon yoga pants, a clean sports bra, and my gray Nike shirt. It is cut high in the front and long in the back, showing off my abs. I'm grabbing my purse and groaning when I put it over my shoulder, and the phone rings. I look down and see Viktor's number.

He never calls me, so something must be wrong. Before I send it to voicemail or talk myself out of answering it, I connect it and put it to my ear.

"Hello?" I say, holding the phone with my shoulder. Walking down the stairs, I hold the railing because my legs feel like jelly.

"Hey, are you around?" he asks breathlessly.

"Depends where around is and what you want," I tell him, walking out of the gym toward the subway. Better yet, I should just take a cab.

"Near my place," he says. "I am sort of stuck, and I need

help."

"I'm about five minutes away. I just left my class," I tell him and start to walk toward his apartment. "How urgent is this situation?" I ask him when I spot Starbucks.

"Um ..." he starts to answer.

"I'm in front of Starbucks, and I'm thinking I should get a drink." I stop in front and hear him huff out. "Jeez, Louise, I was going to offer to get you something too."

"Fine. Get me an iced coffee with milk," he says. "And check and see if they have any protein bites."

"First, you huff, and then you even order food." I shake my head and joke with him. "I'll be right over."

I try to tell myself that I'm just going over to help him as a friend, I would do it for anyone. I buzz his number, and when I get to his floor, his door is open. I step in, and it looks like a warzone.

Boxes are scattered everywhere, and everything from the boxes are laying on every surface that he has. "Oh my God." I look around to see if anything looks like it's in its place. "Did you get robbed?"

He looks over at me, his face full of scruff, his eyes a touch darker than normal, and the circles under his eyes also back to being a bit darker. "Why are you naked?" he asks me, his eyes almost glaring.

I look down at my outfit. "If this is what you think a naked girl looks like, I feel sorry for the women who actually got naked for you," I say, walking in and deciding where to put the drink. When I walk to the island, it's full of everything that you could need in a kitchen. And then some knick-knacks you never use but always have. The only free space to put anything on is the stove. I walk over and place the tray on it, and my purse falls to the floor. I turn back at him. "But seriously, what in the fuck is all this?"

"My life," he says, and I grab his coffee and bring it to him. "I thought it would be a good idea to unload all the boxes and then put things away."

"Okay," I say, looking at the clothes covering his couch.

"Well, then, by the time I looked around, I just don't know where any of this shit goes," he says, taking a sip of coffee and looking around to see if he can sit anywhere. "I didn't even know I had half this stuff."

"What do you mean?" I ask, walking to the kitchen table and seeing that he has about ten different tablecloths. "Didn't you buy this stuff?" I run my hands over the tablecloths, thinking maybe an ex did, and then having a need to just toss it out and have him start everything fresh.

"No"—he shakes his head—"I had a designer who did all this." Well, then, the tablecloths can stay.

"I think the first thing you need to do is put away the big things," I say, going to the counter. "Like this Kitchen Aid mixer."

"It has ten different pieces," he says, throwing up one hand. "Ten." I laugh at the way he tries to flash his hand twice to give me a picture of ten.

"Well, because you can use it ten different ways," I tell him and see the frazzled look on his face. "Have you ever used it?"

"Zoe." He says my name almost like he's groaning, and I have the sudden image in my head of what he would sound like if I perhaps put his cock in my mouth.

I blink and try to erase the image from my head. "I'm trying not to judge you." I try to roll my lips together. "How do I know you're not some secret baker?" I can't hold it in anymore.

"Are you done?" he asks.

"It's too early to tell." I look over at another machine. "Ten bucks if you know what this is." He looks at the machine in my hand and stutters. "It's an electric juicer. Usually for orange or lemon," I tell him, and he looks at me like I have two heads. "Zara made me do her registry with her." He gets up and comes to me and takes it in his hand. "Now, I take it you've never used it."

"No, but it would be cool to use," he says, and I shake my head.

I grab a box. "This box is going to be stuff to donate."

"That's a good idea," he says. "God, I'm glad I called you," he says with a smile on his face, and just like that, the little devil in my head whispers to me.

"You like him."

No, I don't. I'm just his friend.

Keep lying to yourself, is the last thing I listen to before I finish helping him.

FIFTEEN

VIKTOR

"WHAT YOU NEED to do is look at things and think about the last time you used it," she says, holding up ... I don't even know what she is holding up. All I know is it's white and you plug it in. "If you don't even know what it is, you donate it." She puts it in the box.

The past couple of days have been a clusterfuck. I've been all over the place, attending two meetings a day. I thought getting back on the ice would calm things but not after my fuckup in the first game. Yes, I did come back and score to tie the game, but the pressure was so much. I was drenched every single night I woke up after just sleeping for three hours at a time. I'd get up, unpack a couple of things in my bedroom, and then go back to bed. This morning, I rolled out of bed and had a plan, a plan in my head that was going to be awesome. I was going to unpack everything and then place everything accordingly. Well, fifty-seven boxes later, my house looked like a tornado. I didn't know who to call because I didn't want to bother anyone really. But that nagging voice in the back of my head kept chanting her name, so I caved and called her.

"Yes," I tell her. "It'll be easier that way and maybe"—I pick up something else I don't know—"you can help me by naming things."

She shakes her head. "No, if you can't name them, that means you aren't going to use them." She takes the tool out of my hand. "By the way, this is a hand blender."

I look at it before it disappears into the box. "Interesting," I say.

"Who should we donate this stuff to?" she asks, waiting for me to pick up the next item.

"I have no idea," I say, grabbing another item.

"There are a bunch of people you can donate to. Women's shelter, homeless shelter."

"We can donate to the people who are coming out of rehab." I look at her. "You know sober living places."

She nods. "Yeah, that's a good one. Plus, it will mean more to you if it's close to your heart."

I don't answer her as we fill more boxes than I care to admit, even giving them extra now that I know where it's going. I was lucky that I could start over fresh and have the financial means to do it. Not everyone is this lucky. While we fill the boxes, she goes on and on about this show on television about dating abroad and having ninety days to wed.

The whole time, I'm mesmerized by the stories and the way her hands get all animated. She goes on and on about how it works, and I have to admit I'm a little curious myself.

"I can't believe we did all that in six hours," I say, looking at the clock on the stove and seeing it's just after eight.

"I'm surprised my arms could hold anything," she says and puts her hands up again and her shirt rises. "I swear it was a tough class today." I swallow, but it feels like I have a mouth full of nails.

I don't bother answering her. Instead, I turn around and go to the fridge, grabbing a water bottle and giving it to her. "Are you hungry?" She shakes her head while opening the bottle and drinking.

"No," she says when the water bottle leaves her lips. "I'm still full from the pizza you ordered. I am going to get going," she says, walking to the living room and putting on her shoes.

"Let me order you an Uber," I tell her, and she looks up. "It's the least I could do."

"Fine," she says, giving in. "You do owe me." I nod and order her an Uber.

She looks over at the boxes we stacked on one wall. "Don't forget to call the shelter tomorrow."

"I won't. I'm going to ask my sponsor and see if we can give a bit to everyone."

"That is so nice," she says and bends to pick up her purse. I almost groan when my eyes go straight to her ass. "I'm out," she says and opens the door, then turns back around. "Let me know if you start watching."

"I will keep you posted," I tell her, walking to the door and holding it open until she gets in the elevator. When the door closes and I don't see her anymore, I let out a huge sigh of relief. I know we are friends, and I know that I shouldn't even be thinking of her like that, but every single time our hands touched, it was like an electric shock to the system. I close the door and turn off the lights. I don't bother putting the chairs back in their place since I know I'll be up in the middle of the night anyway.

I strip out of my clothes and toss them in the basket and finally walk into the shower. I let the hot water run over me, closing my eyes. The only thing that comes to my mind is Zoe and the way her toes are now painted a deep red. The way her skin shines in the sun, the way her stomach goes in at the side showing you her abs, and the way her ass fills out those yoga pants. I don't stop my hand from gripping my cock. *One time*, I think to myself. I'll just fantasize about her this one time, and then next time, I'll watch porn. I think about her riding me, her hair swinging from side to side as my hands grip her hips. My mouth taking one of her nipples in my mouth. Another one of her on her hands and knees in front of me, my hands still gripping her hips while she looks back at me.

I don't think I stroke myself more than ten times before I come with her name on my lips in a whisper. When I open my eyes, the guilt washes over me, so I switch the water from hot to cold and stand in it to clear my thoughts.

The official start to the season is next Saturday. I already asked my parents if they wanted to fly in, but with my father and his own coaching schedule, it was impossible. So I gave my tickets to Jeffrey, and he and his son-in-law are going to come.

The whole week goes off without a hitch, and nothing out of the ordinary happens. Matthew tells me that my mandatory urine test came back clean. No surprise at that. I've only woken up drenched in sweat three out of the five days in the past week. I've also binge watched two seasons of *90 Day Fiancé.* I'm dying to talk to her about it, but I don't text her. After I let myself think about her in the shower, I knew it was getting just a bit out of hand, so I've kept my distance. But it's the game opener tonight, so I know I'll see her, and whether I want to admit it, I'm really excited.

The organization is going big for the season opener, as they usually do, and all the family members are invited to an after party at a pub close to the arena. They are shutting it down for us, which is good, and I have also invited Jeffrey. I wanted my parents to be there, and I don't know why it bothers me because I should be used to it by now.

I slip on my blue suit jacket and look in the mirror. My eyes are a lighter blue today, and it's probably because of the color of my suit.

I grab a taxi and head to the arena. I'm walking in the same time some other players are walking in, and I spot a camera crew setting up to film the arrivals of the players for the season openers. I keep my head down the whole time and don't look up for them to see me. But it doesn't work because one of them calls out my name. I look up and smile right before walking into the arena and away from their prying eyes. The beating of my heart is so hard and loud it echoes in my ears. My hands are clammy, and my whole body feels like one giant nerve ready to explode or vomit.

The hallways are packed with people and the press. The music coming from the outside pounds through. "This is going to be fun," Mark, our goalie, says to me. "Don't get undressed right away. Oliver wants us to go out there and meet some of the fans," he says, walking to the locker room. He and I have spoken a bit but not much which is why he has the nickname of Private Mark. He seems like a decent guy, but he's huge at six feet four.

I walk into the locker room, and Mark was not wrong. Oliver stands in the middle of the room wearing a suit that has the team logo all over him. "Is that custom made?" I ask him.

"Of course, it is," he says, looking down at the suit. "Every year, I get one made."

"Interesting," I say, trying not to laugh.

"I need you to take that sexy Russian behind out to greet some of the fans," he tells me. "Half the team is out there already." I am about to ask him if I really have to when he says, "You really need to. Now go out there. Max twenty minutes."

I nod at him and walk out to the masses. A couple of fans come up to me and ask me to sign their jerseys and pose for some pictures. I spot a couple of the rookies, Jeremy and Benjamin.

"It's a madhouse," Benjamin says. "I think I saw one of the *Game of Throne* chicks walking around here somewhere."

"Forget her. Have you seen Evan's sister-in-law?" Jeremy says. "I got a boner the second she turned around." It takes everything I have to put my hands in my pockets instead of around his tiny little punk ass throat.

"A little advice," I say, looking around for her. "It might

not be a good idea to go for the captain's sister-in-law." I look back at them. "Besides, you really don't want to piss off Matthew." They both swallow now, and I see their Adam's apple move.

It doesn't take me long to spot her, and the minute I do, I smile. She is squatting down talking to Max's little girl while she holds her hand. When she stands up, I take in her outfit. Dark blue jeans that mold her with rips on the front. Her long-sleeved light gray sweater is fully conservative; it even goes to her neck. Her wavy hair is down, and her shoes match the color of her sweater. *I don't know what the big deal is*, I think to myself. And then she turns around, and I stop breathing. I hold my breath as the back of her shirt swoops all the way down to her ass, showing you her whole bare back. A back that is perfect, a back that has way too much skin showing, and a back that has no bra strap.

I make my way to Evan, who is standing near her. "How long are you here for?" I ask him, and just then, Zoe finally looks over, and our eyes meet. I try to steady my heartbeat and make it as casual as I can by nodding my head at her. She smiles at me and repeats the same thing to me.

"I'm trying to keep the rookies away from that one," he says, pointing at Zoe. "M&M gave me orders to cover her up with my jacket if I have to," he says, and I look at Zoe, who can hear him and just rolls her eyes.

"How am I supposed to find a man if I have everyone covering me up?" she asks us. We all look at her, but no one answers her.

"Here," Matthew says to her, handing her a plastic bag with the team logo on it. "I just bought this for you." Max is beside him, trying not to laugh.

She snatches the bag from Matthew, and Max bends to pick up his daughter, kissing her neck. I watch as she puts her arms around his shoulders. "You will never give me trouble like Auntie Zo Zo, right?"

"I'm not wearing this," she says, throwing the bag back at Matthew.

"It's the team jersey," he says. "You have to support."

"It's a men's large," she says, and then looks at him, and I see she is spinning something, and I can't help but smile. "Actually, I can wear this with a belt, and it can be a dress." She tries to snatch the bag back, but Matthew is faster. "I mean, these shoes don't go with the outfit, but I can make it work." And just like that, I picture her wearing nothing but the jersey. I also picture her against a wall somewhere with the jersey pulled way up there while I'm buried in her.

I'm taken out of my daydream when Matthew claps his hands. "Okay, we have to go," he says, then leans over and kisses Alex in Max's arms. She blocks her neck, so he has to kiss her cheek. "You are pretty just like your mommy," he says to her, and she smiles.

"Give her to me," Zara say, reaching for her, but she shakes her head.

"Come on, sweet pea," Zoe says, holding out her hand, and she lunges for her. Zoe sets her on her hip, and I take her in as she whispers in Alex's ear, "Tell Uncle Evan to break a leg."

"Break a leg," she says softly, then turns back to Zoe. "Now can I have candy?"

We all laugh but turn to walk back into the dressing

room. I take a second to look back over my shoulder. I know I shouldn't, but I do anyway. She is walking away from us now, her hair swinging left and right while she does it. The only one who actually sees me looking at her is Alex, who waves at me and then turns around to talk to her aunt.

"Get your head in the zone," I mumble to myself. "The zone is the only place you have to be."

Sixteen

Zoe

"How long is it again?" I ask Zara while I sip my wine and watch the game. Usually, I sit up in the suite, but now, I'm sitting in the chairs right outside next to Zara and Karrie. Allison and Vivienne are sitting in front of us, having their own conversation. From back when Matthew started playing here, my parents bought a lodge in the arena, and Karrie's father, Doug, who owns the team has the lodge right next to us, so there is one huge room with couches where you can watch the game and eat and drink. It's almost like a living room. A counter with four barstools separates you from the seats in the arena, which is where we are sitting now.

"How"—Karrie turns to me—"do you have hockey all in your family, and you don't know anything about it?"

I throw my head back and groan. "What don't you guys understand! I don't actually like hockey?"

"She never did," Allison pipes in from in front of me, taking a sip of her wine. The good news about having a suite is that the kids have their own section so they are always busy and not all over us.

"It's not a foreign concept," I tell them. "I come so I can eat and drink for free. It's called socializing." Taking another sip of my wine, I try not to see if I can spot Viktor from the players on the bench.

"And take pictures," Vivienne says, turning to nod her head. "You have the best selfies."

"Thank you," I say, smiling. "See, someone actually gets me."

"You know who else gets you? Viktor," Zara says from beside me, and I whip my head in her direction. "What? I swear he was looking at her like he hasn't had a meal in a year."

"He was not," I say, shaking my head and thinking he looked so good in that suit he had on. He stood with his hands in his pockets, and that pose made his arms fill it out even more. I swear it looked like he was going to bust out of it a la hulk style. "We are friends. How many times do I have to say it to you?"

"Would you bang him?" Vivienne looks at me to ask the question, and I shake my head and lie. It's such a lie I'm surprised my nose isn't poking her in the face. "Seriously, you can't say no to that. He's hot. Look at him," she says, pointing at the jumbotron that now shows his face. When the game started, they introduced the team one at a time, and they skated out by number. The only ones out of place were the captain and the two assistants. Viktor was second to last because he was assistant. Something that apparently just happened tonight also. The crowd went wild when he came out, and I just watched him skate to center ice and hold up his hand to the spectators. His eyes were blue, and his smile tight, but you could tell he was nervous when he skated to the blue line with the rest of the players and he shook his hands at his sides.

"I don't bang hockey players," I tell her, "unlike someone I know."

"Please," Vivienne says. "I'm still so thirsty, you have no idea. It's like I'm a camel in the desert. Dry. Seche." She says the French word for dry. "I swear, I went to the gyno the other day, and he had to use extra lube."

"Dryness comes with age," Karrie says, and you would think that she just slapped Vivienne in the face.

"Bitch, I'm as old as you are," Vivienne says. "How much lube do you have to use?" The minute she asks that, Allison, Zara, and I all groan. If we didn't have wine glasses, we would have covered our ears.

"Don't answer that!" I scream, and it happens at the same time as the other team scores, and boos fill the arena. "Shit," I say, looking at the replay and seeing that it was the third line on the ice.

"Well, at least it wasn't our guys," Zara says quietly.

"*We* don't have guys. You have a guy," I tell her and get up to refresh my drink. I'm pouring another glass when I hear the whole crowd gasp.

I look at the television screen and see that one of the guys on the other team tried to hit Viktor in the back of the head. Of course, Viktor turned around, and then the pushing started. I don't know what the guy said, but one second, they are face-to-face, and the next second, the stick goes flying, the gloves go flying, and all you see is Viktor grab the guy by the shirt and punch him square in the face. "Oh my God." I gasp when the guy tries to hit Viktor, but he doesn't stand a chance. The referee has to break them up, and Viktor skates to the penalty box. "Dad," I call my father, and he turns from the bar and comes over. "Why is he in the box?"

"What?" He looks at me confused.

"Why did he get put in the box? He was defending himself," I tell him. "The guy tried to hit him."

My father looks at the replay on the television screen and then at me, back and forth maybe four times. "You're asking me about hockey."

"Oh my God, Dad," I groan. "Just … I don't get it."

"It's retaliation," my father says. "If he would have let it go, the other guy would have gone to the box, but Viktor dropped his gloves."

"Well, yeah, but," I start saying, and I look at my father.

"Honey," he says softly, "I really think …"

"Dad, seriously, I'm not the least bit interested in him," I say, and with him, he can't tell if I'm lying, so he just smiles.

"Are you coming back to our house for lunch tomorrow?" he asks me.

"No, I have a showing for a special client," I tell him and look back at the screen and see Viktor on the screen. "How long is he in the box for?" I ask, and he points at the timer under the score of the game. It's a tied game, and there is forty seconds left in the game and ten seconds left in his penalty. Viktor stands up in the box, waiting for his time to get back on the ice. Just when they open the door for him to get back on the ice, Evan poke checks it out of the zone, slipping the puck straight to Viktor. It looks like he's running on the ice, but I think it's him skating faster. I hold my father's arm as I watch him go one on one with the goalie. Holding my breath, I watch as he goes left to right and then he fakes one way and the goalie goes that way, but he stays there, and he actually scores. "Ahhhhh!" I scream and jump. My mother looks over at me, her eyes fixated on me while my father turns to high-five Matthew. The horn goes off, and the crowd stands on their feet and cheers.

The announcer says Viktor's and Evan's name, and the crowd is still on their feet. They line up for a face-off again, and this time, the only thing that happens is they drop the puck and the horn sounds, telling us the game is over. I walk over to the entrance of the box and the seats and stand there when they announce the three stars of the game. I'm watching when they announce him as the first star.

He skates out and does a turn, tossing pucks into the crowd, and then they pull him for an interview. The jumbotron shows him standing next to the reporter, and I watch him with a sense of pride.

"Viktor, game one of the season and already on the scoreboard." He smiles at him, and Viktor cracks a little bit of a smirk. "How did it feel?"

"It's great," he says, and I am so happy for him I could explode. "It's great to be a part of this amazing organization."

"The fans have been sporting those Petrov jerseys. How does it feel to see them?"

"It feels amazing," he says, looking into the stands, and I see the nervousness he had before the game is gone. He was quiet, and I knew this was because he was "getting in the zone."

"I'm just thankful they have welcomed me with open arms, and I can't wait to make them proud." I want to clap my hands and applaud him.

"Well said," the reporter says and then shakes his hand. Viktor skates back to the bench and then makes his way to the back.

The lights in the pub are dim, and tables are scattered everywhere. No one is here yet, so we grab two tables in the back corner where we always sit. By the time we sit down and order drinks, the room has started filling up. Evan comes in about thirty minutes later, and the music is starting to play now. "Hey," I say when he nods at me and grabs Zara for a kiss. Matthew and Max follow him and go to grab their wives. "I have to go to the bathroom," I say, getting up and going to the bathroom. My eyes scan the room, looking to see if he's here, and I smile at a couple of wives who I recognize on the way. When I walk out of the bathroom I come face-to-face with the man who I'm going out of my way to avoid and not think about.

He spots me and smiles. "Hey, you."

"Hey there, Rocky," I say, laughing while he shakes his head. "A nice right hook," I say, chucking his chin, and he throws his head back. He then looks to the right where an older gentleman stands next to him, and I wonder if it's his father. "Hi," I say, putting out my hand. "I'm Zoe."

"Jeffrey," he says, grabbing my hand and smiling.

"Jeffrey," Viktor says. "This is Zoe, my friend and real estate agent." I try not to cringe at friend. "Zoe, this is my sponsor, Jeffrey."

"It's nice to finally meet the one who got him settled," Jeffrey says, smiling.

"Did you enjoy the game?" I ask him, and my voice is a touch louder than normal since the music is playing. The pub is now full, and it's getting hard to move without bumping into someone.

"It was amazing," he says, looking at Viktor. "Minus the whole 'Rocky' moment."

"Yeah, well, not every day you get called a junkie," Viktor says. My head snaps back to him, and the smile is gone. In its place is anger.

"What did you just say?" I ask him. "I don't think I heard you properly." I watch him and ignore that Jeffrey is now looking at me intently.

"Nothing," Viktor says. "Just words on the ice. They say things to get under your skin and into your head."

"I thought all you guys talked about was fucking each other's sister and mothers," I tell him, crossing my arms over my chest, and Jeffrey starts to laugh, shaking his head.

"She's a feisty one," he says and then slaps Viktor's shoulder. "I should head out."

"I'm going, too," Viktor says, and I want to tell him not to go. I want to tell him to stay and talk to me. I want to drag him back to the table and have him sit next to me and talk about nothing and everything. But I don't do that. I just smile. "Will you tell Evan I took off?"

"Yeah," I say, acting like him leaving is not ruining my

night. "Sure thing," I say and then look at Jeffrey. "It was so good to meet you." He sticks out his hand in a fist, and I fist bump it.

"I'll see you soon," he says, and I push his shoulder.

"See you around," Viktor says. I look at him, and he just nods at me, so I turn and escape into the crowd of people, not once looking back. I go back to sit in my chair and pick up the glass of wine that has now turned hot and tastes gross. "I think I'm going to head out." I look at Zara who is yawning.

"Us, too," Evan says. "I was just waiting for Viktor."

"He just took off," I tell them, and Zara watches my face. "He was here with his friend."

"Do you want to go home, sweet pea, or do you want to say with Zoe?" Evan asks her, and she yawns again.

"I would rather go home," she says, getting up, and I look at her stomach.

"You won't be able to hide that little bump for much longer," I tell her, and she gently caresses her stomach, her face beaming.

"Let's go. I'll drive you home," Evan says. We say good-bye to everyone, and once again, I'm leaving alone. I sit in the back of the car looking out into the road, and I'm thinking about the broken man who fights every single minute to be the better person. The one whose eyes hold the key to his soul, yet it's locked up so tight no one can get in.

Seventeen

Viktor

You're nothing but a washed-up junkie.

My eyes fly open, taking in the dark hotel room. My body is aching, and I need sleep more than ever, but nothing is restful about my dreams.

We just played a game against Colorado and then got on a plane headed to Florida. We won the game by the skin of our teeth. It wasn't just a fast game; it was a physical game also. The checks into the board got harder and harder as the time went on. Although no one has thrown the junkie word in my face in the past two weeks, it's still the little voice whispering to me at night.

I toss the covers off me and get out of bed. Looking at the clock, I see it's 4:00 a.m. I was asleep for three hours, give or take, so I get out of bed and open a seven-dollar bottle of water, not caring at this point. I open the television and flip through the channels, stopping at some movie. I let it play, but my head is elsewhere. In two weeks, I will have been clean for six months. One hundred and eighty-four days.

My throat goes dry, and I drink more water, but nothing is helping tonight. Nothing. My hand starts to get clammy, and my chest suddenly squeezes too tight. I get up and my breathing starts to come in little pants. My whole body starts to tremble just a touch, and little beads of sweat form on my upper lip. The nausea starts in my stomach, and I sit on the side of the bed. I know I'm having panic attack because it happened to me in rehab when I was closing in on the six-day mark. I needed something to calm my nerves, and nothing would put me in a calm place like my drug of choice.

I look at the clock and focus on the numbers going from one minute to the next. One second more and I use all the tools they taught me at rehab. I start with trying to calm my breathing by taking a deep inhale and then exhale. I open my eyes and try focusing on one thing in the room. I reach for it all, but nothing is working this time. Not looking at the numbers, not counting it in my head, not repeating the serenity part. Nothing. I close my eyes and think about my happy place, which is the stupidest thing I have ever heard of, but I will try anything.

I'm taken back to my apartment, my empty apartment with a picnic in the middle. I've tried to block her smile out of my head since the pub. I've tried not to look for her or even think of her. I have somehow lost this battle, and tonight is no different. I think of her face when she has no makeup on and it's just her little freckles. I think about her green eyes that turn blue most of the time when she laughs. I think about that little speck at the bottom of her left eye that looks like a black spot. The sound of her laughter echoes in my ears, and my heart suddenly starts beating normal. My breathing is coming in normal now and not in soft pants. I open my eyes now and take a deep breath.

"Maybe I should learn yoga," I say to myself and finish the water bottle. I get back into bed and turn off the television, then turn on my calm app to the sound of waves. I don't know how long it takes before I fall asleep, but the blaring alarm has me groaning. I shut it off and roll over. Blinking my eyes open, I see the sun outside shining.

My phone buzzes, and I grab it and see that it's Jeffrey calling

"Hey," I grumble out.

"Were you sleeping?" he asks me, and I hear cars honking in the distance.

"I just got up," I tell him. "It was a rough night."

"It's why I'm calling," he says. "I remember when I was almost to my six months, my head was a mess, and it was all over the place. I would wake up in a pool of sweat. I would also get violently sick."

"Yeah, I had a panic attack last night." I tell him all about last night, not bringing up Zoe. That is mine and mine alone. No one is getting that. "At one point, I thought I was having a heart attack."

"When are you back?" he asks me, and I roll onto my back.

"We play tomorrow, then we are on the plane back," I tell him. "Why?"

"Well, six months is a huge deal, and I think we should do something to acknowledge it," he tells me.

"I'm not throwing myself a 'I've been clean for six months' party," I say, grabbing the pillows to prop me up a touch.

"It's not a party," he says. "It's a little mixer. It would be good for you to do it mentally. To see faces there that have been there holding you up."

"I don't know," I tell him.

"Okay, can we even sit down and have a coffee or maybe a burger? I can order you a cupcake," he says.

"I have to get up and get to the rink. Can we talk about this when I get back?" I tell him.

"Sure, and, Viktor? You can call me at any time of the night. It's what I'm here for," he reminds me and disconnects. I get up and take another shower and slip into jeans and a shirt, then head down to the bus taking us to practice. I go through the drills; I go through the motions. I make small talk, I grunt at most of them, and when I slip back into my room, I'm exhausted mentally, physically, and emotionally.

The team goes out for dinner, but I pass on the invite and order room service instead. I have been binge watching *90 Day Fiancé*. When I turn off the lights at nine p.m., I fall asleep right away. This time, when I wake up at two, I'm almost ready to fist pump, thinking of the five whole hours I slept. I turn on the television and switch the it to *'90 day fiancée'* and I grab my phone, sending Zoe a text.

Me: She's fifty-three, and he's twenty and from Nigeria. Why does she not see he's using her?

I put my phone down, not thinking she'll actually text me back. But two seconds later, my phone beeps.

Zoe: She just wants the D.

I smile at her answer and then text her back.

Me: What are you doing up?

Zoe: Why are you texting me?

I am about to text her back when the phone rings, and I see it's her on FaceTime.

"What are you doing up?" she asks me as soon as her face comes through the phone.

"I could ask you the same," I tell her, tucking pillows behind my head so I can sit up more.

"I'm working with a guy in Paris," she says. "The time difference makes it hard for us, and he needs to get a place asap." I look at her, and she looks like she woke up not too long ago. Her hair's piled on her head, and she's sitting at her desk instead of in her bed. "So what's your excuse?"

"I'm a recovering addict," I tell her. "The most I sleep straight is five hours."

"When does it get better?" she asks me, looking at me.

Shrugging, I answer her. "I don't know. It's been almost six months."

"That's a big deal," she says with a smile. "Six months doesn't seem long, but it is."

"Yeah, it's a big deal," I say. "Jeffrey wants to do a dinner and stuff."

"Why wouldn't you?" she asks and hides her mouth when she yawns.

"Because I still have a long way to go," I answer her honestly.

"Yes," she agrees, "but you've also come a long way."

"Not going to lie. I never thought I would be this far in," I tell her quietly. "It's just I don't want to make a big deal out of it. Because …" I trail off.

"Because what?" she asks me, now leaning her cheek on her hand.

"Because what if I fuck up again, and then it's …" I start saying.

"I mean, if you fuck up and have to start over, it's almost like going to a wedding and getting them a nine-hundred-dollar gravy boat and then they get divorced and you sit there wondering who the fuck got the gravy boat. Then you wonder if you can ask for the gravy boat back because it cost you the same as it would to buy a new pair of shoes," she says, her head shaking.

"Did you just compare my falling off the wagon to divorce?" I ask her and then shake my own head. "And are shoes really nine hundred dollars?"

"Yes," she answers. "Wait here," she says. She gets up, and she is suddenly moving with her phone, and she turns on a bright light. "See these shoes?" she says, holding up black booties with studs on them. "Fifteen hundred dollars."

"I think my sister has those," I say, looking at them. "Why are they so expensive?"

"Because it's art," she says with a smile, and for the next thirty minutes, she shows me all the shoes she could have bought with the money she spent on the gravy boat. "So, in the end, have the party." She looks at me and now climbs into her bed. "When is it?"

"The first of November," I answer her. "The last time I was high was April thirtieth."

"It's a Tuesday," she says, and I look at her weirdly. "Halloween is a big deal, so they are having a party at Karrie's house for the kids. It's the day before."

"Yeah, I got the invite." Evan sent me an invitation.

"Why don't you let me plan the dinner?" she says, and her eyes look like they are getting sleepy. "It will be low-key. You can invite Jeffrey and a couple of people from your meetings."

"I don't talk to anyone at my meetings," I tell her. "I get in there, I listen, most times I share my own story, and then I leave."

"Well, then it can be the three of us," she says. "Or even just you and Jeffrey, but either way, I think you should acknowledge it and accept it."

"I'll think about it," I tell her, and she yawns. "Go to sleep. I'll talk to you later."

"You should go to sleep yourself," she tells me. "Night, Viktor." She smiles and then disconnects. I put the phone back on the side table and turn off the television, then fall asleep with the sound of her voice playing in my head.

"Go, go, go." I hear ushered next to me, and I jump over the bench and get on the ice. It's almost the end of the third, and we are winning two to one. All we have to do is hold it off them scoring for the next three minutes, and we can leave with the win under our hat. I skate down the line and look over at Evan who has the puck. He tries to go around the defenseman, but the guy poke checks the puck out of the way, and then the forward takes the puck and turns it around, heading back into our zone. I hustle it to get back there before him, and I put my stick out just in time for the puck to hit it and go out of bounds. The referee blows the whistle, and we take a face-off in the neutral zone. Evan gets into position, and I look up and see that the goalie for the other team is ready to take off for the bench and give them an extra man advantage.

Evan loses the face-off, and we hustle it back into the zone, taking the position of a baseball diamond. Evan stays up in the middle between the two defensemen, and I grab the right winger while Jeremy grabs the left man. The other team starts passing it from one to the other, and we all move with them, not giving them a chance to take a shot on the net. The defenseman gets the puck, and he slaps it toward the goalie, but I get down on one knee, putting my stick on the floor, and the puck hits the inside of my foot. The pain courses through me, but right before I fall to the ice and leave my team one man down, I swing my stick, pushing the puck to Evan who shoots it down the ice and scores an empty net goal.

I put my other knee down and wince out as I try to stand, but putting pressure on my foot feels like someone is stabbing me. "Fuck, are you okay?" Evan says, coming to me and helping me up, and I wince.

"It hit the inside of my foot," I hiss and make my way to the bench with Evan on one side as I skate with one leg. I get to the bench, and they open the door, and I hop up and then look at the doctor. "Inside of my foot."

He helps me walk to the back, and I sit in a little room the size of a shoe box. "Take the skate off so we can see," he says, and I take off my helmet and gloves. The equipment guys come in and grab my stuff and start packing up since we are leaving as soon as we are ready. I take off the skate, wincing right when Matthew comes in and looks at me.

"How bad?" he asks, putting his hands on his hips.

"No idea yet," the doctor says.

"The puck hit the inside of my foot," I say and finally take my sock off.

The doctor picks up my foot wearing rubber gloves. He presses it, and I wince. "He is going to need an X-ray," he says. "He can use the crutches until we get home. I have some painkillers he can take for now."

"Pass," I tell him. "I can handle the pain." He takes the gloves off and wraps my foot in Elastoplast, and I grab the crutches in the corner. "I'll have someone waiting for us when we land," he says and walks out of the room.

I look at Matthew. "How bad is the pain?"

"Not bad enough that I want to take a pill," I tell him. He just nods, and I make my way to the changing room. Undressing and taking a shower is beyond challenging because I am afraid to put pressure on it.

I'm the last one on the bus with Evan right in front of me carrying my bag for me. I grab my phone and see three texts.

One is my mother.

Mom: Is it broken?

The other from Jeffrey with the same question.

The third is from Zoe.

Zoe: That looked like it hurt like a motherfucker. Is it broken?

I answer my mother and Jeffrey with the same text.

Me: Don't know yet going to have it X-rayed once we get home. I'll let you know as soon as I do.

Then I text Zoe.

Me: It did hurt like a motherfucker. Not sure. Will have to check it once I get home.

I put my phone away once we get to the plane and ignore the buzzing until I'm in my seat.

Zoe: Don't be a wuss. Let me know.

I shake my head and put my phone away when Matthew sits next to me.

"We land in two hours and thirty minutes," he says. "Someone is going to be there waiting for us."

"You don't have to come with me," I tell him. "Go home and I'll call you when I'm done."

I put my head back on the seat and close my eyes ending the conversation. I send out a little prayer, hoping it's not fucking broken and that my season won't be derailed because of this. I've come too far to stop now.

EIGHTEEN

ZOE

"CONGRATULATIONS," I TELL my client on the phone. "The offer was accepted, and they are drafting it up as we speak." Leaning back in my office chair, I smile at another house sold. It's been over twelve hours since I've last spoken to Viktor, and I'm trying not to text him and ask him he's okay.

I've also held out on texting Zara, Evan, and Matthew. It would be suspicious, and that is the last thing I want. I listen to my client go on and on about how happy she is and that she can't wait to get in there. I hang up and then look over at the clock. It's almost five, and it shows since it's starting to get dark outside. I start to pack up my office and stand, slipping on my suede pumps. I'm almost all packed and ready to slip on my jacket when the phone rings again. I see it's Viktor, and I think about not answering for about one point two seconds until my hand snatches the phone and presses the green button.

"Hello," I say instead of greeting him by his name.

"Hey," he says, and I sit in the chair as I take in his voice. He sounds like he just either got up or is fighting sleep. "Did I catch you at a wrong time?" I hear the television quietly in the background.

"No. I was just packing up my office and heading home." I wait a beat. "Did you go to the doctor?"

"Yeah. It's bruised," he says with a huge sigh of relief. "I have to stay off it for the next two days, which means I can't play, and they want to see it before they leave to go to Washington in five days," he says.

"That's amazing," I say, happy that it's not as bad as everyone initially thought. "I mean, it's better than being broken, right?" I ask him. I don't tell anyone that I was actually watching the game while I was in bed working and that my heart sank the minute I saw the play. I also don't tell anyone about the amount of time I spent online afterward getting the 4-1-1 on a broken foot in hockey.

"Definitely better than being broken," he says, laughing a bit, "but it still hurts."

I laugh now. "Stop being a pussy," I tell him. He full-on belly laughs, and it just makes it even better.

"I was just wondering …" he says softly, and I wonder if he's lonely.

"Did you want me to get you something?" I ask him, suddenly hoping he says yes but not wanting him to say yes. The thought of seeing him and spending the night with him is very high on my list, but I know it won't help me get through this crush I have on him. I need to stop looking for him in a crowd. Stop watching the hockey games just to catch a glimpse of home. "I can swing by on my way home." The words come out even though my head just said no.

"I don't want you to go out of your way," he says.

"Just tell me what you want to eat, and I'll bring it over," I tell him, ignoring every single sign telling me not to.

"You don't have to," he says, and now he sounds more awake.

"I'm already stopping for myself, so I'll just get you stuff also." I mean, I was going to have to stop, ignoring that I planned on having leftover pizza tonight.

"I don't want you to just dump and go," he tells me.

"Aww, aren't you sweet? Are you asking me to have dinner with you?" I joke with him, laughing. "I mean, I thought we established that you just don't cut it for me."

"Hilarious," he tells me. "You know, if the real estate thing doesn't work out, you can always work as a comedian."

"Whatever," I say and hang up on him. After the driver stops at the place around the corner from my place, I think about going home and changing, but I veto it, expecting to just dump and go. When the car drops me off, I bring in the big bag of soup and then grab the other bag with assorted sandwiches. I didn't call him, and when I buzz, it takes him a bit to finally let me in.

"Sorry," he says to me when I make it to his front door and then see him in shorts and nothing else. He's walking with crutches under his arm, but all I can do is take in his perfectly sculpted body. I don't think I notice anything else. I don't take in the couch where it looks like he's been sleeping or that the lights are dim. I notice nothing but him. The way his back muscles ripple while he uses his crutches to get to the counter. "I don't know where you want to eat," he says. After blinking a couple of times, he looks over at me, and his eyebrows are pinched together. "Are you okay?"

"Um …" I snap out of my daze. "Why don't you go sit on the couch, and I'll bring the soup over?" I tell him, walking into the apartment and slipping off my shoes. "And if we can maybe turn on some lights, so I can see," I tell him, and he just stands there at the counter.

"Whatever you want to do, we can do," he says, smirking.

"Also, maybe put a shirt on in case you spill the hot soup." And I about groan as soon as the words come out of my mouth, but I don't face him. I put the bags on the counter, and then slip off my jacket. "Or not if you're good with burn marks." I look up and see the twinkle in his eye for the very first time.

"Does me being shirtless bother you?" he asks. I really fucking hope I don't drool all over his floor.

Instead, I roll my eyes at him, avoiding his eyes. "Did the puck hit your head after your foot?" I ask him, turning my back on him and grabbing two bowls. "Leave it off. It doesn't really bother me," I tell him, grabbing the tub of warm soup. I open the cabinet and take out a pot to put on the stove. I hear the stool scrape the floor and then look at him.

"I would help, but I only have one foot," he says, turning and then putting the injured foot on the stool next to him. "Fuck," he hisses.

"Are you okay?" I ask him, and he just nods. I turn and start the stove, emptying the container into the pot. "I got sandwiches." I point at the paper bag on the counter next to him while I grab a spoon to stir the soup. "I got a couple of different ones since I don't know what you like."

He opens the bag and takes out some of them. "What is your favorite?" he asks me, and I look over my shoulder at him.

"I'm good with just soup," I tell him, grabbing a bowl and then filling it up. "How much soup do you want?" I ask him and see him taking a bite of the sandwiches, and he moans. "I take it that's good."

"I haven't eaten today. I tried to order something and then gave up," he says, and I put the plate in front of him. "Then I napped."

I sit on the empty stool next to him with my own soup. "I love this soup," I tell him. "When I got sick last year, Zara got it for me, and I was waiting for the fall to come, so I can ask her where to get it."

"Glad my injury could help in a way," he tells me, laughing while he takes a spoonful of soup.

"Well, he did score an empty net goal because of it." I look over at him, and he gives me the side-eye.

"I thought you didn't watch hockey?" he says, and I have to really think fast.

"I turned on the television and was working, and I didn't realize I didn't change it from when Zara was over. When I looked up, you were looking like you were proposing to Evan."

"I thought my foot was broken, and you thought I was proposing," he says, shaking his head and eating more soup. "This is really good," he says.

"Good. I got you some for tomorrow," I tell him and finish

my own soup. "This was exactly what I needed."

"Dinner with me?" he asks, and I look over at him, and he winks at me.

I put my hand to my stomach. "I suddenly think I'm going to barf."

"Thanks again, Zoe," he says softly to me. I move over to bump his shoulder, but instead of going away from him after, I just stay there, next to him. Our arms touch shoulder to shoulder, and all I smell is him all around me. It would take nothing for me to lean in, and my lips would be on his. I look up into his eyes, seeing if he is thinking the same thing, but before anything happens, his buzzer rings. I spring away from him as if I got caught doing something I shouldn't be.

He looks at me and then at the door. "Did you invite any hookers?"

"Yeah, a whole harem," he jokes. "That's why I'm shirt-less."

I scoff as I get up. "And to think it was all a ploy to lure me into bed." I shake my head and press the button, asking, "Who is it?"

"Um, Jeffrey, but I think I have the wrong apartment." I hear him through the speaker and press the button for him to come up.

"It's Zoe," I tell him and then hear him open the door. I unlock the door and stand in the hallway for the elevator.

Jeffrey walks out of the elevator and smiles at me. "Well, there is no better sight than that," he says, walking toward us and pointing at Viktor. He stops in front of me holding out his hand and giving me another fist bump. "How is the patient?"

"He's waiting for his harem to come and give him a sponge bath," I joke with him and walk back into the apartment with the sound of Jeffrey laughing.

"Hey," Jeffrey says, going to Viktor. "I thought I'd come over and check on you." He looks at me. "Looks like you're in good hands."

"I just came over to deliver soup, and now I'm going," I tell them, and Jeffrey looks at me. "You are saving me."

"I'm right here," Viktor says, and I shake my head, grabbing my jacket.

"This was fun." I look at Viktor and then back at Jeffrey. "Especially seeing that handsome face," I joke with him as I grab my purse and stuff. "You take care." Then I look at Viktor. "Good luck with the harem."

I close the door and walk down the hallway away from the two men who are laughing as I exit. "It was just a good deed," I tell myself. "The same I would do for anyone," I say under my breath to no one standing next to me in the elevator.

Lies, I hear in my head. *All lies.*

NINETEEN

VIKTOR

"THAT WAS A nice surprise," Jeffrey says the minute the door closes behind Zoe. "She's a beauty."

"I thought you were married." I look at him.

"Married isn't dead," he tells me, and I just shake my head.

"Is she going to be a problem?" he asks me. I get up from my stool and hop over to the couch and sit down, putting my foot up on the table on top of a throw pillow.

"No," I answer him, and he comes over and sits next to me. "We're friends."

"Well, that is good to hear," he says, and I'm suddenly pissed.

"And why's that?" I snap at him.

"Because you haven't started to like yourself yet, let alone have the time to like someone else." I roll my eyes at him.

"I like myself just fine," I tell him.

"Do you?" he asks me, and I want to tell him to leave. "How bad do you want to tell me to fuck off right now?"

"On a scale from one to a hundred," I tell him. "A million."

"Why?"

It's a question with three little letters. Why? Except it's a loaded question.

"Is it because you like her and think you aren't good enough for her?" he starts, and I don't interrupt him. "Is it because all the rules tell you that you can't fall in love until after a year?" He takes a deep breath. "Or is it because you're a scared little shit who thinks that a good woman will never ever love you because of who you are?"

"One and three are the same," I tell him, and he shakes his head.

"That's where you're wrong," he tells me. "One is, are you good enough for her. Three is, can she love you for you." He looks at me. "Two totally different things."

"She knows that it's not an option, and she also let me know that I'm not her type, so ..." My stomach burns while I say this. "We are going to be friends."

"She brought you soup," he points out.

"So? She's a good friend," I tell him, then I finally look at him. "I won't do it to her. I won't lead her on or get involved with her because it's not fair to anyone. I need to fix me. I'm making me my number one right now."

"Good," he says, then looks at the television. "What are we watching?" I toss the remote at him without saying anything. I don't say anything to him for the rest of the night, and when he leaves, I lie in bed, awake most of the night.

"The swelling has gone down," the doctor says when he examines my foot two days later. "How is the tenderness?" he asks, pressing down on my foot, but the pain is dull.

"Not as bad as it was when it happened," I tell him, and he goes over to his chart where he starts to write the notes. I hate this part, not knowing what he's writing in there.

"My advice is to keep off it for another four to five days," he starts saying. "But you hockey players never listen." He laughs, shaking his head. "For it not to give you any other problems, do yourself a favor and just rest it."

"But …" I start to say, and he holds up his hand to stop me.

"I get it. Your team needs you." He closes the file. "But the season just started, so take the time to heal."

I nod my head at him and put my sock and my sneaker on. "Thanks, Doc," I say to him and walk out with him to the waiting room where I'm shocked to find Matthew. "Jesus. First rehab and now this." I smirk at him.

"Figured you needed another ride," he says, putting his hands in his pockets. "What did he say?"

"He thinks it's healing fine, and that I should stay off it for a couple more days," I tell him, and he nods at me. We walk out to his truck. "Aren't you supposed to be on a plane?"

"Yeah," he tells me. "I'm going to grab the private plane with Doug."

"Am I dropping you off at home?" he asks me, and I just shake my head.

"I was going to hit up the gym," I tell him, and he just looks over at me.

"How about you listen to the doctor and just rest it for the next couple of days?" he asks, and I roll my eyes. "Take advantage of the break."

"Yeah, yeah," I say, and he makes his way to my place. "You, of all people, know how hard it is for a player to take it easy and not be on the ice with his team."

"I know, but you do us no good if you get on the ice before you're ready," he says, turning to me. "Listen to the doctor," he says to me right before I shut the door on him talking and turn to go into my house.

I let myself in, going to my apartment and tossing the key on the counter when the phone rings in my pocket. "Hello?" I say, not even looking at the name.

"So what's the verdict?" Zoe asks me, and I smile as I sit on the couch with the sounds of cars honking in the distance. "Are we keeping the foot, or does he want to cut it off?"

I laugh. It's been a couple of days since she brought me soup, a couple of days since I've seen or spoken to her. A couple of days since we almost fucking kissed. I want to say I haven't thought about her, but I would be lying. She is there always in the back of my head. "They just cut it off."

"Well, that solves everyone's problem, then." She laughs.

"Yeah, I have to stay off it for the next couple of days," I tell her. "I'm bored shitless, and"—I sigh—"I'm done with *90 Day Fiancé.*"

"Isn't it the best?" she asks. I can picture her smiling as she asks me. I can picture her eyes lighting up, and her hands getting animated while she says it. "So what's next?"

"No clue," I tell her. "I'm going to go through Netflix and see if there are some shows I should binge."

"There are a bunch. *Ozark* is amazing." She names all the shows I should watch. "Anyway, I have to go and show some houses," she finally says. "Let me know what you decide to watch."

"I will," I tell her and disconnect the phone. I try to ignore Jeffrey's nagging voice in the back of my mind. I grab the yellow legal pad that I started writing on and the pen. I thought putting my resentment and fears on paper was a good start, but while writing it, it gets harder and harder.

There is so much wrong with me, so much that is broken. The first thing on my list was guilt. I felt guilty, and to be honest, I'm not sure if I felt guilty for doing it or for getting caught doing it. I harp on the list, going over and over it for hours. So long that when I look up, it's dark out.

I pick up the phone and call Jeffrey, who answers on the third ring. "Hello," he says, and I can hear him chewing.

"Hey, it's me. Are you busy?" I ask, knowing he is probably eating with his family.

"Not that much. What's up?" he asks, and I hear the chair in the background scrape against the floor.

"I'm done with step five," I tell him. "I mean, I wrote my list."

"How was it?" he asks me.

"Painful," I tell him the truth quietly. "I kept playing over the past four years, and I was a horrible person."

"You probably were." He doesn't sugarcoat anything. "The good news is that you can see it now," he says quietly. "Admitting to ourselves that we aren't perfect is a hard thing."

"I swear there is nothing good on this list," I tell him. "I look at it, and I cringe at what that person was, what I was."

"The big question is who are you going to tell?" he asks me. "Who are you going to choose who will listen to the inventory of yourself?"

"I don't know," I lie because I know who I want to share this list with. I also know who I can't share this list with, and it's the same person. Zoe.

"Sure, you do," he says. "I remember when I did mine. I sat down, and the whole time I was writing, I knew who I wanted to share it with. I knew exactly who I was writing it for."

"You're better than me then," I tell him and change the subject. "I'm having a dinner at my house on November first."

"Really?" He knows I'm changing the subject, but he doesn't call me out on it. "Good. Count us in for two."

"Bringing the missus finally?" I joke with him. "Perfect."

"Thank you," I tell him. "For listening and always being there."

"It's my job," he says. "And I like you," he says with a laugh and disconnects. I toss my phone back on the table and get up to go to the fridge. I pop the pizza in the oven and go take a shower.

It feels like I'm washing my sins away, washing the bad away, except the need to just go into a daze is strong. To not accept it, I never thought letting go of the drug would be this hard mentally for me. I expected to have a couple of days with tremors. I wasn't expecting the soul searching I would have to do in order to beat it away.

I stand at the stove and eat my pizza and then collapse onto the bed. I don't know what to expect, but it's not to sleep a whole blissful six hours. Six. I have to wonder if it's because I finally let go of the awful person I was before. To write down all your wrongs and purge it from your soul. And for the next two weeks, it's the same thing. I sleep just under six hours each night, and I'm finally back on the ice right before the "monster bash."

I slip into my costume and then grab the accessories, shaking my head the whole way down to the car as I make my way over to the arena where everyone is meeting. From what I heard in the past two weeks, it's going to be a party extravaganza. Oliver's exact words.

I get out of the car and head to the dressing room, stopping at Oliver, who is just wearing a suit, a short white wig, and a mustache. "Why aren't you dressed up?" I ask him.

He looks down at his costume. "I am." He smiles and puts on dark sunglasses. "I'm Stan Lee."

"Oh, dear God." I shake my head and then look past him at the guys who have arrived. Max leads the way in ripped jeans with his whole body painted green. I look at Matthew, who is dressed as Spider-Man, and I laugh.

"What are you supposed to be?" Matthew asks me, and I hold up my shield with the American colors and the star in the middle.

"I'm Captain America," I tell them, looking down at the costume that cost me way more than I wanted to spend.

"But you're Russian," Evan says, and I look at him dressed as Batman.

"I'm American." I shake my head, and we walk into the dressing room and it looks like a comic con.

"Okay, people," Oliver says. "We are opening the doors and letting the fans in," he says, and I look at Evan.

"They invited four hundred special guests from the hospital," he says. "Max's sister Denise runs the kids' ward."

"Yeah, I met Zack." I mention Zack, who also retired the year after he got here. His son, Jack, is a cancer survivor, and they moved here just to get Denise to take his case.

"It's part of the Horton Foundation," Evan says, and I just nod.

"All of the players will line up and give out candies," Oliver says, and we make our way out of the room and onto the ice. The lights are dim, and everything is decorated with hanging bats and flying witches. The ice is covered and looks like it's all grass with pumpkins everywhere.

I stand in line next to Evan, who's looking for his wife, no doubt. "Where is she?" he asks, and I start looking around, but I don't spot her. I do spot Zoe, though, and she is standing there in a black latex outfit. And if that wasn't bad enough, she has thigh-high boots on. "I spot Zoe," I tell him, and everyone looks up at her.

"What the fuck?" Matthew says from behind me. "Who let her in like that?"

I roll my lips, trying not to laugh. "She's practically naked," Max adds. "This is not good. It's a kids' event, and now half the guys are going to be walking around with semis." He looks around also. "If she brought a whip, she's grounded."

"Hey there." I look over to see Zara, followed by her group of girls minus Zoe, who stands there talking to some guy

I've never seen before. I try to tear my eyes away from her and focus on the girls arguing with Max and Matthew, but my eyes go to her, then move away every fifteen seconds. Then she turns and struts over, literally.

"Happy Halloween," she says with a smile, and I look at her, then at the guys seeing them glare. "Oh, come on."

"Who bought you that costume?" Evan asks, and she shrugs. "Burn it."

Oliver runs over before the bickering starts and looks at us frantically, then looks at Zoe. "If I was straight, I would so date you." He points at her and then turns to Max. "They want you to say something." He looks at Max, his hands going up and down. "I didn't prepare for this. I don't have a mic or anything."

"It's fine," Max says. "Just breathe. It'll be okay," he says, and everyone walks away to handle the situation.

"I see the foot has healed," Zoe says, smiling and then looking around. "Don't tell them, but I fucking hate this costume. I have sweat forming in places I didn't think was possible, and if I didn't think they would make a big deal, I would go change. But now …"

"Now you have to stand your ground," I tell her, shaking my head. "I know it's last minute," I say, and then I actually hear the words coming out of my mouth, "but tomorrow, I'm having a little dinner in order to celebrate."

Her eyes go big. "Count me in," she says, and then she hears someone calling her name. "I have to go. I promised I would help a couple of the kids." She looks back at me. "But count me in," she says and then grabs my arm. "So happy that you are doing something. I'll text you later for all the info."

I don't say anything as I try to ignore the heat from her hand on my arm. I've had women touch me in more intimate places in my life, yet her touch runs through me.

TWENTY

ZOE

"And if that wasn't enough, when I finally did get the costume off, it looked like I was taking a sausage out of its casing," I tell Zara while I walk around my bedroom.

"I told you it was a bad idea." She laughs at me. "It took four of us to zip you in it, and you had to lie down to do it." I shake my head, thinking about how it took the four of them with two pushing it together and two zipping it up. "I thought it was going to bust open when you bent down to pick up Alex."

"Can you imagine? I would have died," I tell her, and I cut the conversation before she asks me where I'm going and then proceeds to let me have verbal diarrhea about Viktor and my non-relationship with him. I get dressed in my black jeans and dark gray long-sleeve sweater and matching booties. As I make my way over to his house, I know I'm an hour early, but I wanted to decorate. I knew he wouldn't let me if I asked, but if I show up with it, he can't say no.

I call him right when I get there. "Hey," I say when he answers. "I kind of need a little help."

"Okay," he answers. "With what?"

"I'm downstairs, and well, you just need to come and help," I tell him and look over at the truck of balloons that I had delivered. He comes out a second later dressed almost like me, except his shirt is pushed up to his elbows and he has sneakers on his feet. His hair looks like he just ran his fingers through it, and I wonder if it's as soft as it looks.

"What did you need help with?" he asks me, and I stand here with a cake box in my hands courtesy of my driver.

"Don't freak out," I tell him, "but I need you to take this box upstairs, and then I need you to go into the cinema room and only come out when I tell you to." He looks behind me at the truck with the words PARTY DECORATIONS across it. "Trust me."

"I was thinking low-key." He leans in and whispers to me.

I lean in really, really close to him. "Me, too," I whisper back to him. "Now go so we can get the show on the road." He shakes his head at me, and I shoo him away.

I wait for the guys to get out of the truck and hand me two bunches of balloons and then the man brings in a tank and the rest of the balloons. I lead him to the apartment, and I see the cake on the counter and see that Viktor isn't there, so I let the guy in. I let the balloons go and they float to the high ceilings one at a time. I separate them and look at the fifty blue balloons I ordered. He is just finishing up blowing up the balloons that spell 6 MONTHS.

When he finishes tying the balloons together, I shake his

hand and call out for Viktor. I hear the door slam and then hear him walking down the stairs. "Surprise," I say, throwing up my hands.

He smiles and looks at the balloons. "You have a thing with balloons, you know that?"

"I do," I say, shrugging my shoulders. "I think I always did; it just screams happiness to me." I look around. "And also, let's celebrate, bitches."

He shakes his head and puts his head down, then he looks up at me, and I take him in. He's different than he was at the beginning. In the three months since I've known him, he feels a bit less constricted, a little bit lighter on his feet. His eyes are lighter, the circles around his eyes are almost nonexistent, and he smiles and laughs more. "You really are the ray of sunshine."

"I don't know about that," I say, and I'm suddenly nervous around him. My heart beats a touch faster, and my hands are clammy. I rub them together in nervousness. "What time is everyone else coming?"

"I only invited four people," he tells me. "Well, six actually. With us, it will be eight." The buzzer blaring lets us know someone is here. I look around and see that he set up a bar in the corner with some wine, vodka, rum, gin, and scotch.

"Sorry we are late." I hear Zara and look at her. "There was traffic, and Matthew is parking the car." She shrugs off her jacket, and then she looks at me. "Fancy seeing you here," she says, and I look down and feel like I've been caught by my parents doing something I shouldn't be.

Evan is right behind her, handing Viktor his coat. "Matthew and Karrie are fighting about where to park, so they should be up in a second." He then looks around. "Jesus, Zoe, did you need to get so many?" Evan says, shaking his head. "Nice place." I stand here and watch them chitchat, then look at Zara who walks over to me.

"Don't," I whisper to her. "Not right now." I look down, and I try to steady my breathing, then I look up. She must see the emotions I'm going through. I'm too close. I'm lying to myself and to him. I like him, I like him a lot, and he's unattainable. "You feeling okay?" I ask her, trying to change my thinking, and she just nods and grabs my hand, making it a little worse.

"Breathe," she whispers. "Go to the bathroom and fix yourself." I nod and make a quick exit to the bathroom. Running the cold water, I wet my hands and put them on my face to bring the redness down and blink away the little tears about to form. I hear laughter, and I'm about to open the door when a soft knock sounds. "It's me."

I open the door, and Zara comes in. She is wearing black pants with a black shirt that molds her body, and you can see her five-month belly that is slowly becoming bigger. I sit on the toilet and look at her. "I didn't know you were coming."

"That makes two of us." She leans against the counter in front of me. "This isn't good."

"I know," I tell her. "It's fucking insane," I whisper. "He's so emotionally out there it's crazy."

"You need to walk away, Zoe," she tells me. I know she's right, but it hurts, and I don't want it to hurt. "Before you get so far in that you can't go back."

"I'm trying," I tell her honestly. "But it's just …"

"A pull," she answers me. "You're pulled to him, and you don't know why. You can't explain it."

"Yes," I tell her, nodding. "That all that …" She's about to say something when there is another knock on the door. "Is this a meeting?"

She opens the door, and Evan comes in holding a bottle of water and looking at her and then at me. "What's wrong?" His eyes go big. "Are you okay?" he asks, his hand going to her belly.

"I'm fine." She smiles and turns to me. "I was trying to get the baby to kick so Zoe can feel it."

"When are we finding out what it is?" I ask her, and she shrugs.

"We want to be surprised," she finally says, "so we aren't finding out." I'm about to roll my eyes and yell at her when there is another knock on the bathroom door. Evan opens it, and I see it's Matthew and Karrie.

"What's wrong?" Matthew says, looking at us. "What happened?" He pushes into the bathroom, then sees me. "I didn't know you would be here."

"I'm his realtor," I tell him, standing up and nodding to Karrie. "Now, can we go back out there before he thinks we're crazy hiding out in his bathroom?" I say, walking out in time to see him open the door for Jeffrey.

"Welcome," he says with a smile and moves out of the way for him to walk in with a beautiful woman. "You must be Becky," Viktor says to her. "The better part of him."

"Knock that shit off," Jeffrey says, blocking his wife from Viktor's outstretched hand, making us laugh. Jeffrey comes in and smiles when he sees me, and then Viktor introduces him to everyone.

The buzzer rings again, and this time, it's the food. Two people come in and set up in the kitchen. "Can I get anyone anything to drink?" Viktor looks around. "Sorry, I'm new at this hosting gig," he says nervously, and Jeffrey just slaps him on his shoulder.

"Relax," Jeffrey says to Viktor. "Everyone here knows that it's a big day for you," he says, and I see Evan reach over and hug Zara, pulling her to him and kissing her head while her arms go around his waist. I look over at Matthew, who has Karrie in the same position. "It's a day that you need to celebrate and acknowledge. I'm the first to know that it isn't easy. Every single day is a struggle, and some days are easier than others, but as they say, it takes a village." He looks at his wife and then looks at each of us. "Surround yourself with people who can help you up and who can carry you when you fall down. Not the ones who help keep you down." Zara lets one hand fall from Evan's as her hand reaches for mine, and I try to blink away the tears. "My sponsor said that to me on my six months sobriety, and looking around at the people who were there for me, I knew he was right." Jeffrey looks at me. "Looks like you have a good village."

"Damn straight," Matthew says, and it has all of us chuckling. "We are here for anything you need."

Becky walks over to Viktor and hugs him. "You can do it."

"Dinner is ready to be served," the guy in the kitchen says, and we walk to the table. I let everyone else take their seat and stand back with Viktor next to me.

"You can do this," I tell him. He puts his arm around my shoulders and brings me close to him.

"I think I can," he says. I don't move from under his touch. I stand here for as long as I can. Feeling his touch is like a lightning bolt going through me.

"This looks delicious," Zara says, looking down at the plate in front of her.

"Let's go grab a seat," he says, and his fingers grip mine and pull me to the table. I ignore the tingle that it leaves on my fingers. The meal is light with the guys telling stories from the road. I look over at Viktor who sits right beside me at his eight-person square table.

After the food is all eaten, the cake is served. When Karrie yawns, Matthew gets up, and I follow suit. "We are going to head out," Matthew says, and I look over at him.

"Will you give me a ride?" I ask him, and he just nods his head at me. I hug Jeffrey and Becky goodbye and then walk to the door to get my purse and see the small box on the top. I leave it on the counter instead of making a scene with everyone watching. "Thank you for inviting me," I tell Viktor and walk over to him and give him a hug. It's actually the first time I've hugged him. I don't know what I expect, but I'm not expecting to be taken into his arms into a big bear hug. He hugs me with both arms, pulling me close to him. One hand going to his back while I hold my purse in the other dangling next to me.

"Thank you, Zoe," he whispers. "For everything."

I don't say anything to him. I can't because the lump in my throat stops everything and anything from coming out. Instead, I do the only thing I can. I smile and nod, then turn and walk out the door. Zara walks next to me on one side and Karrie on the other side. Both of them are there to hold me up, regardless of what they know. The men are oblivious to what just happened, and even if they asked me, I couldn't answer.

TwentyOne

Viktor

"THANK YOU FOR coming." I hug Becky and ignore the way my head feels like it's going to explode. Having everyone here was everything. Knowing I could count on these people means everything. The pull of wanting to go to Zoe and just grab her face and kiss the ever-loving shit out of her was more than I thought it would be.

She was off the minute her sister walked inside the place, or maybe a touch before that. I can't pinpoint it, but I knew there was a shift, and I didn't like it. She was usually the one cracking jokes, and tonight, her smile didn't make it all the way to her eyes. "You take care," Jeffrey says, grabbing Becky's hand and ushering her out.

I close the door after them and look around. The chairs are still out as everyone left them. The caterer left the kitchen just as he found it. I walk to the table and push in the chairs and pick up the last of the straws and glasses, bringing them into the kitchen and putting them in the sink. My eyes landing on the little white box on the counter with the blue bow. I walk over and pick it up, turning it in my hand.

I pull the satin bow, and it falls to the floor and I pull off the cover. My heart stops when I see that it's another key chain. This time, it's a circle with the words.

I believe in you

06-01-19

I grab it out of the box and that, too, falls to the floor, and I don't notice or care. My finger runs over the words. *I believe in you*. Four words that push me over the edge. Four words and I know I have to build a wall around my heart, if not for her than for me. She deserves better than me. She deserves someone who doesn't have a cloud over his head the whole time. She deserves to have perfect, and that isn't me. I grab my phone and send her a text.

Me: Thank you for the key chain.

I wait for her to answer me, but she doesn't. I don't know if I'm happy or sad when she doesn't.

I'm in the middle of packing my bag the next day for a six-day road trip when my phone finally buzzes.

Zoe: Glad you like it.

I sit down, and my hand itches to reply to her. I rub my finger over her name on my phone, and then I put it down gently, walking away from it. Six days away is going to help; it's going to be a good time. I make sure the days are spent either on the ice or in the gym. I spend extra time on the ice each day by myself or with a few other people. I get my head in the zone, washing away everything that is going on.

The nights are still a mess. The hours that I do sleep

are filled with Zoe in them—her smile, her laugh, her glare, even her rolling her eyes. It's the only time I let myself go, the only time I let my guard down, and she sneaks in.

"Good news," Evan tells me halfway through the road trip. "I spoke with Candace, and she says she can take you on."

"Great," I tell him. "I tried to venture onto Facebook two days ago, and I swear there just were so many red notifications that I closed out of it."

"Yeah, I just stick to Instagram," Evan says. "It's easier. Anyway, I'm going to text you her number," he says, and my phone goes off. "She's waiting for your call."

"Thank you," I say, looking down at her number.

"Hey, are you okay?" he asks me quietly. "You've been a little withdrawn lately, and I know how much being on the road sucks," he says quietly, and I look around and see that no one else is paying attention to us.

"Yeah, it's been okay. Nights are rough, but nothing I haven't done before," I say, looking down at my phone.

"Well, I'm here if you need me," he says, putting on his suit jacket. "A couple of us are headed out to dinner if you want to join us."

"I'm actually going to go to a meeting not too far from here," I tell him, getting up and putting on my jacket and beanie on my head. "But thanks for the offer." Evan nods at me. I follow him but go in the other direction, calling Candace as I walk. We chat for thirty minutes, and I hire her on the spot. The only thing she said I should handle is Instagram just because it's more hands on and people like the stories. I hang up with her and make my way to the meeting.

I nod at the person who looks like he is in charge and sit down.

It's a little easier to go to meetings where I don't see the same people all the time because I can let go of a little bit more each time. When it's my time to talk, I take a deep breath.

"I'm Viktor, and I've been clean for six months," I say, and the people sitting in the circle clap. "I just finished step five," I say and then look down at my hands. "Almost. I still have to tell someone."

"It's not easy to find that person," a woman in front of me says.

"I know," I continue. "The thing is, I know who I want to share it with. I just …" I swallow the lump in my throat. "I'm scared or, better yet, afraid she'll realize I'm not good enough for her."

"Then she isn't the person you think she is," someone else says, and I shake my head.

"That's the thing. She's the right person." I sit up now. "She's the only person really. The only one who really matters, if I'm honest." I look around and see a couple of people nod. "She didn't know who I was. She only knows who I am."

"But who you were is what made you who you are today," the woman says. "You aren't two people." I nod at her. "You're still the same person, just different. There will always be a Viktor; there is just going to be a Viktor now."

"Yes," I say, agreeing with her. "There is the old me, who I'm not proud of, and the new me, who is starting to be worthy of people."

"You have to let go of the Viktor from before. Whatever

or whoever that was, you have to let that person go. Leave all the defects from the old Viktor and start with positive Viktor, the new Viktor. Instead of looking at it as if she will see what's wrong with me, you should be thinking she will see how much better I am. How far I've come. It's the positive that is needed here."

"I guess being scared is never going to leave no matter how far we come. Fear is there regardless. Before the fear was people knowing I was high and trying to hide it. Now I fear that people think I'm still that person."

"That is what step six is all about." She smiles at me, and I nod to the next person, and he starts to talk. I listen to everyone, and when it's over, I'm the first one to leave. I walk out of there with my head just one touch clearer than it was when I walked in there.

For the next couple of games, it's almost like I'm more comfortable in my skin or on my skates. We head back home with three wins on the road and me with five points. We have one day to rest and then a big game on Saturday. I've stuck to my guns about not seeing or texting Zoe.

I dress in a black suit and try to steady my heart, knowing tonight I will probably see Zoe. Saturday night games, we usually have a dinner afterward with most players and their families.

Walking into the arena, I nod at Matthew, who is talking to Max and Evan.

"Hey," I say when I get close enough to them. They are huddled outside of the locker room. "What's up?"

"Nothing," Evan says and then looks down. "M&M are a bit aggravated."

I try not to laugh at the way he says M&M, but it gets me every time. "Why? What's the matter?"

"Zoe is bringing a date," Matthew says, and I try not to let my face change as my heart sinks. Just the thought makes my stomach burn. This is what I've wished for, for her to date and find that perfect guy for her. *Keep telling yourself that.*

"It's not a date," Max says. "Allison says that she's known him since forever, and they work out at the same gym."

"So what's the problem?" I ask, and Evan just watches me without saying a word. "She's a beautiful woman, so she's bound to go on dates."

"Don't talk about my sister like that," Matthew says, and now Evan laughs. "You can't call her beautiful. It's weird."

"But she is." I shrug my shoulders. "But if she says it's not a date, then maybe they're just friends." I look around. "Anyway, I want to hit the gym before we have to warm up," I say, walking away from them to the locker room. I change and head to the gym, but I don't push myself too hard, saving the energy for the game.

When I skate out for the warmup, I try not to let my eyes go to the box where I know she's in. I try to force myself to look anywhere else but there. But I'm a glutton for punishment because I look up anyway. I spot her immediately, but she isn't looking at the game or the ice. She's standing there holding a glass of wine in her hand and talking to a man who looks like a grease ball. Okay, maybe he is clean cut and proper, and he looks like he works out, but he's standing there, and all he's doing is talking while she looks at him with a fake smile. Anyone who knows her knows it's a fake smile. I force myself to take my turn in the warmup and focus on the team and the game, and when I score the first goal of the game, I force myself not to admit that I did it for her to see me.

We skate off the ice after a win of three to two, high-fiving some fans while we skate off. "It's always good to win on a Saturday night," Mark says, taking off his goalie mask.

"It's always good to win, period," I tell him, sitting down. The coach comes in and does his whole good and bad speech. No one really undresses, knowing that the press will be coming in right after. Once the coach leaves, the press comes in, and after twenty minutes, they are ushered out, and we can finally undress.

"Are you going to join us?" Evan says. "We are going to the pub."

I think about it for a minute. The choices are either go home to the darkness in my apartment, or go and sit down, watching Zoe and her boyfriend. "No, I think I'm going to pick something up to eat and just crash."

"Yeah, Zara already told me she wants to be in and out," he says. "Did you get the email for Thanksgiving?"

"I did this morning," I tell him. "It sounds like a good thing." I got the email this morning asking whoever didn't have plans to think about spending the day giving back to the community.

"It started a while ago when Allison was the PR. We all went to the hospital and celebrated. Last year was amazing. Most of the team and their families came out."

"Aren't we traveling that night?" I ask him. "We have a game the night before, and then Friday, we are in Philly and then back that night, right?"

"It's going to be tight, but we'll make it happen," he says.

"I'm going to tell Max to count me in," I tell him and then go to the shower. When I finally finish dressing, I'm one of the last ones left since I have no need to rush.

That night I eat standing up in the kitchen and when I finally crash, my dreams are of me smiling and happy, holding Zoe's hand. But right before I kiss her, the blackness comes, and I'm down the rabbit hole. I fight off the blackness, trying to focus only on the light. I always focus on finding the light these days.

When I slip on my black jeans and jersey to go to Thanksgiving, I'm feeling just a touch lighter on my feet. I know I'll see her, but I don't know if she'll be alone. I have to be honest, I don't give a fuck. I just want to see her, talk to her, even if it's just to ask her how she's doing.

I look at myself in the mirror, which I've been doing a lot of lately. "It's going to be a good day." I've been taking the positive approach. "If she's there with someone, you are going to happy for her." The voice inside my head laughs."No, you're not. You're going to just wish you were him." I shake my head and walk out of the apartment with my bag for tonight.

I get out of the car in front of the hospital, and I'm about to walk in when I turn and see her walking toward me. Well, she's walking toward the hospital. I take her in before she knows I'm watching her. She's wearing blue jeans and a white knitted sweater with a brown jacket open and a thick scarf around her neck. She must sense I'm watching because she turns her head. Our eyes meet, and it's there. Her smile's not a fake one, not one she has to put on, but one that fills her face. One that makes her eyes twinkle, and all you want to do is lean in and kiss that smile.

"Hey there, stranger," she says as she gets close to me. She gives me a hug, something that she's only done once before. "Happy Thanksgiving." I hug her with one hand since the other is holding my bag.

"Happy Thanksgiving," I say. I don't want to let her go, but she steps away from me. "Are you by yourself?"

"Just little old me, why?" she asks me, and the wind blows her hair to the side. "Oh, God, is Matthew still going on about that date?" She shakes her head. "He's ridiculous." She turns and starts to walk into the hospital, and I follow her. "It's good to see you," she says. I look over at her, and I can't help the smile that fills my face.

"It's good to see you, too." I tell her the truth, and that's all I'm able to tell her before the elevator comes and we are pushed in together. Then the madness of Thanksgiving starts.

TwentyTwo

Zoe

I STEP INTO the elevator, and I can still feel his hand on my back from when I hugged him. I hugged him like a love-sick puppy. We've never hugged, I mean, one time we did, but that was the night I realized that I liked him. A LOT. It was also the night I told myself that I had to let him go and stop thinking about him.

The elevator gets crowded, and I'm pushed up next to him. If I turned to face him and got on my tippy toes, I could kiss him—just a peck with some tongue—but I don't. I form an invisible barrier between us and force myself not to even let our feet touch. When we get off together, we can hear the voices already. The nurses are decorating by hanging paper turkeys. "I think we should just follow the noise," I tell him, and he nods as we walk past some of the patients' rooms. Most of the doors are open, and the closed ones have turkeys taped to the door. "Is it always this loud?" Viktor asks, and I just smirk.

"You haven't seen anything yet. Wait till they decide who does the toast. It's goes on like WrestleMania," I tell him. "Last year, Matthew begged to be the one to talk. He's never gotten to do it. Denise usually says something or Max, since it's his foundation and her work. Max and Matthew tried to do rock, paper, scissors for an hour. In the end, my father was the one who said something as Matthew and Max both glared at each other."

We make it to the room where the tables are being set up. It's half empty, and the only people I see are Zara and my mother. "Where is everyone?" I ask, looking around and hearing their voices.

"They are making an executive decision on moving the dinner," Zara says, sitting down with her hand on her belly. "Max thinks we should move it down to the cafeteria since it's big, but Denise just wants to do it here in two sittings."

"Happy Thanksgiving." I smile to my mom and go over to hug her.

"Happy Thanksgiving, honey," she says, smiling and then looks over at Viktor. "Happy Thanksgiving, Viktor. We are so happy you could join us."

"Happy Thanksgiving," he says, then looks at Zara with a smile and then back at my mother. "I don't think I would miss any of this," he says, and then Matthew comes into the room with Max and my father following him.

"Okay, we are going to do tables in this room," Max says. "And then food in the other one."

"That is a great idea," my mother says_and Matthew groans. "Matthew Grant."

"But, Mom," he huffs. "It's just bigger downstairs."

"It's just too hard to move some of the patients," Denise says, and I look at her with her little baby bump finally showing. "It will be fine here. We've always made it work." Her voice goes soft. "The main thing is that we are all together," she says and hugs her husband and her stepson Jack. "Thankful that we have our health and that we can bring some joy if only for just this one day."

"Great," Max hisses. "She's the one doing the speech now." I try not to laugh. Denise starts laughing, and then everyone else follows.

"You were not kidding," Viktor says next to me. "Does it get better?"

I lean in to him. "Yes, they stop talking when they eat." I turn and see the smile on his face. I've refrained from looking into his eyes, but I can't help it. They are a lighter blue than normal. "Follow me," I tell him and walk out of the room and then grab one of the bags from the table in the hallway. "These bags have stuff from the Stingers," I tell him. "What we do is go room to room and give out a couple of things, usually you sign it, and then if they feel up to it, they sometimes ask for a picture."

I walk into the first open room I see. A little girl sits in the middle of the bed, already covered in New York Stinger merchandise. "Happy Thanksgiving," I say to her, and then she says it back to us, raising her hands over her head.

"Happy Thanksgiving," Viktor says from beside me.

"Let's see what I have this year." I open the bag and see we've got pucks. "I think I got the best bag I've ever had," I say, taking out the silver Sharpie that is in there and handing it to Viktor. "This is for you." His fingers graze mine, and our eyes fly to look at each other. My heart beats fast, and I try to swallow.

"What do you have in the bag?" the little girl asks. "It looks heavy."

I blink out of my trance and reach into the bag. "I have pucks," I say, bringing a puck out and showing it to her. "Did you want it signed or not?"

She puts her hands together. "Signed please," she says with glee, and her parents just laugh. "Then can we take a picture?" she asks, and I look over at Viktor who just blinks and looks at her.

"You can have whatever you want, sweetheart," he says. I see tears in his eyes, but he blinks them away. "What's your name?" he asks her while he signs the puck.

"Savannah," she says to him.

"A pretty name for a beautiful little girl," he says, handing it to her, and she shrugs her shoulder smirking. "Now"—he turns to me, handing me his phone—"can you take a picture?"

"I can take that," Savannah's father says. "So you can be in the picture."

I don't have a chance to tell him no before Viktor grabs my hand and pulls me to the side of Savannah's bed. He stands there and pulls me in front of him, putting one hand on my shoulder and leaning down a touch to be next to Savannah. "Smile big," Savannah says, making us all laugh.

"Thank you so much," her mother says, and she blinks away her own tears. "Today is a good day."

"One day at a time," Viktor tells her. "We can only go one

day at a time. Slow and steady wins the race," he tells them, and we walk out of the room. "I think I'm going to need a minute," he says, and I just nod at him. "I didn't expect …"

"You didn't expect for it to hit you in the gut," I tell him.

"Yeah," he says. "I thought I had it bad."

I walk over to him, and I put my hand on his arm. "Everyone has their own struggles," I tell him.

"How old is she?" he asks me. "She's, what, ten, maybe younger, and she is fighting for her life."

"Yeah," I tell him. "It's why it's important that we take the day to be thankful for what we have." Walking to him, I get on my tippy toes, and I hug him, dropping the bag to my feet while I do it. Both of my hands go around his neck, and his arms wrap around my waist so naturally, like he's always been doing it. "I'm thankful that whatever happened led you here," I whisper in his ear, and his breath hitches.

"Zoe," he says my name in a pained whisper, and I close my eyes. I take it in, the feel of me in his arms, and right when I'm going to let him go, I hear Zara calling me.

I let him go and then hand him the bag of pucks. "You can do the rest without me," I tell him and turn to walk away without looking into his eyes because I'm pretty sure they'd tell me something I don't want to know right now. I avoid him the rest of the meal and make sure I sit far away from him. When the guys have to leave, I make a beeline for the toilet, and then when I come back out, my mother is there waiting for me.

"Hey," I say, drying my hand with a paper towel. "Is everyone gone?"

"Yes," she says coming to me and tucking my hair behind

my ear. "My sweet and strong, beautiful girl."

I look at her, trying not to laugh. "What did I do?"

"Nothing," she says. "Absolutely nothing."

"Why are you acting like this?" I ask. She looks around and sees that it's just the two of us. Everyone else is cleaning up and putting things away.

"He's going to see it," she tells me. "I can see it."

"Who is he, and what do you see?" I ask her, swallowing and knowing she's seeing right through me. She could always see right through us no matter how much we tried to hide it.

"He walks with so much baggage that he can't stand up straight," she starts to say.

"Mom," I say, looking down. "He's a friend."

"Yet you can't seem to stop yourself from being drawn to him. You can't seem to look at him and not want to be next to him. You want to help him carry all his baggage."

"Isn't that what you taught us?" I ask her, blinking away the tears. "Help people when they are down."

"Yes," she answers. "And to carry the ones we love."

"I don't love him," I say, rolling my yes. "I might like him a bit, but love is a big—"

"Step," she finishes the sentence for me, and I'm saved by my father, who comes looking for her.

"There you are," he says. "We're almost done." He leans down to kiss her. "What's wrong?"

"Nothing," my mother says. "We were just talking about Christmas and New Year's."

"You going to come with us, right?" my father says, and I look at my mother.

"The team is going to be on the road again this year," my father says, and I groan.

"Again?" I tell him. "It's been four years in a row."

"Now, here's the good news," he says, smiling. "They play in the afternoon and will be back by seven p.m., and then Oliver is transforming the whole arena into a supper club kind of thing."

"Oh, thank God," I say to them. "I was so not wanting to spend it in a hotel."

"Doug also rented rooms for anyone who wants," my mother says. "But it makes sense for you to go home."

I help everyone clean up, and my parents drop me off at home before taking the drive all the way back to Long Island with Zara in the back complaining about having heartburn. When I wave to them, I walk into my house. I don't bother turning on any of the lights before I get undressed in the dark and slip into bed. Hoping that somewhere in my dreams, it'll give me the answers I'm searching for.

Twenty Three

Viktor

My FINGERS TAP on the steering wheel with the beat of the song. One hour ago, we finished our last game before the Christmas break, and I took the six-hour drive home instead of waiting until the morning. We are off for five days, and it'll be a good break, so there was also no excuse to stay away from my family.

The drive to Canada is dark, and not many cars are on the road. I stop once to fill up and grab another cup of coffee from a twenty-four-hour diner. When I pull up to my rental property I got for the holidays, only the porch lights are on. I get out and feel the cold right away, my breath puffing out in front of me. Opening the back door, I take my bag and walk up the steps, entering the code on the door I was given.

When I open the door and step in, there is a light on in the hallway so I can see. I kick off my shoes and take the stairs on the right, going straight up to look for a bed. I slip my suit jacket off and toss it on the chair in the corner of the master bedroom. Or it could be the guest bedroom. I didn't really look. I just walked into the first room I saw. When I finally slip into the bed, my body finally relaxes just a touch, and I fall asleep.

When I get up, I see it's almost noon, and the sun is trying to peek into the room around the closed curtains. Grabbing my phone, I see that my sister texted me this morning asking me where I was. Instead of texting her back, I call her, and she answers after one ring.

"Hey," she says, and I hear Christmas music playing in the background. "Where are you?"

"I'm at my rental house. I decided to drive after the game instead of this morning." I turn in the bed.

"Mom said you could have stayed here with them," she says, and my body gets tense.

"It's easier this way," I tell her softly. "I'm going to get up, shower, and make my way over. Do you guys need anything?"

"Mom," Natalia says, calling my mother. "You need Viktor to get anything?" I hear my mother in the background along with pots banging. "She said just her baby boy," she groans.

"I'll see you soon," I tell her and then disconnect, tossing the phone on the bed and getting up. My body starts to tense just thinking of going over to my parents' house.

When I finally walk up the steps to the house I spent maybe two years at, I don't know whether to knock or just walk in. My hands are already clammy as I anticipate our dinner. It's the first time I've seen my family face-to-face since I left rehab, actually since the day I entered rehab. The front door opens even before I decide whether to ring the bell, and my sister comes flying out the door, calling my name. She jumps into my arms, and her hair flies in my face. I laugh and catch her. "Crazy nut, I could have dropped you," I tell her, and she moves her face back, and I see her. We do look alike in some ways. It's mostly our eyes that are the same.

"You would never let me fall," she says and slaps my shoulder as I let her down. "Come on. Mom has been cooking for the past two days." She grabs my hands and pulls me inside. The smell of apples and cinnamon hits me right away.

"Mom, Dad!" Natalia yells. "He's home; he's here." She pulls me through the house that still has the same décor as when I lived here. A couple more pictures have been added to the wall, but overall, it's the same furniture. We walk past the winding staircase toward the French doors that lead to the kitchen and family room. Walking through those doors, my heart speeds up just a touch more than I want it to.

My mother stands just behind the counter, and when she spots me, she smiles, taking off the oven mitts. "There he is," she says, coming to me and grabbing my face in her hands. "Look at you." She looks me in the eyes, moving my face side to side. "Look at you."

"Hi, Mom," I tell her, taking her in my arms and smelling her. She's always worn the same Chanel No. 5 perfume.

"Let the boy go." My father's voice breaks up the smile on my face. "You coddle him too much," he says, coming over to us. He walks over, and we have the same build, and our eyes are the same. The only thing different is that his hair is now salt and pepper and his stomach a bit more protruded.

"Dad," I say, walking to him and having the most awkward hug in my whole life. He tries to pretend, but when he taps your back like a stranger, you step away from him.

"Glad you could grace us with your presence," my father says sarcastically. "How long has it been since you've come home for Christmas?" he asks me, then looks at my mother. "What is it now, five years?"

"Well, living on the West Coast, it was hard." I try to come up with an excuse.

"Is that what you're blaming this shit on? The West Coast? It's 'cause you were too busy snorting shit up your nose."

"Andrei," my mother hisses at the same time my sister yells at him. "Dad."

"That's fine. You're right. I was too busy getting high to care or come home," I tell him, and he nods and just turns away, shaking his head.

"He doesn't mean it," my mother says, and I look at her.

"Yes, he does," I say under my breath.

"Come and tell me all about New York," she says, trying to defuse the situation.

"Yeah, tell me all about living in New York City and make me jealous," Natalia says, and I walk over to the counter, pulling out one of the stools.

We talk about New York, and I show her some pictures of my apartment. "Betty." My father calls her name from over his shoulder. "The Hendersons will be dropping by for a drink later."

"Great," my mother says and goes about getting the

plates out. "Help set the table." She smiles at me, and I grab the plates and follow her into the dining room. She puts on the same red tablecloth she uses every year.

"I'm going to go over and say Merry Christmas to Ilyana's family. I'll be back in an hour," my sister says and then ducks out.

I go about setting the table the way my mother taught me when I was younger. "You look amazing," my mother says, her voice quiet and her eyes down.

"Thank you," I tell her, keeping my voice down as well.

"Your eyes, they are almost back to when you were …" She tries to come up with the word to describe my eyes.

"You mean when I wasn't high," I tell her, and she looks up now. "It's okay to say it, Mom. I'm a recovering addict."

"I don't mean to push you or anything," she says, and at that moment, it's almost like an elephant in the room trying not to walk on eggshells.

"It's okay to talk about it," I tell her. "It's healthy to talk about it."

She sits down in the chair and looks at me. "I was so scared that you were going to die," she says to me and then looks out the bay window to blink away her tears. "I would pray every single night."

I reach out and hold her hand in mine. "I'm …" I start to say, and my father comes into the room.

"What's all this?" he asks, looking at us.

"We were talking about how good he looks," my mother says, smiling at me. "Dinner will be ready as soon as Natalia returns." My father nods at her and doesn't say a word to me. "He worries about you too."

"I bet he does," I say, getting up. "What else can I do?" I help my mother prepare the plates. She tells me all these little cooking tips, and I'm about to laugh since I don't even know when I would ever cook all these foods. My mind goes straight to Zoe, and I wonder how her Christmas is going.

When Natalia comes back, my mother declares Christmas Eve dinner ready. She lights the two red candles in the middle of the table, and we say a little prayer before digging in and eating. Natalia fills the awkward silence by telling me about all her trips she's taken this year for modeling.

"Wait a second, have you met Zara Stone? She has this Zara's Closet online," my sister asks me after cutting into her piece of apple pie.

I nod at her. "Zara Richards now." Smiling at her. "Yeah, she's the captain's wife."

"I am dying to get on her list. Do you think …?" She smiles at me and bats her eyes.

"I'll see if she is taking anyone new," I tell her, and when I leave the house a couple of hours later, I realize I have never been more uncomfortable in my skin. The night is awful, and sleep doesn't even come. I walk around the strange house, trying to keep my heart from beating out of my chest. I take two showers since I keep sweating through my shirt.

When I drive back to my parents' the next day, my father is the one who answers the door. "Merry Christmas," I say to him, and he steps back to let me in the house. I give him a hug, and he grumbles something and then takes off up the stairs.

"Merry Christmas," my mother says, coming out of the

kitchen and wiping her hands on her white apron. "I'm just putting the bacon in the oven."

Walking into the kitchen, I see that she has already started cooking. "Go sit and watch television," she says to me, and I walk into the family room and sit down on the chair. This is supposed to be my home, yet I feel like a stranger. I take the remote and turn the television on, but then I get up and walk to the wall of hanging pictures. My father is in all of them in his coach's uniform with different players.

I stop at the one in the middle of me and him. It was taken right after we won the state championship. "You were one of the best," my father says from the entrance of the living room.

"Some people would say I'm better now," I tell him, turning.

"Well, you definitely are much better this year." He steps into room, and I shake my head and laugh. "This is funny to you?"

My eyes snap to his. "Nothing about this is funny to me."

"Did you use your drugs last night?" he asks me, and I look at him, hoping he sees the hatred in my eyes. "You come over today eyes all dark like you didn't sleep. Your hair all over the place and the scruff on your beard."

"You think I used last night?" I ask him, my voice raising in pitch. "Do you think if I used drugs, I would even be here?" I put my hands on my hips and shake my head. "Jesus, I don't even know why I try." My voice gets just a touch louder, and now my mother comes into the room with Natalia next to her.

"Watch your voice in my house," he says.

"Yes, heaven forbid I have a voice," I tell him. I wasn't coming here for this, but the opportunity is right in front of me. "Do you know what it was like growing up?"

"Don't you try to turn this around on us," he says.

"Oh, yes." I throw my hands up in the air. "Heaven forbid we point out your flaws. Do you know there was not one time that you came to me after a game and said 'good game, son.'" I look at him, and he crosses his arms over his chest. "No, everyone else got it. I got a rundown on what I fucked up on. How I could be better. Whatever I did," I start to say and then take a deep breath, "it was never good enough."

"Oh, please," my father says, and I laugh now, shaking my head.

"Yeah, I know you're the perfect one in everything you do. Meanwhile, how many Stanley Cups did you hold over your head?" I hit him where I know it hurts him most. "I was always the first one on the ice and the last one off. I had to skate faster, and I had to shoot harder, but it just was never good enough."

"It's because I pushed you like that that you held that cup over your head," he tells me. "Why settle for second place when you can be number one?"

I look at my mother, who stands there with tears running down her face. "I'm sorry that when I came to Christmas four years ago, I was high the whole time. I don't even remember the weekend, but you know what I do remember?" I look at my father. "How you brought out the DVD you had made with all my fuckups of the season." I look up. "Every single one of them, and you sat there for four hours going over everything you would have done differently. Everything that would have made it perfect."

"I was trying to make you better!" he shouts. "Everything that I did was to make you better so you would have it better than me. So you could achieve the things I couldn't."

"Well, you didn't. Instead, you pushed me to bury my head even more." I take a deep breath. "I think I'm going to go."

"You can't go. It's Christmas," Natalia says. "You have to stay."

I look at my mother and then at my father, whose face is pulled tight with anger. "Let him go."

"Andrei," my mother says. "Don't you dare let him go off angry like this."

"He wants to come in here and blame us for him taking drugs. He wants to point fingers. I didn't snort that cocaine; he did that."

"I did," I admit. "That's all my fault, and I take responsibility for my actions." I walk to my father. "But when are you going to take responsibility for yours?" I walk past him and hug my mother.

"I'm sorry I'm leaving like this," I tell her. "I'll call you when I get home." I hug Natalia who tells me she loves me.

I pack up my car with my stuff and drive away from my hometown with a weight lifted off just a touch.

TwentyFour

Zoe

MY PHONE BUZZES on my dresser, and I walk over.

Zara: We will be outside in ten minutes.

I walk back to the mirror and take one last look at myself. I don't even know what look I'm going for. It's been a month since I've actually been out. After Thanksgiving, I put my head down and pretty much avoided everyone. When I showed up for Christmas, everyone gushed about how they missed me.

I use my job as an excuse to skip most of the home games, claiming that everyone wants their house on the market in time for January. I wasn't lying, but I wasn't honest either. I closed a couple of deals and just laid low at home or in the office.

I have lunch with Zara at least once a week, but no one brings up Viktor, or at least I don't. I know he is at a record high with scoring. I secretly watch the hockey games from home but avoid going to the rink, claiming that I need to close deals. Meanwhile, I'm on my couch with my blanket as I watch them either win or lose. I'm starting to get some lay of the land, and I'm starting to understand more calls.

Matthew gave me a headlock when he finally saw me at Christmas Eve and rubbed my head, trying to get me to tell him what was bothering me. I couldn't come out and tell him I had fallen for Viktor, so I lied. It was good to be surrounded by the family. I just need to clear my head, and once that's all done, I'll be back.

I made the mistake of telling Zara I wanted to wear something to knock everyone's socks off, and well, she did not disappoint with that request. I look at the one-piece dress she got me. It's rose gold and sparkly. The sleeves are long, the front goes down in a V, and it's so tight it's stuck to me. A belt of the same colored sits at my waist and then the dress falls down straight. It's the slit right down the middle that makes it drop-dead sexy. Every single move I make, you see my long, toned leg. I have my hair tied up in a high ponytail. Slipping the white cashmere cape over my shoulder, I grab my purse and phone and walk down the stairs to wait at the door.

When I see the car in front, I turn off the lights and lock the door, making my way to the car. The driver opens the door for me, and I get in, seeing that it's just Zara. "Hey," I say, sitting next to her. "Where is everyone?"

"They are meeting us there," she tells me. "I was just not ready, so I left a little after them." She smiles at me. "You look amazing."

"I love your blue dress," I tell her and see that her little stomach is sticking out. If you look at her from the back, you would never know she's pregnant.

"Yeah, well, wait till the mister sees it," she says. "I don't know if he'll like it as much as I think."

I shake my head because Evan likes Zara to be covered from head to toe. If she could walk with a bag covering her, I think he would love it. We get out, and I'm not surprised to see him waiting for her. He opens the car door, and I get out first. "Happy New Year." I smile at him and go and kiss his cheek to block his view of Zara getting out of the car. He rushes me out of the way to see Zara.

"Hey, you," he says, kissing her lips, and he hasn't seen her outfit yet. "You look …" he starts but then looks down at her. "Why is there a missing piece in your dress?" he asks her, and I have to roll my lips. There is a little keyhole under her boobs and right before the belly. I don't think he knows it's off the shoulder either.

"Look at Zoe," Zara says, pointing at me, and I just shrug and take off my wrap. "See, there are boobs and leg."

I look at Evan, who looks at me up and down, and then turns to Zara. "Matthew is going to have a heart attack," he says, laughing.

"Why don't you take off your jacket, Zara?" I turn the tables on her, and she glares at me. Evan panics just a touch as he pulls off her jacket and finally sees it's an off-the-shoulder dress that crisscrosses. The tight dress shows off her cute little bump.

"What happened to the top of your dress?" he asks her, and she just rolls her eyes. "You have to wear my jacket," he says, shrugging off his suit jacket. She just ignores him and walks around him.

"She's carrying your child, so I think it's safe to say that no one is going to try to get with her," I tell him and turn to walk next to Zara. When we walk into the players' entrance, you can hear the music. "I'm starving." I look at Zara, who nods, and then we come face-to-face with the man who's been in my dreams every single night. He's wearing a black suit with a white dress shirt and no tie. The collar is unbuttoned, and if I was his woman, I would kiss him right there on the exposed skin.

"Hey," he says, his face smiling at me and then looking over at Zara. "Happy New Year." He puts his hands in his pockets, and his jacket pulls on his arms, making me wish I was in them.

"Happy New Year," Zara says, kissing him on the cheek. I suddenly want to pull her away from him, and then I want to ask her how she's in the kissing on the cheek relationship.

He kisses her cheeks and then comes to me, and I stop breathing when his bearded scruff touches my one cheek and then the other, the scent of his musk lingering. "Happy New Year," I say quietly. Thank God, Zara must sense something because she makes it not awkward.

"Let's go see where the party is at," she says, clapping her hands and grabbing Evan's hand. "I'm going to hold your hand just in case people think I'm single and pregnant."

I laugh and watch them walk off. Viktor and I follow them. "How was your Christmas?" I ask him, suddenly nervous.

"Good. I went home for two days, which was a mistake," he says the last part quietly. "But I'm happy that I did."

I don't have time to ask him anything or say anything to

him because we finally make it into the arena. "Jesus," I say, looking around. Half the ice has white tables and matching white chairs, and on the other side are little couches and tables. Waitress and waiters are walking around with trays of drinks. I grab a wine glass from a passing waiter and look around, trying to spot my family, but they are all over the place. The kids are all running around and playing together.

"Why don't we sit down over there?" Zara says, pointing at an empty table. I place my wine glass on the table and look around to see where the food is. "The food is over there." She points to the side where buffet tables are set up.

"I'll wait here while you guys get your food," I tell them and expect for them to go except only Zara and Evan walk off. "You can go. I'll be here."

"Think I'll keep you company," Viktor says and pulls out a chair. I sit in the seat next to him. "I need something to drink." I look over at him. "I mean, water." He stops a waiter and asks them for a bottle of water. "So where've you been, Zoe?"

I shrug. "I've been around. Work has been crazy busy."

"Yeah," he says, and the waiter comes over with the bottle of water. "So I heard."

"Why?" I ask him, crossing my legs, and the dress falling to the side so all you see are my legs. He hisses.

"I've just not seen you around. I asked about you a couple of times," he says, and I tilt my head. "Zara said you were busy with listings."

I turn at look at my sister, who is standing beside the food. She hasn't mentioned once that he asked about me. "It's a crazy time of year. Everyone wants to be in a new house come summer."

"Is that the real reason?" he asks, and I grab my glass of wine and drink the whole glass. "Didn't think so."

"Well, you didn't text me or call and ask me." I turn and look at him, and now I stand. "Not once did my phone ring, so if you really were worried about where I was, you sure as shit didn't make an effort to find out."

"I couldn't," he says softly, and before I could ask him what that means, my mother and father come over.

"Hey there," my father says and sees my cleavage and then glares. "Zoe, there are men everywhere here," he says and looks at my mother. "Did you know about this?"

My mother somewhat ignores his question and smiles at him. "She looks beautiful," coming to me and hugging me, then looks at Viktor. "Besides, Viktor is right here. You think anyone is going to come up to her?" I look at Viktor, who just smiles at my father and then gets up to kiss my mother on the cheek. When the fuck did this happen? "You look so nice," she tells him as if they are long-lost friends.

I want to yell what is going on, but I know I can't, so I just look at them as my mother and Viktor chat about the Christmas vacation. "I'm going to grab a plate," I say and walk straight to Zara, who is walking back to the table alone with her plate.

"Who pissed you off?" she asks. "You look like you're stabby."

"I am stabby," I say through clenched teeth and look around to see if anyone is around and listening. "What in the fuck is going on?"

"You are going to have to be a bit more specific than that," she says, looking around. "We are at the arena, and it's

New Year's Eve."

"Cut the bullshit. Viktor said he asked about me, something you never brought up," I tell her and don't give her an option to talk or answer. "And then he kisses you on the cheeks and Mom also."

"One, I didn't think you wanted to know that he asked about you. Two, you deserted the whole family for a month while you planted your head in the sand. He's been at every single function we've had. I think he was coming to see you, but you weren't there."

"What?" I whisper, and then Evan comes over.

"Zoe, that dress is a bit much," he says, looking at the deep V. "You need to burn that dress, actually." He looks around. "M&M!" he shouts to the side and both Matthew and Max turn around. "Look at Zoe!" He points at me, and the smile on Matthew's face disappears, and then Max throws his head back and bursts out laughing. It's no surprise that Matthew charges over.

"Are you crazy?" he says, taking off his jacket and throwing it on me. "Your boobs look like they are going to pop out," he hisses, looking around as I knock his hands away from me.

"Knock it off," I tell him. "I'm going to get something to eat. Besides," I smile at him, "did you see what your wife is wearing?"

"You need to go home and change," Matthew says, and Zara laughs now. "She is wearing a …" he says, turning to look at her. "Where is her jacket?" he says, looking back at her and seeing that Karrie is wearing an off-the-shoulder black dress that's tight all the way down with a slit on the side.

"You might need this," I tell him, giving him the jacket as he stomps away.

"You guys are going to be the death of me," he says between his clenched teeth.

"I swear, one of these days, his head is going to combust," Evan says and then turns to look at me. "Seriously, I already got asked by five guys if you were single."

"Well, I'm single and ready to mingle," I say, grabbing a glass of wine from a passing waiter. "I am going to get food. I'll meet you at the table."

I grab a plate of food and then go back and sit down with Evan and Zara. My parents, Matthew and Karrie, Max and Allison, and Viktor beside me now occupy the empty table. The night is filled with jokes and laughter and dancing, so much dancing I know my feet will kill tomorrow. It's a basic night of dancing with the girls while the guys sit at the table looking on to make sure no one actually approaches us.

The waiters and waitresses pass out party favors, hats, beads, and headbands all with the blinking Happy New Year. "I'm going to go to the bathroom before the ball drops!" I shout over the music to Zara who dances with Alex. I walk out of the arena, fanning my face, and head down the semi empty hallway. Some people linger, but it's no more than two or three.

After using the bathroom, I wash my hands and look in the mirror. My face is red from dancing, and my ponytail is moving to the right a little bit. I fix it and pull open the door, walking out with my head mostly down. When I look up, I see Viktor walking my way, his head down looking at his phone. He is wearing his caramel cashmere jacket, and it looks like he's leaving. "Are you leaving?" I ask him, and he looks up in surprise to see me.

"Yeah, I was going to head out before the ball drops," he says, looking around. "It was safer if I left." His hand comes up, and his thumb is rubbing the bottom of his lip.

"Safer?" I ask him, and then we hear everyone counting down in the distance starting at ten.

"Safer," he repeats the word, looking at me, and all I can see is him. Everything around us fades, and everything seems far in the distance. The sounds of people chanting five, four, three, two, one, and then …

"Happy New Year, Zoe," he says, and I don't know who goes for who first, but it ends with his hands on my cheeks, my hand holding his wrist, and his mouth crashing down on mine.

My eyes close as his tongue slips into my mouth, and then his one hand moves from my face to my waist, pulling me closer to him. The kiss is all tongue, it's all soft, and it's everything that I've thought it would be and more. It's natural, it's perfect, and it feels right. I move my head to one side, and he moves us around the corner to a dark hallway, our lips never parting. My heart beats so fast I think it's going to come out of my chest. I want him closer. I want all of him.

"Zoe." I hear Zara call my name, and he lets go of me. His hand falls from my face, and he steps away from me as if he just came out of his daze. As if he was in a trance. Both of our chests rising and falling. My arms just hanging by my sides. I just watch him, and he does the same. "Oh, shit." I turn to look at Zara beside me. "I'm so sorry. I'll just …" She points her thumb.

"No," Viktor says, his eyes finally leaving mine as he looks down at his feet. "I was just heading out." He heads down the hallway, and I follow his every single move. My lips still tingling from his kiss. "See you guys later," he says and just walks away from me. I don't say anything. I can't say anything. I'm a little in shock. Okay, a lot in shock. The sound of the door slamming makes my eyes close and my heart break.

"I swear I didn't mean to," Zara says softly, coming closer to me.

I roll my lips together to try to keep his touch there. "It's fine," I tell her, and then I look at her.

"Zo," she softly says my nickname.

"I need for you not to say anything right now, and I need to not talk, or I think I'm going to have a breakdown, and I'm not ready for it." I look at her, and the tears already form. She grabs my hand and squeezes it.

"Let's get you some water, yeah?" she says, and I let her lead me away from the spot where I just had the wildest kiss ever. It's also where I had my most heartbreaking moment.

TwentyFive

Viktor

THE COLD AIR hits me as soon as the door slams behind me. My hands burn like I've touched fire, and my lips tingle with the taste of her still on me. The sweet taste of perfection. That is the only way I could describe it. Perfect, pure, and not for me.

When I saw it was almost time for the countdown, I knew I had to leave. I knew the only one I wanted to kiss at midnight would be her. I wanted her in my arms any way I could get her. I hadn't seen her in over a month, and I thought what I felt for her was all in my head and just a figment of my imagination. And then I finally saw her, and my heart stopped. It literally stopped beating, or maybe it finally started beating again. Fuck if I know.

I attended dinner parties I didn't want to go to just to see her, but she never came. Not once. Then going home for Christmas was a disaster. I was an addict, it will forever follow me, especially with my father who made sure to mention it to me each time.

Tonight, I knew she would be there, and I knew I would see her, but I wasn't expecting it to come crashing around me. I walk away from her and replay the scene over and over in my head. Face-to-face with her, our eyes locked. I don't know if it was her or me, but either way, my hands were holding her face and my lips were on hers and everything that I told myself was a lie. I couldn't just be her friend. I walk all the way home, the wind hitting my face making it cold as ice. But I fight the need to go back and see her.

I get home, the soft light from the salt lamp that Zara gave me fills the room. I slip my jacket off and toss it on the couch. I throw myself on the couch and run my hands through my hair.

I avoid everything and everyone the next day by just lying on the couch and flipping through channels while I read the guide to step eight. I only get up at around five to attend a meeting. I don't say anything at this one, passing my turn and just listening to everyone else. The holidays are the hardest, I'm told. Walking back home, I make a list of everyone I've harmed when I was high, everyone who got harmed from me being high. The list isn't long since I never spent time with anyone except the addicts around me. Too scared to start something and then for them to discover my big secret.

I have four names on the list, which isn't a surprise. I put the pad down on the table and close my eyes. Tomorrow will be my biggest test because my old team is in town. That night, I dream of the old days, the days when I didn't have to care, didn't want to care.

When I walk into the arena, I try to keep my head down, but I hear my name being shouted as soon as I step onto the carpet. "Vik." I would know that voice anywhere. I look up and see Kevin. "Look who it is," he says, walking to me with a huge smile on his face. Kevin and I were brought to LA at the same time. Both rookies, we shared a room when we traveled. We shared an apartment. Fuck, we even shared women. But what we shared most of all were the drugs.

"Hey, yourself," I tell him and shake his outstretched hand. "What's up?"

"Not much. I was just chatting with Mika and Chris, and we were talking about the last time we were here." He laughs out loud, and I just nod at him. "What are you doing after the game?"

"Not sure yet," I tell him. "Probably nothing."

"We have to catch up," he says and then calls over to Mika and Chris. "Guys, look who it is."

Mika comes to me first with a huge smile on his face. We played together for two years before I got traded. He was an occasional participant at some of the parties we went to, depending on the chick he was with, but more often than not, he was over at my place crashing on the couch. "There he is. I've been texting you."

"I had to get a new number. I lost the old phone," I lie. The first thing I did was change my number.

"Figured as much," Mika says. "We getting together after? We can go grab a bite to eat."

"Um, yeah," I say, knowing I shouldn't, knowing I should just shake my head and walk away.

"Cool," Chris says. "The team isn't the same without you," he says. "But what can you do?"

"All right," I say to them. "I'm going to go get ready. See you out there." I nod at them and walk away to the dressing room.

"Everything okay?" I hear from beside the door and turn to see Matthew. "You good?" he asks with his chin up.

"Yeah, we were just catching up," I tell him.

"Is this going to be a problem?" he asks, and I just look at him, shaking his head. "Good. I'm here if you need me."

I don't say anything to him, I just nod and go into the room and undress. I don't chat in the room before we take the ice, and I don't dillydally, but I do make the mistake of looking in the box, and I hope she isn't there. Deep down, I hope it's been like all the other times I've looked up there and haven't seen her. But not tonight. Tonight, she's there, standing in jeans and a white shirt. She isn't talking to anyone. No, tonight she's looking straight at me. Our eyes meet, and I can see the hurt in her eyes. I can see the questions she's probably asking herself.

I look down at my skates and begin my warmup by skating a lap around, and then I see the kids all down hitting the glass and calling my name. I smile at them and toss a couple of pucks over. *Get in the zone*, I chant to myself over and over.

"You going to be okay out there?" Evan turns to me and asks me when we line up to go back on the ice.

I snap at him and regret it the minute I do. "I'm going to be fine. Everyone just needs to get off my case." He nods at me and walks away, and I want to apologize, but he's gone on the ice. I'm the last one out there, and we stand, and I take off my helmet for the national anthem. I bounce on my skates as the surge of energy radiating out of me is too much to control.

I skate to the center ice on the right side and meet Mika. "I fucking can't wait for it to be over," he says, and I just nod at him. "This team sucks," he says, hitting my leg with his stick. "Good luck."

I knock his legs with my stick. "Good luck," I tell him and then get into position, my stick fighting his as Evan and Chris take the face-off. Evan wins it and sends it to me, and I skate around Mika, easily bringing it into the zone. Passing it to the rookie who is playing on our line tonight, he takes a shot on net, and to everyone's surprise—his especially—it goes in. I skate over to the kid and knock his head. "Look at you."

He beams with happiness and skates to the bench to give everyone high-fives. We win five to one, and when we get off the ice, everyone is happy and smiling. I take a shower and dress before everyone else, hoping to slip out. "You going to come with us to the pub?" Evan asks, and I just shake my head.

"Not tonight. See you tomorrow," I tell him and walk out of the dressing room where the guys are waiting for me.

"Thank fuck. You took so long," Mika says. "Let's get the fuck out of here."

I'm about to bow out when Kevin slaps me on the shoulder. "Fuck, it's good to see you."

"Yeah, you, too," I say and then walk out with them. We walk out into the street, and my head is swirling with everything, and by the time I look around, we are walking into my apartment. I toss the keys on the table.

"This place is a shoe box," Kevin says, taking off his jacket and going over to the window.

Mika on his phone texting away. "Pizza should be here in thirty," he says, and I just nod at them.

Mika goes over and looks outside, and then twenty minutes later, the door is buzzing, and when I answer it, I step back. The blonde runs in and goes straight to Mika. "There she is, Mrs. Hoover." He uses the nickname he does for a girl who sucks his cock like a vacuum.

She throws her head back and laughs, and her four friends come in and toss their jackets and purses everywhere. "Where is the bathroom?" one of the brunettes asks, and I point down the hall. I look around the apartment at Mika, who is dry humping the blonde against the wall.

Chris is sitting on the couch with a girl on each side of him, both girls petting his chest. Kevin sits in the single chair with another girl in his lap, his hand already halfway up her skirt. My heart starts to beat fast, and I know I have to get out of here. I know I have to get as far away from this situation as I can. And right before I'm about to walk out, the brunette comes back out of the bathroom, wearing garters and a bra. "Did someone say this is where the party's at?" she says, her hands going out to the sides. From one hand hangs a bag of bills, and from the other hand hangs a bag of coke and a couple of baggies of pills.

"Fuck, finally," Mika says, dumping his blonde and coming over to snatch the bag of pills from her. He takes a couple and then tosses the bag to the guys. I just watch, and it's almost as if I have left my body. That I'm not really here. One of the girls turns on the radio and the other lowers the light as they start to dance in the middle of the room together. I feel sick, my whole body tingling everywhere. How did this happen to me, how did I allow this to happen to me is more like it. "What color, bro?" Mika asks me, and I just shake my head.

"He wants the coke," Kevin says, laughing, and then buries his face in the woman's tits.

The brunette walks over to me, swinging her hips, her tits fake are full and not even moving as she walks. "So, big boy," she says as her finger moves down my chest, my skin crawls and my stomach burn the bile starting to come up, "where are we doing this line?"

She turns and goes to the counter next to me. Tossing everything aside, she moves the stools leaving in front for the counter empty. She empties a baggie on the counter and then grabs a card out of her bra and cuts a line. I swallow hard, the sound of my heart beating so fast and so loud, I can't hear anything else. She leans over with a rolled dollar bill in her hand and places it against one nostril. Blocking the other one with her finger, she snorts the whole line, then gets up and wipes her nose. "Fuck," she says, putting her head back. "It's so good," she says, and then she hands me the rolled-up bill. My arm lifts on its own to grab the dollar bill.

I turn to the counter and see the line there waiting for me. The tiny little pieces that look like salt, little, little pieces. The music fades away, the voices fade away, and the only thing I can see is the line in front of me. The only thing I can think of is the rush it's going to give me.

The door buzzes, and I don't even notice or care at that moment. The only thing I care or see is that line, waiting for me. "Come on, hurry. I want another hit," the woman says next to me, and I look at her and then turn to look at the line on the counter, the line right next to my keys. The key chain right next to the line. My eyes again go back and forth from the rolled-up bill in my hand to the cocaine "What the fuck am I doing?" I say to myself as I step back, but then I look at the door that swings open.

My eyes fly to her, standing there as she takes in the whole room. The women in the middle of the room still dancing with Mika. Kevin getting head from the woman, and then Chris who has the woman half naked. Then her eyes come to me, first to my eyes, and then to the counter. The tears in her eyes now falling, and she just turns and walks out.

TwentySix

Zoe

I TAKE IN the whole scene in front of me, and I want to throw up. Guys I've never seen before but I know are from his old team are scattered around his apartment half naked with women who look like they are paid by the hour. My eyes finally fall on the man who has taken over my life. I see the counter with its white powder on it, and the rolled-up bill in his hand, and I know I've lost.

Everything I thought we had was lost in this one second. The tears come, and I don't stop them. I don't wipe them away. I do the only thing I can do. I turn and walk away. I walk down the hall to the elevator, and all of a sudden, the purse on my shoulder is too heavy for me and slips down my arm. I'm so focused on getting to the elevator that I don't notice I'm dragging it. My hand comes up and presses the button once, twice, three times. When the ding finally lets me know that the elevator is here, I walk in and turn to press the lobby button. I look up and see him rushing out and toward the elevator with my name on his lips.

"Zoe," he says and slips his hand into the doors right before they close, and they open again. "Zoe, please."

"Get out of the way, Viktor," I tell him, surprised my voice isn't cracking.

"It's not what it looks like," he starts saying, and I look at him, not knowing anything. I look at him, and I know nothing except that my heart will never beat again the way it should. "I swear I didn't do anything," he says, coming into the elevator and grabbing my arms in his hands to turn me to look at him. The elevator doors close, and I start moving. "They came over, and it was just out of control."

"You really don't have to explain this," I tell him, moving out of his touch so his hands fall to the sides.

"You're my friend," he says the words, and I see his turmoil. I see the pain in his eyes; his face ravished in pain. "A friend doesn't just leave."

"A friend." I say the words softly, and the door opens to the lobby. "A friend." I look down and then look back up at him. "You warned me," I start to tell him. "Told me that all we would be is friends." I shake my head, and the tears just don't stop. It's like the dam has been opened, and it's all rushing out.

"Zoe," he says my name, his voice breaking.

"I can't be your friend," I tell him, walking out of the elevator, and then stop, taking what little bit of strength I have inside me. He watches me, his own tears in his eyes. "I can't be your friend because I'm in love with you." I say the words out loud instead of just in my head, and his breath hitches, and he opens his mouth. "I'm in love with you with every-thing that I have," I tell him, "but it's not enough. I can't love you for both of us."

I take one more look at him before I turn and walk away from him. I walk out the door and turn to walk away from him, but I have to stop at the corner and lean against the wall. My sobs come out, my mouth flying to my hand to stop the noise. Help, I need help. I turn the corner and sit on the concrete sidewalk, ignoring the cold going through me like knives. I grab the phone out of my purse, my hands shaking like leaves falling off the trees in fall.

She answers after one ring. "Hey, did you find him?"

"Zara," I say, and the sob rips through me again.

"Where are you?" she shouts. "Zoe," she says, and then I hear her talking to someone. "Turn around!" she shouts. "Turn around now." Then she comes back to me. "Zoe, I'm on my way. I'm going to be there in seven minutes. I need you to stay where you are."

"Okay," I whisper.

"Are you alone?" she asks, her voice low. "Tell me you're okay."

"I'm not okay," I sob out. "Not even one bit," I say, and then I listen to her telling me that she's going to be right here, and everything is going to be okay. I don't know if it takes her seven minutes; I don't know anything except see-ing a truck slow down in front of me and the door opening before the truck comes to a full stop, and I hear her calling my name. She takes me into her arms, and I sob, clinging to her. "I love him. I love him so much," I say into her neck, and she rubs my head.

"It's going to be okay."

"Sweetheart, you need to move, so I can pick her up." I hear Evan's voice. "Let me put her in the truck, and we can take her home."

She slowly lets me go, and Evan scoops me into his arms. Zara runs ahead of him to open the back door of the truck, and she gets in. Evan sets me down, and Zara puts the seat belt around me. I don't know what they talk about. I know nothing because I'm living in a nightmare, a nightmare I can't wake up from.

I close my eyes and try to forget it all. I try to block it out. I don't know where we are going, and I don't care because I know I'll be safe now. Zara will make sure I'm okay. I hear Evan talk.

"I can't right now," he hisses. "I don't give a shit what he fucking needs. I can't be there!" he shouts, and I blink my eyes open and see he's on the phone. "Fine," he hisses. "I need to take care of something, and I'll be right there." He tosses his phone on the empty passenger seat. "Change of plans." He looks into the back. "We are going to go to the brownstone."

"Okay," Zara says, not asking why.

"Why does it hurt so much?" I whisper to her, looking up at her. "Like right here," I say with my hand to my chest. "It's feels like little shattered glass is being sliced into me."

She doesn't answer me because the car comes to a stop, and Evan gets out of the car, opening the door in the back for Zara, and then he is suddenly at my side of the car. "Hey there, beautiful," he says to me, and I sit up. My hair falls in front of my face, but he pushes it away and tucks it behind my ears. "You're going to be okay."

"Carry her in, Evan," Zara says from beside him now. I didn't even feel her get out of the truck and walk around it.

"I can walk," I tell him. He holds out his hand for me, and I grab it. He squeezes it, and I can't help the tears that fall and one of them land on his thumb. He looks up at me. "Promise me."

"Anything," he says, looking at me.

I put my hand on my stomach, Evan's eyes watching as it shakes. "Don't tell him. I don't want anyone to know." It's the only thing I can say before my legs give out, and he takes me in his arms.

"We have you," he says. "Zara, get the door." He scoops me up again for the second time tonight. Zara gets the door open, and he walks upstairs straight to my room. He places me in the middle of the bed and kisses my head. "I need to talk to Zara for a second, and then she's going to come back, okay?" I don't listen to what he says. Instead, I fall into my bed and get into a fetal position and watch Evan pull her out of the room by her hand. He talks to her, and she just crosses her arms over her chest. He kisses her, and then he's gone.

She walks back into the room. "Do you want me to run a bath?" she asks me, and I start to shiver, the cold ripping through me all of a sudden. Or maybe it's the shock of what just happened.

"Cold," I say, my teeth chattering together. "So cold." She puts her hand on her mouth, blocking out her own whimpers as she runs around the room, grabbing blankets and tossing them on top of me. "So cold."

She gets into bed with me, wrapping her body around mine to help heat me up. "Promise me." I look at her. "We don't tell anyone."

"Zoe," she says, her hand coming out to wipe away my tear.

"Promise me," I tell her. "Twinsie."

"Okay," she whispers. "It will be our secret." I nod at her and then turn back to look at the doorway.

My eyelids get heavier and heavier, my pillow becoming more wet as time goes on. "I can't stop the tears," I whisper. "No matter how much I try, I can't stop the tears." My eyes now stay shut as I listen to everything around me until I finally sink into the darkness.

TwentySeven

Viktor

"I CAN'T BE your friend because I'm in love with you." She says the words out loud, and I stop breathing. Everything around me closes in, and I suddenly feel the bottom open under me, and I'm falling. I open my mouth to say something, to tell her that she can't love me, but nothing comes out, and she continues to talk. "I'm in love with you with everything that I have," she almost whispers. "But it's not enough. I can't love you for both of us."

I watch her walk away from me. I watch the only thing that was pure and perfect walk out of my life. I watch it walk out of my life because, at the end of the day, I'm just a fuck-up. I stand here looking down at the floor, and the tears just come, my hand holding my chest that suddenly feels like it's being crushed. The elevator doors close, and I collapse on the floor, sliding down the back of the elevator until my ass hits the floor. I look at my hands that are trembling uncontrollably now, and I shake them, trying to get them to stop. The elevator doors open again, and I'm still in the lobby. The darkness from outside left the only thing for me to see is Zoe walking away from me, the pain in her eyes cutting through me.

The elevator doors open on my floor, and I get up and start walking down the dimly lit hallway. The sound of music coming from my apartment fills me with rage right now, rage that I lost another thing in my life. I open the door and find pretty much the same scene I left with, though a little less clothes. Kevin is half naked, and Mika is about to fuck a girl on my table while another woman sits on her face, and I just can't take it. I turn on the lights, and I hear a groan from everyone.

"What the fuck?" Chris mumbles from under his own girl. "Shut that shit down."

I walk or more like I pounce to the radio and turn it off, and now Kevin sits up, pushing the girl off him. "This guy obviously needs more blow." He laughs.

"Get out," I say softly, and then they all look at me. The bag of pills sits on the middle of my coffee table along with more bags of coke. "Get out," I say again, and this time, Kevin stands, and Mika has his back.

"Just like the good old days." I laugh bitterly as my blood boils. I want to hit something, I want to smash things, and I want them out of my fucking apartment now. "Here is something not like the good old days," I tell them and walk to Kevin. Chris gets up, and the girls looking around, trying to figure out if they should get dressed or just keep going. My head held high, my hands itching to move. The pull to look over at the counter and see if the line of blow is still there. "I want you guys out of my fucking house, now!" I yell the last part and advance on them. "Now."

I turn to look at the girls, and it takes a split second for Kevin to lunge at me, but because he's flying fucking high on whatever he's taking, I see his arm swinging for me. It might be my reflexes or the fact that every single nerve in my body is tingling, but I swing my right hand and knock his jaw with it, and he falls back into Mika and Chris who now hold him back. "GET THE FUCK OUT NOW!" I roar out, the girls now run around, grabbing what pieces of clothing are theirs and getting out. Kevin sits up and touches his lip that has a little bit of blood leaking out.

"You're a fucking waste," he says to me like his words can hurt me, like I don't know all of this. "What, you think you're a bigshot now that you're playing for New York?" He laughs now. "You can take the scum out of the gutter, but he still lingers with scum."

I throw my head back and laugh. "You're so fucking gone you don't even make sense." I advance on him. "I don't think I'm a bigshot, far from it." I look at Mika and Chris. "I just know that I deserve better than this fucking shitty cycle."

"Oh, here he is, Mr. Therapist," Mika says.

I shake my head and grab the phone out of my pocket. "I'm going to make it really easy for you assholes. If you don't take your shit out of my fucking house, I'll call the cops." I chuckle. "Can you see the headlines? I know my team is going to piss me, but unlike you three, I'm going to come back clean. So, what's it going to be, boys?"

"Fuck this shit and this asshole," Kevin says, grabbing his

clothes from the couch. "You're a waste."

Mika and Chris grab their things also and then walk out, slamming the door behind them.

I look around the apartment and see that the chairs around the table have been knocked over as well as some of the stools at the counter.

I look down at my phone, picking it up, and I know I have to call someone. I need the help, so I dial the first person I can think of. He answers right away with a groggy voice. "Hello."

"Jeffrey," I say, my voice cracking. "I fucked up."

"What do you mean you fucked up?" he asks me, and I hear him moving around in the background. "Where are you?"

"I'm at home sitting on my couch," I tell him. "There is stuff everywhere."

"I'll be there as soon as I can," he says into the phone. "Whatever you do, don't you dare give up." The phone disconnects, and I make the second biggest call of the evening.

"Matthew," I say, my voice cracking. "I need help." I don't know where he is. He is probably at the pub because I hear him shout for Max.

"Where are you?" he asks me, and I hear him running somewhere.

"Home," I tell him. "I'm at home."

"Are you alone?" he asks frantically, and then I hear a car door. "Or are you with someone?"

"I'm alone," I tell him, and he shouts out the address to someone.

"We'll be there in fifteen minutes," he says, then his voice gets lower. "Did you take anything?"

I shake my head while the tears run down my cheeks. "No," I say, my hands start to suddenly shake uncontrollably.

"I need you to just stay where you are. Can you do that?" he asks me. "That is what you need to do. You need to sit down and not move. Did you call Jeffrey?"

"Yes," I whisper. Leaning my head back, I close my eyes, but it hurts too much because all I see are Zoe's eyes. "He's on his way."

"We'll be there in ten minutes," he says.

I put the phone beside me and look outside in a daze as the night plays over and over in my head. The sight of her watching me, the sight of her walking into the room and seeing what I used to be. The hurt in her and knowing I put it there just makes it that much worse. A buzz makes me get up and move toward the door to buzz them in. I open the door and wait for them in the doorway.

Matthew sprints out of the elevator door as soon as it opens on my floor. He rushes over and must see that my knuckles are swelling; something I didn't even feel. "Viktor!" he shouts when he sees. Walking over to the door, he pushes it open. "What happened?" he asks, coming in with Max behind him. They look around the apartment, and then he must see what's on the coffee table. He walks over to the table and picks up the little baggies. "What the fuck is all this?"

"I don't know how it happened," I say, rubbing my face. "It was like I was out of my body, and I just watched it snowball out of control."

"What did?" Max asks, and he just looks at me.

"Mika, Kevin, and Chris. It was supposed to be just to visit, and then the next thing I knew, women were at the door, and then the drugs came out," I tell them, rubbing my hands over my face. "I can't place blame on them." I shake my head. "It's my fault I allowed this to happen."

"Motherfucker," Matthew hisses. "Where are they?" he asks, looking around.

"I kicked them out." I look at him and wonder if I should tell him, if I should tell him I put Zoe in this situation. "Zoe showed up." His eyes go big, and it takes Max a second to step between him and me. "She's gone," I say the two words that hurt me more than anything in my whole life. More than letting everyone down, more than seeing how disappointed my parents were when I told them just how much I was actually using. "She showed up, and it was seeing her that made me see through the haze. See through the fog."

"Where the fuck is she, and did they fucking touch her?" Matthew says between his clenched teeth.

"Of course not. Do you think I would have allowed that?" I look at them, and Max looks at Matthew and then at me. "I swear on my life I will never ever let anything happen to her."

The three of us stare off against each other, and none of us says anything because the door buzzes again, and I walk over and let Jeffrey in. No one says anything until Jeffrey comes into the room, and he looks at me.

"What is going …?" he says, his voice stopping when he looks around. "Holy shit," he says, rubbing his hands through his hair. "How much did you …?"

I shake my head. "Nothing."

"You know we're going to piss you," Matthew says, and I nod.

"You can piss me right now," I tell him. "I didn't fuck touch it."

"We need this shit cleaned up," Max says, and then the buzzer buzzes again. "It's like grand central station in here."

"It's Evan," Matthew says, and I press the button.

"We need to get rid of all of this," Jeffrey says, then looks at me. "You sure you want to stay here after we clean it? You can get a room somewhere."

"I'll be fine," I tell him, and he goes to the kitchen and grabs some cleaning supplies, and Evan walks in. He doesn't make eye contact with me; he just looks at Matthew.

"I'm here for you," Evan tells Matthew. "Just so you know."

"Is she okay?" I ask him, knowing why he said what he did.

He shakes his head. "Is she okay?" The sarcasm oozes out of him. "You tell me. Is it okay that you have to pick her up when she's sitting on a cold cement sidewalk? Is it okay that I have to carry her in the house because her legs give out and she is going to collapse?"

"Evan," Matthew says, and I see him taking his phone out and sending out a text.

"I had to carry her to the car," Evan tells me, coming closer to me. "I had to watch my wife hold her in the back seat like a child." He pushes me. "I had to fucking hold her up because she couldn't walk." The image in my head is too much to bear, and I let him push me again. "I promised her I

289

wouldn't tell anyone. I promised her that I wouldn't fucking tell you but ..."

"But what?" I ask him, almost afraid of what he has to say.

'But you deserve to know," he says and then looks over at Matthew. "She's home. Zara is with her." Then he slips his jacket off. "It's a good idea that it stays here with just us. Zoe is a proud woman, and the last thing she would want is to know that we feel sorry for her."

"Allison is going, too," Max starts, and Evan shakes his head.

"Then you let Zoe tell her," Evan says. "Now let's clean this shit up so I can go home." He looks at Max, then at Jeffrey who is now wearing gloves so he doesn't touch anything.

Matthew comes over. "How's the hand?" He looks at my hand, and I clench it into a fist.

"It hurts," I tell him quietly as the three men clean up and pick up shit. "I need you to know that I had no idea she was coming here. I would never ..."

"She deserves a man who will put her first," Matthew says. "She deserves a man who is going to love her with every single part of his being." I listen to the words. "She deserves a man who is going to fight for her."

"She deserves someone else," I tell him, the pain of those words cutting right through me. "She deserves perfect, and that isn't me." He doesn't argue with me; he just nods his head. "What can I do to help?"

"You need to get the fuck out and take a shower," Jeffrey says. "The last thing you need to do is touch any of this."

"We've got this," Matthew says. "Go take care of your

hand." I nod at them and head to the bedroom and sit on the bed, putting my head into my hands.

I feel hollow like a shell. Everything is moving around me—my heart is beating, my lungs are exhaling and inhaling—but I feel empty. My eyes close, and I fall on the bed. The last thing I see before the darkness comes to take me are her eyes, and the voice that meets me in my dreams repeating over and over again.

I can't love you for both of us.

TwentyEight

Zoe

"Hey," EVAN WHISPERS, and I open my eyes. At least I try to, but they feel heavy and puffy.

"Hey," I hear Zara sit up beside me. "Did you just get in?"

"Yeah," he whispers and goes to her side of the bed, and I feel the bed dip down. "I missed you." I hear them kiss, and if it was any other time, I would fake gag, but instead, my heart just aches.

"It's almost six a.m., she says to him. "You look exhausted."

"I'm past exhausted," he says to her and then lies down next to her, and she pushes into me more. "I didn't mean to wake you," Evan says, and I turn over to see him lying behind Zara with his arms around her waist and his hand on her stomach. "How you doing?"

"My eyes feel like they weigh seven thousand pounds," I tell them, and Zara reaches out and wipes away a tear that

I didn't know was falling. Our eyes meet now, and she has her own tears. "My whole body hurts."

"If it makes you feel better, you aren't the only one," Evan says, and Zara whips her head around and looks at him. "Don't you dare."

"Sweet Zara," he says, using her nickname. "Don't cry."

"I'm not crying," she says. "It's called hormones." She sits up and struggles a bit since her bump is getting bigger by the day. "You know, before you, we would already be planning his demise."

"Zara," Evan says, groaning. "I didn't want to do this, but if I have no choice, I will."

She folds her arms over her chest on top of her baby bump. "Meaning?"

Evan sits up now and looks at her and then me. "Matthew was at Viktor's when I got there."

I get up myself now, tossing the covers over and getting out of bed. "I don't care," I say, going into the bathroom and turning on the cold water in the sink. I avoid the mirror at all costs. I don't need the mirror to tell me I look horrible. Splashing the water on my face, I dab it dry with the hand towel. I open the door and hear them still talking.

"I'm just saying that I would want you to know," Evan says.

"Oh, please," Zara says. "What would you want me to know exactly?"

"Guys," I say to them, and they look over at me. Zara now sitting on my side of the bed. "How is this? You have three minutes to tell me what you want to, and then you aren't going to bring it up ever again."

"Zoe," Zara says. "It's not …"

"Three minutes." I look at Evan, ignoring Zara. I get ready for what he will say, or at least, I think I'm ready. I'm not.

"He's just as broken as you are. He hasn't said three words to anyone except to explain how it went down. I got there when they were cleaning up, so I don't know what happened after you left. But," he says, looking down at his hands, "from what Max told me, he called Matthew after he tossed everyone out." He looks at Zara and then at me. "He didn't touch it."

My heart lets out a little flip that at least he fought through the urge. "I'm glad that his recovery is still continuing, but it doesn't change the fact that I can't …" I stop talking and roll my lips, the lone tear escaping and falling out over my eyelid and onto the floor. It splatters like my heart feels. "I can't be in this. I can't be there."

"But …" Evan says, and I shake my head.

"I love him," I tell him, and it feels just a bit better to have it out into the open. "I love him, and I know it's not his problem, it's mine. He told me not to fall in love with him. He told me that he couldn't do this, and I stupidly fell in love with him anyway."

Zara gets off the bed and comes over and takes me in her arms. "You are not stupid," she whispers in my ear.

"I am stupid," I tell her and Evan. "And I wish him nothing but the best, but I can't even go there. I can't handle it." Zara releases me, and I stand next to her now with her arm around my shoulder. "My heart can't take it." Evan just looks at me, and I'm about to say something else when the doorbell rings.

"Who can that be?" Zara asks, and Evan shoots off the

bed and walks out of the room. We follow with him in the background, and I'm on the stairs when I hear the soft voice.

"I know it's early," Jeffrey says, and I stop in the middle of the staircase on my way down. His eyes fly up to mine. This man is pretty much a stranger, yet he is the closest thing to Viktor that I have. "I wanted to see if you were okay." I take a deep breath and walk down the remaining stairs.

"Why don't we make coffee and give them a chance to talk," Evan says, going to Zara, but Zara doesn't move until I give her a silent nod.

"Do you want to come in?" I say softly, and he nods and follows me into the living room. I sit on the couch, and he sits next to me. His hand comes out, and he puts it on my knee.

"How are you doing?" he asks me. I look at him, and I try not to let it show on my face, but I can't.

"I want to be all proud and tell you that I'm fine, but I'm not," I tell him softly.

"It's hard loving someone who is an addict." I want to correct him, and he just smiles. "Once an addict, always an addict." He moves his hand from my knee and then puts his elbows on his knees and folds his hands together. "You love him."

"Why does everyone care how I feel about him?" I tell him, getting up to walk off the nerves. "You guys should be focusing on him and helping him through whatever the hell he is going through."

"Well, that answers that question," he says.

"He's a broken man." I stand in front of him, and I let it all out. "A man I knew was broken yet still fell for. He also warned me that he can't get involved. He can't go there with me, and I agreed with him."

"But love is love," he says, leaning back. "It happens when it wants to happen and not when it should. The thing is when you're recovering, especially in that first year, you are so afraid that the love you find is actually love and not just something to replace the addiction."

"He doesn't love me," I tell him, and he shakes his head and laughs.

"The man almost washed away eight months of being clean less than ten hours ago, and the only thing he told me was to make sure you were okay," he says with a smile. "He's a broken man, there is no doubt about it, but even broken men love." He looks down and then up. "Even this broken man."

"Jeffrey," I say softly.

"I sat there stoned while my child cried because she had a needle stuck in her leg from crawling," he says, and my hand goes to my heart to hold my chest. "I was past the point of being broken. I was a hollow broken man, and I had nothing left. Nothing, but slowly, I accepted the love that people gave me."

"He's stronger than anyone I've ever known," I say to him. "He deserves to have that love. He deserves to have it all. The love, the happiness, everything and …" I hold my breath as I say the last part. "I hope he finds it." The little pieces of my heart that weren't broken now explode into little shards, pinching and stabbing my chest. "I hope he finds it, and he has the best of everything."

Jeffrey looks at me and just nods his head. "I can't love

him for both of us." I tell him what I told Viktor.

He just nods and gets up, coming over to me. "You're a good woman, Zoe, and you deserve that happiness. You deserve the love that you want for Viktor."

"I do," I say, holding back the tears. "I know I do."

"Stay in touch," Jeffrey says, hugging me and then walking out. The minute I hear the door slam, the sob escapes from my throat. I try to block it with my hand, but I can't. It's bigger than me. This whole thing is bigger than me. Zara runs into the room and sees me violently shaking as I try to stand. My knees shake so badly I barely make it to the couch.

"What should we do?" Evan asks, and Zara looks at him. I fall to the side of the couch and just curl up, the sobs slowly trickling off as I stare into space. I don't even hear what they are talking about. I hear nothing. I just close my eyes and pray that the pain goes away.

I feel a blanket put on top of me, and I just stay here with my eyes closed. Eventually, I doze off, but I don't know how long I'm out for. I feel little kisses on my face, and I slowly open my eyes, and I see my mom. The tears fill her eyes, and she tries to blink them away, but she can't. "Hey, baby girl." She tries to smile big, but you can see it's forced.

"Mom," I say, confused and then look around and see Zara sitting on the other couch with Allison beside her with her arms around Zara as she just looks at me helplessly.

"I didn't know what to do," Zara says quietly. "I'm sorry, Zoe," she sobs, and Allison just pulls her closer.

"It's just us," my mother says. "Just us girls."

"Mom," I say, my throat feeling harsh and dry. "I fell in

love," I tell her, and now she just lets the tears escape. "And it hurts."

"Oh, baby," she says, bending down to hug me, and her hug makes me feel safe, like everything is going to be okay.

"He doesn't love me," I tell her. "And no matter how much I tried not to love him, I couldn't stop."

"You can't stop love," my mother says. "If anyone knows that, it's me." She sits up and looks at me. "When I met your father, the last thing I wanted or was looking for was love."

"When I fell in love with Max, I fought it," Allison says. "I didn't even know I loved him until it was too late." She wipes her own tears away from her eyes.

"Except you guys ended up with the one you fell in love with, and well …" I say, getting up and sitting next to my mother. "It's just …" I shake my head and say the words. "It will never happen for me."

"Well, it's his loss," Zara says angrily. "Fuck him," she says, standing up. "Maybe it's not love."

"Okay, there," Allison says, getting up. "Let's get you some water and maybe you need a snack. You sound hangry." She grabs Zara's hand, and they leave the room.

"I love him so much it hurts everywhere," I tell my mother, and she just nods her head. "I knew falling in love with him was wrong. I knew that it was." I shake my head. "But it just happened so slowly that I couldn't stop it once it was all there in front of me."

"It sneaks up on you without an option," she says. "No matter how much you would have fought it, it would have happened anyway."

"But shouldn't it happen with a man who would love me

back?" I ask her. "A man who looks at me like I hang the moon and stars. A man who is going to put me before everything?" I shake my head. "I kissed him once." I look at her. "One time. One kiss. And I know it's a kiss that I'll be looking for, for my whole life."

"Zoe," my mother says, grabbing my hand and squeezing. Zara and Allison come back in the room.

"One kiss and I knew," I say softly and take a drink from the water bottle that Allison handed me. "One kiss, one little kiss that lasted maybe a minute, and it just …" I laugh bitterly. "It made sense. It made me finally click everything into place." I look at Zara and Allison and then my mother. "It was like all those other kisses were a lead up to the perfect one."

"You'll have other kisses," Allison says. "And this one will just linger in the back."

"You aren't going to get over him," Zara says, and my mother and sister just look at her. "What? I'm not lying to her. If she loves him the way I know she does, she will never get over him." Then she looks at Allison. "Would you be able to get over Max?" Allison glares at her. "And you," she says to my mother. "You still look at Dad with all the hearts and all the gross things that I don't want to think about when it comes to my parents."

"She's right," my mother says. "You will never forget him, and a piece of your heart will always love him. But," she says, "I refuse to let you not fall in love again. Because it's beautiful, it's everything, and I want you to have it. To love with your whole heart and wake up every single day knowing that the man you love thinks you walk on water. I want you to be worshipped and cherished, and I want someone who is going to put you before them," she says. "You deserve nothing but that," she says, silently crying. "You deserve it all, Zoe. You are a warrior," she says. "You play this tough girl, and you always have. The girl who doesn't show her emotions, but when she loves, she loves with everything she has."

"That isn't me," I tell her.

"That is you one hundred percent," Zara and Allison say at the same time.

I look over at my mother. "When is the hurt going to not hurt?"

"I wish I knew, baby girl," she says. "How about we just do one day at a time?"

"One day at a time." I whisper the words that Viktor used to say all the time. "One day at a time." I look at the women in my life; the ones who will be hereto help hold me up. I can't help but think of Viktor and wonder who is holding him up, who is there with him. I block out the answer, but my head whispers, *You want to be that person.*

TwentyNine

Viktor

"It's clean," Matthew says, hanging up the phone. He tells me what I already knew, but it still feels good to hear. It's been two days since I had those people at my house, two days since I stood up to the drug and said no. It's been two days since I've seen her, and it's been two days since my heart stopped beating normally.

I've spent the past two days sitting on my couch in the dark, then the light, not moving as I replay it over and over in my head. The only time I smiled was when Jeffrey came over and told me he saw her. Zoe. The name that is on my lips each and every single time I wake up in a pool of sweat. The name that I linger on when I look down at my phone. The text thread I keep reading and re-reading.

"Well, at least one good thing is going right," I tell him and turn to walk out of his office and then stop and turn around. "She okay?" I ask him, and I see his jaw get tight.

"No," Max answers. Then he looks at Matthew. "Tell me if it was Karrie you wouldn't want to know."

"Zara had to call Parker and Allison to come down because she didn't know what else to do." The pain I had in my chest is now fifty times worse than it was before, and if I didn't know better, I would think I was having a heart attack. "She is kicking everyone out tonight," he says, and I want to puff out my chest and be proud of how strong she is.

I don't say anything to him. I just nod my head and walk to the gym. I spend two hours running—two hours trying to clear my head—but for once, I'm not thinking about me. I'm thinking about Zoe. When I finish in the shower, the locker room is empty since it was an optional day. I'm walking out when the phone buzzes in my pocket, and I see it's Zara

Zara: Do you have time to talk?

I answer her back right away

Me: Name the time and place.

Zara: Coffee shop at corner of your house in twenty minutes.

Me: I'll be there.

I rush to get there, and when I walk in, I'm not surprised that Evan is with her. Zara gets up, and I know she and Zoe are identical twins, but Zoe's eyes are bigger and brighter, and her smile is fuller, and she just is more beautiful than Zara. I walk over to the table, my eyes never leaving hers. "Hey," I say, sitting down at the table that they are sitting at in the back. It's a tiny round table with only three chairs.

"I'm only here to make sure that my wife leaves you in one piece," Evan says, and I just nod at him.

"You fucked up, Viktor," Zara says. I look at her, and I'm

not the one saying anything. Instead, it's Evan.

"Sweet," he says, and she holds up a hand to stop him.

"I don't mean like that. I mean that you fucked up by letting her walk away."

"You have me there. I fucked up by not chasing her, but I have to take care of me before I can take care of her."

She crosses her hands over her chest. "Do you love her?"

"Yes," I answer her without having to think about it. I love her, and I didn't even know how much I did until it was in front of me. I was too busy trying to get better that I didn't know I was doing it with the end prize being Zoe. "With everything that I have," I say and then look up into the sky and blink away the tears. "Even though it isn't much."

"So what's your plan?" she asks me the loaded question.

"Right now, today, it's to get better, stronger," I tell her.

She shakes her head. "Where does Zoe fit in all that?" Her voice is tight.

"I want her there with me, beside me, holding my hand when they hand me my one-year chip," I say out loud, and the words cut through me, but I know it's the truth. "But she definitely deserves someone who doesn't have so many things trying to take him down."

"I agree with you there," she says.

"Sweetheart," Evan says, and she just gives a side-eye glare.

"You can't disagree with me," she says, looking at Evan. "She deserves better, but it's her choice. He is who she chooses." Then she turns to look at me. "Now the question is what are you going to do about it? What's your game plan?"

"I don't have one," I tell her.

"Well, then it's a good thing I'm here. Because I'm going to tell you what your plan is. You're going to get better. You are going to complete your one year of sobriety, and then you're going to go to her and beg her to take you back. You are going to prove to her that you're the man she thinks you are. You are going to do all that," she says and now she blinks away the big tears, "because she deserves that."

"That's five months away," I tell her. "It's almost one hundred and fifty days."

"And?" she asks.

"And?" I answer her. "How am I supposed to not see her for five months?" I look at her. "How would you feel not being able to see Evan for five months? Knowing that he is right there yet not be able to see him?"

"It would be hell," she answers softly. "It would be my absolute fear." She looks at Evan. "But if I knew that in the long run, it would be me with him at the finish line, I would."

"What if she forgets about me?" I ask my most feared question. "What if she starts dating and falls in love with someone else? What if someone finally gets their head out of their ass and realizes that she's the best that there is out there? That no one comes close to how perfect she is."

Evan tries to roll his lips, and Zara rolls her eyes. "She isn't perfect."

"She is," I say softly. "She's the definition of what perfect is."

"Oh, God," Evan says. "I just about threw up." He looks at me, and I glare at him. "I get it now when Zoe says it."

"Fuck you," I tell him, and he just laughs.

"She isn't going to fall in love with anyone. She's getting

over a broken heart, so she isn't going to jump back out there."

"I want to go to her," I tell her the truth. "I want to go to her so much that it's the only thing I think of, but then I know I can't."

"You have one hundred and fifty days to make sure she knows it was worth it," Zara says, and then she looks at Evan. "We should get going."

"Are you going to her?" I ask them, jealous that they are going to see her.

"No, she kicked us all out," Zara says. "She has an appointment tomorrow, and she has to get ready for it, so she needs to focus."

I just nod at her and get up with them. Zara comes over and hugs me. "Don't fuck this up." I just smile at her. "And if you do, it's going to take a lot more than Evan to stop me from slicing off your dick." She raises her eyebrows. "I'll be in touch."

"Sweetheart," Evan says as they walk out, "you aren't going anywhere near his dick."

"God, Evan," she says, and the door closes behind them. I look at the time and see it's almost time for a meeting.

I walk to my normal meeting and nod to a couple of people who I've seen before when I walk in. I sit down and look around the circle. Only four of us sit while the others just linger talking to each other. When the meeting starts, I listen to the first guy go, and then I speak.

"I almost fell off the wagon two days ago," I start, looking down at the floor. "The coke was lined up on the table, the bill was in my hand, and all it would have taken was me leaning over, and it would have been over," I tell them and then look up. "My heart was beating a million miles a minute, and I knew with just one hit, it would take it all away. I knew with one hit, it would all be okay. But then ..." I look at everyone, their eyes on me, and I know that none of them will sit there and judge me. "Then something caught my eye. My key chain telling me one day at a time. I was so close to losing everything that I'd fought for, and I stepped back. I knew that as good as that hit would be, the aftermath wasn't worth it. Then to top it off, I looked up and saw her." Now a couple of people nod. "I knew I liked her, but I didn't know that I had fallen in love with her." I rub my face now. "I fell in love with her, and she walked away from me. And at that moment, I hated myself more than ever before. I hated the drug more than ever. I hated everything that had to do with the drug. Knowing that it had that power over me."

"But it didn't," one guy says. "Did you go after the girl?" he asks, and I nod. "Then you had the power over the drug. If the drug had the power, you would have stayed there and snorted the line. You would have said fuck her and just lost yourself in the high."

"You aren't supposed to fall in love in recovery," I tell him.

"Doesn't mean it doesn't happen," he says. "My wife now, I fell in love with her four months after rehab. I just didn't know it because it was so pure. I wasn't used to something that didn't have anything to do with the drugs. I never knew what it was to feel without being high."

Everyone nods now, including me. "Then it makes recovery just a touch easier because I wanted to be worthy of her.

I wanted to be the man she could be proud of. That she can stand behind. Even if I wasn't perfect, I wanted to be perfect for her." He crosses his arms over his chest with a smile, and I see his wedding ring. I nod at him and then someone else starts talking. The whole time, my eyes never leave sight of his finger. The gold band so simple yet so perfect.

The snowfall is thicker when I leave, so I jump into a cab and make my way home. I walk in and toss my keys on the counter and shrug off the winter jacket. I walk over to the fridge and open it, pulling out a meal I had delivered. I turn on Sports Net and watch whatever is on there. My mind doesn't really pay attention. I can't shut it off Zoe, and I don't want to.

THIRTY

ZOE

I BURY MY head in work and then planning the baby shower for Zara. I have over twenty showings on houses, and it really is my busiest time of the year. When Candace comes in, I am not even ready. I'm still in my yoga pants. "You look amazing," she says, coming into the house and greeting me with a hug. She wasn't always so nice. When Zara started dating Evan, she was a bitch.

"Yeah, well, apparently being really busy and skipping meals is great for the waistline," I joke. Yes, I'm busy, and yes, I'm eating, but it just is what it is.

"I have to go meet with a client," she says when she finally settles into the guest room. I'm sitting in the middle of the bed putting up another listing. "Do you want to come with? It shouldn't take me long, and then I'm thinking of hitting up some shops."

I know what my answer is, but I have to get out. "That

sounds like fun," I tell her. "Let me just put on some jeans, and I'll meet you downstairs." She smiles, and I put on my black jeans and thick green sweater.

We walk out, making small talk about all her new clients, and it doesn't even dawn on me who she might be meeting until I'm sitting at the table and see Viktor walk in. The whole world stops, or maybe it's just my world that stops.

They say a picture is worth a thousand words, but they lied because there are no words to describe him. Just looking at him makes everything hurt, yet it makes me feel like I'm okay. That today will be just a touch better than yesterday, and it all happens in slow motion or maybe it's the fact that everything around me suddenly quiets. There are no clinking plates, there are no spoons stirring coffee, and no chattering from the other tables—it's just me and him. And when he finally looks around the restaurant, and our eyes meet, his face changes. The darkness of his eyes suddenly gets just a touch lighter, and they shine. He pulls off the beanie he was wearing, and he just stands there. Just looking at him makes the past three weeks just fade away.

"There he is," Candace says from beside me, and she gets up to go meet him. He nods at her and takes her hand, but his eyes keep coming back to me. She turns and walks back to the table. "I think you guys already know each other, right?" We don't say anything when he sits down in front of me. The table is suddenly too small. Everything is just smaller, and he's too close and the smell I couldn't remember is back; everything is back. I'm getting ready to jump out of my chair and make an exit when Candace's phone rings, and she answers it. "Sorry, I'll be right back."

I want to yell at her to get back here, but nothing comes out. Nothing, not one single word. I think it's going to be okay, and then he says my name. "Zoe." And it's just too much. I look down and blink away the tears.

"I didn't know it was you," I say, my eyes not coming up to see him. "I wouldn't have come."

His voice comes out soft, softer than ever. "I'm glad you did," he says, and I look up at him. He looks like he is going to say something else, but Candace returns.

"Sorry for that. It was my mother. She's on her way out here, and she's nervous." She sits down and doesn't pick up anything.

"I'm going to leave you to do what you need to do," I say, getting up, and with Candace here, he doesn't say anything even though his eyes say everything. Defeat, sadness, hopelessness. I know because my eyes mimic his.

"How about I just meet you at Neiman Marcus?" I put my jacket on, and she just nods at me. I force a smile on my face and just nod and walk out.

The cold air cuts right through me, but I don't feel it. I feel nothing. I just walk away from him, away from the pain, except it follows me. Everything follows me—the memories, the laughter, and then the heartache. The memory of him so tempted to slip back to what he is fighting so hard to run away from. But no matter how hard or how far I try to run, he's there with me, and there is nothing that I can do to close it off.

Thirty One

Viktor

Candace goes on and on, and I can't even focus on what she's saying. And if I'm honest, I couldn't care less. She could be telling me all the secrets in the world, and the only thing I can think of is getting my heart back to beating normal.

Seeing Zoe for the first time in three weeks knocked me back. I imagined how it would be, kept playing it over and over in my head how it would go. What I would say, how I would beg her to wait for me, but the minute I finally saw her, it all went out the window, and the only thing I wanted to do was to feel her, hug her, make her laugh, and kiss her.

Instead, all I could do was sit and look at her. She looks like she lost weight and isn't sleeping, and it's all my fault. I did that, no one else but me. For the past three weeks, I've been trying to find out what I can about her. I listen to Max and Matthew talk about their family things, hoping one of them will drop her name. I sit next to Evan to see if he says anything, but they haven't said anything.

Not one single word about how she's doing. The only time I get a glimpse of her is on Zara's Instagram. The only thing in my life not suffering is my game. I'm faster, I'm stronger, and I'm meaner. My points are through the roof, and I'm playing so much more physical than I've ever played. Everyone sees it, yet no one is saying anything except for Max. He pushes me even more when we are in the gym. It's like he knows that it's my outlet.

"If you have anything else to add, I'm more than happy to take any suggestions," Candace says, and I just shake my head. "You have to be the easiest person to work with," she says and gets up. "But I'm here if you need anything." I follow her lead and get up and walk out with her. I shake her hand and then turn. My hand goes straight to my phone, and I call Jeffrey.

"I saw her," I say when he answers the phone. "I saw her, and it was worse than I ever imagined it would be."

"Where are you?" he asks right away. For the past three weeks, he's been by my side every single time I wanted to talk about Zoe, even if it was about nothing.

"I'm standing in the middle of the street kicking myself for not going after her. For not running after her and begging her to give me a chance to stick it out. Letting her know that I made the decision not to go down that road before she walked in," I tell him, my chest hurting as I say it. "Letting her know that I'm stronger than that."

"Well, then, why didn't you?" he asks, and I give him the answer that hurts the most.

"Because fear got me. The fucking fear that she didn't care that I didn't do it and that it wasn't good enough," I tell him, and I just shake my head.

"You stupid son of a bitch. How about you come over here and let Becky fawn all over you?" he says sarcastically.

"I think I'll hit up a meeting first, then maybe I'll come over," I tell him and walk toward the meeting. I don't talk during this one, and when I get out, all I want to do is go home and chill. I open the door, and the place is as quiet as can be. Sometimes it's too quiet, and I play music just to make it a bit livelier.

The next day, I hit up the gym knowing that no one will be in since it's Evan and Zara's baby shower. They both invited me, but I kindly declined and sent a gift anyway. There was no way I could take being in a room with Zoe and not going to her to make sure she was okay. To make sure she knew she didn't have to love me for both of us, and I would do everything and anything in my power to do that for her. But it wasn't time yet. I have to do it right. I have to do all the steps right, and then I hope that, in the end, she accepts me with all my pieces put back together. Will they all ever be fully back together? I fucking hope so.

That night, I scroll through Instagram and see that Zara put up some pictures from today. There is one with all the girls and then one of her and Zoe. Like the creep I am, I zoom in on Zoe and her smile and save the picture.

I get a text from Zara, and when I open it, my heart stops as I read it.

Zara: Thank you so much for the Gucci diaper bag with matching outfits. The baby will be styling. Thought you would like to see a picture of her smiling.

Then she attached a picture of just Zoe looking at something, and her head is thrown back and she's laughing. I smile and rub my finger on it. "Soon." I turn off the light and head to bed, leaving her picture on my phone.

The nights are getting easier; the pull toward the darkness dimmer every single day. It's a cycle, everyday getting up only to cross off another day on the calendar. We will be on the road for twelve days. Our longest one to date.

Getting to the arena for tonight's game, everyone is in high spirts. I laugh to myself because three days into the road trip and everyone will be bitching to each other about not being home.

The road trip is even worse than I thought. It only took two days before everyone started to get irritated. And it didn't help that we lost the first two games on the road. I spent most days either on the ice or in the gym.

Two days before we head home, everyone is hurting. "Can we just play a game without it becoming a wrestling match?" one of the rookies asks.

"That's what happens when you're in the run for the playoffs. Every single point counts," I tell him, walking up the stairs to the plane and sitting in my seat. Next stop is LA. Before, I would be nervous and anxious, and I still am, except this time I'm nervous that I'll fuck up by killing one of those fuckers on the ice. I'm not nervous that I might slip this time. No, this time I know I won't slip. For once in my life, I have something good—something that no amount of money or getting high can get me—and I'm not going to lose it.

I sit in my seat, not expecting anyone to sit next to me only because we usually spread out, but Matthew sits in the chair next to me. I look over at him, but he doesn't say anything, and the plane takes off.

"So what's going on?" Matthew starts the awkward conversation. There is a lot to be said about Matthew but beating around the bush isn't one of them.

"You should just come out and ask what you need to ask or say what you need to say." I laugh. "For both our sakes."

"Karrie says I need to be more approachable," he says, scratching his neck. "This is me trying."

"Don't tell Karrie, but you suck at it," I tell him. "Now what do you really want to ask?"

"Is being in LA going to be a problem?" he asks me, and I look at him, turning in my seat.

"That's a loaded question," I tell him. "If you are asking if I think I might slip and it becomes a scene like it was in New York, the answer is no. Without a second thought." I look at him straight in the eye. "If you're asking if I'm going to bring my A game, the answer again is yes."

"That's good to hear." He puts his head back on the rest and crosses his hands.

I lean back in my seat and turn to look at him. "I also won't hesitate to drop the gloves if one of them even looks at me sideways."

"Oh, for fuck's sake," he says.

"Just laying it all out there for you," I tell him, laughing, and I feel like something has lifted from my shoulders. "I have too much to lose."

"That so?" he asks with a smirk.

"Yeah, that is so. And I'll be damned if I throw it away for them," I tell him and look around, then lean in. "Bottom line, at the end of all this, I'm planning on making Zoe mine if she'll have me."

"What makes you think she'll want you?" he asks me seriously, and I think about how I should answer this.

"I pray that she will want me," I tell him honestly. "Every single night, it's the first thing I ask for, and I know I don't have any right to ask for or expect anything, but if I get anything in my whole life, it will be her love."

"What if she's in love with someone else?" And the pain is there again, the pressure pushing down on my chest like a herd of elephants stomping their feet.

"If she loves someone else and she's happy, then I have to give her that." I swallow, and it feels like I have a whole mouth full of nails. "I want her to be happy, and if it's without me, when she deserves that, then I just walk away and give it to her."

"How hard was that to say?" he asks me.

"I felt like I was swallowing nails," I answer him honestly. "Is she dating?" I finally ask him about her. I don't even know I'm holding my breath while I wait for him to answer. He doesn't answer. Instead, he takes out his phone and turns it to me, and I see that it's him in the middle of his sisters.

"That was taken at the baby shower," he tells me, and I know because I have the picture saved on my phone of her in that dress. He swipes to the side, and then she's there again, this time with Alex on her hip. "She puts on a good front," he says, looking at the picture again. "So to answer your question, no, she isn't dating."

I nod and slowly let out the breath I've been holding, my heart starting to beat semi normal again. "Can't say I'm sad about that news."

He lets out a huge laugh. "Well, said," he says, and for the rest of the plane ride, we talk about all the teams trailing us in the standings. It's nighttime when we land but when we get off the plane, it's hot and just a touch muggy.

When I get dressed to go to the arena, I do it with my head held high and my shoulders back. It's the first time I've been back since I've been traded, and I honestly don't know what to expect. It's always weird coming back to the arena that made you into that hockey player and then made you into the drug addict. It's where I started to do most of my drugs while I chased the high. I think back to the times I played high, and I'm still shocked that it took them that long to figure it out. I step onto the bus on the way to the arena, and all I can do is look out the window and replay in my head everything that has happened since I left. It's not as scary as it was the first time or the second time; it's easier, and the road is lighter.

I walk off the bus after Matthew and Max. Evan is behind me, and I spot the reporters right away with their cameras rolling. I know this will be playing on *SportsCenter* for the next twenty-four hours, but I'm not walking down the dark concrete by myself, no not with this team. I walk down next to Matthew on my right side and Evan on my left and Max beside Matthew. A united front, a team, a family. "Hey, Viktor." I hear one of the camera guys say, and I just look ahead to the brown metal door that I've walked into a thousand times before, but this time, when I walk in, I walk to the opposite end of the hallway.

When we walk into the bleak dressing room, I look around. "My room in rehab was nicer than this," I joke with Evan, who laughs. I take a deep breath in and let it out slowly and go to my seat. Taking off my jacket, I start getting my exercise shit out. "I need to run," I tell Evan who is on his phone.

"Whatever you do, don't fucking wear yourself out," he says, looking up for a second and then down again. "We need to win."

"You don't have to tell me that," I say and get ready to run on the treadmill. I'm by myself for most of it and then a couple of the guys come in while I'm walking to cool down. The music blares as we get dressed, and Matthew has closed off the room for reporters. The only one allowed in has a three-minute slot to walk in and just do a camera shot. Not surprisingly, the camera stayed on me as I was getting ready. I blocked it out, I blocked it all out, and the only thing I had in my head was going out there and winning.

When I slip the jersey on and pull up the sleeves, I bounce on my skates. "I can't wait to get this shit over with," I tell Evan, and he grabs his gloves.

"I'm ready to go home to my wife," he says. "I swear her stomach got so much bigger, and I'm scared she's going to have the baby while I'm not there." He shakes his head. "Knowing my luck, that kid is going to come early and shock us all." I laugh.

When the door opens, we start to walk down the hallway, and I know we will come out on the other side of the ice as LA. This is where I called home for four years, coming out of the other side is weird as fuck. "Guys, don't fuck this up for me." I smirk at the team. "Everyone else who has been traded has lost their game once they come back, and I don't want to fall in that category." I laugh, and everyone just shakes their head.

The doors open, and I skate on with the team, the booing already starting. "Welcome home," Evan says, laughing beside me. "Fuck, when I went back to Dallas, they had a shrine of me," he jokes and pushes my shoulder. I warm up by skating around a couple of times and then shooting the puck. When we leave the ice for the Zamboni, I have my skates sharpened just a touch and then take my place on the ice as they do the national anthem.

When I skate to center ice, I'm expecting to see Kevin, but it's Mika. "Hey, douchebag," he says. One look at him, and I can tell he's high. How did no one on the bench notice? Oh, wait they probably did and didn't say anything. "Ready to get your ass handed to you?"

I laugh. "Who is going to hand it to me?" I ask him and see Evan look over at us, Chris in the front of him chirping.

"Look, it's Larry and Curly," Evan says. "Where is Moe?" he asks him, laughing at his own joke.

"Pretty boy has a big mouth," Chris says, and it makes me chuckle because Evan is a pretty boy.

"Yeah, the difference is my mouth can deliver," Evan says, and Chris does what I know he's going to do.

"You know who else has a mouth that delivers?" Chris says, and now Evan stands straight.

"If you want to keep any of your teeth, I suggest you don't fucking finish that sentence," Evan says, advancing just a touch over the line, and the referee pushes them away.

"Save it for the game," he says, and Chris just laughs.

"Pussy ass bitch," he says, looking over at Mika. "Let's make it rain."

"Seriously, you fuckers still doing code words?" I shake my head and now crouch down as the puck comes out of the referee's pocket. "Just one thing wrong with that." I look over at Mika. "I'm the one who created the code words," I say, and the puck drops, and I'm already away from Mika.

Evan and Chris battle for the puck, but Evan is faster than Chris and sends it to Andrew, the right winger, who gets it on his stick and then sees me waiting at the far left. He crosses over the line, and I can see Mika charging for me, but I move to the right just as he comes crashing into the board, leaving me in the center of the ice right in front of the goalie.

Andrew passes it straight to me, and I tip it right over the goalie, hitting the back of the net. I'm about to throw my hands up and celebrate when I'm hit from behind. I have a split second to look to the side and see that it's Mika. The defenseman comes over, trying to stop him, but he shakes him off. I look over at Evan, who is pushing Chris and saying whatever when Mika pushes me again, and I snap. The sticks go flying and then the gloves come off, and Mika does the same thing. No one is going to stop this; everyone is backing up as they see us skate. I grab him by his jersey with my left hand, and I swear my knuckles are white for how hard I'm holding him. I hit him once and then twice in the head, and he ducks down. His right hand tries to swing, but his movements are a touch slower. And when he's mid punch, I knock him from under, and my fist connects with his jaw. He falls to the ice, and I hit him one more time before the referee comes out and breaks us apart.

One of them pushes me away, and the other tries to get Mika up, but he looks confused as to how he got there. I see the trainer come on the ice, and the referee tries to get him on his feet, but he loses his legs again, and they have to hold him up. I look over at Chris, who just glares. "Pussy ass bitch can't even make it rain," I tell him, then the ref pushes me toward the penalty box. "He cross checked me," I tell him, and he laughs.

"You knocked his ass out cold. Get in the box," he says, and I get in the box, and they finally announce my goal and then my penalty. Luckily, the two minutes go by with nothing going on. Chris smashes Evan's stick, and he hits it so hard, the stick breaks, and Evan tosses it to the ice and then blocks the puck once it's passed in our zone. He kicks it over to me, and I take it on my blade and skate up the ice, the defenseman one on one with me. I look around to pass it and don't see anyone. I'm almost to the goalie so I try my luck and shoot it over his shoulder, and to everyone's surprise, it goes in. I kick up one of my legs and scream out in celebration. Some of the fans are on their feet celebrating, but none more than Evan, who jumps up once he gets to me. I skate to the bench and give everyone a high-five and then get on the bench. Evan sits next to me, and then they announce my name. I look up and then see that they are doing one of those video montages of all the times I was here.

The fans stand and clap, and I get up and raise my hand.

I ignore the ache in my hand, and I ignore that my fist is getting bigger and bigger in my glove. I don't say anything to anyone, and when we start the third period, Mika is still not back. Word in the dressing room is that he's being looked at for a concussion. I don't give a rat's ass. I'm ending this game with another goal.

The third period is a joke. It's just hit after hit, and it's to see what they can get away with and what they can't, and we don't play that game. The hits keep coming, but we are ready for them, and when one of them tries to hit Evan in the middle of the ice when he doesn't even have the puck, he's had enough at this point. He throws his stick and his gloves down and grabs a hold of the other guy's shirt, punching him. Evan grabs him in a headlock, and they both fall to the ice. The referee tries to break them up, but Evan flips the guy on his back and knocks him two more times before they get him off him. "Pussy ass bitches," he says, smiling and wipes the little trickle of blood from the corner of his mouth. "Who's a pretty bitch now, cocksucker?" He skates backward toward the penalty box, smirking the whole way and chirping.

I get to the bench, and the coach comes over. "Matthew says stop fucking around and get that fucking hat trick." I just nod at him and look up at the replay. It's 2-0 for us with four minutes to go. "They are going to pull the goalie any minute, boys," he says, walking behind the bench. "Get the fucking puck into the back of the net, and let's get the fuck out of here with two points, yeah?"

I don't listen to him as I pick up the water bottle. When I squirt some into my mouth, I can't help but wince at the pain. I look around to make sure no one has seen me, and when it's my turn to get on the ice, I jump over the bench at just the right time. The goalie is leaving the net, and I intercept the pass and shoot it down the ice, scoring my hat trick. Right before the goalie gets on the ice and they have six men on the ice.

Evan stands up in the penalty box and hits the glass when I skate by. The last ten seconds of the game, the LA coach decides to put on his fourth line to start trouble. He then puts on the fighter of the team who starts to comes for Evan and me.

"You guys think you can come into our building," he starts chirping, and I have to look up because he's huge.

"And fuck you in the ass, Donnie," Evan finishes the sentence for him, and the referee comes over.

"Knock it the fuck off. You start something, and I'll throw your ass out of here," he tells us all.

"We've just fucked him in the ass," Evan says. "You might want to be gentle on him." I laugh, but Donnie doesn't, and he tries to grab Evan, but he doesn't get a chance to. We skate to the center ice and then they switch the center man for Donnie. And you know shit is about to go down. When the puck drops, the gloves drop everywhere. The horn sounds, and the referee throws up his hands.

"It's over," he says, pushing Donnie away from Evan, and then everyone skates off the ice.

"Well, that was fun," Evan says, walking into the room, and I put my stick there and slowly peel off my glove.

"I need ice!" I yell to someone, and the trainer comes over to look at my hand.

"What in the fuck?" he says, and then Matthew comes in to look at my hand.

"Stupid son of a bitch," he says, then looks at me. "Can you move it?"

I make a fist a couple of times. "Yeah, I'm good."

Then he looks at Evan. "Zara told me to tell you that you're and I quote 'you're a punk ass bitch and a stupid fucking idiot.'" Evan laughs. "Okay, boys, let's get home," he says, and for the first time in a long time, I can't wait to get home.

Thirty Two

Zoe

"I'M SO NOT talking to him when he gets home," Zara says from the couch beside me as we sit up way past our bedtime. I'm trying to get my heart to beat normally. It's the first time I've actually sat with her and watched the game. He's back in LA. "He is such an idiot."

We are watching the game, and I swear the number of times I almost threw up is over five. The minute he got hit in the back, I knew this game would not go well. I knew the tension was high, and he looked so much better than the last time I saw him. His eyes sparkled when he played, and when he scored, it took everything I had not to jump up and celebrate with him.

For the whole game, I heard Zara gasping and shrieking, and I pretended not to even care, but when Evan got into the fight, she rolled off the couch and dialed Matthew.

"Get him off the ice now!" she yelled into the phone

and then put it on speakerphone so I could hear Matthew laughing.

"It doesn't work like that, Zara," he told her. "Just let him do his thing."

"Let him do his thing?" she yelled. "I'm having his baby. He doesn't get to do his thing while I'm doing this thing."

"I have to go now," Matthew said.

"Give him a message. Tell him he's a punk ass little bitch and that he's also a stupid fucking idiot."

"I'll see if I can remember all that." Matthew laughed and disconnected.

"I'm not talking to him if he calls," she says, sitting down, and we both know she's lying. The announcer and the cameraman keep going back to Viktor every chance they get, and when they finally show footage from the last game he played for LA, and I sit here cringing for him. He literally fell into his own goalie after trying to get the puck right in front of him.

"Oh my God," Zara says. "That's hard to watch." I agree with her, and then for the rest of the game, they comment on his every single move. "It's like a brand-new player."

"Yeah," I whisper and put my head down on a pillow, and by the time the game ends, it's almost two a.m.

"This baby is going to be a night owl. I know it," Zara says. I get up to feel her belly, and sure enough, the kid is everywhere. "One more month to go and I can finally fucking see my toes when I stand."

"One more month and I can finally have my sane sister back," I joke with her, and her phone rings from beside her.

"I'm not talking to you," she says and puts the phone on

speaker. "Punk ass bitch."

"Sweetheart," Evan says. "I'm fine."

"I don't care if you're fine, Evan," she says. We all know she's lying, and he just laughs. "I'm not even kidding." Then she starts on him. "It's not WrestleMania; it's a hockey game."

"It's not even our fault. They are the ones who said they would make it rain," he huffs.

"How's Viktor?" she asks him, and I know she's doing it for me. I look up at her.

"He's been better. Fucker hurt his hand in the fight and didn't tell anyone, so now it's the size of King Kong's." I try to hide my feelings that I'm worried about him, but Zara just puts her hand on mine on her belly and the baby kicks. "Anyway, we should be home at eight. Go get some rest and rub the belly for me."

"I love you," she whispers, so I don't hear her, and I just smile.

"Let's get to bed," I tell her, turning off the television. Holding my hand out, I help her up the stairs. "Not going to lie. I'll be happy to sleep like a starfish tomorrow night."

"Lies," she tells me and slides in bed with me. When the front door opens, and I hear footsteps coming up the stairs, I open one eye.

"Morning, Zoe," Evan says quietly and walks right to Zara's side of the bed. He gets down on his knees and kisses her softly and then rubs her stomach.

"You're home," Zara says to him and then I feel the bed move. I get up and go to the bathroom and then when I come back out, they are both in the bed.

"This is really getting out of hand," I tell him, and he just laughs and hugs her closer. "I'm going to make coffee," I say and ignore the ping in my heart. Knowing that Viktor is at his place with a swollen hand, I wonder if he's found someone. I wonder if he has someone now who is there for him. Maybe he has met someone who is also like him, and they have more in common than we did.

I start my coffee, and the day is a blur after Zara and Evan wake up and leave. I have my own routine now, or at least, I say I do.

If I'm not at work, I try to hit up the gym and meet with Vivienne a couple of times but for the most part. I just stay home and try to binge a new series on Netflix.

Vivienne: Are you becoming a nun?

Vivienne: Why are you leaving me all alone with married people and all the sex they are having while I'm here thirsty?

Vivienne: Come back to us. It's not the same.

I answer all of her texts with my standard I'm exhausted and so busy at work. We all just communicate via text until it's time for me to attend another hockey game.

I don't want to go, and I tell everyone who is going to listen to me that I don't want to go, but Justin is finally in town to play against New York, so it's not an option. "Sorry, honey, you have no choice. Your father is already starting to suspect something, and it's just a matter of time until Matthew breaks."

"There is nothing to suspect, Mom," I tell her. "I'm busy."

"He hasn't seen you since the baby shower a month ago. You can't push it off." Okay, fine, it's been a month, but I have been busy. I've closed on over thirty-three houses. If I continue at this rate, I'll be the best-selling real estate agent in our firm.

"Fine," I huff. "I'll come tonight, but, Mom …"

"I know, honey," she says softly. "And the minute you want to escape, you can, but just let him see you."

I roll my eyes, not wanting to go, not wanting to sit there and know he's in the building so close to me and not be able to talk to him. I'm even getting annoyed with myself. I look for him when I go out, hoping to randomly bump into him. I watch every single freaking game just to get a glimpse of him and see that he's doing okay.

After the game in LA, he was injured for two days, and I found out from Zara that it was for his hand. I'm lucky that most of the home games have been during the week, so I have that excuse, but I can't do it tonight. Standing in front of the mirror, I look at myself. I'm wearing my blue jeans with holes in the knees and a white T-shirt tucked into the front and going long in the back. A brown leather jacket completes the outfit with matching booties. Zara sends me a text that she's outside, so I grab my purse and walk downstairs, turning off the lights and locking the door. The snow falls just a touch now, and when I get in the car, I look over at her, and she smiles just a touch tight.

"What's wrong?" I ask her, and the car starts to go.

"I've been having cramps," she says, and my eyes open. "But it's nothing strong."

"Since when?" I ask her, now starting to panic. "We should just go to the hospital."

"No, no," she says. "See, it's gone."

"What does it feel like?" I ask her, grabbing my phone to check Google.

"It's like the first couple of days when you get your period. Kind of like a little bit of cramps," she says, and I google that.

"I still have another week and a half to go," she says, and I look at her. "You can't tell anyone."

"Are you crazy?" I tell her. We get to the arena, and she grabs my arms.

"Promise," she says, and I glare at her.

"I swear, Zara, the minute that I think it's not okay, I'm telling at least Allison. She should know what to do, and if she doesn't, Karrie will. She has like a litter of children." I try to make a joke, and usually, Zara laughs at that one. This time, she just smiles.

"Are you having another cramp?" I ask her, and she lies and shakes her head.

We walk to the suite—at a snail's pace, I might add—and I'm rushing to get there for someone else to see her but when we walk into the box, Zara is all smiles, and she literally doesn't even show anything. "See," she whispers. "It was a false alarm."

"How many false alarms are there before the full-blown let's evacuate the building?" I ask her and look around to see if I can ask anyone else the question, but my father comes over.

"There she is," he says, grabbing me around my shoulders and pulling me in to kiss my head. "My beautiful girl," he says, and then my mother comes over, and the whole time, I watch Zara. I see the times she closes her eyes, and then her eyes find me as soon as they open. My heart starts to speed up a bit, and when the second period ends, she comes over to me.

"Don't freak out," she says softly. "But the cramps are back." I sit up now and look over to see if I can get Alison to look at me when Zara grabs my hand and groans. "That one hurt."

"It's okay," I say to her, and I see the pain and fear in her eyes. "It's okay. It's going to be okay," I tell her, and I swear I can feel her fear. "It's going to be okay."

The horn starts, and we know that the third period is about to start. "Oh my God," she says and then looks at me and then looks down.

"Holy shit, did your water just break?" I ask, and then I look around and see Allison watching us. "Her water just broke," I say louder than I planned to. So much for keeping my calm. Everything and everyone spring into action. My father comes over with a chair, and my mother comes over and grabs her other hand.

"We need to call an ambulance," Matthew says, grabbing his hair in both hands. "Get the ambulance."

"No!" everyone yells at him.

"She can't have the baby here in the middle of the suite," he says, and Karrie goes over to him. "Babe, she's going to have a baby," he tells her and grabs her close to him and kisses her head.

"Okay, we need a plan," Allison says, then looks at Zara. "How long have you been having contractions?"

"Um …" She starts to talk and then stops to groan. My hand goes to her stomach, and it feels rock hard.

"She was having them in the car on our way here," I tell Allison.

"Yesterday," Zara says. "I mean, I wasn't sure, and then, well, in the car, they came more regularly."

"How is your back?" my mother asks her, and I look at her confused.

"It's been killing me for two days," she answers and then stops for another contraction.

Allison starts, "Okay, Karrie, can you get the kids and make plans to get them home?" Karrie nods at her. "Mom and Dad are going to take you to the hospital."

"But you're coming, right?" Zara says to me, and I just nod my head. "You have to come with me."

"Um, hello, favorite aunt right here," I say and then look at Allison and Karrie. "Sorry." They look at me.

"Now you," Allison says to Matthew. "You are going to calmly go get Max, who is downstairs with the team, and tell him that you need to speak to him."

"I can do that," Matthew says at the same time Karrie says, "He's not going to be able to."

"What the hell is going on in here?" Max finally says when he comes into the room. "Why is there water all over the floor?" he says, and then he looks at Matthew. "We need an ambulance, and someone needs to get Evan."

"No!" Zara yells. "It's fine. I'm going to go with Mom and Dad and Zoe." She then stops and looks at me, and I breathe in and out and she mimics me. "It's twenty minutes, give or take, and by the time they put me in a room, he'll be there."

"Okay," Allison says. "Mom, Dad, and Zoe are going with Zara," she says. "Karrie, Matthew, and I will follow you. Max is going to bring Evan there."

"We came in one car," Matthew says. "Fuck, no more carpooling."

"Okay, so we are all going with Mom and Dad," Allison says and looks at Max. "And then you bring Evan as soon as he gets off the ice."

"Got it," Max says, and then we walk out with me holding one of Zara's hands and my mother holding the other hand. Zara has to stop on the way there, and Matthew looks like he's going to lose his mind.

"Can I just carry her?" he says to Karrie. "She's in pain, and it's …" Karrie has to stop him, and I see the fear and pain in his eyes when she holds his face in her hands.

"She's going to be okay," she tells him, and I have to blink away my own tears. "It's fine. She's going to make you an uncle again."

"But she shouldn't be walking," he says, and then Zara speaks up.

"Matthew," she says, looking at him. "Can you carry me?"

He doesn't say anything. He just walks to her and picks her up like she's as light as a feather. "It's going to be okay," he says, and she just nods and tries to keep her tears at bay but fails when she wraps her arms around his shoulders and tucks her head into his neck. "It's going to be okay, baby girl. I've got you," he whispers. She sobs out, and one of her hands go to hold her stomach.

"Son," my father starts, "not going to lie, but you need to pick up the pace right about now. Those contractions are about two minutes apart." Matthew almost runs to the car, and when we all get in, we hear the horn go off, and you know someone just scored. My father zooms out of the parking garage, and we make our way over to the hospital.

"Someone needs to get my bag," she says. "It's in my car."

"The car that is at home." Allison says. "We will get you the bag."

"I have one," I tell everyone. "At my house. I had one ready in case." Everyone looks at me, even Zara. "What? It was a backup."

She has five more contractions by the time we get to the hospital, and Matthew doesn't even wait for the car to come to a stop before he jumps out and goes inside for a wheelchair. Zara starts to get out of the car when a big one rips through her, and she almost collapses. Matthew and Dad catch her. She screams so loud I'm surprised security doesn't come out. She finally sits down, and another one hits, and now she groans. My father kisses her and then goes to park the car. We all run in, and everyone is asking for the maternity ward. I swear if anyone was looking at us flying through the lobby with Matthew pushing the wheelchair, they would stop and laugh.

We get into the elevator, and then she looks over at me and then at everyone else. "I don't feel so good."

"That's normal," Karrie says, and she just shakes her head. "If you're going to barf, then barf."

"It's not that. It's my stomach." We don't have time to answer as the elevator door opens. Matthew's phone lights up, and we see it's Max.

"Where are you?" he asks, and you can hear him pacing.

"Just got to the hospital. Where is he?"

"One minute left and it's done," Max says, and then Zara screams out again. "Text me the room number."

We get to the nurses' station, and the nurse rushes

around the desk and Zara sobs. "Something is wrong. It doesn't feel right," she says, sobbing. "I know something is wrong."

"Hey," I say to her, getting down next to her, my own tears coming out. "You are going to be okay," I tell her, and she just shakes her head. "I promise you everything is okay."

"How about we get her to the room and get her undressed?" The nurse pushes the wheelchair now, and we walk into the room. "Can you guys get her undressed, and you"—she looks at Matthew—"are you the dad?"

He looks at her with almost disgust. "That's my sister," he says, and the lady laughs, and his phone rings again. "It's Dad."

"Okay," she says to him. "You go get Dad." Then she turns to us. "Undress her and I'll get the doctor." Matthew runs out of the room, and Karrie and Allison try to get her up and start to take off her top. I grab her tights and pull them down, and I stop midway and look over at my mother.

"Is that blood?" Zara asks. "Why is there blood?"

"It's fine." I swallow down my fear. "I remember Allison had this also. It's like the plug or something."

"Yeah," Allison says while Karrie now runs out of the room. "Can we hurry up and get you in the bed?"

"Before another contraction comes," my mother says, and she wipes away the tears dripping out of her eyes now. The nurse comes back in, rushing with Karrie behind her, and she sees the blood trickling out of Zara onto the bed's white sheets.

The nurse runs over to the button in the back of the bed and presses it. "We need an ultrasound machine in room three ten," she says, and now she pushes everyone around Zara away as she puts on the monitor on her stomach. "This will get the baby's heartbeat and tell us how strong the contractions are."

"What's wrong with my baby?" Zara asks right before the contraction rips through her again and this time, more blood comes out. The sound of the baby's heartbeat fills the room, and I don't know about everyone else, but I sigh out in relief. And from the look on the nurse's face, she's happy also.

Matthew and Dad now come in the room, and Matthew gasps. "Why is she bleeding?" He starts to panic, unlike us, who were playing it cool. "There shouldn't be blood," he says. My father grabs his shoulder, and he quiets down.

Another nurse comes into the room with the ultrasound machine, and now my mother is standing beside him, trying to hide her tears. The doctor walks in and smiles at everyone, trying to hide the worry in her face also.

I stand next to Zara with my hand in hers as we share a look. "Hey, it's going to be okay."

I put my head next to hers, and she whispers, "It hurts so much, Zoe, and ..." She holds her stomach with the other hand as she has another contraction, and now the baby's heart rate goes lower than before. "Where is Evan?" she asks after the contraction.

"On his way," Matthew says. "He's on his way," he says and holds Karrie beside him who tries to hide the fact she's crying also.

The doctor puts the gel on Zara's stomach and then turns on the machine. "There is your baby," she says, and we all look at the screen, and Allison sobs out in happiness that the baby is moving. "Well, don't we have a stubborn little one. Your baby must have had a party in there and moved everything around."

"Oh my God, the head was down last week," Zara says.

"Okay, folks"—she turns the machine off—"we are going to have to do an emergency c-section to get the baby out."

"I can't do this without Evan," she says, and the contraction comes again. Blood now just comes out in a puddle.

"Okay, people, we need to get her in there," the doctor says, and the nurse moves everyone away.

"What's going on?" Zara asks and looks at me, and I just look at her and then I shout at the doctor.

"Someone needs to tell her what is going on!" I shout. "She is scared and about to give birth, and she should have some answers."

"Zoe." I hear Allison beside me, and I just shake her hands off me.

"Now can someone please tell her what is going on?" I say in a lower tone.

"Your baby has turned, and your placenta has detached, so we need to get your baby out of there now," the doctor says, and then they wheel her out of the room at the same time as Evan runs through the door. He's still in his full uniform; the only thing he took off was the skates and he's wearing his Adidas flip-flops with no socks.

"Evan," Zara cries, and he rushes to her. He looks down and sees the blood, and his face goes white.

"The baby."

"Everything is going to be okay." I follow her down the

hallway on one side while Evan is on the other side. We get to the entrance of the two doors, and it says authorized personnel only. "I promise you it'll be okay," I say to her, and the door closes in my face. My hand flies to my mouth to stop the sob from echoing in the hallway, and my legs suddenly give out, and I feel myself falling except I never hit the floor. Instead, I'm picked up into strong arms, arms that hold me close.

And through the tears and the sobs, all I hear is his voice. "It's okay, Zoe. It's going to be okay." I look up to see his blue eyes. "I've got you, baby," he says to me, and I don't question it. For the first time in a long time, it's where I'm supposed to be.

THIRTY THREE

VIKTOR

WE SKATE OFF the ice, and the minute I see Max's face, I know something is up. "Where's Evan?" he says, and his hair looks like he has been running his hands through it like a madman.

"What?" I ask and look behind me to see Evan coming off the ice. "What's wrong?"

"It's Zara," he says, and I'm already taking off my skates when Evan comes into the room, throwing his stuff everywhere.

"I have to go," he says and takes off his skates and slips on his Adidas flip-flops, and I do the same.

"There's a little bit of a problem," Max says, and I see the worry on his face. "Allison has the keys to my truck."

"Oh my God," Evan says, and he starts to panic and freak out.

"Mark!" I yell into the room for the goalie. "Zara is at the hospital; give me your keys." He doesn't even bat an eye and tosses me the keys to his truck.

"Let's go," I say and walk out with them.

"You don't have to come," Max says, and his phone keeps blowing up.

"You have that thing going nuts," I tell him, "and this guy can't drive anywhere because he's shaking," I say, getting into the truck.

"The only reason I'm shaking is because you assholes left me on the ice when she was in fucking labor," he hisses. "Did you not think it would be important to be at the hospital?"

Max gets into the back and closes the door. "What hospital?" I ask, and I plug it into the GPS.

"Her water broke at the beginning of the third period," Max tells him. "She didn't want us to tell you."

"Here's an idea," he says, turning in the front seat. "Don't listen to her."

"I was given orders, and I'm not about to fuck with a woman in labor." He puts his hands up, and the phone rings. "Matthew, we are on the way."

"Where is she? How is she?" Evan starts to freak out and grabs the phone from Matthew. "Let me talk to her."

"They kicked me out of the room," Matthew says, and I'm not surprised at this not one little bit. I'm surprised he lived to tell us about it, if I'm honest. "Um.' He starts to talk, and I hear the quiver in his voice. "You guys need to get here as fast as you can, okay?"

"Where the fuck is my wife, Matthew?" Evan yells now. "Put my wife on the fucking phone now!" he screams the last part. "I want to talk to my wife."

"Evan," Max says silently. "Why don't we get there, and you can see her for yourself."

"I swear on everything I have—"

"Don't," I tell him. "If there is one person who will take care of her, it's Matthew."

"I want to talk to her," Evan says softly. "I want to hear her voice."

"Evan," Matthew says, and you know he's crying right now. "You need to get your ass here now," he says, and he disconnects, leaving Evan just staring at the phone.

"She's fine," I tell him as I speed the whole way there. We get there in under seven minutes, and I run out with him. Security is there, and once he sees us in our jersey, he starts to fan all over us. "I parked my truck at the curve, can you take care of it?" I ask him and then turn to look at him. "Maternity?"

"Third floor!" he yells, and the elevator ride is the longest of my life, but it must be longer for Evan. He bounces on his feet, and the tears are in his eyes. He runs out of the elevator at the same time as I spot everyone, and then the gurney comes out of the room with Zoe standing beside the bed.

I don't know what is going on as Max stops beside Allison and takes her in his arms. I spot Cooper and Parker in the same position. By the time I look down the hallway, Matthew is giving me a nod to Zoe, and I start walking to her when her sob rips through her, and nothing will stop me from getting to her. I make it to her just in time to catch her.

"It's okay, Zoe. It's going to be okay," I say when I wrap my arms around her and bring her close to me. She must sense that it's me. She looks up, and I see the pain in her eyes, the fear, everything that she has gone through has led to this moment with her in my arms. "I've got you, baby," I finally whisper. She just buries herself in my neck, and my arms go around her waist. Her tears run down my neck, and all I can do is hold her.

"What is going on?" I finally turn and ask everyone. Cooper doesn't do anything except look at me with his eyes almost glaring at me. I know we will have a conversation at another time, and I'm ready for it.

"She started bleeding," Parker says, and then the nurse comes right out.

"If you want to wait in the waiting room, we will come out as soon as we have some news," she tells us, and Zoe now looks at her.

"Is she okay?" she asks her. "You need to tell me she's okay." I put my arm around her and pull her to my side.

"She's fine, but she is losing a lot of blood," the nurse says, then looks at Zoe. "I'll come out as soon as I know anything." She turns and walks back into the restricted area.

"We should sit down," Parker says, coming over to Zoe. "You should sit down."

"I'm not going anywhere," Zoe says, her eyes still on that door. "I'm staying right here."

"Do you want me to get you a chair?" I ask her, and she just shakes her head. "Someone get her some water or something," I start to say to Matthew, and she turns to look at me.

"I can't lose her," she says, and the tears pour out of her

eyes. "I can't lose her."

"You aren't going to lose her," I tell her, and I stop talking and start praying. I don't know how long we stay in that hall-way, but I never move away from her. I stand next to her, giving her all the strength I have.

We see Evan walking down the hallway, and he walks out of the sliding door wearing his scrubs. He's sobbing, and I grab Zoe. "We have a daughter," he says, and Parker sobs out along with Allison and Karrie.

"What about Zara?" Zoe says, her chest quivering as she tries to get the words out.

"They are taking her to recovery," he says, and then goes to Zoe. "She's going be okay," he says to her and takes her in his arms. "And wait till you see our little girl," he says, sob-bing with her. "She's so beautiful," he says, now smiling so big it's going to break his face. "I'm going to go and get her," he says, turning around and walking back inside the doors.

"Her clothes," Zoe says. "She needs her clothes." She looks around. "I need to go get her clothes."

"You need to stay here with Zara," I tell her. "I can go and get all the stuff. Just tell me where it is."

She looks at me and nods. It takes her a couple of min-utes to tell me where everything is because every single time the door opens, she stops talking, and the tears come again. "She's here," Evan says, tears running down his face again with a megawatt smile. The nurse pushes a cart on wheels with a clear plastic box on top, and in the middle, wrapped up in a white blanket and matching hat, is the baby.

Zoe just drops her hand, and her keys fall to the floor as

she walks over to the little bed. Her hand goes to her mouth as she cries out. "Oh my goodness, look at you," she says, and the nurse just looks at her with a smile. "Isn't she the most beautiful baby ever?" she says, laughing and crying at the same time. "You can lie." She stands, and Evan hugs her around her shoulder and pulls her to him and kisses her temple.

"She really is," the nurse says. "Mom is going to be out in thirty minutes if all goes well."

"Can I go and see her?" Zoe asks. "I promise not to be in the way." The nurse nods, and she turns around to look at Parker. "She's going to be okay." She rolls her lips to stop from crying and tries to smile, but the tears come anyway.

Parker goes over to her, followed by Cooper, and I stand in the middle of the hospital wanting to hold her. Matthew comes over to me and slaps my shoulder. "She'll be okay."

I just nod my head. "I should go and get the stuff," I say and then look at Parker consoling Zoe.

"Do you want company?" Max says, and I shrug. "We can get some coffee and stuff to bring back." He looks at Allison. "It's not like you guys are going to let me hold the baby now anyway."

Matthew's phone now rings, and he looks down and then up. "Did no one get Justin?" And just like that, everyone laughs. "Hello," he says, walking away from us as he answers the phone.

"So, get Justin, the bag, and coffee," Max says, kissing Allison and then looks at me. I take one more look at Zoe and then walk out.

We step onto the elevator, and both of us sigh in relief.

The security guard sees us as soon as we step out of the elevator and walks over. "Here are the keys. You are parked just to the right." He hands me the keys, and I just nod at him.

The doors open, and the crisp air hits us right away. "I don't really need to come back," I tell Max when we step out and walk toward the truck.

"You think that's a good idea?" He looks over at me, stopping at the passenger door.

"It's not time yet," I tell him and look down and then up. "It's not the time. I had a plan."

"Well, I hate to be the one to tell you this, but sometimes, plans change," Max says. He gets in the truck, and I follow him, getting in the driver's side of the truck. I start the truck. "Do you know the first time I saw Allison again, I ran right over her and then called her a bitch under my breath?"

I chuckle. "Did she not hand you your balls on a platter?"

"No." He laughs now also as I make my way over to Zoe's. "I mean, she definitely didn't like me much."

"But you won her over with your charm?" I ask him, and he just shakes his head.

"Fuck no," he says and then looks at me. "I didn't even know that I was in love with her until she showed up at a bar and saw me talking to another girl." He puts his hands up. "It wasn't my finest moment, but it made me see that she was the one. She is everything."

I don't say anything else as I park in front of Zoe's house and walk in. Without her here, I feel like I'm invading her space. "Do you want to run up and get the bag?" I ask Max, and he looks at me.

"Are you insane?" He looks at me. "What if I see her bra or, fuck it, something more personal? That is not my woman," he says and motions me with his head. "You go get it, and I'll wait for you here."

I walk up the stairs and then turn the light on in her room. I look around, and I can smell her all around me. I walk to her bed and see that her pajamas are in a puddle at the end of the bed. I pick it up and bring it to my face and smell her. I sit on the bed now and take in her private space. A space I've never been invited into, a space that is hers. Her little touches are everywhere. Pictures on the side table of her and Zara and another of her whole family that looks like it was taken at the baby shower. And then a little picture in the back of the ultrasound of Zara's baby.

I sit on the bed and wonder if I'm going be the one who will have this picture with her. Will I be the one who makes her my wife? Is waiting really going to change anything? Will our baby look like her? The thought of her having this with someone else makes my heart stop beating right.

"What is taking so long?" Max says from the doorway. He sees me sitting on her bed, still in my fucking gear from the game. "You okay?"

"No," I answer him honestly and put the picture back where I took it from. "Not in the least."

"Do you need me to call someone?" he asks, and I look up at him.

"What if she's with someone?" I ask him the question no one has answered for me or talked about. "What if she's dating, and she's with someone but hasn't told you guys?"

"She would have told her sisters," Max says. "Trust me,

she isn't with anyone."

"What if she doesn't want me?" I ask him. "What if all this is too much of a burden for her to carry or too much for her to handle?"

"You aren't giving her enough credit." He leans against the doorjamb.

"What if she freaks out when I wake up gasping for air in the middle of the night?" I ask him. "What if she gets tired of always wondering if I'm going to fuck up today?"

"What if she holds your hand during all that?" he counters. "What if she is the one who makes tomorrow a better day?"

"Yeah," I say. Getting up, I go into the closet and see all her clothes hanging, and then there in the corner is the Burberry bag she told me about. "We should go," I say to him and turn off the lights.

We walk out into the night, and the roads are almost empty. I park now, and I get out of the truck with the Burberry bag in my hand. It feels so heavy, and my mind is playing tricks on me, going back and forth about me being here.

But when I step off the elevator and walk with Max down the hallway and into the room, I see her turn to look at me, her eyes full of tears and a huge smile on her face while she holds her niece in her arms. I know that the decision was already made for me.

THIRTY FOUR

ZOE

THE NURSE TAKES me back to see Zara, and she looks exhausted. Her face is still very pale, and after she cries she wants her baby, I semi threaten the nursing staff until she was sitting in bed holding her daughter to her chest.

"You are so perfect," she says, kissing her hand. "Look at her," Zara says to me. "Look at her eyes." Then she takes off her hat, and we see that she has blondish hair. "I wonder if she is going to have our hair color." I don't say anything because I can't. The words are stuck in my throat over the huge lump. Zara looks at Evan. "Should we tell her?"

"Yeah," he says and smiles at me.

"I'd like you to meet Zoey with a y Richards," she says, and I put my hand in front of my mouth. "Aka your goddaughter."

"Oh my God," I whisper and go closer to her. Right before I am about to take her, the nurse comes back in.

"Okay, let's get you back into your room, so we can clear

out the hallway," she says. "We are going to make an exception for one hour, but then your family has to leave and come back tomorrow," she says, and I roll my eyes at her. She pushes the bed, and when the doors open, I see that everyone is exactly where I left them. Justin is now there in his suit, and he just looks at us and smiles.

"Figures you couldn't just give birth and be on the down low." He laughs and comes over to hug me, and I try not to cry. Matthew is the next one to come to me when the coast is clear.

"Are you okay?" he asks me quietly. "I know you two are two peas in a pod."

"Yeah," I tell him and hug him around his waist. "Not going to lie, I almost throat punched the nurse."

"We heard," he says, putting his hand around my shoulder, and we walk into Zara's hospital room.

My parents are beside her bed, my father watching my mother and Zara bonding over the baby. His chest is puffed out, which he does when he's super proud. Karrie and Allison talk in the corner with Justin. "Come and hold her," Zara says, smiling through her tears. Evan stands beside Dad, doing the same puffed-out chest.

I walk over, and my mother places Zoey in my arms, and I swear she reaches out of her blanket and waves at me. "What are you naming her, besides princess?" Matthew asks beside Karrie now.

"Meet Zoey with a y," Evan says, and my father laughs and hugs him around his shoulders.

"You never stood a chance," he says, knowing that even if Zara wanted to name her after the solar system, he would have gone with it.

"Hello, little Zoey with a y," I tell her while I rub her soft cheek with my finger, and she opens her mouth as if to say hi. I'm smiling through my tears as she blinks her eyes at me and opens and closes her perfect plump lips. I'm lost in the moment of having her in my arms. Lost in the unconditional love she brings out in me. I will do anything for her, and then I look over at the door and see him. He stands there in jeans and a jacket with a stupid beanie on his head and in his hand is the Burberry bag I packed as a backup. All I can do is smile. I don't know why he's here, but it doesn't matter. Nothing at the moment matters except for Zoey.

"Hey," he says softly, walking in beside me, then turning to look at Zara. "Congratulations."

"Thank you," she says, leaning back on the bed, her face showing her exhaustion.

"Thank you," I tell him when I see the bag in his hand. "You didn't have to."

"It was nothing," he says and then looks at the baby in my arms. "She's beautiful."

"She is," I say, smiling. "This is Zoey with a y," I introduce her, and he just smiles. Zoey starts to make noises now, and the nurse comes back in.

"Okay, folks," she says. "It's time to clear out. She can have two people stay with her." I look at my mother who just smiles at me.

"Mom, why don't you stay with her?" I tell my mother. "We can switch in the morning."

"Are you sure?" my mother asks me. "I don't mind coming back tomorrow either."

"Nah," I say, kissing Zoey, who is not happy at all. "You know what to do. I'll just threaten people to make it happen." I laugh, and my mother just shakes her head.

I hand Zoey off to Zara and then kiss her head. "Call me if you need me," I tell her and then hug Evan. "Text me if you need anything."

"Will do," he says and looks at Zara. We walk out, and everyone is making plans about where everyone is sleeping tonight. My head just replays everything that has gone on in the last four hours. "Zoe." I hear my name being called and look up at Viktor who is walking beside me.

"Sorry, what?" I ask and see that everyone has gone in their own directions. "Where is everyone?"

"Your father went to get his car," Viktor says. "I was wondering if we could talk." I look at him as he puts his hands in his back pockets. "I know now is not a good time, but there are things that need to be said."

"What?" I look at him. "We really don't have to do this," I tell him, my neck starting to get hot, and my heart speeding up. "I think I got the picture crystal clear," I say without thinking.

"That's the problem. You didn't," he says and then a honk stops him from talking. "I have to go, but we are going to have this conversation," he says and just walks away, leaving me standing in the middle of the sidewalk. As the night creeps by, my eyes never shut, and at six a.m., I finally give up.

I put on my shoes, and I leave a note on the front table. I've had enough of this wishy-washy bullshit, and it's going to stop. I get into the Uber I ordered when I made the plan in my head and thought this was a good idea. But now standing here and pressing the button, I want to turn around and run away, but it buzzes, and I walk into the lobby I said I would never go back to. Up the elevator that holds the darkest day for me.

My heart starts to speed up, my hands start to get clammy, and I'm suddenly worried he's there with someone. What if he wanted to talk to me because he's with someone else? My hand flies to my stomach, and I swallow down the bile that keeps rising.

The elevator door pings, and I think about changing my mind. I think about leaving and just denying I was ever here, but when the elevator finally opens, he's standing there in the middle of the hallway just looking at me. "Well, here goes nothing," I say, getting off the elevator.

THIRTYFIVE

VIKTOR

THE DOORBELL RINGS the second the coffee machine stops. I look at the clock over the stove and see it's a little past six thirty. I walk to the buzzer and buzz up the person. I wonder if maybe it's Mark coming to get his truck. I open the door and stand in the hallway, and when the elevator doors open, I see her. She's wearing black rubber boots with a sweater and a black vest. Even wearing a baseball cap, she is the most beautiful thing that I've ever seen. I suck in a breath when she sees me, and our eyes meet.

She walks out of the elevator toward me, and my heart just speeds up, and I swear I think I'm going to have a heart attack. "Um," I say, at a loss for words.

"Sorry, I couldn't sleep, and I kept replaying the words you said over and over in my head," she says softly. "Can we talk?"

"Yeah," I say, walking back and motioning to the apartment with my hands. "Come in. Do you want coffee?" I ask her, scared as fuck she'll walk into this room and see the scene from when she was here last.

"I can make a coffee, and you can go put on a shirt," she says, and I secretly smile, hoping that I have that effect on her. That she still cares for me and I haven't ruined what was the best thing I've ever had. I nod at her and walk toward my bedroom and grab a T-shirt and then walk back out while I put it on. She's taken off her hat and the vest, and she sits on the couch.

"Sorry to barge in on you," she says, and I go and sit next to her. I've sat next to her on so many other occasions, but something about this time is different. "Listen, I know that the last time we saw each other …"

"I really want to start," I say. She looks at me, and I have to get up or I'm going to grab her by the ponytail and just kiss her instead of saying what I need to say. "I've rehearsed this speech over and over in my head so many times, and now I'm drawing a blank," I tell her, and now I start to pace.

"Do you want to sit down?" she asks me, and I just shake my head.

"No," I say and shake my hands to get the nerves out of them. "I don't even know how to start this," I tell her. "There is so much I want to say, so much that I need to say, but …"

"But?" she says, waiting for me to continue.

"But it's not pretty. And you come from a family that's pretty and perfect."

"No one is perfect," she tells me.

"You," I finally say. "You're perfect."

"There is a reason that a recovering addict can't fall in

love the first year," I start there. "And that is because you replace one addiction with another." She blinks away tears. "I'm fucking this up." I snap my fingers. "When I first saw you, I was like whoa," I say, and she smiles. "But then the only thing I could think is look away."

"Okay," she says.

"But then I got to know you, and every single time, I ignored the pull, and then you gave me these gifts, and I knew I was in trouble." I look down and then up. "Even if I wanted to, I don't think I could have stopped falling in love with you." Her mouth opens now in shock. "And that kiss, that kiss has been the star of every single dream I've had since you left." I run my hands through my hair. "I didn't touch the drugs."

"Viktor," she whispers.

"No, if you hear anything else today, it's that I never touched the drug. Not that day. Not since I was clean." I rub my face. "Right before you walked in or the door opened, I have no idea, but I was standing there and the key chain was there, and it took me maybe half a second to think 'What the fuck am I doing?' Everything that I fought for was almost gone in that one second." I take a deep breath.

"You're strong." She moves to get up, and I hold out my hand.

"There is so much that we have to talk about and so much more that I want to say." I take a deep breath. "So much more that you need to know. But know this. I want you to be proud of me. I want you to be proud to stand by my side. I want to be the man you beam with pride at when you introduce. I want to be the man who holds your fucking hand because I can." I look up at the ceiling and then look down at her and see the tears running down her face. "There was a plan. I made a plan that I would come for you after I was sober for one year."

"How much longer do you have?" she asks as her chest trembles.

"Doesn't matter because I'm learning that some plans need to be altered. Some plans need modifications."

"Is this one of those plans?" She tries to smile while she cries.

"If you'll have me," I tell her. "We have to go slow because I'm not okay with fucking this up."

She gets up now and walks over to me. Standing in front of me, she's so close I can smell her.

"Can I talk now?" she asks, and I just nod my head.

"For the record, I *am* proud of you," she starts. "It's not easy to admit when you need help, and you did it."

"I didn't have anything to do with the first part," I try to joke, and she shakes her head.

"You went to rehab, and you stayed the whole ninety days. No one forced you to be there," she says. "So I'm proud of you and the man you are. I'm proud, so proud that you fight each and every day to stay clean. The struggle is not easy, but every day is one step ahead." She licks her lips. "I'm happy." She smiles at me, "Well, not happy, but I'm glad you see it."

"See what?" I ask her.

"That you are that man. The man who you want to be. You are that man already." She smiles, and my hand comes up and cups her cheek and my thumb wipe away her tears. "Viktor," she says my name. "This is when you kiss me."

"Are you sure you're ready for this?" I ask her, knowing there will be no turning back. "I don't know how it is going to go, but I know that I didn't go through the hell I went through to not have you in the end."

She steps in closer to me and puts her hands on my chest. She can probably feel my heart beating so fast. "I'm sure," she says. She moves her hands up my chest and gets on her tippy toes. I lean down, and it happens in slow motion. Or that is just how it feels in my head. Our lips meet, and I swear it is so much better than I remember. My hands go into her hair, pulling out the elastic from her ponytail, and her hair cascades around my fingers. I turn my head and slide my tongue into her mouth, both of us groaning the minute we touch. We kiss each other softly at first, and then I can't get her close enough. She is plastered to the front of my chest, and my cock is harder than it's ever been. I could spend all day lost in her kisses, and I'm planning on it. I'm lost in her kiss, in her touch, in everything that she is.

"So," I say, my lips lingering on hers, "are we going to do this?" Her eyes look up at me. "Dating."

"Yes," she whispers out on a sigh of relief. "I don't care what we call it as long as …"

"As long as we do it together." I kiss her lips again. "Are we doing this secretly?"

"I think the secret is out of the bag after last night." She tilts her head to the side. "But if you think we should keep it undercover …?"

"I'd rather not," I tell her. "If that is okay with you."

She nods her head. "It's more than okay with me." Her fingers go into the hair on the back of my neck. "How are you feeling?"

"Overwhelmed," I finish for her. "But in a good way."

"I'm dating Viktor," she says with a huge smile on her face. "I'm dating you."

"You are dating me." I nod my head. "What are your plans for the day?"

"I have to visit Zara, and then I'm open. What about you?"

"I want to attend a meeting, and then I was hoping that …" I say, and then she smirks at me.

"That I would come back over and continue this make-out session?" She winks at me, and it's just like her.

I throw my head back and laugh. "Yeah, that's exactly what I was thinking," I tell her and kiss her again.

"That sounds like a plan," she says and then I walk her to the elevator and kiss her before she gets in. "It's about time you got your head out of your ass," she says with a smirk. The doors close, and I put my head back and laugh.

I walk back into my apartment, and I can say it's the happiest I've been in forever, and now my phone is ringing.

"Hey," I say, answering it when I see it's Matthew. "Is Zoe with you?" he says, his voice going low.

"She just left, yes," I tell him. I'm going to have a conversation with him.

"Good. My father and I would like to come by and see you if you have time," he says, and I know exactly what they want to talk about.

"Come on over," I tell him. "I'll be here until about ten."

"We'll be there in ten minutes," he says, and he disconnects. Well, I guess it's going to happen sooner than later. I don't even think it takes them ten minutes when the buzzer goes off after I finally got dressed. I open the door when they knock, and I'm shocked to see Evan and Max are with them, too.

"Hey," I say and move out of the way as they walk in.

"I'm not here," Max says. "I'm here to make sure that one," he points at Matthew, "is okay."

I raise my eyebrows, and then Evan says, "I'm here because Zara says that I'm not allowed to go back until everyone leaves here." I shake my head.

"I'm here because my father wants to have a sit-down," Matthew says.

"Jesus," Max says, going over to the couch and sitting down. "You sound like he's the godfather or something."

"It's fine," I tell him and look at Cooper who hasn't said anything. "Can I get you something to drink?"

"No, I'm good," Cooper says, and I look at them.

"Do you want to sit at the table?" I ask, and suddenly, I get nervous. Maybe I should have called Jeffrey to have at least one person in my corner.

"That would be good," Cooper says and goes to the table and pulls out a chair. I sit in front of him and then look at Matthew sitting between us. I look over at Evan who goes to the couch and lies down. "I'm not here to start anything or get off on the wrong foot."

"I understand," I tell him.

"I thought she was okay," Cooper starts. "She was always busy, she did lots of sales, and her skipping the games was not unusual." I nod at him, and my mouth is suddenly dry. "Then with everything yesterday, it clicked into place." I let him talk, knowing he has to get it off his chest. "When you showed up at the hospital and took her into your arms, she let you. She clung to you."

"She was going to fall," I point out.

"Yeah, I got that, but you didn't let her." Cooper points at me.

I look down and then look back up. "I'm a recovering addict," I say. "First thing they tell you when you go into rehab is do not fall in love. Dating should be the last thing you want to do. And if I'm honest, I didn't want to fuck anything up." I look at Matthew. "I was given a second chance, and I didn't want to mess it up. I was finally able to see how much damage my drug use did to me and the people around me."

"Where does Zoe play into all this?" he asks, folding his hands on top of the table.

"I love her," I tell them without skipping a beat. "There is no question about how I feel for her."

"So now what?" Cooper asks me. "You love her, and she obviously loves you."

"I had a plan to finish my one year and then go after her." It's not a surprise.

"But now that plan has changed?" Matthew asks, and I nod at him.

"I think I'm strong enough to have her by my side and continue my recovery," I tell them.

Cooper shakes his head. "I don't want you to think. I want you to know."

"Then I know," I answer him. "I know that with her I can be the man she should have. I know I don't want to be with anyone else."

"All I want is for her to be happy," Cooper says. "I want a

man who will put her before anything else."

"He basically doesn't want you to fuck this up," Matthew finally says, and Max groans. "What?" He looks over at Max and asks.

"Seriously?" Max says, and Evan just opens one eye and then closes it back.

"Seriously, what?" Matthew asks him.

"Don't fuck this up?" Max laughs. "You think that is what your father is getting at?"

"He's beating around the bush, but yeah." Matthew crosses his hands over his chest. "Besides, you don't get to be a part of this conversation. You stole my sister," he says loudly.

Now it's Evan's turn to groan. "This again?" he says while Max laughs quietly. "They are married and have children."

"Doesn't change the fact he stole her." Matthew shrugs.

"Call it what you want," Max says, smiling big now, "because tonight I get to go home with my stolen property."

"Guys, I really get what you are doing here," Evan says. "My daughter is not even twenty-four hours old, and she's never getting married or dating. But you really think Zoe would let anyone fuck her over?" He looks at me now. "Not that you're planning to fuck her over."

"I get it," I tell them now. "I get all this, and I'm not going to lie. I'm scared shitless." I look down and then up. "I don't want to fuck this up. You know this," I tell Matthew. "She's the best thing to ever happen to me."

"That is all you had to say," Cooper says. "Now we have to get to the house or your mother is going to send out a search party," he says, pushing his chair away as Matthew does the same. Max smacks Evan, who jolts awake.

"Thank you," I tell him. "For giving me a chance to explain and for not judging me because of my past mistakes."

"We all have past mistakes," Cooper says. "It's making sure those mistakes stay in the past and don't mess up the future." I nod my head at him. "Now are you going to the hospital?"

"I'm going to catch up with everyone. I just need to attend a meeting first," I tell them, and I watch Cooper to see how he handles this. I don't know what I'm expecting, but his eyes don't change. They don't judge, and they don't drop down. He doesn't avoid contact; he just looks at Matthew. Evan mumbles he will see me later, and when the door closes, I grab my phone and text Jeffrey.

Me: Let me know when you're free.

He answers me right away.

Jeffrey: No time like the present.

Me: I'm hitting up a meeting at ten. Can you do it before?

Jeffrey: Just running out to drop off a couple of things. Meet you there?

Me: Great.

When I finally walk out, the sun is shining, and it seems a touch warmer. I make my way to the meeting a little earlier than planned, and Jeffrey is there waiting right outside the door. He is on his phone and his fingers are moving.

"Hey," I say when I get close enough, and he looks up at me. "I hope you weren't waiting for long."

"No, I just got here. I had to drop off some images to a client," he says. I found out not long after we started talking that he is a photographer. Retired now, but he's got some great shots out there in magazines that I've seen more than one time. He looks at me. "You look good."

"I feel good," I tell him honestly. "I didn't sleep well last night, but I have this sudden weightlessness to me."

"Really?" he says and looks around. "How about we go grab a coffee before we take in the meeting?" We walk to the coffee shop at the corner and go in, grabbing a table, the hustle and bustle quieter since it's past nine a.m. and most people have started their workday.

I grab a bottle of juice, and Jeffrey grabs a coffee. We sit in the corner, looking out the window. "What brought on this sudden weightlessness?" he asks, taking a sip of his coffee.

"Zara had her baby yesterday," I tell him with a huge smile on my face.

His smile matches mine. "Did she? What did she have?"

"Baby girl. Zoey with a y," I say, smiling, then looking down. "It didn't go as planned, and there were complications."

"Oh, no, is everyone okay?" he asks with concern. I fill him in about everything that transpired in the hospital.

"I went to her," I finally tell him, and I'm not sure if I'm ready for him to tell me if he agrees or not.

"And …?" He waits for it.

"And I knew at that moment I was done waiting. I was done with this whole rule about making her wait another two months. What if something happens to her, and she doesn't know how I feel? What if something happens to me, and all I want is her, but I was waiting?"

"The rules are there—" I put my hand up.

"I know why the rules are there," I tell him. "Trust me, I get it. I don't think I would be where I am today if I had started dating her six months ago." I take a deep breath and look up at him. "I'm not that person I was. They say you know when you hit rock bottom."

"You think you hit rock bottom?" he asks me quietly, leaning back in his chair.

"I don't think I hit rock bottom. I know I did," I tell him. "And I didn't just do it once. I hit it twice." He raises his eyebrows. "I hit rock bottom, or I was forced to admit I was at the bottom when I entered rehab. I accepted the help because I had no choice. But ..." I look out the window and blink away the stinging in my eyes. "When I lost Zoe because I let the wrong people in, because it was the old habit, that was my rock bottom. Having her walk away from me and letting her do it because I knew I wasn't strong enough was my rock bottom. I just did it sober, and I have to say"—I chuckle—"it sucked so much more than the first time."

"No one can tell you when the right time is for anything," Jeffrey says. "Everyone has their own journey with how they heal and grow from it." He leans on the table. "No one is going to tell you that you are wrong or that you're right. It is for you to know. You know the steps, and you know the struggle. No one else."

"Thank you," I tell him, and he tilts his head. "For not telling me what to do, but for listening."

"That's my job as your sponsor," he says. "It's not for me to sit here and dictate how you should do things. It's for me to help you be that person who you were always meant to be."

I nod at him and take a long sip of juice, and we sit here for the next little while talking about hockey, and when I sit in the meeting, I do it with different eyes. I do it knowing that it's a struggle, but I have the strength in me to do the right thing.

ThirtySix

Viktor

"ANY PLACE IN particular you want to eat at?" I ask her a couple of hours later. We walk out of the hospital holding hands, but not only that, I walk with my head held high. I'm proud that she is beside me.

"I just want to lounge around, so we can pick up something to eat and go to my house if you want?" she says, but I shake my head.

"Let's go back to my place," I say and then tell her why. "It's closer to the hospital if Zara needs you."

She smiles up at me like I hung the moon. "Oh, you're good," she says, and I lean down again and kiss her lips. Just a soft touch, but it's everything.

"Let's just go over to my place," I say, walking to the edge of the sidewalk and putting up my hand. "And we can Uber eats something while you relax." A yellow cab stops right there, and I open the door for her to get in, and then I get in next to her. I give the guy my address and then smile down at her. I'm not expecting her to be so close, but I'm also not expecting to want to touch her so badly. My hand comes out and cups her cheek and then she leans up and kisses me, leaving her lips lingering on mine for a bit. I turn my head just a touch, and my mouth opens at the exact time she slips her tongue into my mouth. We kiss the entire way to my house, not stopping or letting the other one go. We kiss softly and deeply the whole time, and my hand never leaves her face. When the cab driver clears his voice, I finally let her go, grabbing her hand and exiting the cab.

We walk into the house together, and she takes off her boots at the door and then shrugs her vest off and places it on one of the stools. "Do you want something to drink?"

"Water," she says, and she walks into the kitchen with me standing right next to me. "When are you going to order?" she asks me, putting her hands on my hips.

"Now," I say, smiling down at her as she bites her lip. "Why?"

"One, I'm starving," she says, her hands wrapping more around my waist. "And two, I would like to continue the kissing thing." She gets on her tippy toes right up against me.

"One, I can order right now, and two …" I lean down and kiss her with my tongue, picking her up and placing her on the counter. Her legs open so I can fit between them, and my hands itch to slip under her sweater. As I move my mouth from one side to the other, our tongues are dancing with each other. The kiss leaves us both breathless. "I need to order some food," I say, kissing her lips softly. "So we can eat." I kiss the side of her mouth. "We need to talk."

"More talking?" she moans, throwing her head back. "Fine. Order me food and then we can talk." She smiles. "And then we can make out."

"Is pizza good?" I ask her, stepping away but then going back to her when I miss her touch. I place the order and then put my phone down. "I spoke with Jeffrey today," I tell her and lean in to kiss her neck. She scrunches her shoulder and giggles.

"The beard tickles," she says. "What did he say?"

"I told him we're together," I tell her, then smile. "It was a great fucking day."

"Was it now?" She looks down. "How was the talk with my father?"

"Good," I tell her. "I mean, Matthew came with Max and Evan." Her mouth falls open. "It was fine. It was more of a what are you going to do."

"Jesus." She hides her face with her hands. "You aren't asking for my hand in marriage." She takes her hands off. "Right? You aren't asking me for my hand in marriage?"

I laugh now and kiss her, and she kisses me back, something that comes so naturally. "No, I didn't ask for your hand in marriage. But I did tell them my intentions."

"This is 2019, right?" she says. "I can date who I want."

"They love you," I tell her. "Accept it."

"I don't see your father calling me to talk to me," she says, and I laugh.

"My father would have to give a shit first," I say to her and then see her look at me with worry. "Don't get me wrong, I love my father, and he loves me, in his own way."

"What way is that?" she asks me, not judging or feeling

sorry for me but wanting to know

"From as far back as I can remember, he was always hard on us. Well, me. My sister pretty much could do what she wanted, but I had to play hockey. Had to. There was no getting around that one. He was always a coach before he was a dad. I had to skate harder and skate faster. We would have team practices, and he would yell at me the whole time." I shrug now. "It is what it is. I guess it made me the hockey player I am today." I smile at her. "So yeah, I thought it was a good talk."

"Nothing that has Matthew involved is a good talk. Last year, he had my father buy a summer home near Max's and then buy kayaks." She laughs changing the subject and I let her.

"What's wrong with that?" I ask her.

"It's in the woods. Like literally a hunter's cabin," she says. "They didn't even tell anyone; they just bought it."

"It's nice that he wants to be closer to Max," I tell her and try not to laugh.

"The kitchen is from nineteen forty-two," she says. "He had to gut the house and have one rebuilt or my mother was not going."

I shake my head. "Anyway, it was fine," I tell her. "Then I told Jeffrey, and then I went to a meeting."

"I'd like to go with you one day," she says quietly, and I try to hide my shock with a smile. "I mean, if it's okay." She then hides her eyes. "I mean, I don't want to pry and all that." I lift her chin with my finger.

"I would love for you to come to a meeting with me," I tell her, and she smiles at me with everything she has. The door buzzes, and I walk away from her to get the pizza, and by the time I turn around, she has the plates out.

"Where did you want to eat?" she asks, and I point at the table. She grabs the stuff and meets me at the table, and I open the top and we both grab a slice. While she's eating, Zara sends her a video of Zoey crying and then my phone pings, and she sees my screen saver. "What is that?"

"Nothing," I say and try to hide it, but she snatches the phone from me, and she sees that I made her my screen saver. You can't really see it with the apps in front of it, but her hair is everywhere.

She looks down and then looks up at me. "When did you take this?"

"New Year's Eve," I tell her, and then she just looks down at it and then up at me again. She puts the phone down and picks up her own phone.

"If you go into my pictures, I have a folder with your pictures," she tells me, and now it's my turn to be shocked. "I have only a couple I took of you live." She looks down and then up again. "The rest are taken from television."

"What?" I ask her, confused. She opens the folder, and I see that the pictures she's talking about are taken in her living room, and they are from the games I've played. "You watched the games?"

"Um, yeah," she answers like it was an obvious answer.

"You hate hockey," I remind her.

"I mean, I don't hate it, hate it." She rolls her eyes. "It grows on you."

"Does it?" I say. Now my heart is so full I wonder if it can possibly be this good. "Are you done eating?" I ask her, and she just nods her head. I push off from the table and grab her hand, pulling her up. "I fed you, so now it's time to lie on the couch and make out."

I lead her to the couch and sit down, pulling her down with me. But instead of sitting next to me, she throws her leg over me and straddles my lap. "This is much better," she says and takes my face into her hands. We both lunge at the same time, our mouths opening at the same time as we devour each other.

I pull out her ponytail, and my hands get lost in her hair while I turn my head to deepen the kiss. I let her lips go and kiss down her neck. She grinds her pussy right over my cock, and it's been so long I swear I'm about to come. "Viktor," she moans my name, and it's like an angel calling me. Her hands go around my head as I nip and bite my way down her neck and then my hand goes under her shirt, my fingertips touching her back. She groans as she moves her hips up and down, and I take over by flipping her to her back, her legs wrapping around my hips as my arms hold me up from crushing her. Her hands start to lift my shirt, and my body shivers under her touch. I stop kissing her and close my eyes just to feel her touch and relish in it.

"Viktor," she whispers, softly kissing my lips, then the side of my lips, and then trailing kisses down to my chin. Her hands stop moving, and she waits for me to look at her. I look down, and I see her eyes so, so clear they sparkle. Her lips are swollen from my kisses, and she has little red dots from my beard. "Hey," she says and moves one of her hands to my face.

"I pictured this," I tell her softly. "Us here like this." She smiles now. "It was my end goal."

"Really?" she says.

"Really," I say. "After you walked out, I swore that one day I would make you mine."

"You are really sure of yourself," she jokes, and I smile.

"I'm not going to lie to you," I say and kiss her. "I will never lie to you. I was scared as fuck you would move on and forget me."

"I tried," she says, and it hurts more than it should. "I won't ever lie to you either. I tried, and then I failed miserably. But I never told anyone. I just ignored that it was there. Tried to anyway and then I would turn on the television and pretend you weren't playing and then change to that channel." I smile now, and she rolls her eyes.

"You like me," I tell her with a smile so big that I think it's going to hurt my face.

"You could say that," she tells me, and I bend my head again this time, biting her lower lip and then slipping my tongue into her mouth. Her moan is swallowed by my mouth, we spend hours, literally hours, lost in the kisses. We settle on my couch on our side with her leg hitched over my hip. Her head is on my shoulder and my face is pressed down to her head when I tell myself I'll just close my eyes for a second. But all it takes is that second with my lips still tingling from her kiss and her hand on my chest for me to fall into the best sleep of my life.

ThirtySeven

Zoe

"I MADE YOU coffee," Viktor says when I come out of the bathroom after waking in his arms. I basked in it for as long as I could before my bladder let me know it was time to get up. Waking in his arms was everything. At first, I was unsure where I was until the memories of the past couple of days came rushing back.

"Hmm," I say, picking up the coffee and bringing it to my nose. "God, why does coffee smell so good?"

He doesn't answer me; he just laughs from the kitchen where he stands wearing the same thing he did yesterday. He reaches up to scratch his neck, and his shirt goes up just a touch, and I see that his pants are hanging low on his hips.

I close my eyes and take a sip of the coffee, and it's heaven on my tongue. "Good morning." I laugh and then see him shaking his head. I sit on one of the stools at the counter. "How did you sleep?" I ask him.

"Better than ever," he says, and I tilt my head to the side, trying to hide the huge smile creeping over my face. "I usually only sleep five to six hours a night."

"Why?" I ask him, the smile now slowly going away as I listen to him.

"It's part of being in recovery," he says, taking a sip of his own coffee. "Nights aren't always easy."

"What do you do when you have a hard night?" My mind runs wild, thinking about how long the night can be when you aren't sleeping. I didn't sleep well in the past two months, and the nights were the worst. Waking during the night and just staring into the darkness was the worst.

"I get up, sometimes watch television or surf the internet until my eyes get heavy again." His voice still soft. "Usually, I just replay everything over and over again."

"It's the worst," I tell him, and he just looks at me. "The past couple of months have not been good for me at night either." I look down, not wanting him to see.

"Look at me, Zoe," he says my name, and I look up. "I want to know everything."

"It's nothing. I should check my phone and see if Zara texted me," I tell him, trying to change the subject.

"No," he snaps. "You aren't going to change the subject that easily."

"I'm not changing the subject." I get defensive because I know that I'm changing the subject and he called me on it. I look at him, and he crosses his hands over his chest. "What?" I say, throwing my hands up. "It was just a hard couple of months. I was busy, work was crazy."

"Did it have to do with me?" he asks, and I roll my eyes.

"No," I lie to him.

"You're lying," he says, shaking his head. "What was it?"

"What was what?" I'm confused at his question.

"What kept you up?" he asks me but doesn't give me a chance to answer him. "I would wake up the minute I would finally get to you. The minute you would finally smile at me and I would go to you, my eyes would fly open." He sets his coffee down. "What was it for you?"

"The scene I walked into," I tell him softly. "The whole scene of opening the door and seeing you."

He shakes his head and rubs his face. "That is not something I'm proud of."

"I know that." I pick up my coffee to keep my hands busy.

"But it's a part of who I am, and a part of my recovery, so I have to take responsibility for putting myself in that situation."

"Do we have to talk about this?" I ask, my heart speeding up thinking about that scene and trying to erase it from my mind forever.

"Yes," he says. "Yes, we have to talk about it if it's bothering you so much that you wake from it."

"What is there to say?" I look at him. "What could there possibly be to say? It was awful, and heartbreaking, and I wanted to puke."

"And …?" he asks quietly.

"And what?" I put my hands up. "It made me angry that you fought so hard to get there, and that this temptation was there."

"The temptation is there every single minute of every single day," he says. "It's everywhere."

"But you're better than that," I tell him. "You are so much better than that. Than what I walked in on. I can't even imagine you being that person."

"But I was." His voice doesn't waver. "I was that guy who did nothing but chase my next high. I'm not proud of it, but that was me in all my glory."

"No." I slap the counter. "You said the right words. That *was* you. That isn't you now."

He comes to me now and turns me to face him, his hands going to my face. "Why are you getting mad?"

"I'm getting mad because I get that you were that guy," I say, taking a deep breath. "I get that that man is the reason you are this man. But I don't want you to have doubts about being this man."

He shakes his head, laughing. "You really are cute when you get all riled up," he tells me, coming and slipping his tongue into my mouth.

"I know that it's hard," I say between kisses. "And it's not pretty. But it's who you are," I tell him, hugging him now with my face in his chest. "And I love all of you."

He kisses my head. "I love you," he says right back to me. "More than you will ever know." I don't move and neither does he. I just listen to his heart beating, and I'm okay with it. I'm happy with it. My phone ringing is what pulls us apart. "That sounds like Zara."

"Who else would be calling me before seven a.m.?" I tell him and go to my phone, seeing it is Zara. "Good morning," I say chipper and then hear her burst into tears. "What's the matter?" I ask her, already grabbing my jacket.

"Zoey didn't sleep all night and I have no milk," Zara

starts to say. "Literally, my boobs are as big as cantaloupes, and I have nothing."

"What did the nurse say?" I ask her and then sit down.

"That it's normal," she says, and I look up at Viktor. "I'm just ... I need ..."

"I'll be right over, and I'll bring you some decaf coffee," I tell her, and she just sniffles.

"With some doughnuts."

"Well, obviously we can't have decaf coffee without doughnuts," I tell her and disconnect.

"Is everything okay?" he asks me, and I just look at him.

"Yeah, I think she's just tired and overwhelmed." I get up and grab my jacket. "I'm going to go talk her off the ledge."

"Do you want me to come with you?" he asks me, and I just shake my head. "Am I going to see you tonight?"

I tilt my head and smirk at him. "Depends if you play your cards right, Mr. Petrov," I say. Walking to him, I get on my tippy toes and kiss his lips. "Text me later and we'll see." He laughs. "What's so funny?"

"That you think you have a choice in the matter." He kisses my lips while I laugh and walks me to the elevator. "Text me when you get there."

"Oh, good God," I say, getting into the elevator and pressing the L button. "Don't you start with that man shit of telling his woman what to do."

He puts his hands on his hips. "Call it whatever you want to call it. Text me when you get there."

"No," I say as soon as the door starts to close. "I'll text you later."

"You better not." I hear him say right before the elevator

goes down. I walk out and hail a cab to the hospital, grabbing some coffee and doughnuts from around the corner.

"Good morning," I say, knocking on the door and going in to see Zara sitting up in bed with her head back, and in the middle of her open legs lies Zoey, who just looks around. Evan's sitting on the chair with his head back also with his eyes closed.

"Why are you wearing the same thing as yesterday?" Zara asks, and now Evan opens his eyes.

"I brought coffee and doughnuts," I say, ignoring the questions. "Who wants one?" I say, handing Evan a coffee and then giving Zara hers. "And how is my favorite little Zoey?" I ask her, and she turns at the sound of my voice. Her lips are so plump. "Aren't you the most perfect baby in the world," I tell her. Putting the doughnuts down, I go to wash my hands, then come back into the room. "Let me hold her," I say, grabbing her up from the bed and holding her in my arms while I walk around. "Good morning," I tell her, and she just blinks.

"So are we just ignoring my question?" Zara says.

"I have to be on the ice in two hours, and I'm going to die," Evan says, and Zara glares at him.

"You slept most of the night," she says to him. "Every single time I looked over, you were sleeping."

They bicker back and forth, and he finally gets up. "Give me a kiss. I have to go, and I'll be back as soon as I can." He stands over her. "Love you," he says softly, and she leans in and kisses his lips.

"Love you," she sasses to him and smiles. He turns around and walks over to me.

"Bye, baby girl," he says to Zoey and kisses her head. "I'm going to give you a high-five," he says to me. "Because one, you're wearing the same clothes you were yesterday, and two, I don't know what you did with that."

I shake my head and laugh. "Trust me, it's not anything like you think," I say, holding my hand up to high-five him. He shakes his head and laughs walking out.

"So," Zara says, "cut all this bullshit."

"Your mom is the most annoying sister of life," I tell Zoey. "Nothing to tell. I went over to Viktor's, and we made out on the couch, and I feel asleep there."

"That's it?" she says. "Nothing more. No hand magic or mouth action?"

"Nothing," I say and then look down at Zoey who starts to squirm. "And I'm not going to rush it."

"It's been six months of foreplay. How is that rushing it?" she asks me, and then Zoey turns her head to the side and tries to find my boob. "How can she be hungry again?" she shrieks, and I just shrug my shoulders. Lucky for me, my mother, Allison, Karrie, and Vivienne walk in at that moment.

"Well, well, well," Allison says, looking at me. "That outfit looks a tad familiar."

"I think so also," Karrie says, and now I glare at them.

"Oh, snap, is this the walk of shame?" Vivienne says. "But then is it really shame?"

"Good morning," my mother says to Zara and kisses her. "How are you doing?" She talks to Zara while Allison, Karrie, and Vivienne come over to me.

"So how was it?" Vivienne asks. "Is he all that and a big tall glass of ice water in the desert heat?" she asks, and Allison and Karrie just look at her, shaking their head. "I haven't had sex in seven months. Seven months. I'm dry and so thirsty."

"Is anyone going to tell me why she hasn't had sex in seven months?" I ask while Allison grabs baby Zoey from me.

"No," Vivienne snaps with her voice low. "No one needs to know. It's just a bump."

"I bet you would like to bounce on that bump all night long." Karrie says to her, and Vivienne closes her eyes. "I swear the next time she has sex she's going to be like a virgin boy going off as soon as she's touched."

"From your lips to God's ears," she says, and the next couple of hours are spent with us passing Zoey around. I leave before everyone else and make my way home, grabbing my phone and checking my messages.

Viktor: Why didn't you text me?

Viktor: I'm waiting for an answer, Zoe.

Viktor: This will be discussed tonight in detail.

Viktor: I'm going on the ice, and by the time I get off the ice, I want you to check in.

I roll my eyes and then finally answer him.

Me: Oh my God. Made it to the hospital, going home now. I have a showing at four, so I'll be working from home. You can call me when you can.

I'm not home for more than two hours when the doorbell rings, and I run down and open it, not expecting it to be Viktor with two boxes in his hand and a bouquet.

"What in the world?" I ask him, stepping back, and he comes in, dropping down the boxes on the table and the flowers and coming over to me.

"You didn't call me?" he whispers and then picks me up, and my legs wrap around his waist. "I told you to call me." I'm breathless from him being here, I'm breathless from being in his arms, I'm breathless yet want nothing more than to get lost in his kisses, again. "I waited for your call," he says, walking through the house and to the couch. "I checked my phone five times in two minutes."

"Antsy, aren't we?" I joke with him, but then I see his eyes are a dark blue. He isn't laughing at this. "I was fine."

"But I didn't know that," he tells me. "I spent the past two months not knowing anything about you. I didn't know if you were okay, where you were, or who you were with. I knew nothing."

"But ..." My voice dips down soft.

"But can you just give me this?" he asks me. "Please." And everything in me melts. "Just give me this one little thing."

I look into his eyes getting lost in the depth of the color. and I nod. "Okay," I say right before he claims my mouth.

THIRTYEIGHT

VIKTOR

"WHAT ARE YOU doing?" I ask Zoe when I finally make it to the hotel room and call her. The past three days have been some of my best days yet. I'm either at the rink or with Zoe, and I swear my step is even lighter.

"I just got home," she says, and she sounds tired. "They let Zara go home today, so I helped bring her home and set her up." Evan was not pleased to be away and find out that Zara and Zoey would be headed home without him. He thought they would discharge her tomorrow when we get home, but she and the baby are doing so well, they let her go.

"Why didn't you just sleep there?" I ask her, settling under the covers and then taking my phone and pressing the FaceTime button.

"Are you FaceTiming me?" she asks, surprised.

"Are you going to answer it?" I ask, laughing at her.

"Simmer down, big guy," she says, and I see that it says it's connecting. Her face fills the screen, and I see she's lying in the bed on her side. "Hello there," she says softly with a smile on her face. "Aren't you a sight for sore eyes?"

"You look beautiful," I tell her, turning on my side also.

"Are you still dressed?" she asks me, and I nod my head.

"Yeah, I just got in and called you before it got too late." We played Dallas tonight, and tomorrow we are off to Boston and then finally home for our last game of the season on Saturday.

"You played good tonight," she says, and I laugh now.

"Look at you now being all in the know about hockey," I joke with her, knowing she usually never watches it.

"I'm not a professional, but I do know when you did good and when you didn't." She laughs. "Like when you passed in the neutral zone and then it got intercepted and then you have a three on one."

"Jesus." I shake my head.

"Okay, fine, the guy on the television said it, too." She smiles, and her eyes get lighter. "But I did agree with him," she says and then her voice goes lower. "When are you coming home?"

"Friday," I tell her. "Morning, if I'm not mistaken."

"I miss you." She tucks her hand under her chin. For the past two nights, we've fallen asleep after hours and hours of kissing. The nighttimes are not as hard when she's there, but I wonder if it's because I feel finally strong enough.

"I miss you more." My voice goes soft.

"So you think when you come back on Friday, we could, you know, get acquainted with each other?" She winks at me, and my eyebrows pinch together. "I love kissing you, and I love being in your arms, but ..." She takes a deep breath. "But I want to get naked with you. I don't want to force you or, I don't know, mess up all the recovery stuff. Is it okay for you to have sex?" She starts to talk to herself, not letting me in on the conversation. "I don't want you to get into trouble, or for you, I don't know, to get addicted to something else."

"Baby," I say softly, and she just looks at me. I have only called her baby one other time, and that is when she cried in my arms. "There is nothing more that I want in this life than to get naked with you. But ..." I say, and her eyes open.

"You know but is never a good thing, right?" I can sense the nervousness in her voice.

"As I was saying ..." I smirk. "But I want to do the dating and show you how awesome of a boyfriend I am."

"Um, it's been six months of foreplay," she huffs. "Six months of wanting to get you naked. I think it's safe to say you are an awesome boyfriend, and you'll be even awesomer if we can get naked."

I laugh. "I don't think awesomer is a word."

She throws up one hand and slaps it back down on the bed. "That is the only thing that you took from that conversation?"

"Can we table this conversation until I get home, and I can touch you while we talk?"

She shakes her head. "Do you or do you not want to see me naked?" she asks and doesn't give me a chance to say anything when her voice gets a touch higher. "Do you or do you not want to touch me while I'm naked?" Just the thought of her naked and under me has me rock hard, and

I swear I feel like my cock will bust my zipper.

"Baby," I say softly.

"No, Viktor, no, baby," she huffs. "Friday night, I will let you take me out and then we can say we went on a date and then you are going to take me home and we are going to get naked."

"Is that so?" I joke with her, and she looks at me and glares.

"That is so!" she shrieks. "Now I'm going to go to bed where I'll be meeting you in my dreams." Her voice goes lower now. "Where we will be on a beach and both naked." I laugh out loud to the last part. "Now good night. Text me if you can't sleep."

"Love you," I say to her, and her eyes go soft.

"I love you, too," she says and disconnects.

The next two nights are not as bad as I thought they would be. We talk during the day whenever we are free, and we dance around the subject of sex. When the wheels touch down in New York, I grab my phone and see that it's ten a.m.

Me: Just landed.

I text Zoe and then grab my bag to walk down the steps of the plane. "Where are you off to?" Matthew asks me as I walk toward the waiting line of taxis.

"Probably home," I tell him and look down when my phone beeps in my pocket.

"Rest up. Tomorrow is a big game," he says, walking toward his car. "We might already be in the playoffs, but it's always good to win against one of the six OG's."

I pull out my phone and see a text from Zoe.

Zoe: Why don't you head over here before going home?

Me: I could do that.

I answer her back and see the three dots come on screen while I get into a car and give them Zoe's address.

Zoe: You could, and you should.

Me: In the car, be there in twenty.

I scroll through my emails to see if I need to see anything. I see a couple from Candace about my Twitter account and my suggestions. We pull up to the house, and I get out of the car, grabbing my bag. I walk up the step and ring the doorbell looking around and then seeing her come down the stairs and I start to smile. My heartbeat speeds up just a touch, my palms get clammy, but I can't stop the fullness I feel in my chest.

I hear the doors unlock, and the smile now gets bigger and bigger, knowing I'll see her. But when she opens the door, the smile goes away. It falls from my face because she stands there wearing what is a white knitted sweater that falls off her shoulder, and you can totally see she isn't wearing a bra. Her nipples are hard, and the sweater falls, covering her but just barely. I stand here with my mouth hanging open at this point. I move my eyes from the top of her head all the way down past the measly excuse for a shirt and see her long lean legs naked. She stands there on her tippy toes, and I storm inside, charging right for her. My hand goes around her waist. "Welcome home," she whispers right before her hands go around my neck, and I take her mouth. I've missed her more than I cared to admit. I've missed her kisses, her laugh, her scowl. My hand goes into her hair, pulling her head back so I can attack her neck.

She moans, and I walk into the house, stopping in the entryway and pushing her back against the wall. "You're naked under this," I say breathlessly, my fingers going to her cheek and then trailing down her chin to her clavicle and then her shoulder. Slowly moving my finger down, I go over her hard nipple and then go around it. She shivers under my touch, her chest rising and falling as fast as mine. My finger trails down the middle of her chest, our eyes both looking at the way my finger is moving.

"I said I would go slow," I whisper right before I get to the hem of the sweater. "I lied," I say. Dropping to my knees, I pull up her shirt and come face-to-face with her pussy. My mouth opens, and I lean forward and suck her into my mouth.

The taste of her on my tongue makes me close my eyes. My tongue licks between her lips, and I swear she's the sweetest thing I've ever tasted. I throw her leg over my shoulder and suck her in again. This time, she moans and arches her back against the wall. One hand goes to my hair where she pulls it and pushes me to her. My tongue comes out to flick her clit, and she silently groans, making me even more frantic. The sound of her moaning in ecstasy because of me pushes me over the edge. Her hips move up and down ever so slowly, looking for my tongue.

"Viktor," she says, and it's the hottest thing I've ever heard. Her voice panting, my hand comes up to her clit as my tongue and my finger now tease her. It's too much for her because her hand pulls my hair harder. "Oh my." She stops talking now when I rub my finger down her wet slit and enter her with my two fingers in one motion. Her pussy is soaking my fingers as I fuck her against the wall. My tongue is sucking in her clit as my fingers take her over the edge. My eyes look up when I know that she's a second away from coming and I take in her beauty. Her head against the wall, her hair loose but her eyes, her eyes have clouded over now as she stares into mine and with my name on her lips she comes all over my fingers. "Viktor," she chants my name repeatedly. She rides it out, her hips moving in sync with my fingers and then slowly her hold of my hair loosens.

Her leg falls off my shoulder, and I stand now just looking at her, but she grabs me and brings my mouth down to hers. Her tongue mixes with mine as she tastes herself on my tongue, and my hand goes to her ass where I grab her and pick her up. Our mouths move right to left as we frantically kiss. "Where am I going?" I ask her between kisses.

She lets go of my mouth only to answer. "My room." I walk up the stairs to her bedroom, and I'm lost in the smell of her. I'm lost in her kisses; I'm lost in everything that is her.

As soon as I walk into her room, she slips out of my arms and her hands move up my chest to my shoulder to slip off my jacket. I'm watching her hands so intently I don't even notice that she is getting lower and lower until her hands are on my belt. She slips it out of its loops in record time, and in a blink of a second or maybe longer, I have no idea, the sound of my zipper is the only sound in the room. It is not me breathing because I'm not. My pants slip off my hips or maybe she pushes them off. My eyes are on her mouth as she pulls down my boxers, and my cock springs free, but only for a minute before her hand fists the shaft, and she takes me into her mouth.

The heat of her mouth and the wetness of her tongue make my eyes close on their own. My hand goes into her hair, and I hold it in one fist while she tries to take me all the way down her throat. My eyes open, and I watch her take me, her head bobbing up and down as my cock disappears into her mouth. Her hand moving in motion with her mouth, and then she looks up at me. Her eyes darker than I've ever seen them, and I look at her other hand between her own legs. "I don't want to come in your mouth the first time," I tell her, and then she slowly moves off my cock, and I think I'm going to get to finally sink inside her. But she just goes to the right and then licks my cock from the shaft to the tip and then taking the tip into her mouth, she sucks it in. She does it two more times, and I swear I feel my balls start to tighten. I know it'll be one more time before I come on her face or in her mouth, and I don't want to do that. I move back, and she moans.

With my hand in her hair, I guide her up to me slowly and then tilt her head back and attack her neck. "I said I want to come in you," I whisper to her. "Me planted all the way in you." Her eyes close, and I know she's still playing with herself. My hand finds hers, and she is slowly rubbing her own clit. I bring her hand to my mouth and suck off her two fingers in my mouth, tasting her again.

"You are wearing too much clothes," she says. "I want to see you naked." My hand releases her hair as her fingers pull my tie loose and drop it to our feet. Her tiny delicate fingers open one button at a time, and it's agony. I just want to rip them open and toss her on the bed. "Next time," she says with a smirk, "how about you just wear a sweater like me," she says and peels the sweater over her head, and I step back. Her body is so defined and perfect. My cock gets even harder, and right now, I think I'm going to fucking come without her even touching me. I bend my head, taking one of her pink pebbled nipples into my mouth, and she moans as her hand lowers to my cock. I do the same thing with the other nipple, and this time, her hand squeezes my cock. Her nipple slips off my tongue while I moan. "I thought you wanted to come in me?" I rip my shirt off now, and the remaining five buttons go flying.

I push my pants down my legs, kicking off my socks and shoes at the same time. "Oh my God," she whispers, then steps to me. Her finger tracing across my ribs where my tattoo is.

Grant me the serenity to accept the things I cannot change,
The courage to change the things I can,
And the wisdom to know the difference.

She leans down and kisses me right there, and then she looks up at me, and I push the hair away from her face and kiss her lips. I back her up until her knees hit the bed. "Condom," I tell her and turn to go to my pants. She stops me, her hand grabbing my arm.

"How long?" she asks.

"Since I've been recovering," I tell her. "The same day."

"I'm clean," she says, and I know what she's saying. "And I'm on the pill." So I turn back to her and pick her up and place her in the middle of the bed. She opens her legs for me, and I see her glistening pussy waiting for me.

I get on the bed on my knees in the middle of her legs. "Are you sure?" I tell her, and she doesn't answer me. Instead, she takes my cock in her hand and rubs it up and down, then positions it at her entrance.

"I'm sure," she says, and I lean down on my arms and take her mouth at the same time that I slide into her. Feeling everything, every single thing, I let go of her mouth so I can moan. The feeling of her snug around me has me throwing my head back at the same time as she arches her back. I lean down and suck on her neck, my cock coming out of her. Then my hips move on their own, pounding into her.

Her hips move higher on my hips, and I slip in deeper. "Viktor," she pants, and I move one of her legs to my shoulder and then slam into her. So fucking deep and so fucking hard, my balls slap her ass. I stop and look to make sure she is okay, but she just lifts her hips to get me moving again. "Harder," she says, and I don't go easy on her. I wanted to slow it down. I wanted to cherish every single minute, but she doesn't let me. "Harder," she keeps saying, and I watch her eyes roll back when I don't go easy. Her hand slides between us, and she starts to move it over her clit in frantic circles. "Don't stop," she says, and I couldn't even if I wanted to. "Don't stop," she says again and again as I watch her pussy take my cock. "I'm there," she says, and I know she's there because her pussy has become like a vise. I can't even take it all out anymore. I only take a couple of inches out and continue pounding into her. My balls start to get tight at the same time as she moans out my name, and her eyes find mine, and she comes all over my cock. Her pussy gets tighter and wetter than before, and I slam into her one more time, and I come at the same time she squeezes my cock again.

I lean down and take her mouth and turn to the side, so I don't squash her. "That was …" I say, my chest rising and falling.

"That was good. Let's do it again," she says and leans up, kissing my neck. "I mean, you're still in me." I shake my head. Only she would get me to have the orgasm of my life and then laugh.

THIRTY NINE

ZOE

"ZOE," VIKTOR HISSES while I sink down on his cock with his hands on my hips. We just got out of the shower, and he worked me up so much, I thought I was going to combust. I didn't even dry off when we came out, and I thought about pushing him down on the cold floor, but instead, I dragged him to the bed and pushed him down on the bed, wet and everything. I didn't care; the only thing I could think of was having him in me.

"Yes," I hiss when I finally have him all in me. We've already had sex four times since this morning, and it's now almost after seven. We did nap, but that ended with him slipping into me from the side when he woke up with me grinding on his cock.

He doesn't say anything to me as I ride him, his hands moving to my bouncing tits. He lets me lead this time. I put my hand down on his chest as my hips move up and down on him. My face next to his as I have my way with him. His hands roaming from my tits to my ass. "Fuck," he says as my pace picks up. "Slow down, I'm going to come."

"No," I pant out. "I'm almost there," I tell him. He licks his finger the whole time his eyes remain locked with mine, and then he slips it between my legs and plays with my clit. It is all I needed to push me over the edge. He watches me as I come on his cock, Waiting, I can see his eyes getting dark, so dark they look black. My hips move slower now, but his cock is still hard like a rock.

"You done?" he asks. I move my head over and bite his lower lip, and that is the end of him waiting. In one fluid motion, he pulls me off his cock and flips me over, standing behind me now. He grabs my hips and slams into me. My face to the bed, my ass in the air as he slams into me over and over again. I've never wanted it as hard in my life, and I've never craved it this much. It's never enough; he doesn't say anything and neither do I. I just ride the wave over and over again, and when he tells me he's coming, I wait for it, and he doesn't disappoint. He slams into me so hard that if his hands weren't holding my hips, I would fly off the bed. "Jesus Christ," he finally says, panting, and I giggle. He playfully smacks my ass, and I look over my shoulder at him. "Don't give me that look. I need to hydrate, and you need to put some clothes on."

I shake my head and sigh when he finally steps back, and his cock slips out of me. He walks back into the bathroom, and I hear the water running. I turn on my back and see that we've left puddles of water all over my floor when I pulled him to the bed. He comes back out with a white rag and looks at me. "Let me clean you," he says, and I close my knees and sit up.

"I can clean myself," I tell him, and he laughs, handing me the rag. I walk back into the bathroom to, then grab a towel to mop up the water in the bathroom. I'm surprised when he's already cleaning up the water in the bedroom, and he's wearing his boxers.

"Thank you," I tell him, and he comes over to me and kisses me on my lips.

"You have a rash all over your face," he says, and I have no doubt I have little red marks from his face. "I'll shave."

"No," I tell him and then look down at his boxers. "Are you leaving?"

"Yes," he says, and my heart sinks just a little. "We both are, so pack a bag."

I cross my arms over my chest. "Excuse me?"

"I have to go to my place, and you can't come naked, and you aren't coming home, so pack a bag," he says as if he just didn't order me to do something.

"Did you just order me to pack a bag?" I ask him, and he grabs his pants.

"I can pack one for you if you want," he tells me, sitting down and putting on his pants. "Just get dressed and I'll throw something in a bag."

"Did it ever occur to you to ask me to come?" I tilt my head and go into the closet and put on a bra and panties set. "What if I'm busy, or I have work to do?"

"Then you bring it with you," he says, grabbing his shirt off the floor and buttoning only the top half of it. "Either way it ends with you coming with me."

"Again," I say, "did it occur to you to ask me?"

"It did," he says, smiling, and then I look at him confused. "Right before"—he points at the bed—"I said are you sure about this."

"That was during sex," I say, throwing up my hands. "How does it mean you tell me I'm coming to your house?"

"Do you think that the first night we finally sleep together I would go home without you?" he asks, shaking his head. "Now do you want me to pack, or do you want to do it?"

"I can't believe I'm actually entertaining this," I say, turning to go in the closet and grabbing the bag. I mean, who am I kidding? I would have gone anyway, but he could have asked.

I feel him behind me, and his hand comes up to cup my breast. "I really like this bra," he says softly. "And I'm happy you're coming home with me." His head comes down, and he kisses my neck softly. "Don't forget to pack stuff for tomorrow and Sunday."

"How long am I coming over?" I ask him, turning my head and kissing his lips.

"We'll see. Worst case, we can come back here on Monday." I kiss him. "I'll go order a car," he says, walking out, and I do what I'm told. I pack a bag with clothes until Tuesday. I grab my laptop and planner, and I walk downstairs. "He should be here in five minutes," he says from the doorway. We walk out of my house and into the car, holding hands and then do the same thing once we get to his house. He orders food while he makes space for my stuff in his closet.

We eat at the table and clean up together, and when I slide into bed wearing one of his T-shirts, I have to say today's been one of my favorite days ever. He slides into bed next to me, wearing boxers, and grabs me, pulling me to him. We start kissing, and just like that, we are both naked again. I straddle him again, and this time, I lean in and kiss his tattoo.

"When did you get this?" I ask him, and he looks down.

"Two days after I took control of everything," he says, looking down at it. "I repeat those words every single day at least once. Figured seeing it would help the journey."

I look down and trace the letters with my finger. He grabs my face with his hands, and we make love. Slowly, slower than before, and we do it while kissing the whole time. When I fall asleep in his arms, it's the most peaceful sleep I've ever had.

I wake up to the empty bed in the morning, and when I reach out my hand and feel the bed, it's still warm. A little light comes in from the shades. I stretch and then grab his T-shirt that got tossed during our last round of sex. I walk into the hallway and see him there at the island sitting on a stool drinking his coffee. "Morning," I say, going to him and kissing him on his shoulder.

"Morning, baby," he says, looking at me with a smile on his face. "Did you sleep well?"

I nod at him and walk into the kitchen and make myself a coffee. "Did you sleep okay?" I ask him, and he just nods.

"Better than ever," he says, and then I smile at him.

"What are you doing?" I ask him, looking at his computer in front of him.

"I'm going to email Candace a couple of things, and then I want to attend a meeting," he tells me. "You want to come with me?" he asks me. "I have to get to the rink by four, so I wanted to hit one at around tenish," I look over at the clock and see that it's just past eight. "Want to get some breakfast before?"

"Yeah," I say and take a sip of coffee. We walk out of the house holding hands and then eat at this little diner next to his house.

"Are you nervous?" he asks as we head to the meeting.

"A little bit," I tell him the truth. "I don't know what to expect."

"It's easy," he says, and then brings our hands to his mouth and kisses my fingers. "Relax."

We walk through the door on the side of the building and then down the stairs. It smells old and stale, and when we walk into the room, I see a circle of chairs. Some have already been taken. "Maybe …" I tell him, and then I stop talking when he sits down and nods at the guy next to him.

"See you brought a friend," he tells him and then smiles at me. "I'm Patrick. Welcome."

"Zoe," I say, reaching out to shake his outstretched hand. "I'm excited to be here."

He leans into Viktor and laughs. "It shows she isn't in recovery." My eyes open wider, and my stomach sinks. "I'm just playing with you," he says, laughing, and I shake my head.

A couple of more people come in and sit down, and Patrick greets everyone. They go person by person, and their stories hit really close to home. The struggles that everyone goes through. The darkness and the dread. I reach out and hold his hand so tight during it all, I don't know if I hurt him or not.

"My name is Viktor," he starts. "I've been clean now for almost ten months." I look at him and beam with pride. "Today was the first time I didn't think about the drug when I woke up."

My eyes never leave his. "It's been less and less as the time has been going on, but I didn't even think about it when I was making my coffee." People clap and then I look down, trying to blink away the tears. "I mean, it's not every day, but today, it was really, really good."

I look at him and smile, and he just looks down. When it's over, I say goodbye to Patrick, and then we walk out. He looks at me. "You okay?"

"Yes," I tell him, not wanting to burden him, but then I stop. "No, I'm not. I'm angry that you struggle every single day. I'm angry that everyone in there"—I point at the church—"struggles every day."

"Hey," he says, coming close to me. "That struggle led me here. That struggle made me see what type of man I want to be, so don't be angry." He takes my face in his hands. "And that struggle led me to you, so I'll struggle every single day if it means I end up in this place right here." He kisses me.

"We have to go home," I tell him. "So I can show you how proud of you I really am," I say, pulling him toward his house. And show him I do.

We walk out of the house with him wearing his suit and me wearing black jean and a Stingers shirt with his name on the back and a black leather jacket. It's the first time we walk into the arena holding hands. When he pulls open the door and we walk down the hallway, Matthew is the first one to see us.

"What is that shirt you are wearing?" he asks me, and then his eyes go to our hands. "It better be a Grant shirt."

I laugh but not before Viktor says, "You wish, buddy." He stops at the front of the dressing room. "See you later," he says, smiling. He leans down and kisses my lips.

"Dude," Matthew says. "Seriously, that's my sister."

"Dude," Viktor says. "Seriously, that's mine."

"I have no words," I say, shaking my head and then walking away from them to the box, hoping someone will be there. I walk in and see Karrie and Vivienne sitting at the bar with Allison. "Hey there," I say, and Vivienne looks up at me.

"She had the sex," she says with a gasp, and I look at her shocked.

"How do you know this?"

"You're glowing, and it's written all over your face," she says, and I touch my face. "It's the I got it so fucking good look," she says and slaps the table. "I want that look."

"Then go get that look," Karrie says, picking up her glass of wine. Vivienne just looks over at her and glares. We spend the next two hours snacking on chicken wings and pizza, and when the game finally starts, I take off my jacket and walk to the seat.

"Matthew!" Vivienne yells for my brother when I sit down. He comes forward and looks at her. "Looks like someone just claimed your last sister." He just shakes his head. "It's a losing battle."

I just laugh and then turn to see my father looking at me. He doesn't say anything, but his eyes say it all. He's both happy and sad that his last daughter has found love. In this wild roller coaster ride.

FORTY

Viktor

"WHERE ARE WE going?" Zoe asks me as I lead her to a little park I found one day when I was walking around. "Shouldn't you be at home getting in the zone?"

It's been two months since I've made her mine, and the only time we've been apart is when I'm on the road. Which, thank fuck for us, hasn't been more than we all thought it would be. Tonight, we head into game six of the Stanley Cup. We are one game away from hoisting the cup in the air, but more importantly, I'm one day away from my one-year chip.

One year seems like a lifetime ago, and technically, it was. "It's going to be so warm later on," I tell Zoe who just walks next to me holding my hand like she always does. Our lives have merged effortlessly. Slowly, she has been filling up her half of the closet that I gave her, and hopefully, by the time the summer is over, she'll be "officially" living with me.

We turn down the little path that hides the park. Trees are all around it, and in the middle of the park is green grass with four park benches. The sun breaks through the top of the trees almost like a light shining in from heaven. "What is this place?" she asks while we walk on the pebbled path. "I've never seen this place."

"Don't tell me that I know of someplace that the big Zoe Stone doesn't know of?" I joke with her. My girl is killing it and taking names, and I couldn't be prouder.

"I found this place on my way home one day, and I sat down and just listened to the birds chirping," I tell her and then finally come into the park, and she's the light shining in. I couldn't have asked for a nicer day.

"It's so pretty," she says. She sees a potted plant on one of the park benches, and she looks at me. "What is that?"

"Come here. I have to tell you something."

She stops walking. "If you are going to propose to me, I beg you not to."

I look at her and try not to laugh. "Would you say no?"

"No," she says. "But I don't have any makeup on, and my hair is dirty," she says, and I walk to her and kiss her. It still feels like the first time. It always feels like the first time.

"I'm not asking you to marry me today," I tell her. "This is something a bit bigger." I pull her over to the bench and have her sit down.

"Are you breaking up with me?" she asks, smirking.

"Baby," I say softly. "No one is breaking up with anyone or getting engaged."

"Well, you're scaring me."

"You know that in recovery, one must go through the twelve steps," I tell her, and my heart beats so hard in my chest, the sound echoes in my ears. I take a deep breath, but my mouth feels incredibly dry. "They tell you to work on one step a month, own it, do it, and by the end of your year, you will have achieved the twelve steps." I lean back and take a paper out of my pocket. "Tomorrow is my one-year date." She nods at me and now wipes a tear from her eye. "But I have one more step I have to do."

"Viktor," she whispers my name. "It's okay to go over the twelve months." She tries to tell me it's okay, and if I didn't love her with everything that I have before this moment, it would change instantly. She is selfless in the way she loves.

"Step five is the hardest step I think I ever did," I tell her. "It's writing down all of our faults and finding someone to tell it to." I look down on the paper that has been folded and unfolded more times than I care to think about. "You see, I made this list in October." I unfold the paper. "I wrote it, and even while I was writing it, I knew there was only one person I wanted to share it with. One only person I wanted to know about all my wrongs." I wipe away my own tear now. "It's been you; it's always been you," I tell her, and she leans into me and holds my hand in her lap.

"I'm honored," she tells me and brings my hand up to her lips, and she kisses it. "Read it to me."

I clear my throat and look down at my writing on the paper. "There are so many things that I can put on this paper to tell you about all the wrongs I've done. I think the first thing that comes to my mind is shame. Shame that I let my family down, shame that my mother and father would know I was weak." I feel a tear drop on my hand, but I go on. "Guilt. I had so much guilt in me that it crushed my ability to breathe at times. I remember when it was my father's surprise birthday, and I missed it because I was getting high the night before and slept through the party. Guilt that I wasn't that son he always wished I would be. I had fear inside me also. That everyone would know my secret, fear that they would judge me because of the drugs, fear that I would always be that person. It took all the guilt and the shame and the fear and made me isolated. I spent all my time alone, especially when I had those days when I would try to get clean, and then I would spiral down. I alienated all the good I had in my life. Pushed it all away. I was dishonest with everyone, but especially me. I told myself I was fine. I told myself that everyone felt like this. It pushed me to becoming angry with myself more than anything." I look down at the paper and then look up at Zoe who has her face covered and tears are falling. "It's this list that makes me look at the man who I have become." I shake my head. "I will always have that shame that I let the drugs have the upper hand and the guilt. I will always have the fear that one day it won't be a good day, and I might slip, but I have anger because of the drugs. I'm angry that I let the drugs define who I was. I am not that person."

"You aren't that person," she tells me. "You are so much more than that person. Being an addict doesn't define who you are."

"It doesn't," I agree with her. "Accepting it and having the courage to face it defines who I am," I tell her. "I didn't get here all on my own. I had hands that held me up and helped me, and for that, I can never repay them."

"I think you being the man they know you are is payment enough," she says, and she grabs my face. "I hope you know that I'm going to make a big deal out of this."

I grab the flowers in my hand. "This is for us," I tell her. "I have to say, writing these faults on paper is one thing but actually putting it out there and saying them out loud is a whole different ball game." I kiss her. "Thank you for accepting me with all my mistakes and faults."

"I wouldn't want you any other way," she says, grabbing the plant from me. "Can we plant it here?"

"Yes," I tell her. "I made sure it was okay. I got the permits and everything."

"It's going to be a plant that flourishes just like you," she says, getting up and walking around the park. "Where do you want to put it?"

I shake my head. I just bared my soul to her and told her every single reason she shouldn't be with me in that letter. I told her about all my faults and my mistakes, but instead of judging me, she sat there and held my hand and shared her love with me even more. This woman will cut your balls off in the blink of an eye if you hurt anyone she loves, but she loves me unconditionally and with everything she has. I look up and send out a little thank you to whoever is listening.

"What about here?" she says to a small spot in the shade that gets a sliver of sunshine through the trees. I get up and walk toward the woman who owns my heart and is in all my future memories. "We should hurry up," she says to me. "We have to go back and do the pre-game ritual."

"I'm pretty sure it's just called a blow job." I walk to her and take her in my arms, my cock ready for the said ritual.

"Well, I don't know about you, but every single home game that I suck your dick, you win, so …" She turns in my arms. "I mean, we could test out the theory tonight."

"I think we should continue this tradition every single day," I tell her, and just like that, her laughter fills the whole park. After we plant the tree and wash our hands, we make our way back to the apartment where she does her ritual, and then I suit up for the biggest game of my life.

We stop in front of the dressing room. "Win or lose," she starts saying, and Matthew groans.

"Fuck, Zoe, can we not say lose?" I shake my head and kiss her lips just to irritate him more.

"Can you guys stop dry humping each other? It's not the time."

Zoe shakes her head. "Good luck and break a leg."

Matthew groans again. "Just leave." Then he turns to me. "Don't break shit."

"You need to calm down. You are going to give yourself a heart attack," Zoe says and then walks closer to him. "Then Karrie is going to have to start dating again."

"Why do you hate me?" he asks her, and she smiles and kisses his cheek.

"I'm just here to keep it real," she says and walks away from him.

"I love her," I tell him, and he just shakes his head. "But she's right, you need to relax."

"Do me a favor and go out there and win me a fucking Stanley Cup, and then I'll relax," he says, slapping my arm and walking away. I get into the room and get into the zone. I block it all out.

I have one thing in mind, and that is to hold that cup in my hands. It isn't an easy battle. The first two periods, we race and win some battles and then lose others. When we line up for the third period, I look over at Mark, who hasn't said a word the whole game. I mean, he barely speaks more than five words in a week. His eyes are on the prize. "I am going to need you fuckers to put some goals in the other net, so I can look like a big deal," he says to us, and we all look over at him in shock that he spoke and that he also made a joke.

He is the first one on the ice, and he makes his way over. I get on the ice and clip my helmet on, looking up at the jumbotron. Twenty minutes and we are up by one. I skate to the center ice next to Evan. "I'd really love to win tonight," I tell him, and he laughs.

"I'll keep that in mind," he says and then gets into position. The puck drops, and he wins the face-off, sending it to the defense. They bring the puck up and enter the zone with us on his tail. He shoots the puck, and it rebounds to the right corner, sending everyone rushing for it and getting there at the same time as the defenseman. We crash into each other and try to win the battle of the puck. Evan comes over and takes the puck from between us, sending it back to the defense at the blue line. Making us separate and get into position. The five players from the other team all in the middle of the box we have created, all ready to block the shots to the net.

Jones, our defenseman, looks it over and skates to the middle of the zone, making the other defenseman skate in a bit. I skate ahead toward him, and he moves the puck across to me. I turn with the puck on my stick, and shoot it straight at the goalie, aiming for the top corner and see it hit right over his shoulder. The fans jump to their feet, and Jones skates to me and jumps on me. "Good fucking play," I tell him and then skate to the bench, celebrating with everyone.

We do a shift change, and once we get on the bench, Coach paces behind us. "Still eighteen minutes to play, guys."

We watch the chances go more for us than for them with Mark shutting it down each time. I jump over the bench when it's my turn with Evan beside me. We rush into the zone; Evan with the puck on his stick going to the net and shooting wide. I'm behind the net, getting the puck and shooting it on the board toward Jones, who passes it right to Jamie, the other defenseman, who takes the puck and sees that Evan is all alone in the circle. He passes it straight down the middle, and Evan gets down on his knee and shoots at the goalie just wide, and the puck bounces off the back board and comes straight at me on the side of the net, the puck hitting the middle of my stick in the back and bouncing across the goal line off the goalie's leg.

Evan jumps on me before I even have time to celebrate, and the building is just going nuts. We are up two goals, but it doesn't last long when they score a goal ten seconds after I do. "Fuck," we say and then get ready for us to take the ice. The second- and third-line fight, and we spend more time in their zone than we do in ours.

The whistle blows, and we change line, the puck dropping in center ice. Evan is on point tonight, and he wins again, sending it to me, and I pass it to Jason, the right winger, who dumps the puck in so we can chase it. We get into position, and the crowd is now chanting. Evan battles behind the net for the puck, and he clears it to send it to me who passes it to Jones.

Jones passes it to Jamie who then skates in a bit and shoots it on net, the goalie blocking it with his leg. I rush to get the rebound, trying to get it to Evan, who hits it back to me. The defenseman now pushing me to the board, not giving me a chance to do anything with it. I see Jason, the right winger, and pass it over to him, who passes it to Jones, who is in the middle of the zone, who hammers it to the goalie, going wide, and then bouncing right back to Evan, who has an empty net shot. He takes it, and just like that, we are up by two again. The crowd goes nuts, especially when Evan jumps on the glass, and we all huddle around him.

The countdown is the worst. The longest five minutes of my life, and when they pull the goalie with four minutes to go, everyone has one mission and that is to score an extra goal. We don't give a shit who does it, as long as someone does. I look up again when I have a chance, and I see it clear as day. The clock counting down from twenty seconds. I look around the arena, and everything zones out and is in slow motion. The crowd on their feet jumping with their hands in the air. The countdown on their lips as the whole arena now counts down. I look up to the box where I know Zoe is. It's strange that with everything going on, I still make eye contact with her as she stands there with a huge megawatt smile on her face and tears streaming down her face as she claps and counts down with all the girls beside them. She and Zara are doing the same thing. The clock strikes zero, and I look up and send out a silent. "Thank you."

Gloves are flying, sticks are flying, helmets, you name it, and it's being tossed out there. Evan is the first one to yell. Everyone rushes onto the ice and makes our way over to Mark who is in the middle of the circle probably getting crushed. Camera crews now come onto the ice all around us as the other team gets ready to shake hands in the middle of the ice. The handshake is fast, and then I see the red carpet being pushed out and the table that will hold the Stanley Cup.

A reporter pulls me aside, and my eyes do a quick sweep of the area as I look for Zoe. "Viktor, describe to us how you feel right now at this moment. You get traded while you are dealing with personal stuff, and now one year later, you are raising the Stanley Cup."

I shake my head, trying to blink away the tears. "It's surreal," I say, laughing. "When you go through that, it's tough getting out, but you can do it. Anyone can do it. You just need a support system, and that system was my family in New York. The organization never let me fall and kept helping me strive."

"Matthew Grant, second year of being a GM, and he takes a chance on you. How big of a thank you do you have to give him right now," he jokes, and I finally spot Matthew in the corner hugging Evan and smacking his chest in celebration.

"I owe him more than he knows," I tell him the truth, and then I spot her, standing beside Zara and baby Zoey, who has headphones on as she sleeps in her mother's arms.

"Thank you so much, and we can't wait to see what you can do next year." I nod at him and skate away to the bench where the wives are all lined up at the entranceway, waiting to come onto the ice and celebrate.

"They are bringing out the cup!" someone yells for me, and I just nod, but I walk to the back and grab her in my arms.

"You did it," she says, trying not to cry as she buries her neck into my sweaty and stinky neck. "I'm so proud of you!"

"I love you," I tell her, and she moves her head to kiss my lips.

"Now go raise that cup," she tells me, and I drop her and skate out just in time to see them walk the cup in.

I make it to the team and stand beside Evan who stands by Matthew and Max. "Holy fucking shit, we did it," Evan says, and then someone hands me a baseball hat with our logo on it.

"You guys did it," Matthew says. "All of you did it." He looks at me, and then they call Evan over to accept the cup. "Well, I guess you think because of this, you can date my sister?"

I shake my head at him. "No, this has nothing to do with me dating your sister. But you should know"—I lean in—"I'm going to marry her."

He shakes his head. "Well, if I have to pick anyone, I would pick you," he says. "You did what everyone else said you wouldn't do. They buried you even before you gave them a chance to change their mind." He smacks my shoulder. "Be proud of what you did."

I nod at him, and when Evan comes over and hands me the cup, the last year replays in my head. The ups, the downs, the nights waking up sweating, the nights spent walking around. Everything happens for a reason, and we can only go one day at a time.

I lift the cup over my head and look at my girl who stands there giving me everything that I could have ever wanted.

FortyOne

Zoe

"DIDN'T YOU SAY we could stay in bed all day long?" Viktor groans from beside me. After he won the Stanley Cup, we celebrated until about three a.m., and then we had our own celebration at home, falling asleep right when the sun was coming up.

"I'm hungry," I tell him, nervous, and my heart beat is rushing and beating so hard that I'm afraid he's going to see right through my lies. I open the door to the restaurant that I forced him to come eat at.

"We could have ordered food," he says, his hand always in mine if we are next to each other. "We could have ordered cake with icing, and I could have eaten it." I block his mouth right before everyone yells surprise. "What?" He looks around at everyone there. The balloons everywhere with "1" all over them.

"You didn't think I wouldn't make a fuss, did you?" I tell

him, and then Matthew comes up to us, and he looks like he slept maybe an hour.

"You know, I would not have gotten out of bed for anything today," he tells him. "But this, this I would." He slaps Viktor's shoulder and then looks at me. "You and your balloon obsession."

"It's a party." I roll my eyes. Okay fine, maybe asking them for a thousand balloons was a bit too much, but I did cut it down to five hundred.

I look around the room at all our friends, some of his teammates, and even some of the people he goes to meetings with.

"You did good," Zara says, coming over to us and handing me Zoey. "I am so tired," she says, and then I look over at Viktor as he shakes hands and has words with everyone.

Karrie and Vivienne come to me now. "We couldn't do this in a week?" Karrie says.

"How was I supposed to know that they would win the cup?" I ask them and just shake my head. Vivienne looks around the room and then takes a long sip of her wine.

"This is lovely," my mother says, coming over to us. "It's wonderful, and we are so proud of him," she says, and I look over at my father who is now hugging Viktor and saying something to him. His eyes tear up, and I look down. "Go to him," my mother says, and I nod and hand her Zoey, who sleeps through it all.

"Hey there," I say to him as my father walks away, and he wipes his eyes. "Are you surprised?"

"Your father just said he's proud of me," he says. "He has known me seven months, and he's proud of me." He shakes his head. "My father probably isn't going to text me about the Stanley Cup, let alone tell me he's proud of me," he says, and my heart breaks for him. "I mean, I don't know why it still gets to me."

"Because he's your father and because his love should be unconditional and all that," I tell him, wrapping my arms around his waist. "This isn't about him. This is about you. This whole thing is about you and being here for you." He nods and kisses my lips. "Look around at everyone here who came to celebrate you and everything you've done."

"I must have done something right," he tells me and kisses me. We find our seat and start eating the meal. The whole time, everyone laughs and has a great time. I look around, and this is what I wanted him to see. That everyone is here to support him and is proud of him. To have the peace he deserves to have.

He taps his glass in front of him, and when everyone quiets down, he stands up. "I guess I should say something since you all came out for me," he starts the speech and then holds my shoulder beside him. "I can't believe it's already been three hundred and sixty-five days." He shakes his head. "This morning when I got up, I looked over and saw the date on my phone, and for once, I thought, what took me so long?" He laughs nervously.

"Today, I remember walking into the rehab and listening to them tell me what was going to happen and thinking, I'm just going to do what they want me to do, make everyone happy, and get out of here." He shrugs. "I made notes on how to hide it in the future. I was in rehab, and I wasn't thinking of getting clean. I was thinking of ways to hide it."

He looks over at Jeffrey and Patrick.

"Crazy, right? But then one day led to another day, and I stopped making a list on how to hide it and started making a list on how to change things. How to change me. They say when you are starting in recovery not to make any big commitments." He laughs. "Well, someone should have told them it wasn't an ideal time to pack me up and move me out to a new city, to a new team, to the unknown." He looks at Matthew, who just shakes his head.

"You're welcome," Matthew says, grabbing his glass of water and raising it to toast him.

"It was, in fact, a blessing, a new page, a new beginning. It was a slow process, and that is what made it harder. I expected to wake up every day and be like I don't want that." He takes a big deep breath. "That was the biggest challenge to want it and fight it. As the days turned into weeks, and the weeks turned into months, I carried on, making progress and gaining the one thing that I lost along the way—my self-respect." I turn my head to kiss his hands that squeeze my shoulder as if he is gaining strength from me.

"Knowing I was worth it, knowing I was a good person. Knowing I am a good person. In one year, I got my life back. I mean, I got it back before, but in one year, I know I deserve it. Every single day will be a struggle, and I've come to terms with that. Some days will be easier than others, but no matter what, I will not use. Knowing that I now have the foundation to achieve it is everything. There are twelve steps to the program, and as of yesterday morning, I had completed them all except to share my inventory with another human." I wipe away a tear and try not to look up at him. "I'm lucky to say that I found that human who took all my mistakes and looked past them. She took everything I did and accepted it, and then she turned and looked at me, and I saw that she still loved me." I shake my head, and then Zara reaches over and holds my hand as I try to blink away the tears and fail miserably. "Zoe, you are by far better than any chip they can give me," he says, and now I feel his hand move away from my shoulder, and he leans down. "I love you," he whispers to me and kisses my lips, and everyone claps. "Thank you," he says when he stands up again and then sits down.

"I love you," I tell him, and just like that, everyone goes back to their own conversations.

Slowly but surely, people get up and leave, and then I look around at Mark, who comes up and shakes Evan's hand. "Congrats," he says, shaking his hand and his beard is so thick with this playoff superstition. "I'm going to head out," he says, and Viktor shakes his hand and thanks him for coming.

He looks around, and then his eyes land on Vivienne. I look at him and then Vivienne again, who looks straight at him. He looks from us, then back to Vivienne. I don't know what is going on right now, and when I look over at Zara, wondering if she just saw what I saw, she looks from Mark to Vivienne who is now talking to Karrie beside her. Mark shakes his head and walks over to her, and my eyes go back to Zara who just watches with her eyes wide. The only one who isn't surprised by all this is Karrie, who tries to roll her lips together. "Are you done?" he says to Vivienne, and if anyone knows Vivienne, they know she is the one who runs the show in all aspects of everything basically.

I swear you could hear a pin drop; I don't think anyone actually says anything. I'm not even sure they knew what was going on before Mark just swaggered across the room toward Vivienne. "Yes," she says, flipping her hair behind her shoulder. She pushes her chair away from the table, and the whole time, everyone watches as the scene plays out.

"Good, now let's go," he says, and she walks around the table, her hand slipping in his like they've done it for a long time.

"What in the fuck is that?" Matthew is the first one to ask, then looks at Karrie.

Karrie shrugs her shoulder. "I don't think she's thirsty any-more," she says, and just like that, everyone starts to laugh.

EPILOGUE ONE

ZOE

Nine months later . . .

"I CAN'T BELIEVE it's the last home game of the year," Zara says from beside me as I blow bubbles into Zoey's neck, and she giggles. I call her the mini us. With her strawberry hair in little pigtails and her big blue-green eyes taking everything in.

The crowd claps and then she follows through, shouting, "Da da da da," which irritates Zara since she has only said mama once.

"I can't wait to be off for the summer," Zara says. "Two months off with no work. It will be fabulous."

"Well, no time like the present to give me another niece or nephew," I tell her, and she shakes her head.

"She just started sleeping through the night," Zara says, and then Matthew comes into the room. His eyes fly around the room and land on me.

He walks over to us and then makes faces with Zoey. "Are you the cutest Zoey in the world?" he says to her, and she gives him a gummy smile with her little two teeth at the bottom showing.

"Uh, second cutest Zoey," I tell him. "I'm number one. Don't ever forget that."

"Hey, I need some help. Can you come down with me?" Matthew says to me, and I get off the stool and hand Zoey to Zara. The whole box is full of family. The only one missing is Justin, who is playing his own game tonight.

"What do you need help with?" I ask him, walking down to the locker room with him.

"It's fan appreciation night," he tells me, and we walk into the hallway, and I see other people who are fans there. "I need you to help them get on the ice and make sure that everyone lines up properly."

"I'm not going on the ice. That's awkward," I tell him. "Ask Karrie."

"It's too late," he says, and the horn blows. "It's the last game of the season, so the fans who were selected get a surprise jersey off the back of a player. No one knows who yet until they get on the ice."

I scrunch up my nose. "They smell like ass," I tell him. "You should at least give them a clean one." He rolls his eyes and puts his hands in his pockets.

"Okay, you can lead the way. Go all the way to the end of the red carpet. You will be the first and last one off the ice," he tells me, and I swear I want to kick him.

"I take it back. I don't want to go out there," I tell him. "My boyfriend is out there. People know," I tell him, and they do. After he won the Stanley Cup, *People* magazine came out and did a story on him. He wrote the story himself about his journey, and it's now framed and hanging in our living room. I obviously moved in with him right after he got his one-year chip. I wasn't asked; I was just there all the time and so were my clothes. I mean, he did help by always packing an extra bag when we went over to the brownstone.

"There is no time for this. Do it for the fans," he says and pushes me out, and I smile at the fans who look at me. "Follow her," Matthew says, and I walk down the hallway and then out of the bench onto the ice that now has red carpet on it. I walk all the way to the end and see the team skating to the middle of the ice and holding up their sticks to thank the fans for another year.

I make my way to the edge of the carpet and then everyone lines up beside me and looks out to the glass. Two of the equipment people walk out and hands them Sharpies. The players go toward their fans, and then I look at Viktor who skates over to me. "Hey," he says to me, taking off his helmet. His hair is all wet as he bends down to kiss me.

"Go to your fan," I tell him, and he just smiles at me.

I look around, and something isn't right. Matthew is standing beside the entrance where I came from with Zara under one arm and my mother under the other while she hugs Allison. My father is on the other side of Allison. I look at them and then look back at Viktor, and then finally I hear the crowd going nuts, and I see why.

He is on one knee in front of me, and the tears just come now, pouring down my cheeks. "Zoe Stone," he starts, and I put my hand in front of my mouth. "You are the shining light in a dark world. You have shown me love like no other, and I don't want to know what life is like without you in it." He pulls out a square box from his pants. "I want to wake up with you forever. I want to go to bed with you forever. I want you to wear my ring so everyone knows that you're mine."

"I am yours," I tell him through sobs.

"I want to have babies with you that look exactly like you. I want to hold your hand when you are happy and hold you up when you are sad. Will you do me the honor of being my forever?" He opens the ring box, and I don't even look at it. I look at no one but him. I grab his face in my hands and kiss his lips.

"Yes," I tell him, and then all of a sudden, a microphone is right next to us.

"She said yes!" Viktor's voice fills the arena, and the crowd goes wild. He gets up and picks me up around my waist. "Forever."

He places me down on my feet and slips my ring on my finger. "This is so wild," I tell him smiling and then look over at my family who stands there cheering us on. "But it's us," I tell him and wrap my hands around his waist.

EPILOGUE TWO

VIKTOR

Six years later . . .

"I'M HOME!" I yell, walking into the house and slamming the door behind me. I walk through the house we bought in Long Island in the same neighborhood as everyone else. "Hello," I say at the base of the stairs and hear nothing. I look up and hanging in the middle of the wall is a picture of Zoe and me on our wedding day.

Two months after I proposed to her, we got married quietly with only our family there. My parents and sister also came out, but it was a bigger deal having her family there. Neither of us wanted a big wedding, or if she did, she didn't say, so we got married in her parents' backyard.

I walk through the house, looking at all the little things we've done over the past five years. On top of the fireplace is the letter I wrote to her framed and engraved with one day at a time June 1st.

I walk to the back door, and when I see them, a smile automatically fills my face. "I'm home," I say out to the yard. The three of them look back at the door, and my son runs to me. His black hair flying back, his dark blue eyes staring right at me, but what gets me most of all is the smile on his face. It's always there, always. He was our little honeymoon present. Nine months after we got married, my wife gave birth to him. Lucky for us, I was home, and we were on hiatus that week. After eight hours of torture for me and for Zoe, they placed him into my arms.

"Daddy's home," he says, throwing himself into my arms. "You were gone forever."

I kiss his neck. "It's been two hours since I went over to Uncle Matthew's house," I tell him, and he smiles.

"I wanted to go," he tells and then squirms out of my hands. "He loves me the most."

"I bet he does," I tell him, and he runs away to the clubhouse that Matthew had built for him. You see, we decided to name him Matthew, but we call him Matt so as not to mess everyone up. But when we introduced him to Matthew, he took him in his arms, and they've had a bond ever since.

"Where are my girls?" I say, walking to them as my daughter sits in the sandbox. She looks up at me, and she is the stamp of her mother. A little mini me and now I know how Matthew felt all the times I kissed Zoe in front of him. "What are you building, princess?" I ask her, using her nickname. I'm sure I don't have to tell you what we named her because it was not even an option: Zara.

"A castle," she answers me, and I go and sit behind my wife with my legs on the outside of her, and my face goes to her neck.

"Hi," she says and turns her head to face me. "You didn't go for long."

"It was shorter than we thought," I tell her and kiss her lips. "What have you been doing?"

"I'm trying to get them as much fresh air as possible so I can go to bed as soon as they do."

"Are you still not feeling well?" I ask her and hug her tighter. "You should call the doctor. It's been two weeks." She doesn't answer me; she just nods her head, and we spend the rest of the day outside where I chase the kids, and Zoe swings in the hammock.

I close Zara's door softly so as not to wake her and then check in on Matt who is already fast asleep with the covers bunched around his feet. I walk down the hallway to our bedroom and hear the shower running. I walk into the bathroom and see Zoe sitting on the counter like she did when we first visited the house.

It's one of the top reasons we bought the house. I grab my shirt and take it off and toss it in the basket in the corner. She looks at me as I walk in. "Are they sleeping?" she asks me, and I nod my head at her. I walk to her, and she opens her legs so I can stand between them. I push her cotton nightgown up. The little spaghetti strap falls to her arm, letting the top slip off the top of her breast past her nipple. My cock springs to action right away.

"I love this," she says, touching the ink on my side. After we got engaged, I showed her that I added her name un-

447

der the scripture and then added Matthew and then Zara. Her finger traces all the names. "Looks like there is space for one more," she says, and then I see that she's holding a pregnancy test in her hands. A bright pink "+" in the middle.

"Are you?" I ask her and then look up at her. "Are we?"

"We are," she says, and I lift her up and bring her closer to the edge of the counter, her hands moving her night gown up and then taking out my cock. I slide into her, and we both moan.

"You've given me everything I could want," I tell her as I make love to her. "And more." She doesn't say anything to me; she just tightens her legs around my hips.

"I love you," she tells me as soon as I plant myself all the way into her. She goes over the ledge, and I follow her.

That night, when my eyes fly open, I turn to look over at the bedside clock and see it's a little after six a.m. Our bedroom door opens, and I see little Zara come in wiping her eyes. "Daddy," she says, her voice soft and angelic. "I sleep with you," she says, and she climbs into bed with us. I tuck her into my side, and then just like that, my eyes close again. Gone are the days when I would get up and watch the sun come up. Gone are the heart palpitations that I got at the beginning. Now, my heart beats normally. In this crazy, wild life, I found my love.

THE END

Other title by Natasha Madison

This Is
This Is Crazy
This Is Wild
This Is Love

Hollywood Royalty
Hollywood Playboy
Hollywood Princess
Hollywood Prince

Something Series
Something So Right
Something So Perfect
Something So Irresistible
Something So Unscripted

Tempt Series
Tempt The Boss
Tempt The Playboy

Heaven & Hell Series
Hell and Back
Pieces of Heaven
Heaven & Hell Box Set

Love Series
Perfect Love Story
Unexpected Love Story
Broken Love Story
Mixed Up Love
Faux Pas

Milton Keynes UK
Ingram Content Group UK Ltd.
UKHW020831191223
434651UK00015B/752